WHITE ELEPHANT DEAD

WHITE ELEPHANT DEAD

A DEATH ON DEMAND MYSTERY

Carolyn Hart

AVON BOOKS, INC.
1350 Avenue of the Americas
New York, New York 10019

Copyright © 1999 by Carolyn G. Hart
Interior design by Kellan Peck
ISBN: 0-380-97530-0

First Avon Twilight Printing: September 1999

AVON TWILIGHT TRADEMARK REG. U.S. PAT. OFF. AND IN OTHER COUNTRIES,
MARCA REGISTRADA, HECHO EN U.S.A.

Printed in the U.S.A.

www.avonbooks.com/twilight

With love to Trent and Adrienne

WHITE ELEPHANT DEAD

Chapter 1

Loretta Campbell tugged at the twisted sheet. She was so uncomfortable. And so cold. If she pushed the bell, no one would come. Or it would be that impatient nurse's aide. Never saw a real nurse anymore. It wasn't the way it had been when Robert was a young doctor and she was a nurse. She was so sick. Too bad about knowing so much. Everyone pretended she was going to be all right. But she knew better.

Loretta wished she'd changed her will. It still made her mad. How could Gary ignore the truth, treating Sam and Kate the same? It wasn't right. All these years she'd not said anything. Aloud. Oh yes, Marie knew how she felt. One Christmas Eve, Marie had come up to her bedroom, stepped inside, closed the door and leaned against it. She was small, but that night she'd been formidable. Marie made it clear: Not a word, not a gesture, not a hint of difference or she'd make sure Loretta never saw Sam. Never.

"Not right." She pushed the words out of her tight

throat. The old resentment boiled inside her, blotting out the pain.

"Of course it wasn't right." The voice was calm, soothing as ointment on a burn.

Loretta blinked but she couldn't see, not really, just a dark shape at the bedside. That woman. One of the hospital volunteers. She'd come before. Always so quiet. A listener.

A soft hand gently held Loretta's cold fingers. "Tell me all about it." The voice was as soothing as honey to a parched throat. "Don't hold anything back. No one will ever know but me. It will make you feel so much better. . . ."

Kathryn Girard's hands moved swiftly, competently. She loved the steady, pulsing click of the knitting needles. She sat quietly, as comfortable as a cat in her cushiony easy chair behind the low Queen Anne table that served as her cash desk. She always smiled when customers commented on the lack of a cash register—a cash box served her needs—and the absence of computers or credit card paraphernalia. "I enjoy the simple life," she always said with a slow, satisfied smile. "No credit cards. Not even a car." People were accustomed to seeing her on her sturdy bicycle. Some even went so far as to praise her commitment to a slow pace. As for the store, "Cash or a check," she always said, her lips curving.

When the bell tinkled at the door of her narrow, dimly lit shop on a steamy Tuesday in September, she looked up without much interest. Then her eyes widened. For an instant, her hands were motionless. But the needles were clicking softly as the woman neared the desk, sharp gray eyes scanning the display of Delft china. A careful observer would note that most of the pieces were chipped.

The woman approaching was a very careful observer.

Kathryn looked down at her knitting, ignored the woman. After all, the lighting was dim. Perhaps Frances wouldn't even notice.

The woman was tall and thin, with a jutting-out face and

uncompromising wire glasses; she came to an abrupt stop in front of the table.

Kathryn continued to knit, her eyes downcast.

"Frieda!" The sharp voice rose in surprise. "Frieda! Whatever are you doing here? Why, the police are still looking for you. Someone at church told me the other day that they never close a missing person case. It was a seven-day wonder when you disappeared."

Kathryn looked up slowly. "I beg your pardon?" Her eyes widened. A slight frown marred her heart-shaped face.

Frances Wilson clapped her hands on her bony hips, poked her face forward like a questing turtle. "Frieda March. I'd know you anywhere."

"I'm sorry." Kathryn's voice was slightly amused with just the right dash of kindly condescension. "Actually, you don't know me. I'm Kathryn Girard. I suppose your friend must resemble me. But I assure you, I'm not—who did you say—"

"Frieda March," Frances snapped.

"No." Kathryn was firm. "And where are you from?"

"Winnetka."

Kathryn gave a slight shrug. "Where is that?"

"Winnetka, Illinois." Suspicious gray eyes scoured Kathryn's face.

"I've never been there." Kathryn put her knitting on the table. "I hope you are enjoying your holiday." That was the trouble with resorts. People came from everywhere. "Are you looking for anything special? I have a nice selection of sandwich glass. And some pewter candlesticks from Boston."

"No. No, thanks." Frances was backing toward the door.

As soon as the bell tinkled, Kathryn rose from her chair. She was thinking fast. No matter who Frances contacted, nothing would likely happen for a few days. Today was Tuesday. Kathryn nodded. Thursday would be time enough. She needed a car. Usually her customers came to her. She thought longingly of her sleek black Porsche garaged at her hacienda in San Miguel de Allende. How could she— Oh, of course. She laughed aloud. What fun. What a clever way to make one last run.

Vince Ellis clicked off his computer. He looked at the yellow legal pad next to his keyboard. He was on to a hell of a story. But there was no spring in his step as he moved away from his study, walked softly up the stairs and stopped by the first bedroom. He opened the door gently. In the shaft of light from the hall, Meg's long blond hair splayed on the pillow. But even in a deep sleep, Piggy, the old ragged cloth animal, was tightly clutched to her side. Piggy was all she'd brought from her old life. Meg was doing well now, although perhaps too often silent for a seven-year-old. And she still had nightmares. Doing well, but still oh so vulnerable.

Vince Ellis closed Meg's door. Desperate danger called for desperate measures. He would do what he had to do.

Ruth Yates heard the slam of Brian's car door. He was home early. She'd thought he would go by the church, check to make sure the east room of the basement wasn't flooding. It so often did in hard rains. Quickly, she returned the gun to the dusty cardboard box. She stood, swiping her hands against her navy slacks. Hurrying, she reached the attic door, was out and down the stairs to the second floor as the front door opened.

"Ruth? I'm home."

The sound of his deep, quiet voice, full of warmth and caring, stabbed at her heart. She couldn't bear for him to turn away from her. And he would if he ever knew.

Forcing a smile to her face though her skin felt like leather, she moved to the top of the stairs. "I'm here, Brian. I'll be right down."

Janet Pierce knew the eggshell white of the drawing room flattered her. She could see her reflection in the massive ormolu framed mirror on the opposite wall, ash-blond hair drawn back in a severe chignon, finely boned face, sapphire-blue eyes, pale pink lips now curved in an appreciative smile. She managed to invest every conversation with a breathy attentiveness. She could hear her voice, so well bred, saying, ". . . you don't mean it? Bridget, that's simply shocking! I can't believe a bracelet could disappear without . . ."

Neither her words nor her demeanor reflected the panic fluttering inside. She'd looked forward to this moment for months. She, Janet Pierce, was serving tea at the Thursday Book Club's annual tea, an honor accorded every year to the Most Outstanding Volunteer of Broward's Rock, a pinnacle of social achievement in the small and exceedingly exclusive group of women who ran island society, women who often were only minimally polite to second wives and so assured of their own social eminence that they didn't care how powerful the husband might be. Janet had worked hard, curried favor from old biddies with poisonous tongues and fat purses. This was her moment of triumph and instead of enjoying it, she teetered on the edge of ruin.

"Sugar or cream, Adelaide?" What a supreme moment. She, Janet Pierce, easily using the given name of the island's wealthiest and most prominent resident. "It's just marvelous the way you've lifted the Art Center out of obscurity by bringing . . ."

But inside, thoughts ricocheted in her mind: What choice did she have? None, none, none. This afternoon she had to provide a written assurance that would be returned Saturday morning in exchange for the desired package. It would be madness to make the attempt. But what else could she do?

The jagged bolt of lightning split the sky, the harsh light emphasizing the huge lumps of coal-black clouds. Dave Pierce's hands closed tightly on the steering wheel, his grip so hard his fingers ached. But nothing moved in his smooth face. His dark eyes stared through the heavy wash of rain on the windshield. He used to love these storms. They'd always reminded him of Tahiti and Lynn. He pushed memories away. He didn't permit memories anymore.

Henny Brawley pushed open the shiny white front door, peered through the sheeting rain. The weeping willows that masked the parking lot were scarcely visible through the gusts. But it was pointless to look. If the van was there, Kathryn Girard would have struggled through the rain to the Women's Club Building. Or she could have used her cell phone to call Henny, who was the only person in the building at the moment. Only one car waited in the crushed oyster-shell lot and that was Henny's black 1982 Dodge. Besides, Kathryn's bicycle was still in the green metal stand to the left of the entrance. Where could Kathryn be? Henny checked her watch. Almost six. Kathryn had left two hours ago, insisting the imminent storm was no problem. She'd smiled that ostensibly pleasant, infuriatingly obdurate Mona Lisa smile and said in the patronizing tone that always offended Henny, "We can't let a little rain keep us from our duty."

Henny sighed and turned back to the graceful room, now a repository for boxes, bags and stacks of discarded items that would be offered, once they were arranged and priced, at the Women's Club annual White Elephant Sale, opening at nine A.M. Saturday. The volunteers would arrive tomorrow to begin the pricing. Henny grinned. This year's sale, as always, would be great fun. How much did you ask for a necklace of shark's teeth? Or a basket from India with the dubious claim that it once housed a cobra? Or an Olivetti Lettera 22 typewriter? Henny strode to the bulletin board on an easel. A banner across the top read: THE WOMEN'S CLUB ANNUAL WHITE ELEPHANT SALE, "MORE MARVELS THAN THE BIG TOP." Henny was charmingly modest about her authorship of the slogan. Usually even a fleeting thought of it elevated her to high good humor. But right now, thanks to Kathryn Girard, she was too irritated to take pleasure. Damn Kathryn. If she weren't the most stubborn woman in the world—and a master of passive aggression—she'd have waited until tomorrow to make the collections. It wouldn't have taken a moment to call the scheduled pick-ups and change the time. What was sacrosanct about Thursday afternoon?

Now Henny's own plans were askew because of Kathryn's stubbornness. It would serve Kathryn right if Henny simply locked up and left. See how Kathryn would enjoy riding her bicycle in this downpour!

Henny was tempted. Then she sighed. The Women's Club van was her responsibility. She'd checked it out to Kathryn Girard, and she damn well was going to check it in.

"Four o'clock . . ." she muttered aloud. Now it was almost six. Surely Kathryn would have called if she was stalled somewhere. Reluctantly, Henny pictured the island, the beautiful South Carolina barrier island of Broward's Rock, with its pristine beaches—when not being pounded by a stormy high tide—and miles of wilderness slashed through by only a few roads.

Finding Kathryn should be easy enough, however. Emma Clyde, the island's claim to literary fame, author of the fabulously best-selling Marigold Rembrandt mysteries, was chair of the sale. Henny thoroughly enjoyed the Marigold Rembrandt books and was always more than a little surprised at the contrast between the charming, fluffy sleuth and her cold-eyed, tart-tongued, totally unfluffy creator. Emma Clyde, in fact, was as far from fluffy as a Doberman from a toy poodle. Actually, Henny would never admit it—it would tarnish her own reputation as an intrepid sleuth—but she found Emma Clyde downright intimidating. But so did everyone else, including sloe-eyed, mealy-mouthed, two-faced Kathryn Girard. Emma Clyde had used her computer to create the pick-up schedules and had posted them on the bulletin board with directives to sale volunteers. Therefore, finding Kathryn should be easy enough.

Henny paused on her way to the bulletin board, grabbed up a phone and dialed a long-memorized number.

A familiar cheery voice answered obligingly, "Death on Demand, the finest mystery bookstore east of Atlanta."

"Annie, Henny. I'm at the Women's Club and running a little late. Kathryn Girard hasn't turned in the van." She didn't try to keep the irritation out of her voice. "I've got to track her down, then I'll come by for the books. Do you mind staying open for me?" In the summers the store stayed open until eight, but after Labor Day, Annie closed up at six.

Annie Laurance Darling had long ago embraced the shopkeeper's dictum—the customer is (usually) right—and said agreeably, "Sure. I've got them packed up for you. See you in a while."

Henny was smiling as she hurried to the bulletin board. She scanned the pick-up cards. Hmm. That was odd. The addresses on Kathryn's card were scratched out. Written below the original list in a bold back-slanting script were four addresses: 31 Mockingbird Lane, 17 Ship's Galley Road, 8 Porpoise Place, and 22 Sea Oats Circle.

Henny yanked the card from the bulletin board. What would Emma Clyde think if she saw the changes? Emma didn't encourage improvisation. Tucking the card in the pocket of her slacks, Henny hurried toward the door, pausing only long enough to retrieve her purse and her gray poncho. The sooner she found the van, the sooner she could go to Death on Demand and pick up her wonderful box of books.

At the Death on Demand Mystery Book Store, owner Annie Laurance Darling spoke firmly to the resident feline, although in her innermost heart Annie knew she was on the losing side. "Agatha, you can't eat again."

Green eyes venomously slitted, the imposing black cat stalked to the end of the coffee bar and crouched.

"Agatha, no! Do not attack—" Annie jumped sideways to avoid a hurtling mass of fur.

Agatha thumped to the ground, turned a graceful pirouette and moved toward Annie's left knee, fangs clearly visible.

Annie may not have moved as gracefully as the cat, but she was damned fast as she sought refuge behind the coffee bar. "All right. All right. A snack. A healthy snack. But the vet said you were too heavy and you know it." She rattled dry diet food into a blue plastic bowl, set it atop the coffee bar.

Agatha floated through the air, emitting piercing yowls on the order of, "I am starving. I am neglected. I am riven by pangs of ferocious hunger and you do not care." She poked her lovely face into the bowl and, growling between bites, ate like Joyce Porter's Inspector Dover on a binge.

"You are much prettier than Inspector Dover," Annie cooed.

Agatha continued to eat and growl, growl and eat.

Annie would have liked to stroke the cashmere-soft black fur, but she wasn't stupid. A series of small scars on both forearms reminded her that Agatha in a bad mood was not to be trifled with.

Annie moved a safe distance along the coffee bar. She resisted the temptation to forage in the refrigerator for a Reese's Peanut Butter Cup. After all, fair was fair and she couldn't feed Agatha diet food while munching on delectable candy. Annie glanced at her watch. She, too, was beginning to feel like a starving castaway on a desert island. Where was Henny Brawley, her best—and sometimes most demanding—customer? Henny, of course, was a Serious Collector, which meant the fact that books were available in paperback mattered not a whit. Hardcover firsts only, please. Annie regretted having reported the arrival of the special order, but she was so pleased with her success in finding the books that she hadn't been able to resist. After all, it was quite a coup to come up with hardcover first editions of books that had been published more than a year earlier. Henny had been on a trek to the Himalayas when the books came out. Except for stars like John Grisham and

Mary Higgins Clark, the shelf life of new hardcover books ran about three months. Not to worry, so long as Annie Laurance Darling, bookseller extraordinaire, could come to the rescue. She looked in satisfaction at the box, wonderful books all: *Bellows Falls* by Archer Mayor, *Fertile Ground* by Rochelle Krich, *Death of a Rodeo Rogue* by Robert Greer, and *Killing Time* by Cynthia Harrod-Eagles.

As Annie glanced at her watch—already half-past six— a huge blast of thunder almost coincided with a vivid crackle of lightning. The lights in the store wavered, went out, came on again. Rain gurgled in the waterspouts behind the store. The roads were probably an inch deep in water.

The phone rang.

Annie felt a quiver of relief. That would be Henny, saying she'd turned back, the storm was too much, and Annie would be free to slosh home to Max, who would welcome her with a glass of California Cabernet and homemade ravioli and a Caesar salad. Annie could scarcely begin to count her blessings. Her handsome blond husband was not only a sexy grown-up version of Joe Hardy, he had recently embraced cooking as his latest hobby. Only in quiet moments of reflection did Annie worry about his genetic inheritance. Her mother-in-law Laurel was forever and anon embracing new enthusiasms. But surely Max would never be tempted to raise anacondas or scale forty-story office buildings. Not that Laurel had succumbed to any such peculiar interests. Yet. Certainly Laurel's latest preoccupation was inoffensive. Wasn't it? Annie glanced at the beautifully executed flowers drawn on a note card her mother-in-law had left at the cash desk earlier in the day, a pink rose, a bunch of sweetpeas and a Christmas rose. Each flower was carefully labeled, perhaps for the elucidation of the florally impaired, i.e., Annie. Though she knew she was succumbing to Laurel's ploy, she couldn't resist unearthing an old book on the language of flowers and trying to decipher the message. Annie wasn't at all certain, but she was afraid it translated to something like: Please believe me, your departure would calm my anxiety.

Annie grabbed the phone. "Death on Demand." She loved saying the name of her store. She'd taken the narrow, cramped, admittedly dingy mystery bookstore she'd inherited from her Uncle Ambrose and turned it into a spacious, welcoming enclave with heart-pine floors, the best in current mystery fiction from Albert to Zukowski, a fabulous selection of classic mysteries from Allingham to Zangwill, and a used book section with plenty of collectibles including some super recent acquisitions: *The Blunderer* by Patricia Highsmith, a letter written by Raymond Chandler and a signed map of Maggody drawn by Joan Hess.

"Dinner is served, madame." Max's voice was smooth and deep. Then he spoke in his usual easy tone. "The master chef is producing yet another delicious delight. When may I expect my appreciative audience?"

Annie glanced toward the front window. Even though the boardwalk was covered, wind-driven rain splatted against the front window. "I'm waiting for Henny. She's on her way." Annie frowned. The entire island could be traversed in eight minutes. Even doubling it for the rain, Henny should have arrived. Of course, she'd said she had to find the club van first. But how long could that take?

"Maybe she changed her mind," Max suggested. "It's rugged out there." Static buzzed on the line as another bolt exploded.

"She'd call and tell me." Annie heard the worry in her own voice. This was a small island. A very small island. "She has to be here pretty soon. Do you mind waiting?"

"Nope."

Annie was grateful Max had not assumed the temperamental qualities of a master chef. He was, in fact, his accustomed good-humored self, even though she was delaying the arrival of his oh-so-appreciative audience.

Max continued to win husband-of-the-year awards. "Don't worry, Annie. Everything's on warm. It's probably better to wait until the storm eases anyway. Dorothy L. and I will relax with a good book. I've got Steven Womack's latest.''

Annie smiled as she clicked off the phone. Max was especially fond of the elegant white cat that she'd rescued from the alley behind the store only to find that Agatha was implacably opposed to sharing her territory. Dorothy L. by default became their home cat and she was Max's devoted admirer. Annie couldn't resist occasionally telling the blue-eyed feline that after all if it weren't for Annie, Dorothy L. would be a foundling. In the usual manner of cats, Dorothy L. took no notice and continued to adore Max and ignore Annie. But Dorothy L. was so endowed with charm that Annie didn't hold a grudge.

Annie glanced down the coffee bar. Agatha now sat with her back to Annie as she scrubbed her face with a decisive paw. Okay, so Agatha was short on charm. What she lacked in charm, she made up in intelligence, determination, cleverness—and ferocity. Annie loved every dangerous black inch of her.

Annie reached gingerly for the empty bowl, rinsed it, refreshed Agatha's water. She glanced around the store. Everything was in order. As soon as Henny came, Annie could scoot—okay, splash—home to a wonderful dinner and other delights. Her eyes softened as she thought about Max, her unflappable, good-humored spouse. Not that Max was perfect. He lacked application. He wasn't lazy, of course, but he'd never equated self-worth with work, a concept difficult for type-A Annie to comprehend. He did have his own business. Of sorts. In fact, Max was very proud of Confidential Commissions, which was not, he was quick to point out, a private detective agency, but was a counseling service devoted to solving problems, problems of any sort. Annie had to admit that Max took an interest in promoting Confidential Commissions. He had, in fact, recently revised the ad which ran, boxed, in the *Island Gazette* personals:

> CONFIDENTIAL COMMISSIONS
> 17 Harbor Walk
> Problems?
> Ask Max.

He'd thrust the paper across the breakfast table with a proud grin.

Annie had managed to squelch the tart response that immediately came to mind: Well, honey, that's fine. But how long has it been since you've actually had a client and done any work?

If you have as much charm—and money—as Max, who needs to work?

Annie's eyes widened. She'd not said it aloud but the thought had come so clearly, the words seemed to ring in her ear. Her Calvinistic rectitude immediately protested—it was amazing the dialogues she could manage to have with herself—that charm was no substitute for effort.

Charm, so impossible to define, so joyous to encounter. She'd been thinking a good deal about charm lately. What made a mystery charming? Perhaps that accolade would differ with every reader. But Annie didn't think so and she'd devised a perfect test. Every month, she commissioned a local artist to paint five watercolors, each representing a mystery that Annie considered to be very special indeed. The mysteries always had a common theme: American history, women PIs, romantic suspense, comedy. Always before, the theme had been readily apparent. This time, she was asking the contest winner not only to name the title and author represented by each painting, but to define the quality common to all the books. The prize would be the winner's choice of a current hardcover plus a month of free coffee.

Annie glanced toward the paintings hanging over the fireplace. She grinned. The various books certainly didn't fit into any obvious category.

In the first watercolor, flickering candlelight fitfully illuminated the inside of an old stone burial vault. An old man's body lay in stiff repose atop a tomb. A handsome young man with curly dark hair and vivid green eyes and a slender young woman with long flowing hair stared in horror at the wet cement being slapped on the still form atop the tomb by an old woman with a rhinoceros-wrinkled face and crazed eyes.

In the second watercolor, a muscular, bronze-skinned man in his fifties with a head as bald as a cue ball glowered at two deputy sheriffs as they hitched a twenty-four-foot silver Airstream Excella to the back of a mustard-yellow Chevy truck with Coconino County badges on the doors. A round-faced woman with a short, light brown Afro anxiously watched.

In the third watercolor, pale fluorescent light illuminated the large open L-shaped room divided by book stacks and tables. A yellow plastic tape inscribed POLICE LINE DO NOT CROSS blocked access to the Mo–Ne fiction aisle. Four uniformed policemen and two men in suits watched as a young woman studied the body sprawled face down between the book stacks. Everything about her proclaimed order and neatness, from her short curled hair to her navy heels. The blue of her skirt exactly matched the blue of the Brazilian enameled bird on her burgundy sweater. In sharp contrast, the dead man's brown hair and beard were matted, his jeans and sweater worn and the laces of his Rockports untied.

In the fourth watercolor, two old women energetically jitterbugged in a country and western bar. The big blond woman's turquoise T-shirt featured a pelican peering around the slogan TOUGH OLD BIRD. She swung the small woman, gray-haired and petite, over a glowing inlaid glass boot in the dance floor. Overhead spots glowed red, green and yellow. Neon behind the bar announced SCOOT 'N' BOOT.

In the fifth watercolor, a blinding glare of light speared down into a water-filled pit. Sheer panic distorted the sharply curved features of a gorgeous young woman with light brown skin and almond-shaped hazel eyes. She stared at a massive hippopotamus only a few feet away. Reaching out to her was a determined young white woman with dark brown eyes, auburn hair and an oval face with fine features and a tip-tilted nose.

Would the winner immediately comprehend that these were the first books in series that resonated with charm?

Time would tell.

Time—she glanced at her watch.

Annie grabbed the mobile phone, punched in Henny's home number. Maybe her most intrepid reader had decided to escape the storm. When the voice mail came on, she said slowly, "Henny, this is Annie. It's a quarter to seven—" Annie broke the connection. Forty-five minutes since Henny had called. This was wrong, all wrong. Henny: responsible, thoughtful, punctual Henny. Where was she?

Thunder exploded. Lighting flashed, so near the boardwalk sizzled with a sulfurous glow. The lights went out.

"Sure we can go look." Max Darling cradled the phone under his chin as he snapped the plastic casserole top on the dish and slipped it into the refrigerator. "Don't be frightened, honey." He pictured his wife pacing with the telephone, her curly blond hair rumpled from nervous hand swipes, her usually cheerful face strained, her gray eyes dark with worry, her eminently kissable lips drawn by a frown.

"Max, do you think I'm overreacting?" Static blurred Annie's worried voice.

"No. Henny may just be stalled—"

"She has a cell phone." Annie spoke with finality. A woman with a cell phone was never more than the push of a button away from a connection.

"She may be trying to get a wrecker. Maybe she forgot to call you—"

"Max! Henny would call. And now it's almost an hour—"

"Okay, honey. Let's figure it out. She called from the

Women's Club—'' Max pictured the skillet-shaped island. The club, housed in a restored, very old plantation chapel, was at the north end of the island, Annie's store in the curving harbor on the southwest tip.

"She said . . ." Static drowned out Annie's voice. ". . . had to find the club van and . . . come here."

Max sketched the island on a kitchen pad. "Where was she going to look for it?"

Annie paused before she said slowly, "Henny said something about it being on the way to the store."

Max marked the club on the map. The club was in an isolated area on the east side of the island and perhaps a half mile north of St. Mary's Church. If Henny's search for the van was en route to the bookstore, that meant she was heading south and the only road going south was inside the gated community of the retirement and resort area. The gate was manned at all times, usually by a retired Marine sergeant or former cop. Residents' cars had decals.

"Hold on, Annie, let me call the gate, see if the guard remembers Henny coming through." In a moment, he came back on Annie's line. "Willard's on duty. He said Henny drove through shortly after six and turned right." Sand Dollar Road circled the resort. Streets poked off into exclusive neighborhoods. Narrow dusty roads twisted beneath live oaks to remote homes. Henny's west-side house was one of these, with no near neighbors and a spectacular marsh view.

"Then she intended to look for the van on the west side of the island, somewhere between the entry gate and the harbor. That makes a lot of sense, Max." Annie's voice sounded brighter. Action always pepped her up. "Okay, Henny was looking for the van. We'll find Henny."

Max reached into a cabinet for a flashlight. "Let's check out the west loop of Sand Dollar. I'll drive to the gate and go south. You drive north. And Annie, keep your cell phone turned on."

*   *   *

Rain slid thickly over the windshield like water cascading from a fountain. Max doubted he could find an ark outlined in neon, much less an old black car. The gusting rain cut visibility to a couple of feet. As for the woods to his left and the salt marsh to his right, they existed only in his memory. He knew they were there, but they were shrouded in fog and rain. He was more worried about Henny than he wanted to admit to Annie. Of course, Henny could have gotten stuck, or slid into a ditch, but surely she'd found her way to shelter. Even the most remote houses were not more than a mile or so from a neighbor. She might even now be drying off in someone's clubroom, awaiting a wrecker.

Just in case, Max used his cell phone. There was a recorded message at Ronnie's Wrecker Service. After the tone, he said, "Ronnie, this is Max Darling. Annie and I are out looking for Henny Brawley. Please let me know—" he left his cell phone number—"if Henny's called for help. We're afraid she's stuck out in this storm. Thanks."

He peered through the watery glass. He was speeding along at about fifteen miles an hour, but even so, he should be nearing the first major turnoff, Red-Tailed Hawk Road, which angled south. Annie said Henny was looking for the van used to pick up donations. He was no expert on club duties but it seemed odd to him to frolic about collecting discards in this storm. Maybe the van skidded off the road. Whatever, the sooner he and Annie scoured the area, the sooner he could present Annie with his latest superb repast. Had he used just a touch too much garlic? But the master touch was the freshly grated Romano cheese—

Max braked. Slowly. Carefully. He turned onto Red-Tailed Hawk.

The windshield wipers struggled against the downpour. Annie's eyes swung from one side of the road to the other. She fished out her cell phone, called Emma Clyde. Annie knew that number by heart. Emma was a cherished customer of Death on Demand as well as being one of the star

authors with her very own shelf. Emma had long ago refused to go on author tours. Though she refused to do a
formal signing, Emma did deign to come by and autograph
her new books. Annie was pleased to be able to offer signed
copies of Emma Clyde titles to her mailing list and Internet
customers. Emma had dropped by the store a couple of
weeks ago to autograph the latest Marigold Rembrandt
novel, *The Adventure of the Purloined Python,* and she and
Annie had talked about the upcoming Women's Club White
Elephant Sale. Knowing Emma, Annie could count on her
having a computer file on pick-up routes. The phone rang
and rang. No answer. Damn. Annie thought for a moment,
then took a deep breath and punched in her mother-in-
law's number.

"Laurel? Listen, Henny may have had car trouble. Max
and I are out looking for her—"

"Oh my dear. I knew there was a reason for my concern." The husky voice could have led a dirge. "Out of nowhere this afternoon, I pictured monkshood! Monkshood!"

Annie wasn't about to go down this byway. "Look, Laurel. We need your help. Please get a phone bank busy calling
everybody in the Women's Club. Find out if anyone's heard
from Henny since six o'clock. Call me on my cell phone if
you find her."

"Monkshood," came the sepulchral tone. "Oh, I shall.
But, Annie, the blooms were purple. I am very much afraid.
There could be no clearer presentiment that danger is near."

Annie clicked off the call. Dammit, that was spooky.
Trust Laurel to make her feel like a beleaguered heroine in
a Mary Stewart novel. However, Laurel, in her own dippy
fashion, was dependable. Annie knew that even now phones
were ringing across Broward's Rock. The search for Henny
was in full swing.

Annie slowed as she reached Laughing Gull Road, a narrow blacktop that ran east, intersecting Red-Tailed Hawk.
Winding, reclusive roads poked south from Laughing Gull
in the island's most prestigious development around the Is-

land Hills Country Club golf course. Annie hesitated, then
pressed ahead on the main road, unhappily aware that Henny's car could easily be in a ditch, invisible behind the curtain of rain. Annie was nearing the northern entrance to
Red-Tailed Hawk when her cell phone squawked. She
punched it on.

"Annie dear, picture a fleur-de-lis." A pause while, pre-
sumably, Annie pictured a fleur-de-lis. "Oh, the dear iris,
harbinger of spring, a message of lovely weather to come,
if you will."

Annie wouldn't. She gritted her teeth.

Laurel's throaty voice brimmed with cheer. "Harbinger.
Isn't that a gorgeous way of indicating a message?" To make
the point clear, she said distinctly, "Fleur-de-lis. Message.
Indeed"—Laurel spoke at a brisk clip, perhaps sensing impatience in her listener—"I have an important message. Serena Harris just called—and isn't it a wonder how much her
hair looks like parsley, so spriggy—although only faintly
green—but certainly so appropriate to one imparting useful
knowledge." Just in case Annie's wits were moldy from the
rain, Laurel added sotto voice, "Parsley, useful knowledge."
Then, loudly and very quickly, "Serena reports that she saw
Henny's car turning onto Marsh Tacky Road shortly after
six. Serena did wonder a bit, since that's a dead end, but
she simply had to get home in time for the rerun of Andy
Griffith. Which always brings to mind the red camellia,
which symbolizes unpretentious excellence and—"

Annie forbore saying it sure as hell didn't bring any such
thought to her mind. "Laurel"—forcefully—"is Serena sure
it was Marsh Tacky Road? The little lane that runs west
from Red-Tailed Hawk and dead-ends at King Snake Park?"

"My dear." Laurel's tone indicated disappointment in
such churlish questioning of her source. "Quamoclit."

Annie pressed the receiver against her ear. "What? What
did you say?"

"Truth to tell—"

Always an interesting claim when made by Laurel.

"—I've not actually encountered the quamoclit flower. However, the import is clear: busybody. Add to that a dash of thistle—sternness—and I believe we may rest assured that the message is correct. In fact, we may adorn Serena with a wreath of liverwort, the token of confidence. Of course, liverwort is rather thick, like a bunch of moss on a log. Perhaps it might be difficult to create a wreath but—"

"Thank you, Laurel." Annie ended the connection. Liverwort. She hoped it looked better than it sounded. As she punched in the number of Max's cell phone, she slowed to a crawl, peering through the rain. Yes, she was at the turnoff to Red-Tailed Hawk.

Max answered on the first ring. Quickly, Annie reported the sighting of Henny's car.

"Marsh Tacky Road?" His voice was puzzled.

"Yes. It runs west off Red-Tailed Hawk between Laughing Gull and the south loop of Sand Dollar."

"I'm on Red-Tailed Hawk and almost to Sand Dollar. I must have passed Marsh Tacky. I'll find a drive and turn around."

No matter the static and buzz, just hearing his voice made Annie feel brighter and happier. Was the rain easing just a little? She felt a surge of relief. Yes, oh yes. And they had a definite place to go. "I'll meet you there."

The big black car loomed out of the rainy night, its taillights bright as warning lights on a channel buoy. The interior of the car was dark but the headlights speared through the night, twin beams illuminating silvery slanting rain.

As Annie jammed on her brakes, Max's crimson Maserati roared to a stop behind her. Annie was grateful for her yellow slicker and billed hat and rubber boots. She was already slogging toward the old black Dodge—why had Henny left on the lights?—when Max caught up with her.

"Henny!" Annie shouted. The call sounded as forlorn as the cry of a mourning dove.

They reached the car. Max pointed an oversize flashlight

inside. Henny's cell phone lay in the passenger seat. A crammed-full book bag rested on the floor. Henny never took a step without plenty of books to read.

Max swung the beam to the back. Empty.

Annie bent close to him. "Where can she be? There aren't any houses on this road. It just leads to a little park supported by the Women's Club. There's a big lagoon and some picnic tables. The golf course is on the other side of the lagoon." Not a destination of choice on a rain-drenched night. "Why in the world . . ." She didn't complete the sentence. There didn't seem to be a rational reason why Henny would turn onto this road. Except . . .

Annie turned, moved quickly to the front of the car. The headlight beams shone straight ahead. "Look, Max, look!" Annie broke into a run, or the nearest approximation, her boots squishing and sliding on the muddy road. If she hadn't looked hard, she'd never have seen the dark blue van. Henny had driven into the storm in search of the Women's Club van.

Annie swung her flashlight, and yes, there was the insignia on the door: WOMEN'S CLUB, BROWARD'S ROCK, SOUTH CARO-LINA. But Annie couldn't imagine what had led Henny here, to this remote and unfrequented lane. Oh well, of course she *could* imagine, as could any sophisticated mystery reader: a sighting on the main road, a determined chase, the cornering of the quarry on this deserted road.

But what then?

Despite the warm embrace of her slicker and only a vagrant splash of rain on her face, Annie suddenly felt as cold as Roderick Usher approaching Madeline's tomb. She took a deep breath, tried to stave off a clammy sense of horror. Maybe deep familiarity with detective fiction had its drawbacks. This was no dreary House of Usher, it was simply the club van. And yes, Henny's car was abandoned, but there were no indications of violence or injury. Annie had a sudden mental picture of the sailing ship, the *Mary Celeste*, found adrift off the Azores on December 3, 1872, breakfast

partially prepared in the galley, and not a soul aboard and
never a hint to the fate of the crew and the captain, his wife
and daughter.

Max pulled open the front door of the van. His light
danced across the seats, revealing the disarray of an upended purse on the passenger seat and the gaping car pocket
with tangled papers. Tape cassettes and CD cases spangled
the floorboard.

Annie whirled and ran to the back of the van. She
reached up, grabbed the handle and pulled.

The door swung open. The beam of her flashlight skimmed
across bulging piles of clothes thrown helter-skelter. A broken
wooden chair leaned against the mound of clothing. Wad-
ded brown grocery sacks were stuffed in a corner. A worn
wool blanket covered a lumpy form. The flashlight in Annie's hand wavered as she stared at the exposed sole of a
woman's shoe and at a pale white ankle.

Chapter 2

"Max!" Annie's voice was thin and terrible, piercing the sodden night. She knew there was a body beneath that blanket, an utterly still shell without life.

Max's strong arm came around her shoulders. "Hold on." He swung his flashlight into the van. The beam illuminated the uneven bunching of the thin olive-green blanket, the mud clinging to the black leather shoe, the bare ankle.

"Annie." He spoke quietly. "Go to your car. I'll call—"

But she was already moving, shrugging free of Max's touch, thrusting her flashlight at him, clambering into the van, reaching for the blanket. Yes, she knew the protocol for crime scenes, how the evidence would be handled by Ed McBain's Steve Carella of New York's 87th Precinct, Barbara D'Amato's Chicago officer Suze Figueroa and Susan Dunlap's Berkeley cop Jill Smith. But Annie wasn't a cop, she was a friend. Henny. Dear Henny, so crisp and clever and kind. Annie gave no thought to fingerprints or DNA as she grabbed the end of the blanket and yanked, pulling hard

against a dreadful, unyielding weight. She scrambled next to
the still form, pushed and pulled until the blanket slid away.

Blood matted dark hair.

Annie was so shocked that for an instant she could
scarcely believe what she saw.

Not Henny. "It's not Henny. Oh Max, it's not Henny."
It felt like a shout even though she scarcely managed a whisper. There was an instant of unimaginable relief, but that
was swiftly superseded by a wash of horror as she recognized Kathryn Girard, a brutally dead Kathryn, her skull
crushed by a powerful blow. The ferocity of the attack made
Annie feel sick and frightened.

Unwillingly, Annie reached past Kathryn, making sure
there was not another body there. But no, that was only a
quick nightmarish fear, impelled by the grisly discovery.
There was no room for anyone else in the van.

Dear God, where was Henny? One murder was clear to
see. Had there been two?

Annie heard the wail of the siren, but she didn't pause
in her slow, careful survey of the rain-drenched salt myrtle
and bayberry and yaupon holly shrubs on either side of the
road. Water glistened on ferns. She was looking for some
trace of crushed branches or, worst possibility, another still
form. Back and forth she swung her flashlight. She didn't
bother to hunt for footprints in the sticky mud of the narrow
road. The steady rain would have washed out any trace.
The siren choked off in midsqueal. Bright lights pierced the
darkness behind her, signaling the arrival of the police. Max
was at the van to hail them. He'd been reluctant to let her
seek Henny, but he understood that she must. And, as she'd
informed him, murderers don't linger. Annie felt she was
safe enough. If only Henny was safe . . .

A police radio crackled. She glanced back. A stark light
flared behind the van. The methodical gathering of evidence
had begun. No doubt a careful search was being organized.

Annie followed the curve in the road. The road widened

into a turnaround. An iron grillwork arch marked the entrance to King Snake Park. Annie suppressed a shudder, though a naturalist friend had once waxed rhapsodic about the glorious nonpoisonous Eastern King with its golden markings and its penchant for eating poisonous snakes. Annie took comfort in the fact (surely this was true) that snakes don't like to be cold, so none of the glorious creatures should be writhing about near her on this rainy night. Her light played across a series of picnic tables, the beam poking here and there, as ineffectual in illuminating the darkness as the flicker of fireflies. Beyond the tables was the murky lagoon, undoubtedly home to alligators. Alligators hunt at night. The fearsome creatures reach fourteen feet, weigh five hundred pounds and have mouths with teeth that can rip small dogs into morsels.

If Henny was in the lagoon, she was long past help. If she was lost or hurt somewhere in this rugged terrain, she had to be found and found soon. The rain had eased. Now it was a steady, fine drizzle, but the temperature had dropped into the sixties. Obviously, Henny wasn't on her feet, wasn't able to call for help. If she were to lie unmoving too long, hypothermia would kill her.

Annie whirled and ran back toward the lights and the metallic squawk of the police radio.

A searchlight on the bed of a small pickup threw the back of the Women's Club van into garish relief. Rain misted against the open rear door, beaded the floor.

Max was gesturing toward the woods. ". . . need to round up a search party. There's no trace of Henny Brawley. My wife's looking for her."

"I'm in charge here." Rain dripped from a snap-brim hat sheathed in plastic, rolled down the gray plastic poncho. The voice was gruff, the posture straight and stiff, and both seemed at odds with a youthful, rounded face with plump cheeks, dogged blue eyes and a snub nose. In the blazing spotlight, the earnest young man staring up at Max looked more like a choirboy than a law officer. "Chief Garrett. My immediate duty is to secure the crime scene—"

"Chief"—Max's voice was dangerously quiet—"we have a missing woman. She's elderly, defenseless and—"

"Thought your wife told you this Brawley woman had chased after the victim." He pointed at the van.

Annie skidded to a stop beside Max. "Henny went after the van because she was worried about Kathryn—"

"We'll see what the lady says when we talk to her. You folks can wait over—"

"Chief!" Annie wished she were as imperious as Amanda Cross's sleuth Kate Fansler. "You don't understand. Henny Brawley is missing. There's her car"—it was Annie's turn to point—"and we haven't found any trace of her. None."

"She can't get far. Now you folks need to get out of the way. This is a crime scene." He swung toward the van. "Pirelli, make sure you get a complete sweep with the videocam—"

Lou Pirelli was stocky and muscular. His posture didn't change, but he stared at his boss in surprise for an instant, then said, "Yes, sir."

"—and Cameron, get on the horn, get some dogs out here. Tyndall, check out that car"—he pointed toward Henny's old black Dodge, the headlights beginning to dim as the battery ran lower—"lift some prints from the steering wheel, see if you find a match in the van."

Billy Cameron had been on the Broward's Rock police force ever since Annie had arrived on the island, a gentle, sweet giant, towering at six-foot-three, handsome as a rugby player in a sport drink ad. He ducked his head as he passed Annie, obviously unhappy with his new boss, but Billy followed orders. As would Officers Pirelli and Tyndall, who made up the rest of the Broward's Rock police force. Joe Tyndall had a complete collection of Mike Hammer paperbacks. He liked to kid Annie that the Mickey Spillane novels were the only politically incorrect books still in print. He, too, avoided her gaze as he broke into a trot, heading for Henny's car.

This was Annie's first meeting with the new chief, who had succeeded their old friend Frank Saulter. Frank was celebrating his retirement by going on a round-the-world trip with his oldest grandson via tramp steamers, hostels and hitchhiking. Yesterday they'd received a card from South America: *Going up the Amazon. Found a signed first edition of* The Glass Key *in a little store in Tefé. Cost $2 American. Love, Frank.*

Annie felt the quick burn of tears. She'd shown the card to Henny, who considered Frank an intense rival in the world of mystery collecting. Henny had clapped her hands together. "That's a real coup. We'll have a party for Frank when he gets back."

Annie wished Frank, dear laconic, saturnine, dyspeptic Frank, were here tonight instead of this newcomer who was too busy establishing his authority to listen. Annie forgot to remember her long-standing resolve to curb her quick tongue. "Look here, it doesn't matter whether Henny's fingerprints are on the van. You could find her prints on the murder weapon and it wouldn't mean a thing! Henny would never hurt a soul. And she's out there somewhere"—Annie's arm swept toward the wet shrubs and dripping forest—"and she could die if we don't find her soon."

A satisfied smirk transformed the plump face. Garrett looked like Hamilton Burger confident he'd finally cornered Perry Mason. "Do I understand that you have searched the immediate area and found no trace of the missing woman?" His voice had the stentorian ring of a prosecutor.

Garrett certainly lacked people skills, but Annie was pleased that he finally seemed to get the point. "That's right." Annie once again gestured into the darkness. "I've checked along both sides of the road all the way to the park."

Chief Garrett nodded. "The conclusion is clear. *She* has not been a victim of violence. If she'd been attacked, she

would have been found. Obviously, she left the scene under
her own power. But she won't get far. After all, this is an
island. Not even a ferry crossing until morning. We'll have
her in custody by then." He turned away, moved with stiff
dignity to the van. "Pirelli, label the film case. As a backup,
take Polaroid shots from every angle. Then . . ."

Max reached out to grab Annie's arm, but he was too
late. She bounded after Garrett faster than Craig Rice's Bingo
Riggs and Handsome Kusak on the trail of money, theirs or
someone else's.

Annie flung herself between Garrett and the van. "Are
you an idiot?"

Garrett's round face congealed like a Mary Roberts Rinehart dowager encountering the lower classes.

Too late, Annie realized that maybe on a ranking of in-
terpersonal skills, she and Garrett might be dead even with
slab-faced, monosyllabic Sgt. Buck, the misogynist sidekick
of Leslie Ford's urbane Col. Primrose.

Before Garrett could respond, a gray station wagon slid
to a stop near the chief's car. Garrett brushed past Annie.
"Dr. Burford. Over this way, please."

Max reached her in an instant. "Come on, Annie. It
won't do any good to go after Garrett. And he won't be
thinking about us, since the ME's arrived."

"But Max, we've got to—"

"I know. And we will. Come on."

The first car arrived in ten minutes. Max set up a command post on the hood of his car.

Garrett bustled over. "What's going on here? Who are
all these people—"

The local bird-watching society, splendidly equipped for
a cross-country expedition, was setting off to the south.

"—and what do you think—"

Mayor Cosgrove, who moved like a penguin but earned
more than a million dollars a year in real estate commissions, wobbled up the lane and greeted the young police

chief in a booming bass voice. "Good thinking, Garrett. Time to get the community involved. To think a Women's Club volunteer has been murdered and our own Henny Brawley missing! We'll leave no stone unturned. Though I'm relieved the search won't involve the beach. Think of the sea turtle eggs!" The mayor was a passionate defender of sea turtles. "All right now, Max, I'll give you a hand. Let's get a grid together. Have to know who's going where."

Within twenty minutes, a bus from the First Methodist Church disgorged the women's missionary society, Boy Scout Troop 19 and the a cappella choir. Laurel arrived at the wheel of a produce truck and out spilled the members of St. Mary's Altar Guild.

As Laurel waited in line for her assignment, she called out dolefully to Annie, "Monkshood." Then, chin high, which always showed her aristocratic throat to good advantage, "We must be positive. Think geranium, dear Annie."

Annie nodded absently. Among the calls she'd made on her cell phone was one to Emma Clyde. This time Emma had answered and she was on her way. Annie hated to stand waiting while searchers fanned out in all directions, their flashlights bobbing, but if there was anyone on the island of Broward's Rock who could outthink the world, it was Emma Clyde. Annie had stopped fuming about Garrett's unexpected conclusions and was trying to figure out what could have happened on this remote stretch of road. Though it had taken much longer than it should—she glanced at her watch, it was half past eight—a thorough search was now well under way. If Henny was there to find, she would be found.

As Laurel joined a group striding toward the park, she sang out, "Nutmeg geranium, my dear. It always heralds an expected meeting. We shall meet with Henny, never fear." Laurel disappeared around the bend.

Raincoated figures scurried in all directions. There was an undertone of noise, people talking, the polite but harried directions barked by Officer Pirelli to keep the searchers away from the van, the patter of light rain, the squish of feet on the muddy road, an occasional honking horn.

"Hi there, Emma."

"Emma, good to see you."

"Did you bring Marigold along? We need a real detective tonight."

Annie looked past the brightly lit van at the road leading to King Snake Park. The spill of light from the spotlight illuminated a swath of the road. The cheery hellos were coming from that direction. Annie knew Emma was amazing and her latest car was a pink Rolls-Royce but unless it came equipped with wings, Annie didn't see how Emma had driven from her house on the marsh side of the island over the golf course, which abutted the park, and chugged across the admittedly shallow but very wet lagoon.

Search volunteers split into a V and here came Emma in a golf cart. Oh, of course. Emma's elegant home overlooked the ninth green. The fourteenth hole ran along the other side of the King Snake Lagoon. Smart Emma. She'd figured that the narrow road into the park would be choked with vehicles.

Annie ran to greet her. Emma scared the hell out of her sometimes, but if she ever had to man a barricade, she'd definitely pick Emma as her leader. Max was dear and sexy and swashbucklingly brave, but Emma was tough.

Emma switched off the cart, climbed majestically out, her clear plastic raincoat flapping. Emma was always majestic, tall, broad-shouldered and athletic. She was still golfing though she was now in her late seventies. Her blunt face would have been a natural for a Mount Rushmore of mystery authors, perhaps featuring Emma, John D. MacDonald, Erle Stanley Gardner, and E. C. Bentley, square-jawed all. However, even an accomplished sculptor might find it difficult to re-create Emma's hair. Emma, in fact, seemed to find it difficult to re-create her hair, which ranged from varicolored spikes to tight white ringlets to a bluish pompadour possibly inspired by childhood memories of Marie Antoinette. Currently, she was sporting bronze ringlets bright as a new penny. Emma's hair was no match for the multihued caftans which were her dress of choice. Tonight's glowed beneath the clear plastic, an improbable mixture of lime and purple. Her cornflower-blue eyes swiftly scanned the scene. "Good show, Annie. Good people. They'll find Henny. Now tell me what's happened."

Annie was not celebrated for brevity, though she disputed Henny's calumny that she was as verbose and diffuse in speaking as the amiable narrator of Torrey Chanslor's Amanda and Lutie Beagle mysteries. But not tonight, not with Kathryn Girard brutally murdered, Henny missing, and Emma Clyde's pale blue eyes watching her like Agatha observing an unwary and succulent rough-wing swallow innocently nesting along the eaves of Death on Demand. Annie started with Henny's phone call, described their search and Laurel's report that Serena Harris spotted Henny's old car turning onto Marsh Tacky Road shortly after six. She concluded, "and that idiot cop thinks Henny bashed Kathryn, then disappeared. Isn't that crazy?"

Emma didn't answer directly. Instead, her brilliant blue eyes settled thoughtfully on Henny's car. "A one-lane road. Both cars facing the park. So Henny turned in after the van. She was looking for the van. She saw it turn into this road and followed."

Annie waited expectantly.

"The driver of the van had to know there was a car behind it." Emma's cool voice was uninflected, but the sudden picture in Annie's mind was disturbing.

Annie looked at the old Dodge, pictured it driving along Laughing Gull or Red-Tailed Hawk and Henny spotting the vagrant van. How like Henny to give chase. She must have been puzzled indeed when the van turned off on Marsh Tacky Road.

"The driver of the van could not afford to be seen." Emma's gaze was distant, measuring. Was this how she looked when plotting her Marigold Rembrandt stories?

"Why? The back of the van contained Kathryn Girard's body. The driver turns off—" Emma held up a hand. "Wait a minute. The van turned in here to leave the body, that has to be how it happened. And now there's a car behind it. Can you imagine the murderer's panic? A car following, a car stopping behind the van. What to do?"

But Annie was thinking of Henny, not a murderer, picturing Henny climbing out of her car and walking toward the van, unwittingly marching into danger.

"Turn off the van headlights. Of course. Immediately." Emma's head swiveled toward the van so clearly visible in the flood of light from the spotlight. "Yes, look. The headlights are off. But Henny left her lights on"—a blunt hand pointed toward the black Dodge—"so she was clearly visible as she came up the road. Now the murderer had to work fast, slide across the seat, jump out the passenger door. That put the van between the murderer and Henny. Grab up something—a rock, a branch—and slip around the back of the van. When Henny walked past, the murderer attacked." She stopped, nodding.

Annie hadn't quite expected Emma Clyde to pull crimson silk scarves from a top hat à la Daniel Stashower's magician detective, but this seemed like a pretty lame denouement.

"Where's Henny?" Annie couldn't keep the disappointment from her voice. "How did the murderer get away? How come the van and the car are both still here?"

Emma ignored Annie. Her bright blue eyes focused on the van, and she spoke in a musing tone. "Henny isn't here. There's no trace of her—or her body—close to the van. There would be no reason for the murderer to hide Henny's body. What would that accomplish? That must mean Henny isn't dead."

Annie threw up her hands. "But what happened? I don't get it, Emma. Here comes Henny. The driver attacks. Where's Henny?"

Emma's broad mouth curved in a delighted smile. "It can only mean one thing. Something must have alerted

Henny. Maybe the murderer jumped at her, but slipped in the mud. Oh, that's nice. I like that. I'll use it in a book sometime. Everybody always pictures murderers as quick and efficient. But sometimes shit happens. Right? After all, Kathryn's just been killed. The murderer turns into a deserted road to leave the van or dump the body and here comes a car. That's enough to unnerve almost anyone. And the weather's lousy, the road slick and muddy. The murderer lunges at Henny and skids! Maybe there's only a glancing blow and Henny probably had on a poncho or was holding an umbrella. Oh yes, that's nice."

Annie watched Emma with widening eyes. Emma was scary, scary, scary.

Emma continued and her tone was as pleased as Agatha's purr after an illicit encounter with a cream pitcher left unattended on the coffee bar. "The murderer slips. Henny is struck but not seriously injured. Perhaps the murderer falls down and that gives Henny time to run. The murderer is between Henny and her car so Henny heads out into the forest."

Annie swung to look out into the wet night, punctuated by brief blips of light from bouncing flashes. That was when a faint shout went up from the direction of King Snake Lagoon. In a moment, a flare burst high in the air.

Annie broke into a run.

Annie clung to a limp, cold hand. There was the barest thread of a pulse. Henny's skin was cold, so terribly cold. As they waited for the medics, Annie heard the high chatter of the Boy Scout who had found her.

". . . thought it was just an old rag . . ."

In the circle of light from another scout's flash, Henny's crumpled body looked small and forlorn. She lay on her left side, one arm twisted beneath her, her head jammed against a thick branch that had fallen across the path.

Behind Annie, a crowd of onlookers parted for medics with a stretcher.

Annie gave that limp, cold hand a squeeze, and stood
to get out of the way.

A burly medic with a calm face and bright blue eyes
gently eased Henny onto the stretcher. He carefully strapped
her down to keep her immobile for the trek to the ambulance. "Hypothermia," his tall, thin partner murmured. They
worked together to wrap that still form in wool blankets
until only her face was visible, then expertly lifted the
stretcher and moved briskly up the path.

As they passed, Annie saw that Henny's thin face was
bluish with cold. Her eyes were closed. A swollen lump, the
skin abraded, looked red and angry near her left temple.

Annie followed the medics with their fragile cargo. As
they reached the road and passed by the searchers who were
gathering, called back by the sound of the ambulance siren,
Annie waved at friends.

"What happened?"

"Is she hurt?"

"Is she going to be all right?"

"Yes. Yes, she'll be fine." Annie heard her voice, bold
and confident. Inside, she was terribly afraid. That cold, cold
hand and the uneven pulse. And Henny was old. She never
acted old. She was bright and funny and brave and kind,
but she was old. Dammit, who had hurt her! Annie felt the
beginning of anger that crackled like a lightning-sparked
blaze.

Max sprinted up to Annie. "What does Henny say—"
His flashlight swept the moving stretcher. He broke off.

Annie grabbed his hand. "Max, I'll go with Henny. You
stay here. Try to talk to Billy and see what's going on with
the investigation. And," she called back as they reached the
ambulance, the red light whirring, "ask Emma to come to
the hospital."

Annie paced in the emergency waiting room. The door
marked ADMITTANCE was closed and no light shone through
the pebbled glass. A blond wood counter curved in front of

three desks, two computers and a bank of filing cabinets.
During the night shift, a clerk logged in patients at the second computer behind the counter. Past the end of the
counter, another door led to the cubicles for patients. Metal
chairs with red leatherette seats were ranged against the
wall next to a window that overlooked the emergency drive.
A dumpy woman with wispy white hair huddled in a chair,
her face splotchy from tears. A middle-aged couple held
hands. The wife stared at the door to the emergency cubicles. Her husband spoke loudly, insistently, "He'll be all
right, Maude. Tommy's tough. He'll be all right." But there
was terror in his eyes. A thin black woman stood by the
counter. "When can I go in to see my husband?"

The wan-faced attendant glanced at her watch. "Pretty
soon, ma'am. Please make yourself comfortable. I'll come
and get you when they're ready."

Annie wondered if all the others felt as helpless as she.
The nurse had shooed Annie out of the cubicle, saying
briskly that they needed to get Henny ready to see the doctor and was she a close relative?

A close relative? Annie almost said no, that Henny had
no family, but she caught herself in time and simply said,
"Yes." She was darned if she was going to be banished
altogether. And she was as close to Henny as anyone on
this island. Henny couldn't speak for herself now, she
couldn't fight for herself. But Annie could. It had taken a
few minutes to fill out the paperwork and Annie was
amazed how much she knew about her old friend. As for
insurance, Henny was on Medicare. Annie promised to get
her Medicare number and Social Security number as soon
as possible.

Now she paced, hungry, tired, worried and scared,
knowing those sensations must be the common currency in
every hospital emergency room. There was something so
ominous about the door that didn't open. What were they
doing in there? Was the doctor with Henny? Was Henny
still unconscious? How badly injured was she?

The door opened. The orderly probably never equa⁺
himself with a ministering angel and there was nothing ˌι-
gelic about his crew cut that was alternately pink and orange, the ring in his left nostril and the gap between uneven
front teeth. But he was smiling. No rock star ever had, for
that initial instant, a keener audience. "Mrs. Carson?"

The thin black woman's face was so eager, so hopeful
that Annie blinked away a sudden tear.

Mrs. Carson started toward the orderly, an answering
smile growing, her golden hoop earrings jangling like
Christmas bells.

As the door closed behind them, the room had a deflated
feel, silent as a deserted dance floor.

Annie paced. How long had it been? It seemed like a
long, long time. She checked her watch and for a moment
blinked in disbelief. Only ten o'clock? It seemed more like
midnight. And where was Emma? Surely she would come.
But no one, certainly including Annie, ever had the temerity
to tell Emma Clyde what to do. Annie wasn't certain she
especially liked Emma, but she wanted that incisive, coldly
analytical mind engaged in the effort to make sense of this
night. Had Max been able to find Emma among those mill-
ing along the road after the search ended? And where was
a police guard for Henny—unconscious, defenseless Henny?
Surely the new police chief understood the danger. Henny
must have walked toward the van and a waiting murderer.

Annie scrabbled in her shoulder bag for her cell phone.
She stepped outside but stood where she could see that very
important door. As she punched in the number of Max's
cell phone, she sent ESP messages: Max, turn on your cell
phone. Max, turn on your cell—

"Hello," his easy, familiar, cherished voice answered.

"Max, you're wonderful! You have your ringer on!"

He laughed. "I thought I had other qualities more de-
serving of admiration. And I have to confess, I'm waiting
for a call from Billy. Hey, what's the word on Henny?"

"No word yet. They made me go out to the waiting

room. She was still unconscious when I left her." A light breeze rustled the fronds of a clump of palms near the emergency room door. The rain had ended for the moment, but the air had a sultry, steamy, more-to-come heaviness. The plaintive cry of a mourning dove made the moonless night seem darker and sadder. "Max, did you find Emma and ask her to come over here?"

"Sure. She was sitting in her golf cart, staring at the van."

Annie frowned. That had to have been an hour ago. "Did she say okay?"

"Yes. Isn't she there yet?" Max sounded surprised.

"No." Surely Emma wasn't missing now. No. Annie would as soon imagine Sherlock Holmes deferring to Watson. "Maybe she changed her mind. I'll call her." Annie tossed it off as if a casual act, praying that she could within minutes acquire the smart-ass assurance of Janet Evanovich's Stephanie Plum and the tough confidence of Dana Stabenow's Kate Shugak. They wouldn't mind calling Emma. Okay, okay. Annie would do it. But not right this minute. "Max, where are you?"

"I just got home. I've been ferrying volunteer chauffeurs. Ingrid drove Henny's car and Laurel drove yours." There was an odd silence. "When I dropped Mother off, she rummaged around in her purse and found a drawing of a chamomile plant. It looked like a bunch of peculiar daisies and it smelled funny. She murmured something about scented and how odd that the soothing drink should be a product of a plant that signals energy in adversity. Then she handed me the drawing, kissed me on both cheeks like De Gaulle presenting a medal and wafted out into the night."

Annie might not be a whiz at tea leaves but she was getting the hang of flower messages. "Don't worry. She's giving us a psychic push to help save Henny. I'll call her tomorrow. She might have some good ideas." Annie heard her own words with surprise, since normally she equated Laurel's brain waves with unexplained vibrations from outer space.

For an instant, Max was speechless. Then he said firmly, "You must be hungry. I'll bring you some dinner. . . ." Annie was past caring about food. "Food doesn't matter." She ignored Max's shocked silence. Anyone would think she was as obsessed by food as Selma Eichler's happily pudgy detective Desiree Shapiro! Did Max think she was as desperate for mouthwatering sustenance as Nero Wolfe during the war years ("Help Wanted, Male" in the collection of novelettes, *Trouble in Triplicate*) when he might have traded in Archie for a succulent slice of prime rib? "We can't waste time thinking about food," she said bravely, ignoring the sudden lurch of her stomach. "What's happening with the investigation?"

Now the silence had a markedly different quality, that of a man trying to find words.

"Max?"

"Nothing." Only one word, but it bristled with bemusement, irritation and disgust. "Our I'm-in-charge-here new police chief says the case is closed, all that remains is to arrest one Henny Brawley when she regains consciousness. Garrett announced it's a clear case of women squabbling over charitable works. He was in an expansive mood after the coroner removed the body. He stood by the open door to the van while Vince Ellis—"

Annie wasn't surprised that Vince was on the scene. As the owner of the *Island Gazette,* he often covered big stories himself.

"—shot a dozen photos and interviewed him. When Vince asked what the motive might be for Henny to murder Kathryn Girard, Garrett tossed off a half dozen, ranging from jealousy to a club power struggle. In one superb flight of fancy, he suggested that Henny coshed Kathryn just before you and I turned onto Marsh Tacky Road, that the lights of our cars scared her and she ran out into the forest to hide and that's how she fell down and banged her head."

Annie forgot her hunger pangs. Now she knew how Bulldog Drummond felt when facing an utter cad, ready to scale cliffs, ford rivers and generally raise a little hell with the forces of evil. "That's ridiculous. How does the great detective explain Kathryn's body in the back of the van? If Henny followed Kathryn there to attack her, why wouldn't the body be found in the front seat or on the road beside the van?"

"This guy is unsquashable, Annie. To hear him tell it, poor Kathryn sought refuge in the back of the van against a weapon-wielding Henny, which would argue the intelligence level of a rabbit, and Henny battered her to death and was busy covering her with a blanket when we turned onto the road."

"Where's the weapon?" Annie pictured the front seat of Henny's old Dodge, the cell phone and the bag of books.

"Another point against Henny." Max sounded weary. "The fact that the weapon wasn't in the van proves that she ran off into the darkness clutching it."

"But nobody found—"

"Actually, somebody did. One of the bird-watchers spotted a croquet mallet just off the road in the direction Henny ran. Garrett had Pirelli shoot lots of pictures, then they took it into evidence."

A croquet mallet. For a moment, Annie wondered if she had wandered into a Constance and Gwenyth Little mystery of the absurd.

Max said grimly, "We'd better damn well hope Henny's fingerprints aren't on it. Of course, it won't help if they aren't. Garrett'll just say she had on gloves or wiped it off or something. His mind is closed tighter than a clam."

"Is he sending someone over here to guard her, make sure she doesn't escape?" That was infuriating, but a guard would be a guard. Annie didn't care who or why, so long as someone was on duty.

"Not until she regains consciousness. He's asked the hospital to notify him as soon as she does."

Annie rubbed her temple. She wasn't sure why it throbbed, whether from anger, hunger or general frustration.

Since she couldn't banish Garrett to a remote cabin outside Maggody, Arkansas, with Roz Buchonon as a housemate, maybe she'd better find a vending machine. She needed to think.

And dammit, where was Emma Clyde?

A pink Rolls-Royce slid silently to the curb, majestic as the *Queen Elizabeth.*

Max said, "Annie, I'll bring some food."

And the door to the emergency cubicles swung open.

Chapter 3

Cary Martin was a good doctor. Annie was glad he was on duty tonight. He and Henny had become well acquainted during Henny's stints as head of the Hospital Auxiliary. His long, narrow face was grave as he greeted them. "Hi, Annie." He nodded more formally. "Mrs. Clyde." Was there anyone on the island who didn't know the famous mystery writer? "The hypothermia danger is past, but we don't know the extent of the head injury." They stood in a small cramped office at the end of the hall past the cubicles for patients.

Annie fought a rush of disappointment. She'd hoped for reassurance that Henny definitely was going to be all right. She should have known the situation was uncertain when Cary ushered them in there, instead of taking them to see Henny.

He gestured vaguely at a small sofa, waited for them to be seated, then folded his six feet seven inches onto a straight chair. "She responded well to the hypothermia treatment, hot packs and heated oxygen. One episode of ventricular fibrillation required cardiac massage. She's stabilized. On an IV, of course, with antiarrhythmic drugs. The question now is the coma and whether she'll come out of it. The good news is that the CT scan doesn't show any massive lesions. Moreover, her eyes opened briefly. But edema from the head wound—"

Emma's bright blue eyes bored into his face. "Was she struck, Dr. Martin?" Emma got to the heart of it.

Cary leaned back, tilting the chair. He stared up at a lazily whirring ceiling fan. "From the report of the medics, it doesn't appear so. They said she was found with her head jammed against a fallen tree limb. One of them scraped off a trace of the tree. The bark appears to match particles in the wound. I'll leave that to the police laboratory. I just spoke with Chief Garrett before I came out to get you." He nodded toward Annie.

Annie realized unhappily that Cary's report could be used in support of Garrett's hypothesis, although the medical evidence only proved that Henny ran up a path in the dark and fell. It certainly didn't prove she was a murderer fleeing from her crime.

"Hypothermia and a head wound." Emma tapped her broad, blunt fingers on the sofa arm. "Have you examined her for any other trauma?"

Annie looked at Emma in surprise.

Cary answered promptly, "Her right forearm is bruised. A minor injury."

Annie remembered the way Henny was bunched on the ground. "But she fell on her left shoulder."

Emma's blue eyes glowed. "What kind of bruise?"

Cary looked from one to the other. "A roundish, two-inch discoloration located just above the elbow. Of course, I didn't see her before she was moved. All I can say is that she either bumped her right forearm good and hard or she was struck a sharp blow."

"Is she going to be all right?" Annie asked in a small voice.

Cary Martin rubbed a bristly chin. "She's stabilized. There's no alteration in fluid and electrolyte balance indicating brain damage. But we won't know until—and unless—she regains consciousness. We'll keep her in ICU until then." Slowly he heaved to his feet. He moved toward the door. "We'll take good care—"

"Dr. Martin." Emma was on her feet. She was looking up at a tall man, but nonetheless she dominated the room. "I've arranged for members of the Hospital Auxiliary to take around-the-clock shifts outside the intensive care unit. You know that Henny is a longtime member of the hospital board and has twice served as president of the auxiliary."

The doctor frowned.

Emma continued briskly. "We won't be in anyone's way. Thank you so much for speaking with us."

She sailed toward the door.

Annie scrambled to her feet and followed, feeling as outclassed as a cutter in the wake of a battleship. Obviously, it wasn't lost on Emma that Henny might well still be in danger.

In the hall, Emma headed for the back exit. Annie followed, though she had no idea where they were going or why. Emma pulled open the heavy door with a capable hand and charged up the interior stairs.

On her heels, Annie said mildly, "Do you have a particular destination in mind?" If it was a stop at the women's restroom, Annie knew there was one near the emergency waiting room next to the vending machines that were exerting a tidal pull on Annie.

"ICU." Emma's tone was abstracted.

Max sliced medium rare roast beef, piled it an inch thick on crusty white bread, added a swipe of tart mustard and a thicker layer of creamy horseradish mayonnaise, crisp romaine lettuce, slices of home-grown tomatoes, bread and butter pickles. As he worked, he took hasty bites of his own sandwich. He fixed two sandwiches for Annie, then wrapped three raspberry brownies in waxed paper and poured fresh coffee into a thermos. He worked quickly and efficiently, but his mind was focused on tomorrow and everything that needed to be done. It was clear that Chief Garrett considered Kathryn Girard's murder solved. There was no suggestion he would look deep into Kathryn Girard's background.

Max checked the kitchen clock. Almost ten-thirty. He'd asked Billy Cameron to call with information about the contents of Kathryn's purse. There had to be some personal information, enough to help Confidential Commissions begin a search for information on Kathryn.

Max was filling the picnic basket when the phone rang. He reached for it with a grin. Good old Billy. "Hello."

"Parking lot. Seaside Inn. By the Dumpster. Fifteen minutes." The connection was broken.

The second-floor hallway was long, quiet and fairly dim. A sudden rising giggle sounded as peculiar as an oompah band at a blues nightclub.

When they reached the nurses' station, the night nurse was eating with slow, savoring bites a huge piece of delectable white cake frosted with a mixture of pineapple and crushed pecans. Annie exhibited the kind of character celebrated in John Buchan's *The Runagates Club* and resisted lunging for the uneaten portion. She was so pukka sahib she deserved a ten-ounce filet mignon with béarnaise sauce.

The giggler, well-known to Annie and indeed to all involved in good works on the island, bounced indefatigably to her feet, clutching a notebook. If she'd stood any straighter, Annie would have saluted.

"Annie. Emma." Pamela Potts's dun-colored hair was contained within what looked like a mesh bag made of white netting. Annie dimly remembered her grandmother once talking about a snood, although perhaps she was just

weak with hunger—the nurse took the last bite of cake—
because "snood" didn't sound like a word that would describe anything but a mound of something edible in a Dr.
Seuss book. Pamela envisioned herself as an angel of mercy,
so she was partial to white. Tonight her crisp blouse reminded Annie of water chestnuts and her stiff slacks would
have pleased a meringue chef.

Annie licked her lips. Was there an old bag of gummies
in her purse? She fished in the oversize carryall but her
scrabbling fingers encountered only the flotsam and jetsam
of a purse but no food, not even a stray after-dinner mint.

Pamela's serious blue eyes gleamed with happiness. "I
came on duty at nine-thirty-seven. Patient Henny Brawley
is resting comfortably. No change in status. As a matter of
course, I brought a Tropical Surprise cake for the staff"—a
beaming smile at the night nurse, who gave a sigh of reple-
tion; Annie's hands clenched—"and have endeavored to
make myself useful by answering the telephone. However,
I have not stirred from my post, as I was instructed to keep
the entrance to the ICU under observation at all times."

Emma nodded. "Very good, Pamela. I want to impress
upon you the seriousness of your responsibility."

Pamela stood even straighter, her blue eyes shining in
anticipation. A Serious Responsibility was elixir to her spirit.

Emma's voice had the resonance of The Shadow at his
most mellifluous on his Mutual Broadcasting radio show.
"It is the responsibility of the Women's Auxiliary to protect
Henny Brawley from further attack—"

Annie looked at Emma sharply. Was it wise to be so
open? After all, it wouldn't take long for the word to get
out that Chief Garrett planned to arrest Henny for Kathryn
Girard's murder.

"—therefore every person who enters the ICU must be
logged in by the auxiliary. With no exceptions."

The nurse smothered a tiny belch. "Dr. Woody will take
her head off."

Emma's smile was grim. "Dr. Woody may terrorize the staff, but he understands the power of the auxiliary."

Pamela and the nurse gazed at Emma with profound respect.

Annie knew she was light-headed with hunger but something teased at her mind. Pamela had the imagination of a peanut butter jar—okay, she was seriously hungry—so whatever Pamela mentioned had a basis in fact.

"Pamela, how many phone calls have you logged in?"

Pamela thrust a notebook at Annie. The calls were logged in by time, the first at nine-forty. Six of the calls also listed names. There was no name by the call at nine-fifty-eight.

Annie pointed at it.

Pamela's usually placid face creased in dismay. "I asked for the name. But the caller had such a bad cold—"

Annie felt a prickle down her spine.

"—that I could barely understand. Whoever it was wanted to know when Henny would be moved to a private room."

"What did you say?" Emma's tone was gentle.

Pamela tucked a vagrant sprig of hair beneath the snood. "I said the patient would remain in intensive care until she regained consciousness."

Annie stared at the door to the ICU. Behind that door, Henny lay defenseless. "Emma—"

Emma raised a hand to silence Annie, but their eyes met and Emma nodded in agreement. Emma reached out, gripped Pamela's thin arm. "From now on, tell anyone who calls that the patient's condition is unchanged"—she looked from Pamela to the nurse—"and call me immediately should Henny regain consciousness."

The nurse said placidly, "Head wounds never remember a thing that happened. She may even think it's last week."

"That's a good point." Emma smiled at Pamela. She spoke slowly to impress her message. "Maintain to all inquirers that Henny remains unconscious even if she comes to. *All* inquirers. Make certain that your replacement understands this and agrees to it."

"I shall not leave my post unless I am assured of total cooperation." Pamela had a Mission. She would fulfill it. She combined the doggedness of Bertha Cool confronting Donald Lam with the serenity of Maud Silver quoting Tennyson.

"Nurse," Emma continued briskly, "call me if there is any change in Henny's condition. Please tell the next shift to do the same." Emma opened her purse and lifted out a silver card case. "Here is my number."

Annie glanced at the card. Yes, this was Emma's second line, which was answered always by voice mail. Annie was one of the few on the island who knew the number to the reclusive author's first line.

The nurse reached for the card. It might not be included in the nursing station job description, but once again Annie felt confident Emma's request would be obeyed.

Annie half turned, ready to walk swiftly down the hall. Wasn't there a vending machine by the door to the stairs?

But Emma still stood, frowning slightly, a blunt finger gently stroking her upper lip. The blazing cap of tight bronze curls and clashing colors of the shapeless caftan would have made most women look absurd. Not Emma. Her square face radiated power and her piercing blue eyes glinted with cold intelligence. "Pamela, tell everyone that the nature of Henny's head injury will result in memory loss of recent events and make it a point to discover everything about Kathryn Girard, her friends, her activities, her interests. Report to the Women's Club at nine tomorrow."

Pamela glanced at her watch, then grabbed her purse. "I have my cell phone. I'll get busy right now. I can call the people who watch David Letterman."

Annie looked at Pamela in astonishment. How did she know who watched what? This reflected awesome knowledge of island customs. Pamela's cooperation might prove to be invaluable.

As Annie and Emma neared the end of the hall, Annie's

eyes were on the vending machine. She was reaching into her purse when Emma took her by the arm. Annie's fingers felt the beveled edge of a quarter. So near, yet so far. Emma turned her firmly away from the machine. "All right, Annie. Here's what I want you to do. . . ."

The Seaside Inn parking lot held a couple of pickups, three station wagons and a half dozen sport utility vehicles. The two-story wooden building was L-shaped. Max drove past the near parking slots to an untenanted third line of parking places. At the north end, a Dumpster nestled next to a huge pittosporum bush. A clump of willows hid the refuse container from most of the rooms. Max pulled into the slot nearest the Dumpster, switched off his lights.

He watched the dark shadows near the shrub. A flashlight flicked on, then off. Max slipped out of his car, walked softly on the gravel.

"Over here." Billy Cameron's high tenor voice was as taut as a guy wire.

Max brushed past tendrils of willows, smelled rotting grass clippings and discarded fish heads.

"Billy—"

"Shhh. I'm not here. You never saw me. You never talked to me. Okay?" There was anguish in his voice. Billy tried hard to follow the rules. Sometimes, like a long-ago time when the woman he loved needed help, he forgot about rules. That time, when Mavis was a murder suspect, Henny Brawley helped solve the crime. Billy followed rules. Rule Number One: Don't forget your friends.

"Victim's purse was dumped out in front of the van, but her billfold was there with three hundred and sixty dollars in it. Driver's license in the name of Kathryn Joyce Girard of Broward's Rock address." Billy cleared his throat. "The chief was particularly interested in that since the mayor said Girard didn't have a car. But she had a license. Rest of the stuff from her purse was the usual, lipstick, makeup, comb, change purse. But no credit cards. The chief's going to follow up on that. Maybe the credit cards were stolen. Then we checked out her place. She lived up above her antique store. The front door wasn't even locked. Nothing appeared to have been disturbed and everything seemed to be in order in the upstairs apartment. There was no evidence the murder occurred there. The apartment looked like nobody lived there." There was a puzzled tone in his voice. "Clean. Bare. Closets empty. She was going on a trip. In the living room, there was a suitcase, plus a carry-on bag and a briefcase. All of them were shut. There was no examination by investigating officers"—his clipped tone rippled with disgust—"because the officer in charge said the luggage didn't have anything to do with the crime scene."

"So she was going on a trip. I wonder where." Max wished he could see Billy's face. "I suppose the premises were secured?"

Billy shifted from one foot to another. "Those instructions were given." But not another word did he say.

Max grinned.

As she passed the loading dock behind the hospital, Annie made another cross-hatch on an old envelope she'd pulled from her purse. She spotted a door at the end of the wing that held the ICU and made another check. She glanced up at the line of lit windows. What was it Emma had asked? Annie padded nearer, her rubber boots crunching oyster shells. No, this portion of the hospital, unlike the concrete latticework front, was sheer. Oh yes, there was a fire escape, but the end dangled a good twenty feet off the ground. It was the kind that descended under pressure of weight. Of course, anybody handy with a lasso might be able to snag it, but, as a general rule, lassoing was not a sea island accomplishment.

Annie was giddy by the time she completed her circle of the hospital. In Camilla Crespi's mysteries, everyone ate delicious Italian food all the time. Jean Hager's Iris House mysteries had pages laden with scrumptious dishes like deep-fried turkey and cherry cream crêpes. Annie forced her mind, if not her stomach, back to the task at hand. Seven entrances, not counting the dangling fire escape. She reached the main entrance, a two-story portico, and angled to her right and the sweep of drive leading to the emergency room.

Annie's eyes narrowed. Where the hell was Godzilla the Great who'd sent her off to reconnoiter? Okay, yes, maybe she was getting a little surly. Emma's pink car still sat at the curb. Annie surveyed the sidewalk and drive. No Emma. Sighing, Annie pushed the door and walked into the all-too-familiar emergency waiting room. The middle-aged couple looked up dully. The white-haired lady was gone.

Emma stood at one of the pay telephones. She lifted a broad hand in a commanding gesture.

Annie started toward the phones, once again feeling for quarters in the bottom of her purse. She was almost past Emma when that strong hand fastened on her arm.

The vending machine glittered like the Las Vegas strip. She spotted a Reese's Peanut Butter Cup. Agatha would never know.

Emma hung up the phone and reeled Annie in.

"Seven doors," Annie muttered, her eyes on the coin slot.

"Did you check each one?" Emma's grip never slackened.

"Yes. Nobody can get in this place without a key or a merit badge in skyscraper scaling." Annie leaned forward. Emma effortlessly restrained her.

"All right, Annie. We've secured the area. Henny is safe. I simply wished to be certain. Now it's time to bend our energies to detection. I used a land-based telephone to set in motion an undercover survey of the Marsh Tacky Road area. I called your mother-in-law." For an instant, Emma gave Annie a curious look.

Annie forgot about food. "Laurel? You called Laurel?"

Emma deftly positioned herself between Annie and the vending machine, then loosed her grip. She opened her oversize purse and rummaged, pulling out an oblong card. She handed it to Annie.

Annie studied the—to her—odd-looking, intertwined plants. The legend read: *Balsam, Barberry and Bayberry. Being the best, you excel because of impatience, sharpness of temper and discipline.* A P.S. theorized: *Perhaps Marigold triumphs as a detective because she has suffered cruelty in love? Or dealt cruelty in love? Or is it because she has a restless nature? Whatever, Marigold is Marvelous.*

"An interesting combination of insults and flattery," Emma observed, and once again a little smile twitched her broad mouth. "Laurel was presenting customized cards to some of us at the Women's Club meeting last week. She's quite enthusiastic about creating personalized floral note cards. That's what she will do tomorrow."

"Laurel? You mean you're going to send her to the houses near Marsh Tacky? What if she finds out something dangerous?"

"Don't worry, Annie. The woman is not such a fool as she appears. And she's quite willing to do her part to help Henny."

"But the murderer may figure it out." Annie felt herself being propelled across the waiting room.

"So much the better. We are going to scare hell out of murderer if at all possible." Emma was ebullient. "Oh yes. I've dealt with murder—"

Annie had a sudden, creepy memory of the fact that there had been some question as to whether Emma's philandering, much-younger second husband fell from Emma's yacht some years earlier or was pushed.

"—for a great many years." Emma's tone was confident. "Murderers are damn skittish. We don't want ours to relax so we're going to push every possible lever. We have to catch the murderer to save Henny. And we damn well are going to do it as fast as we can."

Soft-soled shoes slapped behind them. "Hey, lady, aren't you a close relative of patient Brawley?"

Annie whirled to face the emergency room clerk. Emma stood totally still, her square face bleak.

The clerk tossed her head and her wilted ponytail quivered. "We can't look after personal effects in emergency and they won't take it in ICU. Here's her stuff," and she thrust a blue plastic bag into Annie's hands, then turned and shuffled away on her soft-soled slippers.

Emma's eyes glinted as the steps faded away. "There goes my next victim. It will be a pleasure. I'm torn between a garrote and a toppling statue."

Annie clutched the blue plastic bag, wished her heart would stop thudding. "Or drop her into a pool with piranhas."

"I've done that." Emma's smile was as satisfied as an island alligator on a sunny bank. She pushed open the glass door.

Annie looked back longingly at the vending machines.

Emma was unmoved. "You can eat when you get home." She gave Annie an encouraging shove onto the sidewalk. "I'll give you a lift. I want to get to my office and organize for tomorrow."

The steamy air made Annie think of lifting the lid on a pot of chicken dumplings. Visions of delectable golden dumplings parted long enough for Annie to realize they were at Emma's pink Rolls-Royce.

Emma poked into her oversize canvas bag—

Was there any food in there?

—pulled out gold-plated keys linked to a medallion with a likeness of Marigold Rembrandt, and a couple of sheets of computer paper. "I went home and printed out Kathryn's White Elephant pick-up list before I came to the hospital. Here's a copy for you. I am puzzled by it, I must admit. You'll see what's wrong—"

Headlights swept up the hospital drive. Max's crimson Maserati slid to a stop behind Emma's car. He jumped out, waved. "Hi, Annie, Emma. Got some dinner. Plenty for both of you." He held up a picnic basket. Annie would have dashed to the food faster than Mary Daheim's Judith McMonigle Flynn whipping up a feast, had it not been for Emma's implacable grip.

"—the minute you look it over. I'll see you at the club in the morning. Nine sharp."

Annie would have promised to scale the Himalayas to win her release. "Sure. You bet. Nine."

Emma turned to greet Max, and Annie held out her arms for the picnic basket. She managed a thank-you before the first bite melted into delight.

"Oh, no thanks, Max." Emma declined a sandwich. "I had some vegetable juice earlier."

Annie was inhaling the sandwich. She flicked a disbelieving glance at Emma's girth. Veggie juice! And maybe some pork rinds and cashews on the side? Or did Emma eat bat wings and stewed entrails? No way did her ordinary dinner consist of V-8.

Emma reported on Henny's condition and the posting of the auxiliary by the ICU while Annie devoured the first sandwich and grabbed the second. She intended to alert Max that Laurel had her first undercover assignment, but she spotted the brownies.

". . . so we'll get everything in full swing tomorrow."

As soon as Emma's elegant car pulled away from the curb, Max reached for the picnic basket. "Come on, Annie, you can finish eating while we drive."

Annie grabbed the baggie with the brownies and wondered at the urgency in his tone. She settled in her seat and addressed the first raspberry brownie. As far as she was concerned, RBs combined the planet's most exquisite flavors.

"Sam Porter's working the gate tonight," Max said crisply.

Annie licked a vagrant smear of raspberry from her fingers. "That's nice," she observed amiably. Sam was a grizzled Marine veteran who was fond of Parotti's Bar and Grill (coldest beer, freshest bait) and surf fishing. "He's part of the ground crew for the Confederate Air Force. He'll be

sorry about Henny." Henny was a longtime pilot and often
flew her restored P51 Mustang at air shows.

"That'll work." Max was as delighted as Agatha Christie's Miss Lemon upon vanquishing a stenographic challenge. "Okay"—the Maserati turned left—"when we get to
the gate, you can tell him how she's doing and what the
doctor said and—"

Annie glanced at Max's handsome profile. He gripped
the wheel, staring straight ahead, like a Manning Coles hero
coming up on a German sentry. "Well, sure. But what's the
big deal?"

He shot her a grin that was sheer Joe Hardy. "You'll see.
We're going to act on information received—"

Annie loved the police jargon.

"—because it's all up to us."

Navy slacks, navy tee, navy tennies. Max's clothes were
equally dark. The only exception was the gloves. It occasionally drops into the thirties during a Low Country winter,
but mittens aren't required so Annie scrounged around in
the garage and found a couple pairs of white cloth gardening gloves.

"That's okay." Max stood at a kitchen counter, scrawling
a quick map. "We won't need the gloves until we get inside.
Look, here's how we'll go. . . ." Max made a box for their
house on Scarlet King Lagoon. "See, we can take the golf
cart paths all the way to the bike trail that goes through the
forest preserve—"

The island Chamber of Commerce claimed that Broward's Rock boasted more miles of bike trails than Hilton
Head. Annie suspected the Chamber was counting some
trails twice but certainly you could get quickly from one
end of the island to the other on a bike.

"—and skirt the gate. If anybody ever asks Sam, he'll
swear we drove past the gate about ten o'clock and didn't
come out again. Nobody will connect us with a break-in at
Kathryn Girard's store."

As they wheeled their bikes out of the garage, Annie dropped a flashlight in her basket. Max waggled a slender pencil flash. "This will show us enough to find our way and it will look more like fireflies." As they rode, he occasionally pointed the narrow beam on the trail. It was like riding inside a black velvet bag. The storm had done nothing to ease the humidity and Annie felt sweat beading her face and sliding on her skin. The golf paths were fairly easy to follow but once they plunged into the forest preserve, the darkness was so impenetrable that Max said softly, "Let's walk this portion, Annie."

She pushed her bike and followed the dip and slide of the sliver of light. She concentrated on keeping to the asphalt trail and tried not to picture their surroundings and the myriad of curious eyes belonging to bats and raccoons and snakes. A splat of something wet spangled her cheek. She doggedly marched on. It was nothing more than droplets of water from the forest canopy. Where were all the alligators? But surely an alligator would have something better to do with his time than loll around on a bike trail waiting to be bumped. "It's asphalt," she announced. Any self-respecting alligator would prefer a mud wallow.

"What did you say?" Max paused and she swerved to avoid running her bike wheel into his heel. The wheel came up hard against a solid barrier. Annie's heart lurched until she realized there was no movement. She must have struck a log. An alligator would have already made an hors d'oeuvre of her leg.

"How are we going to get inside?" Had Max brought any tools? What if Kathryn Girard's store had a burglar alarm?

Max repeated Billy Cameron's ambiguous answer. "I don't think we'll have any trouble. Besides, I think there's a balcony over the front porch. We'll find a way." Max was moving on up the trail. "I dropped in last Christmas to try and find something for Mother. You remember her musical pig phase?"

Annie remembered Laurel's musical pig phase. Annie
had scoured Web sites around the world in search of a min-
iature pig playing a saxophone and wearing a porkpie hat,
only to receive it in time for Laurel's birthday and be greeted
with a sweet smile. "Dear Annie, so kind of you." A vague
wave of a beautifully formed hand with the palest of pink
nail polish. "Those little dears are somewhere about. Yesterday I awoke and looked out my window and do you know
what I saw?" Annie had doubted if the scene included pigs
playing instruments. Laurel's smile was beguiling. "I saw
flowers. It was simply an epiphany. What speaks to us? Life,
my dear. And what tells us more about ourselves and our
world than glorious flowers?"

"Talking flowers," Annie blurted now at her husband's
back.

"No, no. It was pigs— Wait a minute, Annie." Max
jolted to a stop.

Annie's wheel swerved and she skidded into a fern that
showered her with moisture.

Something moved in the brush to their right. Branches
thrashed. Max swung the pencil beam. A raccoon paused a
few feet from them, his intelligent eyes surveying them
calmly. Then he turned and loped away.

"Wonder if he'd loan us a mask." Annie loved the quick,
confident creatures. She was smiling as they wound through
the rest of the forest preserve. But a mask wouldn't be a big
help if they got caught. She doubted Chief Garrett would
cut them any slack. Would Frank Saulter provide character
references from deep in a rain forest?

It was easier going once they were out of the preserve.
The trail wound past St. Mary's Church, its parking lot
empty, the asphalt shiny from the recent rain. Tendrils of
fog wreathed the steeple. They followed another trail past
soccer and baseball fields and reached the edge of Main
Street. All the businesses were shuttered except for Parotti's.
Bright red neon along the roof line bathed the nearly full,
foggy parking lot in a pinkish glow. Keeping to the far side

of the road, they pedaled fast and within a half block were again in darkness. The rutted dirt road curved inland, out of sight of the bar and grill. Tall pines pressed to the edge of the road.

Annie rolled to a stop. "I see some kind of light," she whispered.

Max's answer was equally soft. "Let's leave the bikes here." Shielding his light, he flicked it briefly off the road. "Behind those palmettos."

While Max stashed the bikes, Annie used her light to scuff around and build up a pile of sticks on the road to mark the hiding place for the bikes. It wasn't high-tech but she had no intention of walking home. She tucked the flashlight in her pocket.

They moved quickly, Annie stumbling once in a deep rut. Max caught her before she fell. A dim glow came ever nearer. Annie gripped Max's arm. "It's the front window of the shop." That was the only glimmer of light. The two-story wooden building sat by itself, tucked into a grove of towering pines. There was an empty turnaround just past the store.

They reached the deep shadow of the pines about ten feet from the front steps. An owl shrieked, a wild scream that resounded in the clearing. A chuck-will's-widow skimmed past, looking for flying insects. But there was no other movement, no other sound. The wooden steps creaked beneath their weight. Annie fished in her pockets for her gloves. Max pulled on his gloves and they eased up to the plate-glass window.

In the back of the long narrow room, crowded with tables and dishes, a single unshaded bulb dangled from the ceiling.

The light went out.

Annie clutched Max's arm. "Who turned it off? Max, what—"

"Shh. Hurry. Over here." He hustled Annie to the side of the porch. As they jumped to the ground, he pointed at a rain barrel. "Hide behind it. See if anyone comes out the front way. I'll go around to the back."

He was gone before she could protest, before she could remind him to be careful, to be very careful. No one had any business in Kathryn Girard's apartment and she doubted anyone else was there in response to a tip from Billy Cameron.

Annie crouched behind the rain barrel, her cheek pressed against the splintery wood. The smell of dank water mixed with a faint odor of creosote. Why would anyone come here? And why now? The second question was easier to answer. It was late, nearing midnight, a good time to move unnoticed around the island just as they had. As for why, Kathryn's apartment had to contain something of enormous importance to the intruder. But what could it be? Annie had a sudden vision of a bag of diamonds or a stolen Titian or—

Rusty hinges rasped.

Annie's heart thudded. She peered around the barrel. If only she'd brought her cell phone. But even if she could have called Billy Cameron, he wouldn't arrive in time.

The front door opened. A dark figure darted across the porch and moved swiftly down the steps.

Annie didn't think. Or actually she did, in a disjointed, unconnected way, sure that this mattered, that she had to know who was there, that Henny's safety and perhaps her freedom depended upon Annie. Annie pulled out her flashlight, turned it on. She glimpsed a dark coat, a dark cap.

The figure whirled, face shielded with a handful of folders, and lifted the other arm.

Maybe it was instinct. Maybe it was a childhood memory of *High Noon*. Maybe it was her recent rereading of an Eve Gill adventure by Selwyn Jepson. Whatever, Annie dived behind the rain barrel, scrabbling like a land crab as the gun cracked.

Face down on the uneven ground, she smelled the acrid tang of cordite as well as rotting leaves and pine straw. Water gurgled out of the barrel, splashing against her leg, cold as the frozen tundra in Alistair MacLean's *Night Without End*. Annie welcomed the icy wetness and the gouge of a root against her cheek. She was alive.

"Annie!" Max's shout shattered the night quiet. A beam of light speared into the night from behind the house. His feet thudded on the ground.

Her shoulders drawn tight, as if that would help against a bullet, Annie crawled on her hands and knees along the side of the house, then pushed to her feet. "Max," she yelled, and if a bullet came, it came. "Stop, wait. Don't go in front. Max, don't!"

They crashed together. Annie pushed and they fell, sliding on the slick pine needles. "Quiet, Max, quiet. Shh." She pulled the flashlight out of his hand, turned it off.

Max tugged at her arm and they crawled over the slippery pine needles until they were hidden behind a thicket of ferns. "Annie." His whisper held love and fear and a terrible relief.

She gripped his hand, felt herself begin to shake. His arms came around her.

"The door opened. Someone came out." She took a deep breath. "I thought I had to see." She lifted her head, strained to see through the night. "No one's there now. But Max"—her voice was stronger—"now we've got something to tell Chief Garrett."

Max got up on one knee, helped Annie and they both stood, looking toward the shop. "I wish we did." His voice was grim.

"But Max, why would anybody shoot at me? Garrett has to listen to that." She tugged on his arm, eager to get to a phone.

"How do we explain what we're doing here?" He resisted her pull, staring through the dark toward the road.

She got his point. "So what can he do, throw us in jail?" She was trying for defiant, but it came out sounding uncertain.

"No. But he'll claim we're trying to divert attention from

Henny." Max absently brushed pine needles and leaves from his trousers.

"The bullet in the barrel!" Quickly, she told Max. "That will prove . . ." Her voice trailed off. Sure, there was a hole in the barrel. Water was trickling out. But it didn't prove anyone shot at her. "Damn." And she couldn't even say whether the shooter was a man or woman. She squeezed her eyes shut for an instant, trying to re-create that fleetingly seen figure. Dark clothes, shielded face, that moving hand. No, she'd seen too little too quickly. It could have been either a man or a woman. Wouldn't Garrett sneer at that description!

"No. I'd like to call Garrett," Max said. "But we have a choice, Annie. We call Garrett or we look in the apartment."

Eve Gill would never hesitate. Annie started for the front porch.

Chapter 4

Max used his flashlight to find the switch for the dangling bulb.

As the dim light spilled down, Annie waggled her garden-gloved hand toward the plate-glass window. "Somebody might see it. We did."

"That's okay." Max looked as comfortable as Perry Mason with Della Street at his elbow. "The cops have already been here. As for anybody else, if they're on the sly like we are, they'll wait until we leave." Not even Mason could have elucidated the proposition with greater clarity.

They looked around the long, narrow store, at chipped figurines on scarred tables, old wooden toys, threadbare tapestries, tarnished silver-plated pitchers and bowls, dull glass, cracked plates, boxes of old buttons and stacks of dusty books.

Annie waved her hand and her gardening glove flapped. "Junk. How did she stay in business?" She looked toward the front of the shop. "Where's her cash register? I don't even see a counter."

Max pointed—pine straw shook free from his glove and wafted to the floor—at the nearby Queen Anne table and easy chair, the cushions dented from long use. "That's where she sat. I didn't buy anything—"

Annie wasn't surprised. Who would?

"—but another woman was paying for a Coca-Cola tray." He stepped to the table, lifted the lid of a rectangular metal box. Coins glittered in their compartments, but the back of the box was empty. A pad of paper lay next to the box. Otherwise, the table was bare.

Annie bent over the desk. A single sentence was printed large on the top sheet:

Women's Club van at four o'clock Thursday!!!!

Annie felt a wash of repugnance. There was something smug and distasteful in the deeply incised, flamboyant printing and the string of exclamation points, as if the writer took a particular pleasure in this pronouncement, a private glee not to be shared but to be savored. Annie shivered. Wasn't she drawing an ugly conclusion from scant evidence? Her gaze swung around the room. "I don't like this place."

"Not high on the charm scale," Max agreed. "But everything looks in order down here." He turned toward the stairs. "I'll go first."

His boots squished as he walked and so, Annie realized, did hers. They were leaving a damp trail. But who would see and who would care? She smiled fondly at Max's back as she followed him up the worn, squeaky wooden stairs. Although she had no intention of being a gothic heroine (saved by the white knight in the last chapter), she appreciated Max's manly intent in taking the lead.

She watched with interest as he eased open the door at the top of the stairs, then gave it a sudden kick and burst through. She wondered if any studies had been done to gauge the effect of James Bond movies on American males.

When the ceiling light flashed on and he stood aside for her to enter, she noted his bright eyes and beaming smile. He was having a hell of a time.

But her answering smile slid away as she stepped into a room that would have made Hercule Poirot's austere apartment look fussy.

Max followed her gaze. "Yeah. I've been in motel rooms with more personality."

No rugs. A single sofa. An easy chair with a floor lamp on one side, a low table on the other. Nothing else. No paintings, no vases, no photographs, no bric-a-brac. Nothing. Unlike the room below, there was a cold cleanliness here, a faint smell of furniture polish, the floor shiny with wax. The only indication of habitation was a coffee mug on the small table, next to a copy of *Architectural Digest*.

And, of course, the floral tapestry carry-on and sleek brown leather briefcase on the dining room table. A matching tapestry suitcase sat near the front door.

Max glanced at the suitcase, then hurried toward the dining room table. Annie walked quickly past him toward a closed door. If anything reveals a woman, it is her bedroom. Somewhere in this featureless apartment, there must be a clue to Kathryn Girard.

Annie pushed open the door and switched on the light. It was easy to take in the whole room in a quick glance: a bare floor, a single bed covered with a white comforter, a plain wooden chest of drawers. No curtains, no mirror, no dressing table, no array of cosmetics or perfumes, no jewelry case, no pictures, no photographs, no books.

Kathryn Girard had existed. Annie knew that. She'd had casual conversation with Kathryn at a dozen social functions. Tonight she'd seen the battered head and still body bunched in the back of the Women's Club van. But Kathryn Girard had to be so much more and so much less than Annie had ever realized to have lived in this featureless, bleak apartment.

Swiftly, Annie checked the chest of drawers. Empty. So what else was new? There was not even a stray button or a crumpled sales slip. It was eerie that Kathryn had left so little trace of her occupancy and no hint to her personality. The bathroom, too, was empty except for some tissues and a crumpled tube of toothpaste in the wastebasket. In the closet, a row of hangers hung unused. No clothes, no shoes.

Annie whirled and hurried back to the living room. "Max, this is crazy! She didn't *live* here. She must have camped out, lived out of her suitcase. There's nothing anywhere."

"But there's something here." Max pointed at the table.

Annie hurried across the room, her boots slapping against the wooden floor. She stopped at the table and stared down at Max's display: Two driver's licenses and an open passport.

"In her briefcase." Max's eyes gleamed.

Annie almost spoke, then her eyes widened and she gazed in disbelief. Yes, each held a familiar picture, Kathryn's heart-shaped face with the big dark eyes and a slight half smile, but one license was for Louise Carson, resident of Chicago, and one for Miriam Gardner, resident of Los Angeles. The passport was in the Gardner name.

Max's gloved hand pushed forward a Visa credit card, also in the name of Gardner.

Max pointed at the carry-on and suitcase. "Why don't you check them out. There's more stuff in the briefcase. Here's a copy of her lease. Did you know Ben Parotti owns this place? And here"—he pointed to a stack of envelopes— "are her bank statements. She closed out her account yesterday. And look at this!" Max held up an airline ticket, opened it. "Apparently, Mrs. Gardner was flying to Mexico City on Saturday."

Annie felt like they'd lifted the lid on a bucket to expose a writhing mass of snakes. She didn't know who Kathryn Girard really was, but Annie had a firm conviction that there was nothing good to be discovered.

Annie opened the carry-on and found a couple of paper-back books, a Robert Ludlum thriller and a collection of crossword puzzles, some unlabeled medicine bottles with pills that could be for anything, a sack of M&M's, face cream, tissues, a black sweater, bottled water, throat lozenges, sunglasses and a small leather photo album. Photo album! Annie grabbed it, flipped it open. The album had plastic sheets for photos to be fitted front and back. She stared at the top picture, a rather ordinary color photo of the Broward's Rock harbor. She turned the page. The second print was another harbor shot from a different angle. She flipped through the pages, more and more puzzled. Every page was full, photos of the library, a sailing schooner that had visited the island over the Fourth of July, the ferry, a half dozen marsh shots, a wood ibis on a piling, the rotting hulk of a bateau, a beach umbrella, a formation of pelicans. There were no people in any of the shots. The photography was unremarkable, no dramatic sunrise or sunset, no artful lighting or telling shadows, just ordinary, run-of-the-mill, snap-a-shot photography.

The store was shoddy, the apartment spooky, but the photo album seemed strangest of all. Annie tossed the peculiar little album into the carry-on and fumbled with the zipper, the thick gloves making her hands clumsy. She stopped, frowned, pulled out the album and tucked it under her arm. Who would know that it was missing? Certainly not Chief Garrett. She glanced at Max, who was busily writing in his small notebook. Maybe he could make some sense out of the album.

She was still frowning in thought as she tipped the large case on its side, unzipped it. When she lifted the lid, some of the tension eased out of her body. Actually, it wouldn't have surprised her to find a shrunken head or bags of bones. That would be in keeping with the weirdness of the apartment and the somehow sinister banality of the album. But the clothes—four skirts, a half dozen blouses, two pairs of slacks, panty hose, lingerie, a gown—were perfectly ordinary and of good quality. Kathryn Girard apparently always dressed in black and she preferred one hundred percent cotton. Even the shoes were black: flats, sneakers and house slippers. Annie shivered, realizing she was touching clothes that now dead but recently living hands had folded and arranged. She ran her fingers in the elastic pouches on either side. One held a leather identification tag. Annie opened the flap and saw a photo of Kathryn, but the name read Miriam Gardner.

She jumped to her feet. "Look at this!" She held open the flap for him to see.

Max nodded, flipping his notebook shut. "Makes sense because the plane ticket's in that name. My guess is that she used the Gardner name when she traveled. Maybe it's her real name. Or as real as we'll ever know about. But we've got enough now to track her." He carefully eased the papers back into the briefcase.

Papers.

A folder.

Annie's eyes widened. "Max." She dropped to her knees beside him. "There's something missing." She pressed fingers against her temple. "Whoever it was—tonight—that's why I couldn't see the face!"

Max understood finally. The fleeing figure clutched a folder or folders. "Annie, think!" Did Poirot use that impatient tone with Hastings? "Was it large? A lot of papers?"

Try as she might, she couldn't dredge up another detail, just the shielded face, hidden behind oblong, stiff paper. "A folder," she said stubbornly, "that's all, maybe several folders."

"A folder. Or folders!" he repeated excitedly. "Annie"—he pulled her to her feet—"that tells us a hell of a lot. Don't you see?"

Folders. Annie prided herself on her deductive abilities. Why should Max act like Mike Hammer spotting a blonde upon learning that their armed intruder escaped with folders most likely filched from Kathryn Girard's briefcase?

Folders didn't take up much room . . . Kathryn obviously was involved in something illegal . . . what could . . . Annie nodded suavely, restraining her impulse to shout eureka. After all, she was the detective here. She tapped her chin reflectively. "Why, it's obvious. It can't be drugs. Or stolen jewelry. Or anything bulky. What fits in folders?"

"Papers," he said grimly. "Papers someone was willing to kill for."

It was almost one o'clock in the morning when they eased their bikes into the garage. They pulled off their muddy boots, which had slogged through all kinds of detritus this night, and dropped them by the steps. Annie reached into the bike basket for the leather album. When they stepped into the kitchen, they looked at each other and laughed. Max had a cottonwood tuft in his thick blond curls, his navy blue polo sprouted pine straw and his pants were splotched with mud. Annie looked like a refugee from a pig wallow, her hair tangled and her face smudged. She tucked the little leather album under one arm and brushed ineffectually at her slacks.

Max glanced at the album. "What's that?"

She held it out. "It was in Kathryn's carry-on."

Max flipped through the album, then shrugged and dropped it on the kitchen counter beside the crumpled plastic bag with Henny's clothes that Annie brought home from the hospital. "Maybe you can frame it as a souvenir, but it's pretty worthless as a clue."

Annie stopped at the sink to wash her hands. Did he think he was Anthony Boucher's Fergus O'Breen? He certainly sounded as cocky. Well, she wasn't going to have her discovery belittled. As was once observed by a long-ago detective, Harvey O'Higgins's John Duff, every crime has a psychological origin. Duff was describing the murderer, but it applied equally well to the victim. "That album's an anomaly, Max. It has to be important. When we know why she carried it, we will know why she was murdered." With that sweeping announcement, Annie moved toward the refrigerator.

Dorothy L. pranced into the kitchen, round white face alert, eyes bright, tail waving.

"No, sweetie, it isn't time to eat." For cats. Annie opened the refrigerator. What was an evening's end without vanilla ice cream topped with fresh raspberries and chocolate syrup? So it was a little past the usual time for an evening repast. Was she in a rut? "Want some ice cream, Max?"

"Now? Actually, I—" He bent down. "Are you hungry, honey?"

Annie thought his tone of incredulity when speaking to her was in marked and not very attractive contrast to the sugary concern when addressing Dorothy L.

"Are you a hungry, starving, mistreated little girl?"

Annie grimly dipped into the ice cream while Max opened the lower cabinet to retrieve cat food.

When her dessert was ready—so yes, she'd gone for three dips, what the hey, it'd been a long night—she settled at the breakfast bar. The first bite was exquisite. She looked fondly at Dorothy L., who was burrowing her little pink nose into a mound of chopped fish. To each his own. Annie lifted her spoon.

The phone rang.

Annie's eyes swung to the clock over the kitchen window. One-eighteen.

Max reached out and snatched up the receiver. "Hello." As he listened, his body relaxed and he began to smile. He looked toward Annie and turned a thumbs-up. "So she doesn't remember anything, huh? Well, that's probably safer. Get the word out, Emma. Yeah. Thanks for calling. Right. Tomorrow. Thanks."

Max fished a couple of oranges out of the fruit basket, peeled them and tossed them in the juice crusher. "Henny's lucid. Has a hell of a headache, but otherwise fine. No vision problems." The crusher noisily crushed.

Annie smiled and spooned. Fresh raspberries coated in

chocolate with an ice-cream base might just be the best taste in the world. Tomorrow she'd fix up a goody hamper for Henny and take her the books that had just arrived. And she'd toss in her newest prize collectible, Ngaio Marsh's *Death of a Fool*. And she would go by Henny's house and get a gown and some clothes. Annie reached for a telephone pad and made a note: *Henny/books/clothes/snacks*.

". . . moved her to Room Two Eighteen." Max held a glass under the spigot.

Annie felt a quiver of unease. "Is she going to be safe there?" A room certainly wasn't as closely observed as the ICU.

Max drank thirstily. "Not to worry, Annie. Garrett's stupidity comes in handy here. Emma said Pirelli's on duty out in the hall. And there will be an auxiliary member in the room with her."

That should be safe enough. Annie scooped up the last portion of ice cream. In the morning, they would help get the word out that Henny didn't remember anything at all of the previous night. But Annie knew Henny wouldn't be safe unless Kathryn's murderer was caught. That dark figure outside Kathryn's store had not hesitated to shoot.

Annie wiggled her toes in the foamy bubbles. Was it decadent to take a bubble bath in the middle of the night? Not after the night they'd put in.

The shower door opened and Max stepped out. Mmmm, mmmm, mmmm. Actually, there was something better than vanilla ice cream laced with chocolate and topped with fresh raspberries. Annie pulled the plug. Mmmm, yes. Max looked across the bath and she saw his smile and its reflection in the mirrors. In two steps he was beside the tub and reaching down to pull her up. So they were wet. Mmmmm.

The banana split dish slid over a mound of meringue and splashed into a lake of chocolate. Annie stood in the prow of the dish, night-vision binoculars at the ready. Cotton candy fog swirled around the dish. If she could just see through—

The piercing peal poked into her sleep-numbed brain.

Annie struggled to regain the dream, dipping her hand into the smooth, velvety chocolate—

"Annie"—a muffled plea—"the phone."

Annie rolled onto her elbow, reached for the screaming banshee instrument. "Hello."

"Surely you don't intend to lie abed when our dear Henny is at risk."

Annie blinked at the telephone. She knew that raspy voice, knew it well. But Miss Dora Brevard, the doyenne of Chastain, South Carolina, was supposed to be in Italy at the Tuscany villa of her cousin, Sybil Chastain Giacomo, who maintained a residence at the family Tarrant mansion in Chastain as well as the Giacomo villa in Sienna. Sybil had long ago divorced the race-car-driving scion of the Giacomo family, yet she spent a part of every year at their villa. Flamboyant and intriguing, Sybil preferred younger men and flouted convention whenever possible. That Sybil had invited Miss Dora to visit was merely another indication of her unpredictability.

"I thought"—Annie cleared her throat; it was hard to talk when your body was still surfing a chocolate lake— "that you were visiting Sybil." Annie glanced at the phone. Oh God, surely it didn't read five A.M.

"I am. I find Sybil . . ."—the pause was long enough to eat up several long-distance dollars considering the rates between Sienna and Broward's Rock—"continues to impress me with her vivacity."

Annie was awake enough to suppress a snort.

"However, I did not call to discuss my holiday, interesting though it is." The ancient voice rippled with amusement. "Sybil's daughter sent us an E-mail about Henny's predicament and I felt compelled to contact you. I knew if I called at a somewhat early—"

Somewhat early?

"—hour I should catch you. Now, please give me the details. Courtney's report was sketchy."

Annie knew the village network throbbed with energy but, nonetheless, she was impressed. Sybil's daughter Courtney and her husband, Harris Walker, lived on the island. Was Courtney in the hospital auxiliary? Yes, that had to be it. And now the word was out all the way to Italy.

When Annie concluded her report, there was another moment of silence. "The White Elephant Sale," Miss Dora mused. "There are possibilities there. Was the woman killed because of something she picked up? Did she observe something while making the pick-ups that placed her in danger? The first necessity is to determine where the van stopped. Then it will be essential to learn everything possible about the occupants of those houses. Here is what I would suggest, my dear. . . ."

Annie scrabbled for a pad and pen, didn't find them. But she could remember the two names Miss Dora gave her. One she knew well, Edith Cummings, reference librarian at the Lucy Kinkaid Memorial Library. The second she knew casually, Adelaide Prescott, an old and very rich lady.

"Tell Adelaide I send my best." A whispery laugh. "Ask her if she remembers the night we slipped away from the cotillion." Annie had a quick vision of two young ladies in white dresses sweeping across a terrace. Did the waiting swains have an early Model T or was that night's adventure begun in a buggy?

A tiny cough. "Well, every dog has its day, young lady. Never forget that. As soon as you obtain this information, call me. And tell Max I'll be bringing him some salami. Very unusual. Spiced with cloves. Tasty."

Annie hung up the phone and poked Max. She didn't intend to be the only person awake at this forlorn hour. Besides, she couldn't wait to tell him about his salami. It was illegal to bring it through customs. But no sniffing beagle would be a match for Miss Dora.

*   *   *

Annie sprinkled raisins on her papaya, contemplated the sugar bowl.

Max averted his eyes and reached for the coffeepot. "More?" he asked.

Annie nodded. Her hand swerved away from the sugar bowl. Not that she was intimidated. It was simply a judgment call. "Why is it clever when a *chef* combines unusual foods and disgusting when hoi polloi do it?"

"If you have to ask . . ." Max murmured, filling both their cups.

They grinned at each other companionably, Annie took an ostentatiously large bite, and Max munched his buttered English muffin toasted with grated cheddar, crumbled smoked bacon and a dash of honey.

Annie popped up, retrieved the leather photo album she had liberated from Kathryn Girard's carry-on, and placed it beside her plate. She slipped into her place, added a few more raisins and opened the album, to be confronted once again by the unexciting view of the Broward's Rock harbor.

Max glanced at the album, but didn't bother to comment. Instead, he flipped open his small notebook. "Miss Dora's ideas aren't half bad," and he began to write, then paused. "Didn't Emma give you the sheet with the pick-up addresses on it last night?"

Mostly Annie remembered suffering voracious pangs of hunger. But yes, at some point, Emma had said something about going home and printing out the list but the list didn't make sense.

Annie pressed her fingers against her temples. "I've got it!" She'd left her purse on the hall table last night before their bike foray, since even well-dressed cat burglars rarely carry purses. Annie dashed into the hall. She returned with the list, scanning the addresses. "I see what Emma meant."

Max took the sheet, read the list, then frowned. "Annie, this can't be right."

"Max," she replied with the authority of Monica Quill's

Sister Emptee Dempsey, "if Emma Clyde says this was the route assigned to Kathryn Girard, this was the route."

"But only one address is inside the resort gate and to go there, Henny would have turned left, not right."

"I know." The guard at the gate told Max that Henny turned right. So where did that leave them?

Max rumpled his thick blond curls. "I don't get it. And if Garrett ever sees this list, he'll claim that Henny wasn't following Kathryn, that they must have arranged a meeting."

"On Marsh Tacky Road!" Annie threw up her hands. "That's crazy."

Max tossed the list onto the kitchen table.

Annie plopped back into her seat and picked up her spoon. She looked again at the album, slowly turning the pages. The album's bland nature scenes were *the* most boring damn pictures. But Kathryn Girard didn't have a single other photograph in her possession. So why these, why, why, why?

The phone rang.

Annie grabbed the cordless. "Hello."

"Annie, my sweet." Laurel's husky voice brimmed with energy and good humor. "I've just popped by the hospital. Dear Henny is sleeping. I left the dearest flower card." There was an expectant pause.

"A flower card!" Annie wondered for a moment if she'd overdone the note of rapturous interest.

Max's dark blue eyes, so reminiscent of his mother's, looked suddenly wounded.

Annie flashed him a sweet smile.

"I propped the card up by Henny's water carafe. They aren't permitting the flowers—and there are so many of them—in the room just yet. The nurse said absolutely not without the doctor's approval. And the *nurse!* Annie, she is Nurse Adams, actually Hilda Adams. I find that a wonderful, meaningful coincidence—"

Even Annie had to admit the long arm of coincidence

sometimes occurred. Nurse Hilda Adams was a sweet-faced, spunky heroine in several mysteries by Mary Roberts Rinehart.

"—and I impressed upon her how important it is to protect our dear Henny. I gave her a card, too. Henny's card is elegant and simple, periwinkle for friendship, morning glory for affection, and dogwood for durability." Another expectant pause.

Annie saw dark blue eyes regarding her intently. So, all right, Max felt his mother needed encouragement. Actually, Annie felt precisely the opposite, but in every happy marriage there are many compromises. "And Nurse Adams's card?"

"Goldenrod for precaution, lavender for distrust, oleander for wariness." A deprecating laugh. "Each of us must contribute as we can."

"Laurel, that's wonderful. I honestly don't know how you do it." Annie had no intention of defining the wonderfully vague pronoun.

"Oh my dear, how sweet of you." Was the emphasis on 'sweet' overlong? "I worked quite late. I've a dozen or so cards with the same striking message."

Annie didn't wait for the pause. "Yes?" she asked encouragingly.

Laurel's husky voice dropped, soft and eerie as a waterfall in a cavern. "Basil for hatred, columbine for folly, and rhododendron for danger."

Danger. Annie said quickly, "Laurel, be careful. Be very careful."

But the connection had already been broken. Laurel was not one to forgo a dramatic finale.

Annie punched off the phone. "I forgot to tell you last night. Emma recruited your mom to survey the area near Marsh Tacky Road."

Max shot her a quizzical look. "On the theory that if Laurel's knocking on doors, she won't be disrupting Emma's fine-tuned investigation under way at the club?"

Annie grinned. "Actually, I think you do Emma a disservice. She said your mother . . ." How to put this tactfully? Perhaps there was no way to completely report Emma's comments. "Was eager to help clear Henny."

"Well, of course Mother's always willing to help out. And she may find out something helpful." He pushed away the computer printout of Kathryn Girard's donation route. "Certainly more helpful than this." He picked up his notebook. "Okay. We know that list doesn't work. So where did Kathryn go last night? Why? What did she pick up? What did she see?"

Annie slapped the album shut and dragged widespread fingers through her curly hair. The album might as well have pulsed out invisible gamma rays, she felt so certain it held a secret. But no matter how many times she looked through it, the blah contents didn't change.

Max glanced up. "You resemble a snowy egret looking for a mate."

Annie smoothed her hair. She wasn't going to talk about the album, since Max so obviously dismissed it as unimportant. As for Miss Dora's suggestions—

She said abruptly, "You're starting at the wrong end."

Max looked surprised. "Annie"—his tone was gentle—"that's where it all began, with Kathryn heading out in the van, and somewhere between the Women's Club and Marsh Tacky Road, she got killed. Something had to have happened—"

Annie held up both hands like Jaqueline Girdner's Kate Jasper quelling a group of fractious Marin County dwellers. Max stopped short, looking a trifle affronted. Okay, maybe traffic cop hand gestures were overkill. But she said firmly, "No. Stop. Wait."

Max put down his pencil and looked attentive, as courteous as Charlie Chan listening to a witness.

"It's not where she went. It's why she went." Maybe she did owe something to yesterday's memory of Detective Duff.

Or maybe it was the result of a mélange of impressions, the heavily impressed sentence on the pad at Kathryn's shop, the stolen folder, a gunshot in the night, too many names for one face, an album that defied explanation. Whatever, Annie pushed back her chair, and fluffed her hair, truly resembling a snowy egret as she paced. "It begins with Kathryn. Yes, I know we have to find out where she went, who she saw, but Kathryn's the key, Max. Who was she? Why did she live in such a weird way? Why is that apartment so bare? Who is Miriam Gardner? Why were her bags packed? Where was she going?"

Max waved his hand in dismissal. "Sure, we'll go into all that. She was flying to Mexico City. As for her apartment, she was probably just an odd loner. I know you thought she might be into something crooked, stolen antiques or paintings or jewelry. But apparently the only thing taken from her place was a folder out of the briefcase. And the most important fact is that her bank account was that of a small and not very successful merchant." He whipped open his notebook, read off modest balances for the past six months. "Don't you see? Even a small-time crook should have more money than that. And Billy said there was about three hundred and sixty dollars in her purse. And there wasn't any money in the briefcase—"

Annie interrupted, "Maybe it was money that was taken. Maybe that's what the intruder came for."

Max shook his head, not quite with the patronizing air of Leslie Ford's Col. Primrose. "In a folder? Nobody carries money in a folder, especially in a folder in a briefcase that had to be carried through airport security."

"Another bank account," Annie said feebly.

Max folded his arms, looked as complacent as a Lillian Jackson Braun cat. "And where's the checkbook?"

Annie's fingers twitched. Max was lucky she didn't have the homicidal impulses so prevalent in Pamela Branch books. She was beginning to feel like Tuppence Beresford when Tommy was trying to leave her out of the action in *N or M?* And she was so sure she was right. So, okay, maybe she was going on intuition, but unlike Ariadne Oliver, she had the inexplicable album.

Annie whirled and snatched up the album and shook it. "This matters. This has to matter. Maybe there's a secret code on the back of the pictures." She flung herself into her chair, opened the album, lifted the first plastic cover and tugged at the picture. But the photo was only halfway out when she stopped and stared.

"Hey, Annie!" Max reached over and poked his finger between the plastic sheets to pull out a crisp thousand-dollar bill. Max reached into the cutlery drawer and found a pair of tongs. Using a dish cloth to hold the album, he eased up the remaining sheets, then lifted each photo with the tongs. Three rows of bills were placed behind thirty photographs.

"Ninety thousand dollars!" Annie's voice wavered between a squeak and a choke. "My God, Max."

Even Max, insouciant, always unruffled Max, was stunned. "Damn, that's clever. Don't you see, Annie, Kathryn had this album in her carry-on bag. When she went through customs, the agent might open the album but the bills would be hidden behind the photographs." He used the dish cloth to carefully polish the page that Annie had handled and the inside and outside of the album covers.

Annie appreciated her fellow cat burglar's concern for her fingerprints. And his. But she stared at the album as if it had suddenly turned into a poisonous toad. "What are we going to do with it?"

"Nothing right now." He tossed the album onto the counter.

"All that money," Annie breathed. "Who does it belong to?"

"I don't know. We can pretty safely assume Kathryn didn't come by it honestly." He looked at her with admiration. "You win, hands down. We were starting at the wrong end. Now we know what to do. We've got to find out every-thing about Kathryn Girard."

Max was pleased with the legend on the plate glass of Confidential Commissions. Beneath the firm name in gold letters, black letters invited: TROUBLED, PUZZLED, CURIOUS? WHATEVER YOUR PROBLEM, WE ARE HERE TO HELP. His eyes wid-ened. The lights were already on. He reached out, turned the knob. The door was unlocked. He stepped inside.

His secretary Barb, big, blond, buxom and bright, looked up from her computer. "I've been here since five," she said briskly. "I heard all about everything at mah-jongg last night. If Garrett thinks he can arrest Henny Brawley, he's got another thing coming!"

Max wondered if Garrett was aware yet that he was trifling with an island icon.

"And Max"—Barb shoved back her chair—"you're not going to believe this, but Kathryn Girard doesn't exist! No driver's license, no Social Security number, no taxes paid. She had a small bank account here in town, but she closed it out yesterday. Apparently, she always paid for everything in cash. No credit card. I've tried to crack the FBI's witness protection program, but I haven't had any luck."

"No driver's license?" His face was intent.

Barb was definite. "Not from the sovereign state of South Carolina."

"That's interesting, because apparently the police found one in her purse. It must have been a fake. Okay, Barb, see what you can pick up on this name," and he wrote down Miriam Gardner.

Annie clicked off the phone. Thank heavens for Ingrid. Ingrid Smith Webb was not only a friend, she was the most agreeable employee in the world and she was quite willing to open Death on Demand this morning even though she wasn't due in until noon. Annie glanced at the clock. How could it already be eight-thirty? She hurried across the kitchen—she wanted to go by the hospital but she needed to be at the Women's Club by nine and the thought of reporting late to Emma Clyde inspired speed—when she skidded to a stop beside the crumpled blue plastic bag from the emergency room. She didn't want Henny's clothes to mildew. In the Low Country humidity, damp things squeezed into plastic could develop a green film faster than Clark Kent crossing the newsroom. Annie emptied the sack: a white blouse, navy slacks, white cotton bra and panties, white cotton tennis socks, navy tennis shoes.

Holding the clothes, she clattered down the steps into the garage and turned toward the washing machine. Last night, she and Max had draped their muddy clothes across the dryer. She decided on a dark wash first. Automatically— her mind focused on seeing Henny and reporting to Emma and talking to Pamela Potts and the club auditorium filled with donations for the White Elephant Sale—Annie turned out the pockets. Nothing in Max's, a bookmark in hers, a folded note card in Henny's.

Annie smoothed out the card, expecting a list of wanted books in Henny's small, neat printing. Instead, she saw a computer printout pick-up list for the White Elephant Sale. A big, dark X covered the printed addresses. Annie immediately recognized the addresses because this was the list that had puzzled her and Max. Next to the big X, four new addresses were scrawled in oversize printing, the same flamboyant, somehow impudent script that Annie had seen only last night in a single sentence deeply imprinted on the white notepad at Kathryn Girard's store: *Women's Club van at four o'clock Thursday!!!!*

Annie stared at the four new addresses—31 Mockingbird Lane, 17 Ship's Galley Road, 8 Porpoise Place, 22 Sea Oats Circle—and knew she was seeing a map to murder.

Annie loved coming to Confidential Commissions. The outer office, where Max's secretary presided with a ready smile and a sunny disposition, was fairly long and narrow but the morning sun poured a golden swath across the heart-pine floors. Barb's white pine desk and assorted white wicker chairs added a casual beach air. Modigliani prints on the walls were not quite as colorful as Barb with her beehive hairstyle and penchant for fiery red dresses.

Max's spacious office featured a red leather chair equipped with everything short of a sauna, an Italian Renaissance desk fit for a Borgia and a rose and cream Persian rug Aladdin might have coveted. The glass-covered bookcases, filled with lawbooks, provided an aura of gravity and sobriety, although Max was always quick to point out that he was not practicing law (he was accredited in New York but the sovereign state of South Carolina denies reciprocity and Max had declared that one bar exam was enough for a single lifetime), nor was he a private detective (the sovereign state of South Carolina has particular requirements for that license). But, he always concluded grandly, there was no law against a man giving advice. When delivering himself of this pronouncement, he looked adorably Joe Hardyish (to Annie), his handsome face ostensibly serious, his dark blue eyes sparkling with delight. Max felt his office was a superlatively tasteful retreat which should not be expected to maintain itself on the cash flow generated by those seeking help. As he often pointed out to Annie, his industrious grandparents had acquired enough money that it would really be rather unseemly for him to add to the family fortune. Annie was rarely impressed by this argument and often suggested he close Confidential Commissions, since it usually was devoid of clients, and devote himself to good works. Max pondered this, wondering if good works included golf, gin rummy and making love to his wife.

But this morning, it gratified Annie's Calvinistic soul to see the office pulsing with barely leashed energy. Barb hunched at her computer, face intent, sparing Annie the briefest of glances and giving a swift wave as a greeting.

Max was on the telephone. His blond brows quirked up in surprise.

Annie held aloft the note card she'd found in Henny's slacks.

Max craned his neck to watch as she crossed to a map of the island. It was a rather fanciful map with a coat of arms of crossed golf clubs and a can-can line of long-toed great blue herons, but the streets were there. Annie spotted the four addresses and felt a tingle of awe.

"Yes, I'm a lawyer for the estate of Walter Grosbeek, and we've been led to understand that Ms. Gardner is a lateral descendant through the Menhaden family . . ."

Never had Max sounded stuffier.

Annie gave him a thumbs-up and grabbed a fresh legal pad from the stack on his desk. Quickly, she sketched the island, the gate to the resort, the south island loop, Laughing Gull Lane and Red-Tailed Hawk Road. All four residences were within the resort. Annie marked the addresses.

". . . imperative we be able to communicate . . ."

Kathryn Girard set out to visit these houses, ostensibly to pick up donations. But these addresses didn't belong on her list. She had put them there herself.

". . . and that address in San Miguel de Allende? Yes"— he wrote swiftly—"thanks so much. And if she should be in contact with you, if you would be so kind as to give her our address, Bell, Bonkers and Billman, 8219 South State Street, Chicago, Illinois, 49424, Attention: Grisham Q. Billman, Esq. Yes, thank you for . . ."

Annie stared at the addresses in that distinctive, extravagant script. Kathryn Girard intended to make pick-ups, all right, but not donations to the Women's Club. Annie pictured Kathryn standing by the bulletin board at the Women's Club, scrawling her substitute list, then turning away with a secretive, satisfied, triumphant smile, ready to use the club van for her swing around the resort area for pick-ups that might better be described as donations to the fund for the enrichment of one Kathryn Girard. Why do people fork over money in secret? It didn't take almost twenty-five

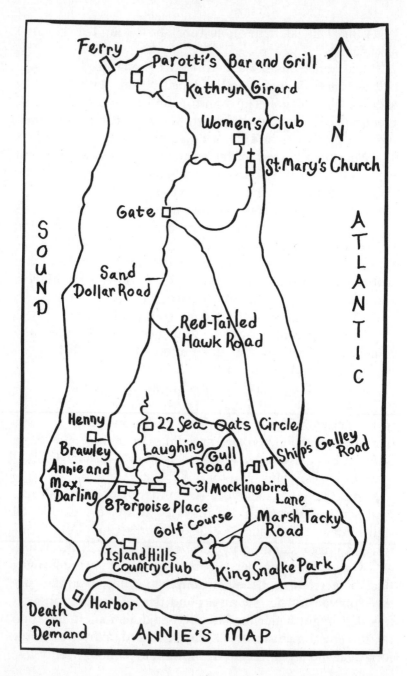

years of assiduous mystery reading—starting with *The Secret of the Old Clock*—to know the answer.

"Blackmail!" she exclaimed. The money-laden album, the packed bags. Yes.

Max threw her a startled look. ". . . your assistance." He put down the receiver, unfurled his six-foot frame from the red leather embrace. When he stood beside her, his arm automatically curved around her waist.

Annie pointed at the revised pick-up list and at her map. "Don't you see? That's how Henny knew where Kathryn planned to go."

"Why did Kathryn leave that list behind?" Max, too, recognized the handwriting, but his tone was puzzled.

"Just for the hell of it. Because she wanted to point to her victims even if nobody else ever understood the joke. She was thumbing her nose at everybody, at the club, at the people she was blackmailing." Annie traced the line on her map to Marsh Tacky Road. "She never thought she was going to end up dead in the back of the van. She couldn't tell anyone how clever she was"— Annie worked it out in her mind, a picture growing of a malevolent personality that had been well hidden beneath the surface charm of a woman eager to be a part of the community, a woman active in charitable works, a woman always willing to listen as others talked—"but this was a way of making a public yet covert announcement." Annie shivered. "Max, she must have been vicious. Why else list the addresses? She was leaving, but she liked leaving behind a little goad for her victims. Some of them might very well have seen that list on the bulletin board and felt a moment of panic. I suppose she was going to enjoy that thought as she traveled. When was she flying out?"

Max bent over the table, studied the map. "Saturday morning. From Savannah to Atlanta to Dallas to Mexico City."

Annie looked at him in admiration. "How did you get the address in San Miguel de Allende?"

"That was easy." He was as casual as Edmund Crispin's Gervase Fen solving the riddle of the disappearing toy shop. "She had an apartment in L.A. in the name of Miriam Gardner, ditto the credit card, passport and airline ticket. I figured the L.A. apartment manager might have her address in Mexico." He made it sound quite reasonable. "But"—he looked at her quizzically—"aren't you making a leap, jumping from these addresses"—he gestured at the map—"to blackmail?"

"Do you have a better idea?" Annie moved around his desk, pulled out a bottom drawer and fished out the cross-directory.

Max studied the map. "Drugs."

Annie looked up the addresses and wrote the names on his legal pad:

Gary and Marie Campbell, 31 Mockingbird Lane

Vince Ellis, 17 Ship's Galley Road

David and Janet Pierce, 8 Porpoise Place

The Rev. Brian and Ruth Yates, 22 Sea Oats Circle

Annie tapped the last name and address. "Drugs? Our associate rector? His wife?"

"Blackmail?" Max asked wryly.

"Blackmail." Annie was decisive. "Think about the money in the album, Max. So much money. Supplying drugs to four people would bring in cash. But not ninety thousand dollars." Annie shivered. "No, it has to be blackmail. That's the only thing that makes sense." She sighed. "People can have secrets, Max."

It was very quiet in that serene and beautifully appointed office. Max picked up the legal pad, his face somber. "Annie, we can't sit on this." He ripped off the sheet and waved it. "We have to call Garrett. But . . ." He rubbed his knuckles against his chin.

"I know." She paced between the desk and the wall map. "It won't mean anything unless we tell him about the money. And how can we do that?" There was no way they could admit to their clandestine visit to Kathryn's store and apartment without landing in real trouble.

A quick smile curved Max's mouth. "Are you game for a little stage-managing?"

"Sure." But after she heard his proposal, she knew she'd better be both game and damn lucky.

Max looked at his watch. "I'll spot you an hour. Okay?"

September is still T-shirt and shorts season on the sea islands. Annie picked a navy top, navy shorts, navy sneakers. It took a minute—she kept checking her watch—to find the particular hat she wanted, a wide-brimmed straw with pink ties. She put her hair up in a ponytail, put the hat on, pulled down the brim, tied the ribbons beneath her chin and added oversize sunglasses, an old pair of Max's.

Dorothy L. rollicked into the bedroom, then jumped sideways, her tail puffing.

"Thank you, Dorothy L." Annie glanced in the mirror. She was definitely generic tourist. Maybe Max's plan was going to be easy after all.

In the kitchen, she pulled the gardening gloves out of the miscellaneous drawer and turned to the album, still lying casually on the counter. She found a brown paper sack beneath the sink, dropped the album into it.

In the garage, she placed the sack in her bike basket, punched the garage door opener and swung onto her seat.

Max buzzed for Barb.

In a second she skidded to a stop beside his desk. "Max, I'm picking up some stuff about Miriam Gardner, credit card history, that kind of thing. But it all starts about five years ago. I can't find anything earlier than that."

"That's okay. Barb, I'd appreciate it if you'd take a break, walk down to the harbor. There's a pay phone near the bandstand. Wait until no one's paying any attention to you, then call here. Disguise your voice. Okay?"

Not even Evelyn E. Smith's Miss Susan Melville could have shown more aplomb. "Sure thing." She turned and sauntered out.

And Hercule Poirot thought he had a gem in Miss Lemon.

Chapter 5

Bicyclists, both tourist and native, were a common sight on the island. Annie was so confident of her disguise that she waved hello as she encountered cyclists in the forest preserve. In the morning sun, the preserve seemed cheerful and welcoming and she was glad to note that the occasional alligator rested somnolently on lagoon banks, not the path. Once out of the preserve, she pedaled faster. No one paid any attention as she rode past the church and turned onto the dusty road that ended just past Kathryn Girard's shop. She rounded the bend. It was quiet except for the chirrup of birds and the rustle of the live oak leaves in the light breeze. There was no car parked in front of the store.

But other people had bikes, too.

Annie hugged the edge of the road, keeping in the shade of a line of loblolly pines. She paused at the edge of the clearing, looking for the best place to leave her bike, finally choosing a willow opposite the back door. She slid the bike deep within the long hanging fronds.

Tucking her sack with the album under one arm, she gathered a handful of pine cones. She threw one hard against the back door, then, clinging to the shade, she moved alongside the store and tossed two cones at a second-floor window. Finally, a careful distance from the front steps and poised to sprint for the forest, she slammed three cones against the front door.

She glanced at her watch. Twenty-eight minutes of her hour was gone. It should only take her a minute to achieve her goal. Her sack firmly in hand, Annie hurried up the creaky steps. Last night, they'd found the front door unlocked and been grateful for their ease of entry. Annie's gloved hand slipped a little on the brass doorknob, but the handle moved. She stepped inside and wished she had a better temperament for this sort of thing. Her ears buzzed and her heart thudded. Linda Barnes's Carlotta Carlyle never seemed to breathe heavily in scary situations.

Annie hurried down the center aisle, ignoring the ricky-ticky furniture and chipped dishes that looked even tackier in the morning light. On the stairs, she paused to listen before thudding up the steps. On the landing, she froze. Last night, Max had shut the door to Kathryn's apartment as they left. Now it was ajar.

A cat?

She'd watched Max tug on the knob.

Cats were smart, but the last she knew not even Rita Mae Brown's gifted Sneaky Pie opened doors. Besides, what she'd learned to date of Kathryn Girard didn't suggest a woman who would love an animal.

Annie's foot gingerly poked out, a pale imitation of Max's lunge the night before. But she'd never pictured herself as 007. Her heroines were Julie Smith's Rebecca Schwartz and Sarah Shankman's Sam Adams, brains and humor over brawn.

The door swung open. Annie edged into the room. Last night she'd felt chilled by the remorseless anonymity. Now she stood still and tense, her gaze traveling over the shambles of the opened, upended and emptied suitcase, briefcase and carry-on, clothes flung and twisted, papers crumpled, bank statements thrown. The single lamp lay on the floor, the shade crumpled, the bulbs broken. Flung down, then kicked.

Annie wanted out. The room exuded malevolence, the basic bare ugliness overlaid now by violent anger. She opened the sack, pulled out the album. But maybe the disorder was useful. Just to give Chief Garrett a little help, she opened the album and draped the pages over the edge of the emptied suitcase. Then, with a little shrug, she lifted up a plastic flap and moved the photo to expose one end of a thousand-dollar bill.

Short of marking the album with an X, Annie didn't know any better way to—

Her thought was interrupted as outside a car door slammed.

"Confidential Commissions." Max cradled the receiver between his chin and neck and waggled his putter. A man couldn't spend every minute working. Annie had given him the putting rug and it was his duty to appreciate such a thoughtful gift. He sighted, swung. The ball dribbled off the green onto the wooden floor.

"This is an anonymous call." The whisper was very artistic, giving no hint to the sex of the speaker.

"Really! As Reggie Fortune would say, 'Oh, my aunt!' " Max raked the golf ball back onto the green. "Tell me something really fascinating, such as how many steps around the sundial before I should start digging. Or perhaps you have a secret formula sought by super agents from around the world." Max gently putted. This time the ball spurted across the green, skimmed over the cup and ricocheted off his desk.

"At midnight"—the whisper was vigorous—"Count Antoine will meet you behind the fifth crypt in the haunted cemetery on Hangman's Lane."

"Cool," Max marveled. "Would you ask him to send Lady Alicia instead?"

A snort of very familiar laughter was quickly smothered. But Max would have no need to report that part of the conversation.

"Hist! The fog rolls in. Footsteps approach. I must flee." The connection was broken.

Max nudged the ball into the hole with his toe and checked his watch. Good. It was time to visit the Broward's Rock Police Station.

Downstairs the front door creaked open.

Annie looked wildly around the littered room. She stared at the door—still ajar; why hadn't she shut it behind her?—which led to the only means of escape, the stairs leading down into the store.

Frantically she turned and hurried toward the bedroom, knowing she was burrowing ever deeper into the trap. She tiptoed past the clumps of Kathryn Girard's belongings, pushed past the bedroom door.

Under the bed?

Soft footsteps sounded on the stairs.

Annie stared at the bed. If she rolled beneath it, she would truly be trapped. So far, everyone who came to this apartment seemed to be looking for something. So, not under the bed.

Annie ran lightly toward the closet, her heart hammering. At the last minute, she whirled and plunged toward the bathroom. Bathroom doors lock. Once within, she closed the door, twisted the lock, an old-fashioned lock.

In the mirror over the lavatory, Annie looked at her reflection and for a minute felt as unsettled as Dorothy L. by the straw hat with its pink ties and the oversize men's sunglasses and the hands hidden by bulky cotton gardening gloves. She looked for a weapon. The towel racks were wooden dowels in ceramic holders. Annie pulled. No give at all. She looked up at the shower curtain. She would need a screwdriver to loosen the rod. She opened the bathroom cabinet. No handy screwdriver. Or machete. Or anything that could offer any kind of defense. Finally, she reached behind the toilet and picked up the plunger. On a scale of one to ten, it maybe came in at one-half. But she could at least poke an assailant. Face or gut? Whichever she could manage the most quickly.

Through the thin door, she heard the muffled sounds of search and the footsteps growing ever nearer.

It came finally, the twist of the knob, another twist, then a rattle. They stood on opposite sides of the door, Annie and the unknown searcher.

Then, maybe because she was so scared, maybe because she was beginning to feel like a miner in a blocked shaft, Annie hefted the plunger and beat the hell out of the door with the wooden end.

The Broward's Rock Police Station overlooked the Sound, a half block from the ferry dock. The cinder-block station was painted a soft cream. Max pushed inside, welcoming the blast of air-conditioning.

Mavis Cameron looked up from her computer behind a counter. Her hair, now a natural glossy brown, fell in soft waves. Her face, which had been so gaunt and strained when Annie and Max first met her, was fuller now and she flashed a quick, bright smile at Max. Her eyes still had a haunted quality that happy years of marriage to Billy had not quite erased.

"Hi, Mavis. How's Kevin?" He'd been a toddler when they first met and was now a stocky eight-year-old who loved to play soccer with his mom and go fishing with his stepfather.

She pushed back her chair, came to the counter. "He's great." She glanced toward the closed door and the frosted glass marked CHIEF. Her voice dropped. "Max, have you found out anything to help Henny?"

"Things are happening. Will you check with Chief Gar-

rett, tell him I've got some information that may be helpful?" Max grinned. "Some stuff that just happened to come
my way."

"A little bird told you," Mavis said with a wink. "Sure."
She started to turn, then hesitated, swung around and whispered, "Max, he's just a kid—"

Mavis was maybe a couple of years older than the new
chief, but she'd escaped a brutal marriage, snatched her
baby and run.

"—give him some slack, if you can."

Mavis tapped on the door, opened it. "Chief, Max Darling wondered if he could talk to you for a minute."

Garrett might be young, but he apparently was quickly
learning the identity of the town movers and shakers. He
came around his desk, hand outstretched as Max entered.
His round face sported a smile, but his eyes were wary and
defensive. "I was talking to the mayor this morning. He
told me you and your wife are outstanding members of the
community." Garrett pulled a straight chair from the wall,
positioned it carefully to afford a great view of the Sound.

"We try," Max said cheerfully, settling comfortably into
the chair.

Garrett sat behind his desk. He added stiffly, "As is
Mrs. Brawley."

Max knew capitulation when he saw it. But it never hurt
to help a man save face. Max had read enough of John P.
Marquand's Mr. Moto to understand the importance of social niceties. "Oh, Annie and I understood your plan right
from the first. I hope we played our parts well enough," he
said earnestly. "It's very clever of you."

Garrett managed not to look too bewildered.

"It's truly brilliant"—Max's tone was admiring—"making everyone think Henny Brawley is the suspect while you
figure out"—he spoke slowly, distinctly—"who Kathryn Girard was and why someone killed her. From what everyone
says, Kathryn was a real loner. Anyway, you're doing a
great job and I may have some information to help. Of

course, I know anonymous calls are always suspect, but the minute I got this one, I thought you ought to know about it." Only an Irish setter gazing at the sunset could have looked more noble.

Garrett yanked a pad out of his desk drawer. "Anonymous call? In reference to Girard? When? What was said?"

Max reached in his jacket pocket for a small notebook. He flipped it open, frowned at the page. He looked up apologetically. "I want to get it just right. Let's see. Time: Nineseventeen this morning. An unidentifiable voice." He looked up at Garrett. "A husky whisper. Couldn't tell if it was a man or woman. The call lasted"—Max checked his notes again—"thirty-six seconds. First, the caller said, 'I want to speak to Max Darling.' And—"

Garrett moved impatiently in his chair.

"—I said I was Max Darling. Then the caller said, 'Are you the blond guy who was helping look for Henny Brawley last night?' I said I was. The caller said, 'She's an innocent victim. You'd better put a double guard on her at the hospital to keep her safe. As for Kathryn Girard, nobody knows the truth about her. Don't let the bitch get away with it. Look for the money in Kathryn Girard's apartment.' I tried to ask who was calling, but the caller hung up."

Garrett scratched notes. "How about background noise? Any hint where the person called from?"

Max looked thoughtful. "There was a kind of squeaking noise. It might have been seagulls."

Garrett wrote down, *Seagulls.* He tapped his pen on his pad. "Man? Woman? Think about the tone, the pitch."

Max turned his hands palms up. "A whisper, Chief. That's all I know."

"Name's Pete." Garrett studied his notes. "It may be a hoax, somebody wants to see the cops hurry over to the woman's place. But"—he pushed back his chair—"can't do any harm to check. I'll get Mr. Parotti to let us in. He's been real cooperative."

Max stood, too. He started to turn away, then, resisting

his impulse to clap himself dramatically on the forehead (shades of the old days when he played Mortimer Brewster in *Arsenic and Old Lace*), Max jerked to a stop. "Almost forgot. My wife found this"—Max pulled the now much rumpled note card from his pocket—"in Henny Brawley's pocket. At the hospital last night, they gave Henny's clothes to Annie, said they didn't have anyplace to keep them in the ICU. And the new addresses are in Kathryn Girard's handwriting," Max said carelessly. "Annie had seen her writing at the clubhouse. Anyway, we figured those had to be the houses Kathryn went to last night and we thought you'd like to know."

Garrett reached for the sheet, looking like a river otter ready to belly-slide into the water for a succulent turtle.

Max smiled pleasantly. "Hope some of this is helpful. And Chief—Pete—we'll let you know if we hear anything else useful."

The silence reminded Annie unpleasantly of an overgrown cemetery she'd once visited, the stones tilted and broken, the old mausoleum almost hidden beneath a growth of fragrant wisteria. The silence pulsed with a heavy, waiting, guarded quality.

Annie looked at her watch. Her hour was up. Actually, she was five minutes past. If Max's mission had succeeded, Chief Garrett should arrive any minute. How long would it take from the police station? Three minutes? Four? Was his car pulling out of the oyster-shell lot while she stood, waiting, the plunger in her hand?

A car motor roared.

Annie twisted the lock and this time 007 would have been proud. Yanking back the door, she burst out of the bathroom, plunger whistling like a samurai sword. She skidded to a stop in the middle of the living room. No one waited to attack her.

The sound of the car was fading. Annie ran to the window overlooking the road, but all she saw was a swirl of dust. Without pausing, she turned and ran to the stairs and pounded down the steps.

The searcher was gone, but Garrett was coming. She loosed the chain to the back door and turned the knob.

A car door slammed. The sound came from the front of the store. Annie closed the back door as the front door opened. Edging along the back wall, she craned her neck, checked around the corner, saw no one and sprinted for the weeping willow.

Max dialed home, Death on Demand and Annie's cell phone. No answer. He frowned. What could be taking her so long? It was almost ten. Certainly it should have been the work of a minute to drop the album in Kathryn's apartment. He dialed the house again, left a message.

Annie flung the straw hat onto the kitchen counter, plucked off the sunglasses and gardening gloves and slid them into the miscellaneous drawer. She glanced at the clock as she trudged across the kitchen, heading straight for the refrigerator. Ten o'clock. How could it be only ten o'clock? Way back there in the dark ages, rather like a weary dowager in a Leonidas Witherall escapade by Alice Tilton (Phoebe Atwood Taylor), she had headed out to see Max at Confidential Commissions, en route to the Women's Club. And Emma, who had all the charm of a coral snake, was no doubt wondering where the hell Annie was. Instead of following her plan, she'd returned home, changed clothes and grabbed the album as per Max's suggestion. What she had packed into a mere hour since surely deserved commemoration, something on the order of a bronze medal with a motif celebrating endurance, courage and steadfastness.

She opened the refrigerator.

Dorothy L. rubbed against her ankle, purred and lifted an enchanting white face, shining blue eyes assessing the possibilities.

Annie picked up the cream pitcher, poured a bit in a

saucer. Withstanding pressure of any sort was simply not to be expected at this point. Back at the refrigerator, she sought the magic potion. Chocolate-covered strawberries? Her hand hovered near the bowl. Covered with cream whipped until it was almost like butter? When Max warned about cholesterol, Annie pointed out smugly that Agatha Christie lived to be eighty-five, imbibing clotted cream at every opportunity. Clotted cream was the result of leaving cream at room temperature for several hours, then beating it vigorously. Room temperature in September in the Low Country was not an option. The nearest Annie could get to the British clotted cream was her buttery version and it was almost as good. Annie's hand closed on the beautiful brown bottle of chocolate syrup. Zero fat grams. Annie walked to the silverware drawer, got a tablespoon and poured. She carried the syrup and spoon to the telephone answering machine, which was blinking faster than Barbara Jaye Wilson's milliner sleuth Brenda Midnight whipping out a summer hat design.

Annie punched the button and leaned against the counter.

"Dear Annie. Just a quick report." Laurel's husky voice burbled with enthusiasm. "I've made so many new friends this morning. Actually, I've been offered everything from guava juice to a ginseng drink. So interesting what people enjoy. And there is such a nice gentleman—Fred Jeffries— who lives just a block from Marsh Tacky Road. Reminded me of that handsome writer you had at the store once, Walter Satterthwaite, dark hair and an interesting face. He's a widower—Fred, not Mr. Satterthwaite—and he just loves to tootle about in his yacht. He's invited me—oh well, that's neither here nor there. Though once our dear Henny is quite safe and well, I may be there, wherever there may be—"

Annie poured another tablespoon of syrup.

"—but that's what makes life so fascinating. I could not miss the significance of the quince tree near his patio. Temptation! Doesn't that sum up life so beautifully? But tempered by a marvelous profusion of jasmine. Amiability is such an admirable quality, especially, I should think, on an extended cruise to—wherever."

Annie licked the spoon. She was contemplating punching the erase button and sending this particular message to—wherever.

"Dear Fred braves the elements." She might have reported the successful completion of a polar trek in equal tones of admiration. "On one voyage to Zanzibar, he and his parrot Alexander plunged right through a typhoon."

Annie wandered back to the refrigerator to return the chocolate syrup. She studied the milk. Whole or skim? Her hand closed on the skim, and she savored the smug satisfaction of self-denial. As for Fred, Annie hoped Laurel might have serious reservations about taking a voyage with a man who confronted typhoons, no matter how much vigor he exuded. Annie poured the milk.

"So, of course," Laurel said briskly, "the storm Thursday afternoon was no hindrance to Fred. At five-thirty, he was on his way to the club for a drink, driving west on Laughing Gull."

Annie sipped the milk, but the mention of Laughing Gull got her attention.

"The blue van passed him going east. Unfortunately, it was raining so heavily, he couldn't see the driver. He didn't see Henny's Dodge. That's all for now. I shall report anon." A delicate pause. "Fred is quite interested in learning more about the language of flowers and he's going to accompany me. I know that sharing with Fred is going to be such a pleasure. Not, of course"—the disclaimer was hasty—"that I shall forget the purpose of my peregrinations."

Of course not, Annie thought, sipping the milk.

The second message was short and crisp.

"Annie, I do expect a report." Miss Dora was too ladylike to snarl. "Have you spoken yet to Adelaide and Edith?"

Annie glanced at the clock. Late afternoon in Sienna. Maybe she should bring Miss Dora up to date, but she'd listen to the rest of the messages first. The sweet comfort of the chocolate was ebbing. There was so much to do and here she stood in her kitchen. Too bad you couldn't fast-forward messages and get the gist even if it made callers sound like Donald Duck. But there might be something important.

The third message made her smile.

"Thumbs-up. I'm sure you pulled off your end. Barb and I are compiling information faster than Agatha swiping a canapé." At a bookstore open house during the summer, Agatha nudged the plate with shrimp to the floor. She had made an interesting sight with shrimp in her mouth and cocktail sauce on her whiskers. "How about lunch at Parotti's? Garrett's well intentioned but the likelihood of his scouring out any hard info on Kathryn's activities is nil. It's up to us. I know we have a good guard system for Henny, but every time I think about last night and that gun, I get worried for her. I'll count on seeing you at one unless I hear otherwise."

The final message put her in motion.

"You're late." Emma's dry, cold voice was unemphatic, but Annie felt guilt piling on her shoulders. She needed to learn how to shed pressure with the insouciance of John Mortimer's Horace Rumpole, who never let She Who Must Be Obeyed get him down. But Rumpole's Hilda was a cream puff compared to Emma.

"I shall assume you have made *some* progress, which you will report upon your arrival here. Henny is doing well, though this is being kept secret. Pamela Potts is bringing her report. I believe it will open up several avenues of inquiry. I have consulted with Chief Garrett and arranged for you to sign for the club van. An officer will drive it to the club. Every item in that van must be checked. That may be our best lead to Kathryn's stops last night—"

Annie was almost to the door, ready to jump in her Volvo. Emma wouldn't be so damn patronizing when Annie showed up with a complete list of Kathryn's route.

"—and I expect to see you shortly."

*   *   *

Every road leads to another on an island, so Annie didn't feel that it was really out of the way to scoot by the harbor and Death on Demand. So Emma expected her at the Women's Club pronto. Well, Henny was stuck in the hospital and Annie knew how to improve that convalescence. Annie almost poked her head into Confidential Commissions, but the memory of Emma's cold voice spurred her directly to Death on Demand. As always, she loved the boardwalk that curved on one side of the harbor. In late afternoon, sunlight bleached the boards, but this morning it was pleasantly cool and shady. The Broward's Rock marina berthed every kind of boat from oceangoing yachts to Zodiac rafts. The water shone like polished jade and beyond the mouth of the harbor a pair of porpoises arched above the surface, sleek and graceful. A man in brief white shorts, his skin as dark as mahogany, patiently scraped the side of his boat. Music drifted from the nearest yacht, the cerebral guitar of Andres Segovia. A crimson and cobalt parrot perched on an awning of a deep-sea charter boat, the *Merry Maguffin*. The parrot screeched and it sounded very much to Annie as though he were commanding, "Hurry, dolt, hurry."

Dammit, she was going as fast as she could. As she passed the Death on Demand window, she scanned her September display. New titles by perennial favorites Anne Perry, Lawrence Block, Nancy Pickard and Diane Mott Davidson. She stepped inside and was greeted by piteous cries announcing cat abandonment and advanced starvation with an underlying threat of imminent application to the Cat SPCA. Annie looked up. Glittering eyes glowed beside the glassy gaze of Edgar, the stuffed raven. The raven occupied a small niche above a glass-encased display of recently acquired collectibles. A very small niche. Agatha's shiny black fur was indistinguishable, so close was the fit, from the stuffed bird's glossy feathers.

"Agatha." Annie spoke pleasantly, confident she was exhibiting the spirit of sweet reasonableness. "You know Ingrid's already fed you." Annie waved good morning to Ingrid, who was not only chief clerk, but friend, mainstay and fellow mystery lover. Ingrid and her husband Duane loved vacationing in New Orleans and always brought back a trunk full of secondhand mysteries. Their latest prize was a first British edition of Ngaio Marsh's *Artists in Crime*, the book that introduced painter Agatha Troy, who would become the love of Roderick Alleyn's life.

Ingrid was arranging a display of first appearances of very famous sleuths: Albert Campion in *The Black Dudley Murders* by Margery Allingham, Joe Leaphorn in *The Blessing Way* by Tony Hillerman, Faith Fairchild in *The Body in the Belfry* by Katherine Hall Page, Charlotte Pitt in *The Cater Street Hangman* by Anne Perry, Deborah Knott in *Bootlegger's Daughter* by Margaret Maron, Amanda Pepper in *Caught Dead in Philadelphia* by Gillian Roberts, and Susan Henshaw in *Murder at the PTA Luncheon* by Valerie Wolzien.

"Agatha has eaten." Ingrid didn't quite speak through gritted teeth, but there was a definite sense of strain.

Agatha lurched. The raven wobbled.

Annie leaped forward, hands outstretched.

Edgar's base—was it ironwood or basalt?—crashed into the display case, shattering the glass.

Annie swerved to avoid gashing an artery. She could see the headlines: AGATHA GUILTY OF ASSAULT or SHOPKEEPER SAYS CAT DID IT.

Annie stepped gingerly around the shards of glass. "Oh Agatha." The plastic-sheathed first editions were okay—*Motor City Blue* by Loren D. Estleman, *The Thin Man* by Dashiell Hammett, *Death in Zanzibar* by M. M. Kaye and *Beast in View* by Margaret Millar—but an elegant and highly decorated hat created and signed by Jeanne Dams was dented beyond repair.

An unrepentant Agatha waited impatiently in the center aisle, her whipping tail a clear signal that she wanted more food and she wanted it now. Annie followed the whipping tail down the aisle to the coffee bar. Behind her, she heard Ingrid sweeping up the broken glass.

Annie poured out more dry diet food. Agatha hunkered over the dish. Annie wished there were a fat-free delicacy for cats. She gingerly gave Agatha a pat, yanked back her hand and hurried to the cash desk. She grabbed Henny's books.

"Ingrid, watch out for her incisors." There was no need to identify the possessor of incisors.

Ingrid added Miss Silver in the *Grey Mask* by Patricia Wentworth to the table. "Annie, Lillian Jackson Braun's cats are charming."

If there was a ready answer, Annie didn't have it. On her way out, she hesitated, then added the M. M. Kaye title to the sack. Henny would get a kick out of that and the book was a recent acquisition which Henny hadn't seen.

As Annie hurried to the parking area, she found herself slipping into a trot and trying not to feel overwhelmed. Usually the waves rolling into Broward's Rock were gentle and low. Occasionally, before a storm, in hurricane weather, the waves crested at six or seven feet, sometimes ten feet. Annie felt like she was standing on slipping sand staring up at a huge breaker, the hospital, the list, Emma awaiting her arrival, Edith Cummings, Adelaide Prescott, and, now, the van. And that damn parrot calling her a dolt. She flung herself into her car, started the motor so quickly it made a worrisome grinding noise. As she pulled out of the parking lot, she had very good intentions. She truly planned to drive straight to the hospital. She opened the sunroof and headed for Sand Dollar Road.

Chapter 6

The phone number of Confidential Commissions registered Unavailable on call recipients' caller ID. Max congratulated himself upon his foresight in ordering that designation. He'd done it at the start of the summer on one of those dogs days when he practiced his putting on the indoor green and Barb surfed the net, reporting that an Edgar Allan Poe Web site had the scariest illustrations of a whirlpool she'd ever seen and he *had* to stop putting and read *A Descent into the Maelstrom* immediately. Max read it, suggested Barb return to cooking as her hobby and called the phone company. After all, he was confident that someday they would once again have a need for sub rosa investigation and, voilà!, the day was at hand.

Max glanced at a name and number procured by Barb from a reporter on the San Miguel de Allende daily newspaper. He punched the numbers. Buzzes, pops and faraway voices were followed by a melodic, *"Bueno."*

"Hello. I'm calling for John Murphy."

"Un momento, por favor."

Max waited patiently.

Finally the line clicked. "Hello. John here." The voice was as smooth and rich and unsettling as she-crab soup with a dash of unexpected cayenne.

"Mr. Murphy, I'm Sturdivant Whist, a freelance writer doing a piece on Miriam Gardner for a new pop magazine out here in L.A., *Life at the Top.*" Max doodled on his legal pad, sketching a palm tree and a smiling mouth with huge teeth. "She told me you could give me a picture of her life there in San Miguel de Allende."

"Marvelous woman." The drawl was pronounced. Max pictured a rotund man with a puffy face, small, mean eyes, and thick lips. "I'm a little surprised she told you to call me. But I guess I am the man about town down here." Satisfaction burbled in his voice. "Actually, I'd like to know a lot more about her. Maybe you could send me a copy of your story—"

"I'll send you a clip." Max drew a paper clip.

"—because she's kind of a woman of mystery. But she's made a place for herself in the community, helps with good causes and gives lots of parties. Of course, we often miss her. She's gone for two or three weeks out of the month, says she has to see to business interests in the States. I think her family was in the import-export business. But she's never really said."

"I'm interested in her house there. . . ."

"Beautiful, just beautiful. Huge house. On a bluff over-looking the town. Olympic-size pool. Previous owner even had a jai alai court. One night I was up there at a party—"

Max rippled a string of dollar signs across the page.

"—and stood out on her terrace and watched the lights come on down in the valley. Great view."

"And how is she perceived among the Americans there?" Max sketched a treasure chest piled high with coins.

"Oh, she fits right in. Except she doesn't have a lot to say. She's a good listener. But she seems to like it here. She always looks"—there was a considering pause—"pleased. Like a cat on a velvet cushion."

Max drew a thousand-dollar bill and another and another. "Oh, that's great, Mr. Murphy. Thanks for your time. I'll be in touch." Max put down the phone and reached for his legal pad. He studied Annie's list of the houses Kathryn had written on the note card and their owners. His eyes rested on one oh-so-familiar name, Vince Ellis, the red-headed, ebullient, energetic owner and editor of the *Island Gazette.* A longtime friend. A man Max wouldn't have hesitated to contact with questions about any island event.

How do you ask an old friend if he was being blackmailed?

Sea air swept through the sunroof as the road curved along the Sound. Yellowing cordgrass rippled in a gentle breeze. Fiddler crabs scurried on a brown bank. A dazzling white plumed egret crooked its neck to poke a long yellow beak near the water, looking for crabs or snails or small fish. Annie loved the pungent marsh smell, a combination of salt water, spartina grass, decay and sulfur. To her right, glimpsed through the groves of loblolly pines, spread the rolling links of the Island Hills Country Club golf course. Many of the island's most expensive homes backed onto the course.

Annie saw the sign, hesitated, then sharply swung the wheel, screeching into Laughing Gull Road. As she turned, she wondered if this had been Henny's route last night. But Henny could well have turned left onto Red-Tailed Hawk, planning to turn right on Laughing Gull. The same was true of Kathryn Girard. Either route made sense because Kathryn planned, of course, to return to Sand Dollar for the drive back to the gate.

Annie knew that Sea Oats Circle was near. Thick forests of pines intermingled with clumps of homes. She passed White Ibis Inlet, Lady Crab Lane, then turned left onto Sea Oats Circle. Number 22 was an attractive two-story red brick with white wood, green shutters and ivy. Banks of azaleas would be glorious in the spring. Two huge magnolias glistened in the sun. A couple of bikes rested in a wooden stand. A battered old VW sported a Braves pennant on the radio aerial. White organdy curtains hung at open windows, and honeysuckle climbed a trellis at the end of the front porch. Annie had been to guild meetings with Ruth Yates bustling happily between the kitchen and living room, freshening guests' coffee or tea, serving candied fruitcake in the winter, fresh peach cobbler in the summer. Ruth was in her late forties with faded gray eyes that looked anxiously out of a thin face. Hearty, bearishly built Brian Yates played pickup basketball at The Haven, the center for the island's disadvantaged kids, managed to remind his well-to-do flock that earthly success is temporal without offending any of them, and wielded a mean hammer at Habitat for Humanity building sessions.

How could this serene house be on Kathryn Girard's list?

Annie turned at the end of the block. These were nice houses but modest by island standards. How could either of the Yateses afford blackmail? Not, of course, that blackmail was something worked out in a budget.

Back on Laughing Gull, Annie spotted a long log-shaped form in the water hazard on thirteen, negotiated a humped bridge over a broad canal and watched the street signs. She turned right on Porpoise Place. Number 8 was three stories, an Italianate villa scarcely visible through a thick screen of pines. A small wooden sign announced SERVICE ENTRANCE about twenty feet before the main drive. Kathryn's stash of ninety thousand would be small potatoes at this residence.

Annie craned to see as she slowly drove past. A bunch of cars were in the front drive. The Pierces often entertained houseguests. Annie was a bit fuzzy on what David Pierce did but he had a private plane that took him to his Atlanta office. And he had offices in New York, Houston and London. Something about satellite communications. He was short, slim, dapper and intense. As for Janet Pierce—a head

taller with gorgeous ash-blond hair and brilliantly green
eyes and a model's figure—Annie had once heard someone
describe Janet as a trophy wife. But the Pierces didn't quite
fit that glib assessment. Dave was a widower. Janet had,
indeed, been a part of his corporate life, but once when
someone complimented her, Annie thought a little snidely,
on the grandness of the Pierce home, she'd said bitterly,
"Dave won't move. Because *she* chose it." Then she'd
swirled back onto the court and played with barely restrained violence. Trophy wives aren't jealous of a dead
mate.

A green Porsche bolted out of the drive, cutting in front
of Annie. As the Porsche roared past, long blond hair
swirled from beneath a pink straw hat with a blue ribbon.
A white hand had lifted in greeting.

Annie waved back. Janet always drove fast.

Annie took two wrong turns, but finally discovered
Mockingbird Lane, a squiggly offshoot from Mourning Dove
Court. The Campbell house was a two-story Tudor that ram-
bled with L's and wings and turrets. All it lacked was a
rope ladder dangling from the east turret and a moat. Annie
had worked with Marie Campbell on a clothing drive to
benefit The Haven. Marie had worked swiftly, cataloging,
discarding, talking all the while, a passionate discourse on
preventing tourists from feeding the dolphins (". . . just
criminal. It teaches them to depend on people. We have no
right . . ."), her dark eyes flashing and her finely boned face
flushed. Her husband Gary was tall and thin and very quiet.
At parties, he stayed close to her side, carefully observing
everyone who approached her, not quite truculent, not quite
hostile. Annie was never certain whether he displayed dog-
like devotion or the dog's instinctive wariness of interlopers.
This morning a small figure knelt beside a bed of petunias,
energetically weeding.

Annie picked up speed as Marie looked toward the
street. Just past the house, Annie realized that Mockingbird
was a dead end. Making the turn, she retraced her path.

Marie stood by the bed, trowel in hand, gloved hand shading her eyes.

So far as Annie knew, she owned the only red Volvo on the island. So much for a quiet survey of Kathryn's addresses. Annie waved.

The trowel flashed in the sun.

The last house—or the first, if Kathryn came the other way around—had once been a home where she and Max were familiar guests. How many times had she and Max stood on the second-floor balcony of the Ellis house and looked down at a sparkling pool. She and Max had known Vince and his wife, Arlene, since those scary early days on the island when Annie was suspected of murdering an obnoxious mystery writer. Vince put out a superb small-town newspaper and knew everybody and everything that happened on Broward's Rock. The house was unpretentious but nice, a two-story, rambling colonial surrounded by magnificent roses, white, crimson, yellow and pink, a profusion of loveliness. Vince no longer was a genial host, flipping hamburgers, teasing guests, planning party games. Not since the death of his wife.

Four houses. The homes of people she knew. Last night when a blue van stopped at one of these houses, Kathryn Girard died. Who drove the van to Marsh Tacky Road?

The *Island Gazette* newsroom consisted of three desks with computers. Ace reporter Marian Kenyon covered news; an ebullient retiree from the *Atlanta Constitution,* Eddie Abel, covered sports; and Ginger Harris, sweet-faced, seventyish, sharp-eyed, did everything else, from Life Style to obituaries to gardening to financial news. Ginger had come out of retirement after Arlene Ellis's death to take her place in the newsroom. Beyond the desk, a door led to Vince's office.

When Max stepped inside, Marian popped up, her frizzy blond hair (a new shade bordering on apricot) quivering. Marian always moved fast, her eagle-beaked face intent, ready to pepper any source with pointed questions. Grab-

bing her steno pad and a soft lead pencil, she balanced on
her toes in Max's path. "Police report states you and Annie
found the body. How come you were on Marsh Tacky
Road?" The question was oddly indistinct and the side of
Marian's face pouched like a squirrel with more acorns
than mouth.

Max found himself being maneuvered to the hard
straight chair by Marian's desk. Since his goal was Vince's
office only a few feet away, he didn't resist. "I'll make a
deal. Fill me in on what you've got on Kathryn Girard and
I'll give you a blow-by-blow."

Flinging herself into her swivel chair, Marian scrabbled
in her desk drawer and pulled out a piece of bubble gum.
Unwrapping it with one hand, she shoved the pink square
into her mouth, distending her left cheek even further. "Quit
smoking. May strangle on sugar. About to go out of my
mind. What have I got on K. Girard? Nada. She must have
landed on the island like Athena out of Zeus's noggin. I
can't find anything on her. Zero. So I told the boss we could
do a three-column head, use a border of question marks, I'd
give it my Arthur Brisbane best, but you know what the
boss is running for the lead story? His rewrite of a handout
from Garrett. Anemic. Puerile. Then he had the"—the next
was indistinct but Max could fill in the blanks—"——s to
tell me we had everything we needed! The lead goes something like, 'Island Police Chief Peter Garrett announced Friday that an arrest is imminent in the slaying Thursday night
of Kathryn Girard, owner of an island antique shop. Girard's
body was found—' "

Vince's door opened. The tall, rangy redheaded editor
hesitated for an instant when he saw Max. Then he plunged
into the newsroom, smiling, but his eyes were hard. "Hey,
Max, sorry I can't stop. I'll get back to you."

Max stood, hand outstretched.

Vince pumped Max's hand, clapped him on the shoulder. "See you later." And he brushed past.

Marian's raspy voice twanged, "So maybe if I get some

stuff from Max, the *Gazette* will have an honest-to-God news story. And what's this crap about Henny Brawley going to the slammer? Hey, Vince, you heard that?" She bounced to her feet, glaring after her boss, pugnacious as Brett Halliday's Mike Shayne when it was time to stand up and be counted.

The front door slammed.

Marian Kenyon's face crinkled in dismay. "Vince, oh Vince, what the hell?"

Marian didn't have an answer.

Max was afraid he did.

Vases of flowers were arranged three deep on either side of the door to Room 218. Billy Cameron dwarfed the straight chair to the left of the door. As Annie came down the hall, his big face creased in a smile, then he clapped both hands over his face and sneezed. Once. Twice. Three times.

"Gesundheit, Billy." Annie saw that the door was ajar.

He pulled a handkerchief from his pocket, smothered another sneeze. "Thanks, Annie." He gestured at the flowers. "Nurse wants doctor's approval, said you have to be sure there's no allergy or anything." He sniffled. "I wish Garrett could see these."

Annie understood. Anyone who evoked this kind of care and love couldn't possibly be a murderess. But Annie doubted the floral tributes would sway the young police chief. "How's Henny?" Henny came first. Annie was glad she'd stopped at the hospital. Emma could just wait.

Billy rubbed his nose, which could soon serve as a beacon in the fog. "Lots better. She doesn't know about"—he lowered his voice—"the other lady. But I think Garrett's going to try and question her pretty soon. So maybe you better tell her."

Annie reached out to push the door. "Has anybody tried to get past you?"

He looked as stalwart and impassable as Rowdy, the masterful malamute in Susan Conant's Holly Winter mysteries. "Naw. Everything's super. Emma Clyde's got a schedule set up. Mrs. Yates is in there right now."

Annie felt like Rowdy had just landed on her shoulders. She shoved into the room, her heart thudding, to find wispy Ruth Yates sitting beside the bed, crochet hook flashing. ". . . and I don't want you to worry about a thing, Henny. I went by your house and fed Dash. I told him you'd be home soon. He is such a handsome cat, isn't he? And I've brought you a fresh assortment of clothes, that pretty red blouse you brought back from Maracaibo and those nice tan slacks from the Talbots catalog. And fresh underwear, of course, and socks and tennis shoes."

Annie reached the bed, clung to the metal end.

Ruth Yates, looking as frazzled as a Girl Scout leader at the end of a week-long campout, shook the fluffy yellow yarn and peered down at the shapeless mass in her lap. "I swear I hate this new yarn. It just slips and slides."

Annie's gaze swung frantically from Ruth's wistful, defeated face to the bed. Henny was propped up against double pillows, a bandage looped around her head, her face a stark white. Bluish patches looked like bruises beneath her usually vibrant brown eyes, eyes that now looked fuzzy and bewildered. She tried to smile, but it slipped away and she touched her temple.

"Henny." Annie was at her side and holding a thin cold hand. "Oh Henny, we were so worried about you."

Henny moved uncomfortably against the pillow. "What happened, Annie?" her voice was thick.

Ruth Yates popped up and leaned close. "Now, Henny, you mustn't—"

Annie saw the water pitcher on the stand. She'd empty it, bring fresh. The IV, surely Ruth couldn't have trifled with it. When had Henny taken medicines? Annie needed to be sure the nurse's aide presented the medicines directly to Henny, didn't leave them to be taken later. She stared at Ruth, who surely was a most unlikely candidate for murderer-in-chief. But she was a candidate.

". . . think about it. It's better not to dwell . . ."

Henny's voice was weak, but she managed to snap, "Dammit, how did I get here?"

Annie gave Henny's limp hand a squeeze. "I'll freshen up this water." She grabbed the pitcher, crossed to the open bathroom door, poured it into the lavatory, all the while watching Ruth's pale face.

Ruth's gray eyes blinked. She brushed back a strand of hair. "I think that's fresh, Annie. The nurse brought it in just a few minutes ago."

Annie turned on the faucet and filled the pitcher. "The fresher, the better." She plumped it down on the bedside stand. "Henny, have you taken any medicine since Ruth came?"

"Turned it down," Henny said sturdily. "Don't like painkillers. Asked them to bring me some ibuprofen." She gestured at a little white cup on the stand.

Annie picked it up, shook two tablets out in her hand, checked them. Water okay. Tablets okay. IV? Annie leaned over the bed. "Were you awake when Ruth came?"

Henny's brown eyes didn't look quite so fuzzy. "Yes."

So the IV couldn't have been tampered with. At least, not by Ruth.

Annie swung toward Ruth, who was glancing back and forth like a spectator watching an unfamiliar sport. "Ruth, who was on duty when you arrived?"

Ruth looked relieved. This was a question she understood. "Pamela Potts."

Annie felt the tension drain away. Henny was okay. No way would anything be tampered with during Pamela's watch. And Henny, though weak and confused, was awake when Ruth arrived. But to stay safe, Henny had to know what was going on and she had to know she was in danger. Annie turned back to the bed.

Henny was looking at her sharply. "All right, Annie." Henny was almost her crisp self. "What's going on?"

"Do you remember calling me from the Women's Club

last night?" Annie poured a glass of the fresh water, put it
on the stand within Henny's reach.

Henny's usually confident face was troubled, anxious. "I
don't remember anything after breakfast yesterday. I sat on
my deck, watched a great blue heron." She gingerly touched
the bandage. "Annie, what happened to me?"

As Annie described the evening—Henny's call to the
bookstore, her non-arrival, the search by Annie and Max,
their discovery of Henny's car and the Women's Club van
on Marsh Tacky Road, Kathryn's body in the back of the
van—Ruth Yates hunkered down into her chair, her hands
tightly clutching her crochet.

Ruth interrupted, her voice high and thin. "What happened to the driver of the van? The way you tell it, Henny's
car blocked the road. Where did the driver go?"

Annie looked at Ruth with respect. She might be fluffy
and uncertain, nervous and troubled, but she immediately
perceived the critical point.

So did Henny. "Wait a minute." Her voice was stronger,
though she still pressed fingers to one temple. "Kathryn Girard was murdered. Her body was in the back of the van.
But if the murderer drove the van to Marsh Tacky Road,
how did he—or she—get away? There's the park and lagoon
and golf course to the west and nothing but forest to the
east."

And it was at least two miles to the nearest of the four
houses on Kathryn's list, not that Annie intended to get into
that with this audience.

"Is that why the police think—" Ruth clapped a hand
over her mouth.

Henny was very still, her dark eyes scouring Ruth's face.
"I see," she said quietly. "Am I the Prime Suspect?"

"At the moment," Annie said grimly. "You'll soon have
a visit from Frank Saulter's fuzz-faced replacement. Just
close your eyes and refuse to speak until you've talked with
your lawyer. Max will call Johnny Joe Jenkins." The person-

able criminal lawyer lived in Chastain, the nearest town on the mainland.

Henny's sharp brown eyes crackled. "If that isn't infuriating!"

"To be suspected of murder?" Ruth Yates asked in a small voice.

Henny's eyes flashed. "To be trapped here and not be able to do a thing. And I'm the best detective on the island."

Annie managed not to smile. "Emma's heading up a task force at the club—"

Henny dismissed Emma with a wave of her hand.

"—and Max and I are busy—"

Henny grabbed the glass of water, drank thirstily, then cleared her throat. "Here's what we need to do, Annie. Check the back of the van, see if there's any trace of dirt or sand or smudges from a bicycle tire."

Maybe Henny *was* the best detective on the island. That had not occurred to Annie. If a bike had been tucked into the van, it might have left some trace. Retrieving the van from the police would give Annie a chance to check out the back.

Henny continued, almost briskly, "See what you can find out about Kathryn—"

"Max is busy on that. And I'm going to talk to Edith Cummings and Adelaide Prescott as soon as I see to the van. Now, Henny, here's what I want you to do." Annie spoke softly but firmly. "You're the only person who came close to the driver of that van. Everyone knows you don't remember anything—"

Henny's hand flew up. "The van was going fast." Her face squeezed tight. "But that's all I remember, the van and the rain. I followed it." Her voice quivered with frustration. She moved restlessly, then sighed and turned her face to the pillow. In an instant, she was fast asleep.

Annie stared at Henny and wished she'd talked faster, harder. Henny still didn't know she was in danger, though when she woke, if her head wasn't pounding, it wouldn't take the island's best mystery reader long to figure it out. As for now, Annie still had to deal with Ruth Yates. She didn't dare go off and leave Henny alone with Ruth.

Annie eased away from the bed, stepped lightly to the alcove with a window and rocking chair. As she pulled her cell phone from her purse, Ruth tiptoed up to join her, her faded gray eyes blinking furiously.

"Annie, you saw the body last night?" Ruth's voice quavered.

Annie kept her face empty of expression. Ruth had enough expression for both of them, fluttering eyelashes, trembling lips, shaking hands. What on earth was wrong with the woman? "Yes." Annie spoke slowly, watching Ruth. "She was in the back of the van, covered with an old green blanket. I pulled the blanket down."

Ruth's hand clutched at her neck. "Did they find the weapon?" Her voice shook and her eyes glistened with a sick apprehension.

The weapon? But they'd not talked of how Kathryn Girard died. The word had spread across the island, of course. But how definitive had it been? Some might have heard about the croquet mallet, but many, obviously including Ruth Yates, had not.

Weapon.

Annie had a sudden, sharp, horrific memory of the figure that had whirled last night and lifted a gun and fired as Annie flung herself behind a rain barrel.

"Ruth, what do you know about the gun?" Her voice was louder than she had intended, sharp and accusatory.

Ruth's face crumpled. She whirled and dashed across the room, her shoes clattering on the floor.

Shocked, Annie stood for an instant, then, questions flooding her mind, she started for the door.

". . . no, no . . ." Henny's voice rose.

Annie turned toward the bed.

Henny's eyes were wide and staring. "No lights. No lights."

Annie held her hands tightly. "It's all right, Henny. You're safe."

Tears spilled irregularly down Henny's pale cheeks. "I walked toward the van. The lights were off. Oh Annie, that's all I remember."

But, Annie thought grimly, Henny's memory was returning in patches. So she wasn't safe at all. "Rest now, Henny. I'll stay with you for now. You'll feel much better soon." Annie kept her voice low and soothing and Henny drifted off to sleep. Carefully, she loosed her grip of Henny's hands, waited to be sure the injured woman didn't rouse. When Anne stood, she knew it was much too late to catch Ruth Yates. However, this was a small island, a very small island. Ruth had no place to hide. Annie would find her. But first, Henny must be protected. Stepping softly, Annie tiptoed to the door.

Billy looked up anxiously. "Annie, is something wrong?" He pushed up from the chair and now he towered over her. "Mrs. Yates looked upset when she came out. Is Henny okay? I almost called the nurse, but you didn't come out." He rubbed his red nose, smothered a sneeze.

"Henny's doing fine, Billy. She's asleep now. But from now on, anyone who comes—and that includes members of the auxiliary—tell them to pull up a chair outside in the hall, that Henny needs quiet and the doctor's put her room off limits."

His big face corrugated in a worried frown. "But he hasn't, has he?"

"He will." That was first on Annie's agenda. She started down the hall, then turned. "What time do you go off duty, Billy?"

"Seven."

Annie felt a welling of relief. Billy could be counted on. There was plenty of time to make sure Henny was safe. By the time she reached the parking lot, Annie was connected to Cary Martin's cell phone, thanks to his office nurse, who was a big Death on Demand customer and who wanted to know if there was a new book by G. M. Ford ("Annie, The Boys are the funniest detectives in the world!"). Indeed there was a new title and Annie promised a free copy. Pronto.

"Hi, Cary. Listen, will you do me a favor and put Henny's room off limits to visitors? Including God's gift to the Broward's Rock police force? Our new police chief doesn't know the difference between a suspect and a victim!" Annie's voice dripped disgust. "He's after Henny, believe it or not. Plus, Emma and I are afraid the real murderer might try to get to Henny, so the safest thing is to keep everybody out."

"Sure. Probably a good idea anyway. Listen, I'm all out of books." He sounded like a waif who hadn't had a square in two days.

"I'll drop a Tommy Hambledon by your office." Cary's favorite books were the World War II adventures by Manning Coles.

Annie dialed the store as she drove out of the hospital lot. She'd better figure out what happened last night in a hurry because the free book count was climbing.

"Death on Demand, where Agatha rules and mysteries flourish." Ingrid sounded more resigned than joyous. Ingrid loved mysteries and cats. Usually.

"Did she bite you?" Annie braked to let a mother duck lead seven large ducklings across the road.

"I swear I don't know how she does it." Ingrid's normally pleasant voice was aggrieved. "I was watching her. And Annie, I'm nice to her."

"I know. Ingrid, she doesn't mean to bite." Actually, of course, Agatha certainly meant to bite. But Annie was confident that Agatha truly loved both her and Ingrid. It was just that cat nature did not take kindly to being thwarted (or hungry).

Ingrid didn't say a word. It must have been a large gash. Often, as in a marriage, some topics are best left unexplored. "Ingrid, put up the 'Closed' sign. I need to have these books delivered . . ." and Annie concluded, ". . . and please see if there's a new Earl Emerson for Billy." Was giving away books getting to be a habit? "Thanks, Ingrid."

The next call was less satisfactory. Voice mail. Annie left a message. "Pamela, will you take the night shift outside Henny's door? Billy Cameron gets off at seven. If you'll take over—and Dr. Martin has ordered no visitors and that means none, zip, zero—I will be absolutely confident that Henny is safe. Pamela, I am counting on you."

Henny was as safe as Annie could manage. But with the way of today's hospitals—get the patients out, keep those beds empty, raise the prices—Henny might be on her way home tomorrow. Henny's house was remote with no near neighbors. But surely they had twenty-four hours of safety.

The memory of that swift gunshot in the night outside Kathryn Girard's store made Annie feel cold despite the summery September morning. As she turned into the Women's Club parking lot, she wasn't sure where to start, talking to Emma Clyde or hunting for Ruth Yates.

Chapter 7

"I'll get us some iced cappuccino," Barb offered, dropping a folder on Max's desk. Iced cappuccino was a specialty at Death on Demand. "I need a pick-me-up."

"Watch out for Agatha," Max said absently as he clicked print on his computer screen. "She's hungry."

Barb tugged at her shift, which fit just a little too snugly over her ample bosom. "What's life without good food? In fact, I think I'll whip up an awning cake. Do us all good."

Sheets slipped out of the printer.

Max kept his tone casual. "Awning cake?" It's hard on a serious chef to admit ignorance.

Barb grinned. "Think beach chairs, alternating stripes of green and white. White cake, green crème de menthe mixed in cream cheese, white cake, white crème de cacao mixed in cream cheese. Mmm, good."

Barb reached out for the newly printed sheets, handed them to Max. Her good-natured face drooped. "You know, just to look at all these people, you'd think they had it made, rich, handsome, secure. But the truth is, everybody's got troubles." She forced a smile, but tears glistened in her large brown eyes. "Back in a flash with a caffeine charge."

Max put the sheets in a folder and watched her leave, head down, hand scrabbling in her pocket for a tissue. This had been a hard year for Barb: Her mother died in a car wreck, her teenage son was arrested for smoking pot, her new boyfriend turned out to be a louse who cleaned out her bank account. On the surface, she was an ebullient extrovert, a great cook, an avid bowler, an accomplished gardener.

But like Barb said, everybody's got troubles and the people on Kathryn Girard's list had more troubles than most.

Max arranged the dossier folders in alphabetical order: Gary and Marie Campbell, Vince Ellis, Janet and Dave Pierce, Brian and Ruth Yates. As he picked up the top one the phrase strummed in his mind over and over, "Everybody's got troubles."

The Broward's Rock Women's Club was housed in one of the oldest structures on the island, a Georgian chapel built in 1770 by a plantation owner. The plantation had fallen into ruin after the Civil War. The only remnant of the fine plantation house was half a brick chimney and one partial wall of stucco-covered tabby, the sea island building mixture made of oyster shells and lime mortar. The chapel, however, was built of brick that had been shipped from Savannah. The beautifully proportioned building had survived war, fire and pillage. Local philanthropist Adelaide Prescott bought the ruins in the early 1950s and oversaw its restoration. She deeded the building and its grounds, including the old cemetery with its leaning stones and age-darkened crypts, to the Women's Club, which met monthly to hear visiting lecturers on topics ranging from the plight of the great cats in Africa to the expected transformation of American society as a result of instant worldwide communications. The interior had been transformed into a spacious room with a low stage at the east end. To afford flexibility, folding chairs were arranged for programs and stored at other times for square dancing, holiday bazaars and, of course, the annual White Elephant Sale.

Today, a half dozen cars were tucked in a row behind a line of weeping willows. Adelaide had insisted that cars not be visible through the sparkling glass panes of the Palladian windows. Annie parked beneath the shade of a live oak and brushed back a strand of feathery Spanish moss as she stepped out.

Crushed oyster shells crunched underfoot as she hurried up the broad central path to the building. Annie decided Adelaide Prescott was a very wise woman. Once past the line of willows, the chapel appeared as it existed in long-ago days, the two Palladian windows on either side of the door, the high roof and small end wings in perfect balance. The chapel nestled against a backdrop of pines, like a small diamond in an exquisite setting. The little cemetery, its iron gate ajar, lay in the shadow of a half dozen live oaks. Silvery swaths of Spanish moss hung straight and still, graceful reminders that life can be drawn from sunlight and air.

Inside, Annie paused while her eyes adjusted from the brilliant September sunlight to the softly lit interior. At first glance, the long room looked like a tidy housekeeper's worst nightmare, overflowing boxes and bags scattered in disorderly piles, broken lamps, a statue with one arm missing, chipped dishes, stuffed animals including a moose head with pink eyes, a model train that was clacking merrily around a mountain and emitting a piercing whistle as it neared the bridge, cowboy hats, a fake cactus, Japanese screens and more, much more. Women wearing blue aprons with the club emblem, an osprey with spread wings hovering high above green water, conferred in low voices, wrote prices, affixed stickers and placed items ready for sale on trestle tables set up against the north and south walls. There was an air of intense pressure and total concentration.

Beyond the disarray on the main floor, the low stage was bare except for a card table and Emma, perched on a small wooden chair. Her cell phone tucked under her square chin, she was gesturing decisively to a drooping figure. It took Annie a moment to recognize Pamela Potts. Emma looked up, spotted Annie and beckoned.

Annie began a snakelike progression toward the stage, skirting a piece of driftwood carved in the shape (roughly, very roughly) of a pelican, stepping over a rolled-up grass mat that made her nose itch, avoiding the moose's immense antlers, squeezing between two huge pottery camels, unhooking her sleeve from a hand trowel attached to an orange Formica pole festooned with a sign announcing, CUTE CLOTHES TREE.

All the while she scanned familiar faces. Muted hellos greeted her, but no one paused to chat. The minutes were ticking away and whether the motley merchandise was tagged or untagged, the doors would open at nine tomorrow. Annie was almost to the base of the stage when she spotted Ruth Yates, who was sidling toward the front door, her thin face averted. Annie waggled her hand at Emma, held up a finger meaning just a minute and hurried after Ruth.

Outside, Ruth threw a frantic glance over her shoulder and broke into an awkward run, veering away from the path.

Annie jogged. In a half dozen steps, she was on Ruth's heels. "Ruth, you can't get away from me." It was not a race. If the circumstances had been any other, if Henny weren't in danger, if a gun hadn't been fired the night before, Annie would have hated herself for bullying this abject middle-aged woman. Only Ruth would have come to the club today. No doubt she was signed up to work so she came, even though she must have known that Annie would seek her out. Poor, bedeviled Ruth.

Gasping for air, Ruth clung to the cemetery gate. "Kathryn wasn't shot." Her voice quavered, but her eyes were defiant. And hurt, like a child who's been lied to.

Annie wasn't sorry. "No. But the murderer has the gun."

Ruth whirled away, plunging into the cemetery, stumbling across the hummocky ground. She finally stopped and leaned against an old obelisk, the name obliterated by time, the outline of a palmetto palm barely discernible. "Oh, I wish I were dead. I was going to shoot myself." Tears trickled down her face, furrowed her makeup. She crossed her arms tightly and shuddered. "I got the gun out when she called. I went upstairs and got it out of the attic. It belonged to my dad. Brian doesn't like guns but I wanted to keep it. My dad brought it home from the war. He was proud of it. It's pearl-handled and has his initials on it. It wasn't loaded. But I know how to shoot. Dad taught me when I was little. So I loaded it."

Cicadas rasped their late summer song. A tendril of Spanish moss caressed Annie's cheek. Sunlight slanted through the live oak branches, touching the weathered gravestones with streaks of gold.

"Nothing's that bad," Annie said softly. "Ruth, it would break Brian's heart."

She was hiccupping now, little jerky sobs. "I was to put the money out with some stuff for the sale. She said she'd be by sometime after four." Miserable eyes, begging understanding, sought Annie's. "I wasn't going to do it. Not again. I lied to Brian before. I told him the car had a big repair job. That's what I said once. Another time I told him my cousin Becky had to have an operation and she needed help. He said of course I must help her. We had to cancel our trip to see Judy and the new baby. Oh God, I hated that woman."

"Yesterday . . ." Annie said gently.

Ruth's tear-stained face hardened. "I'd told her to pull around to the back of the house. I was waiting there with the sack. She got out and opened the rear door. She had on a blue poncho. The hood framed her face and"—the flat voice was wondering—"she looked like an old Italian painting, that beautiful dark hair, the way her cheeks hollowed beneath the bones." Ruth shuddered. "But her mouth was mean. Her mouth was always mean. I brought the sack. Then I opened it and pulled out the gun." Ruth's face crumpled like a Chinese lantern dashed to the ground.

Annie stepped back. The hard edge of a granite tomb poked into her hip.

"Do you know what she did?" Ruth reached out, grabbed handfuls of the Spanish moss, twisted and tore the gossamer gray moss. "She laughed at me. She laughed and yanked the gun away and tossed it into the back of the van."

The cool cry of a mourning dove mingled with the pulsating song of the cicadas.

Annie's skin prickled. She had never seen such a violent mixture of pain and anger and defeat.

"Kathryn took the gun," Annie repeated.

Ruth pushed away from the obelisk, walked heavily, head down.

Annie followed. "What happened then?"

Ruth ignored her, walking faster toward the weeping willows.

"Ruth"—Annie grabbed her arm—"what happened then?"

"She looked in my sack"—Ruth's voice had an odd hollow tone—"and when she didn't see the money she said—" She shook her head. "It doesn't matter what she said, Annie. Kathryn's dead. She took my gun and drove away and someone killed her."

This time, Annie didn't follow. Ruth walked hurriedly, leaning forward, like a swimmer breasting heavy waves.

The burden of guilt.

The judgment came so clearly Annie almost expected to hear the words in a deep stentorian tone. Ruth claimed Kathryn took the gun, drove away. Did she? Or when Kathryn turned arrogantly away to toss the sack into the back of the van, did Ruth pick up a croquet mallet and batter Kathryn to death?

Max nodded in approval. Barb was certainly a whiz. Of course, today's computers could do everything but hold the scalpel in brain surgery, and that would probably be next. The capability to print sharp color photos was pie-easy, certainly easier than making his newest favorite recipe, a mint-flavored chocolate pie in a graham cracker crust, topped with springs of fresh mint and flecks of shaved bitter chocolate. And Barb was a master at scouting out photos that made the dossiers twice as up close and personal.

He picked up the top photo that had run in the *Island Gazette: Spring House and Garden Tour, l. to r., Loretta Campbell, Gary and Marie Campbell, Sam and Kate Campbell.* Gary and Marie stood together on one side of a redwood piano. Gary bent forward, minimizing his height. He looked like a balding stork, a bony, solemn face with bushy eyebrows, deep-set blue eyes and a square chin. His arm curved around Marie's slight shoulders, one thin hand tight on her arm. Marie had the odd quality of being arrested in motion, as if she were just about to move, or had just settled for an instant, like a hovering hummingbird. Curly dark hair framed a piquant face remarkable for vivid green eyes, a bright, quizzical expression and a smile that promised warmth and love and hope. Teenagers Sam and Kate sat stiffly on the piano bench. Sam was an echo of his father, all long arms and legs, but he had a mop of curly black hair and his mother's mouth. Unlike her mother, Kate was solidly built with an athlete's bright cheeks. Long blond hair framed a softly rounded face with spectacular dark brown eyes. Old and frail, Loretta Campbell hunched in an over-stuffed, ornately carved walnut chair near the piano. A slight smile touched her wizened face.

There were individual shots, Gary in a dark gray suit receiving a plaque from the county bar association in honor of his term as president, Marie marching with a placard held high above her head, DON'T KILL THE DEERS!, Sam sitting on a weathered pier with a fishing pole in hand, smoothly muscled Kate handing off the baton at a track meet, the obituary photo of Loretta as a younger woman with tightly permed hair and thin lips.

Max read the obituary first:

CAMPBELL *Loretta Agnes Simpson, 76, daughter of the late Burl Simpson and Gladys Wright Simpson. Born in Columbia, South Carolina, nursing school graduate, married Maj. Robert Campbell M.D. March 7, 1945. Predeceased by Dr. Campbell in 1982. Survived by son Gary and his wife, Marie, and two grandchildren, Kate and Sam.*

Loretta Simpson joined the Army Nursing Corps upon her graduation in 1944. She met Maj. Campbell at Ft. Bliss, Texas, and they were married in 1945. In 1946, Dr. Campbell set up private practice on Broward's Rock, the home of his paternal grandparents, and was a founder of the hospital. Loretta worked as his nurse until the birth of their son Gary. Loretta was a member of the St. Francis Altar Society, the Hospital Auxiliary, the Broward's Rock Women's Club, the Red Cross, the Community Chest, and the Island Hills Golf and Country Club.

A rosary will be said at 10 a.m. Tuesday at St. Francis Catholic Church. In lieu of flowers, the family suggests memorial gifts to the Women's Club or to the Hospital Auxiliary.

Max checked the date. Loretta Campbell had died the previous year. Barb had appended a note: *Congestive heart failure. Died at the hospital, doctor in attendance. She left everything—no surprise—to sonny boy. An estate around four million. The old man never charged a lot as a doctor but he bought up lots of oceanfront property and sold it for big bucks when the island was developed.*

So Gary Campbell didn't need to practice law too assiduously. Max picked up the Campbell dossiers:

GARY CAMPBELL, 44, only son of Dr. Robert Campbell and Loretta Agnes Simpson Campbell. Top graduating senior from high school. B.A. in political science and J.D. from the University of South Carolina. Solo practitioner, specialty wills and estates. Active in county bar, a past president. Shy, retiring, gifted mechanically. Worked backstage in local Little Theater for a number of years. A first marriage to Helen Jimson ended in divorce. Divorce settlement in closed court records, rumored to be substantial. Married to Marie McKee in 1980. Two children, Katherine McKee and Samuel Edward. Served as scoutmaster, active in Parents Club, volunteer at The Haven (teaching chess).

MARIE MCKEE CAMPBELL, 42, youngest of five children born to Michael James McKee and Elinor Bassett McDougal, Shelbyville, Tennessee. Father a small farmer, killed in a tractor accident when Marie was eleven. Moving the family to North Carolina, her mother worked nights in a clothing factory. Marie's brother, Mike, was killed by a drunk driver. The year Marie graduated from high school, her mother was diagnosed with ovarian cancer and died within three months. Marie's SAT scores earned her a scholarship to Chastain College, where she majored in business and minored in ecology. She picketed a university lab which used cats for laboratory research. After graduation, she received certification as a paralegal and moved to Broward's Rock, where she went to work for Gary Campbell. She and Campbell married within six months of his divorce.

KATHERINE MCKEE CAMPBELL, 17, senior at Broward's Rock Prep. Won lead role in *Annie Get Your Gun*. Accomplished at tap, ballet. Member choir. Uses gift for mimicry to do sketches of famous actresses. Loves nineteenth century novels but careless with schoolwork, making mostly Bs and Cs except for drama where she always excels. A superb athlete, holds double A times in backstroke and free style, a quarter miler and relay star, and a state-ranked tennis player. Missed a month of school last year for illness.

SAMUEL EDWARD CAMPBELL, 14, sophomore at Broward's Rock Preparatory School. Belongs to Chess Club, Aerospace Club. Received prize as outstanding second-year Spanish scholar. Has accrued twelve hours of college credit through advanced placement exams. Shares his mother's passion for wildlife preservation and plans to be a marine biologist.

Barb clattered into Max's office, carefully carrying two tall frosted glasses topped with mounds of whipped cream dotted with chocolate and cinnamon. "I left a note. Ingrid wasn't there." She put a coaster on his desk, placed the drink. "Maybe Agatha needs counseling."

Max grinned. "It doesn't take a psychiatrist to read her mind. Agatha thinks 'svelte' is a swear word and she won't listen to a discourse on the dangers of fat to a small cat liver."

Barb avoided his gaze. "She was in a better mood when I left."

Max didn't need a cat psychiatrist to explain that one either. Soft-hearted Barb, who understood hunger. "Don't tell Annie," he warned. He closed the folder on the Campbell family.

Barb picked up the Ellis folder, handed it to him. "More troubles than a man should have."

Annie waited until Pamela Potts completed her report. ". . . had only an hour's sleep." Red-rimmed eyes blinked bravely. "I've compiled a complete report on Kathryn Girard's activities on the island. And now"—a bravely suppressed yawn—"I'll go off duty."

"Very good, Pamela." Emma patted the folder. "You get some rest."

Pamela wove her way unsteadily toward the steps, but

she managed to go down them quite easily. Annie suppressed a grin. She didn't bother to alert Pamela to the message awaiting her, requesting her presence tonight at the hospital. Annie wasn't worried. Pamela would be there.

Annie opened her purse. "When I emptied Henny's pockets this morning, I found the pick-up card for Kathryn Girard. Kathryn had marked out the original addresses and substituted others. Max took the card to Chief Garrett, but we made some copies and I brought you one." She put a sheet on the table in front of Emma.

Emma's eyes blazed with a cold, eager light. She tapped the sheet with a stubby finger. "I researched handwriting analysis once. For *The Mystery of the Startled Widow*." Her finger traced the first address in Kathryn Girard's bold script. "Thickness indicates greed. That loop means care in planning, attention to detail. And this curl simply screams malevolence." She looked as pleased as Frances and Richard Lockridge's Jerry North spotting a martini. Emma's square face exuded satisfaction. And even a hint of admiration? "Good work, Annie. Combined with what I've learned, we're finally on the right track. I have a well-placed source who informed me just a few minutes ago that a large sum of money was found hidden in Kathryn's apartment. Now, juxtaposed with this list, what does that tell us?"

Annie knew better than to upstage one of the world's most popular mystery writers. "What does it tell us?" she asked obediently.

"Blackmail!" Emma's eyes glistened with delight. "And everything reported by Faithful Pamela—"

Was Pamela taking on the guise of Miss Silver's Faithful Frank?

"—confirms this assumption. Kathryn was extremely active in the Hospital Auxiliary and she was especially eager to stay with the dying. Where can you find out more about any family than at a deathbed? It rather reminds me of one of my best, *The Case of the Chattering Crocodile*."

Annie resisted the temptation to say, "Coo!" although

she realized she likely was passing up what might be her only opportunity to respond with the enthusiasm of Tuppence and Tommy's faithful Albert.

"So, our role is clear."

Annie wondered where Emma kept her crystal ball. "Clear?" At this rate, maybe she should change places with the parrot on the fishing boat.

"We shall attack, all guns firing." Emma pulled a stack of papers close.

"Attack? But Emma, these people don't have any idea we know about them. Wouldn't it be better—"

"Annie, you may have read a great many mysteries." The patronizing tone made Annie wish she'd stuck Emma's latest on a bottom shelf down with the W's. "But I write them. I know how a murderer's mind works. And"—this was reflective—"I know how a blackmailer thinks."

Annie didn't doubt that statement. If she'd had the courage, she would have asked snippily, "Had a little personal experience there?" Instead, she made an Agatha-like growl deep in her throat.

Emma waggled her copy of the sheet. "Blackmailers are bullies. They like to see people squirm. Kathryn couldn't resist a final poke at the caged animals."

"Emma"—Annie's voice was eager—"we don't want to make people squirm. That would be awful. Let's keep this quiet. We can try and find out—"

Emma shrugged. "Omelets," she said briskly.

Annie had a vision of broken eggshells surrounding a sizzling skillet. But these weren't eggs, these were people.

"Emma—"

A stubby hand was raised. "Annie, do you think Henny is in danger?"

Last night a bullet didn't miss Annie by more than a few feet. The murderer could have aimed into the air. That would as likely have sent Annie into a dive for cover and afforded the murderer time to escape.

The murderer still had that gun and Henny was remem-

bering occasional patches of last night. Even though Henny
might never recall the moment when she came up to the
van, the murderer had to be frightened. Annie could imagine the scene, the dark road, the misting rain, the lights from
Henny's old car poking through the darkness, the van with
the body in the back. The murderer most likely slid out the
passenger side of the van, carrying the croquet mallet, and
came up behind Henny. But when the mallet was swung,
the murderer slipped. Or Henny moved forward. That explained the roundish bruise on Henny's arm and the fact
that Henny wasn't battered to the ground. Instead, Henny
ran away. Where was the gun at that point? If Ruth was the
killer, her story of Kathryn taking the gun was a lie. Perhaps
Ruth had intended to use the gun but saw the mallet in the
back of the van and grabbed it to strike Kathryn. She must
have left the gun at home, but taken it later that night when
biking to Kathryn's store. But if Ruth was innocent, the gun
was in the back of the van and the murderer saw it when
dumping Kathryn's body on the floor, saw the gun and left
it, but retrieved it after Henny fled.

Whatever had happened, Annie was certain that the gun
was in dangerous, deadly hands and, yes, that Henny was
at risk. But was making the murderer nervous a wise thing
to do?

Annie came around the card table, knelt beside Emma.
"Listen, Emma, last night . . ." Once started, Annie not only
described that terrifying moment in front of Kathryn's store,
she spilled out her confrontation with Ruth Yates.

Emma wasn't interested at this moment in the prove-
nance of the gun. She gripped Annie's arm. "Think, Annie!
You must have some sense of who shot at you. A man? A
woman? How tall was the person? Bulky? Thin? Old?
Young?"

"A coat. A cap. Dark. Black. An arm sweeping up. Folders. That's all I saw," Annie said miserably. "Then—"

Emma gave her arm a squeeze. "Good thing you dived."
Her piercing gaze studied Annie with interest. "So you and

Max opted not to call the cops. Maybe the less said about that episode the better." Her cornflower-blue eyes were busy calculating why they hadn't called Garrett. "Has it occurred to you that the murderer might add you to the shut-'em-up list?" Then she shook her head and her bronze ringlets quivered like sea oats in an onshore breeze. "No, no," she answered herself brusquely. "Obviously, you aren't going to finger anyone or you would already have done so. The murderer's not worried about you. Just like," she muttered, *"The Case of the Half-Hearted Heiress."*

Annie wished Emma would refrain from drawing corollaries with her own books. Annie didn't want to take offense but she remembered that particular title and a rather vapid ingenue who never quite understood what was going on. Emma's sleuth, Marigold Rembrandt, understood everything of course.

But this was no time for personal feelings. Annie pushed to her feet. "Emma, I think we should move quietly—"

Emma held up a stubby hand. "The cat's out of the bag. My source told me Garrett's already on his way to check out those addresses, talk to the people who live there. That will be the beginning of pressure. We'll figure out how to increase the stress. But first, let's go get the van. I got the extra set of keys out of the office this morning."

She was on her feet and leading the way. This morning her caftan was a swirl of black and red and she somewhat resembled a mobile checkerboard. "Who knows what we may learn from it. After all, as Marigold often points out, 'A woman's eye sees more.' " Emma laughed deep in her throat. "Of course, I never explain more of what. But my readers don't seem to care. It rather reminds me of *The Puzzle of the Purloined Pillow*. Marigold deduced the presence of a missing python from a bulge in the clothes hamper."

Max studied an array of color printouts on his desk:

Vince Ellis, freckled face almost as red as his curly hair, legs pumping, crossed the finish line in the annual Save the

Turtles Marathon. He looked stronger than most middle-aged athletes, a shade over six feet tall with a broad chest and muscular legs.

Vince and his wife Arlene danced at the country club's New Year's Eve ball, Vince dapper in a tuxedo, though his black tie was askew and confetti spattered his red hair, Arlene ethereal in an ice-blue gown, her golden hair in coronet braids, a gold necklace emphasizing the slender column of her neck.

Tennis player Vince accepted the silver trophy for men's singles, ages forty to fifty. His red hair was a sweaty mop and his nose peeling from sunburn, but he had a grin big enough to make an alligator jealous.

Vince and Arlene walking slowly, a little girl between them clutching their hands as they entered the church.

An ashen-faced Vince climbing into a Coast Guard search helicopter.

Max opened the folder:

VINCENT HENRY ELLIS, 46, son of William Henry Ellis and the late Margaret O'Hara Ellis, Jasper, Florida. High school track, basketball and football star; editor high school newspaper. Track scholarship to the University of South Carolina. B.A. in journalism. Five years as AP statehouse reporter in Columbia, ten years as business reporter on *Miami Herald*. Used inheritance after mother's death to purchase the *Broward's Rock Island Gazette*. In high school dated homecoming queen and class president Arlene Frances Simms. Arlene received an academic scholarship to the University of South Carolina. She also majored in journalism. They married the day after graduating from college. Arlene worked as a freelance writer, specializing in garden stories. When they bought the *Gazette*, she became Life Style editor and her gardening columns regularly won first in state newspaper competitions. Vince and Arlene had no children until they adopted the orphaned daughter of Arlene's sister, Amelia. Three years ago Arlene's sailboat capsized after a sudden storm. Her body was never found.

Max scanned a very brief dossier:

MARGARET WENDY LASSITER ELLIS, 6, daughter of Richard James Lassiter and Amelia Simms Lassiter. Parents deceased. School record indicates the Lassiters were killed in a car wreck. Adopted four years ago by Vince and Arlene Ellis.

Max picked up the iced cappuccino. But not even the coffee-rich drink lifted his spirits. Vince couldn't have made it clearer that he—and the *Gazette*—wouldn't be investigating Kathryn Girard's death. His name was on Kathryn's list.
Vince, a blackmail victim?
Max couldn't believe it. Or even if he had to believe it, he couldn't believe that Vince Ellis, a man he'd known and liked for years, a man who'd wept at the memorial for his wife, a man who'd walked the beaches, gaunt and thin, staring out to sea, could possibly have arranged her death.
But what else could he believe?
Max shoved the folder aside, picked up the next.

Annie followed Emma and Mavis Cameron around the end of the police station. The parking lot was screened from the street by a line of pines. Annie lagged a little behind. Honestly, she didn't see why she had to be the one to drive the van back to the Women's Club. But Emma, that stubby hand firm on Annie's elbow, had marched her directly to the pink Rolls-Royce. On any other errand, Annie might have enjoyed riding in Emma's car, which breasted the roadways like a stately liner encountering swells. On the short jaunt, Emma had discoursed with pleasure about *The Adventure of The Curious Coon Cat*. Annie was, to put it exceedingly politely, suffering from a surfeit of Marigold Rembrandt.

Did Emma ever talk about anyone else's mysteries? Annie tried a diversion. "Don't you think Jean Hager's Mitch Bushyhead is terrific?" Emma's cornflower-blue eyes blinked, but she kept right on talking about Marigold.

As they neared the van, Mavis said, "Did they tell you to bring another set of keys? Billy had to call the wrecker service to bring it in last night."

Emma nodded, opening her purse, a floppy square of beige canvas sailcloth beaded with sea shells dyed purple.

Annie gave the huge purse a jaundiced glance. The purse was so damn big Emma probably had a half dozen copies of her books in there just to make sure dear Marigold was ever near. Then she focused on the keys in Emma's capable hand.

Why were the keys taken from the van last night? Henny's keys were in her car. Max had arranged for the old Dodge to be driven to Henny's house as well as seeing to Annie's car. Why were there no keys in the van? That seemed odd.

Emma held out the keys.

Annie grimly took them. After all, she read mysteries. She could drive a murder van. Wasn't she as tough as Liza Cody's Anna Lee or Janet Dawson's Jeri Howard?

Unfortunately, no. Her hand shook and she had trouble poking the key into the lock. When it slid home, she turned the key, opened the door.

That smell . . .

Mavis might simply be a desk clerk, but she was married to a cop and she typed reports. She knew the drill. "Step away from the van." Mavis's voice was clipped. "Don't touch anything."

Chapter 8

Carefully skirting the artificial putting green, Barb waggled the sheaf of color prints before dropping them on Max's desk. "Tip of the iceberg. Surprised they didn't get a picture of him when he was teething. If I keep looking, I'll probably find that."

Max stood and spread the prints across the desk, adding them to the half dozen Barb had brought earlier. Ah, the prosperous Pierces. But, as Barb had said, everybody's got troubles. Max stared at a particular photo with an unsettling sense of déjà vu, a haggard, white-faced Dave Pierce, hair tangled, tie askew, hurrying toward a Coast Guard helicopter. A tragic coincidence? Or something much more sinister?

Max riffled through the file, found a copy of the next day's news story in the *Island Gazette:*

LYNN PIERCE
LOST AT SEA
No trace has been found of accomplished island sailor

Lynn Pierce, 42, whose sailboat, Just Funnin', *was discovered capsized and adrift yesterday two miles from the southern tip of Broward's Rock by Coast Guard helicopters.*

Coast Guard Lt. Milton Farriday reported that Mrs. Pierce, wife of island resident Dave Pierce, often sailed alone. She and her husband were founding members of the Broward's Rock Yacht Club.

The accident was the second island boating tragedy this year. Six months earlier, Arlene Ellis, Life Style editor of the Gazette *and wife of publisher Vince Ellis, was apparently swept overboard during a sudden storm. Mrs. Ellis's body was never found.*

Lt. Farriday said yesterday the weather was clear with light winds. Mrs. Ellis, however, had taken her boat out shortly before a thunderstorm.

A spokesman for the Pierce family said a memorial service is being planned. Mrs. Pierce is survived by her husband, Dave, of the home, and son, David Jr., New York City.

The story was accompanied by a two-column picture of Lynn Pierce at the tiller of her sailboat, wind ruffling a sleek cap of dark hair. Despite the grainy quality of the reproduction, the newspaper photograph captured Lynn Pierce's exuberance and, oddly, sadly, an aura of invincibility: lifted head, eager gaze, flashing smile.

The cutline read: *Lynn Pierce came in first in the Europe class race for women 35–49. Pierce is a longtime competitor in Low Country races and is treasurer of the Broward's Rock Yacht Club.*

Max checked the dates. Lynn Pierce won that race two months before she drowned.

There were so many other clips, he scarcely knew where to start. He chose one of the earliest:

COMMUNICATIONS CEO
CHOOSES ISLAND HOME

Dave Pierce, CEO of Almerol Communications, has purchased an island show home and plans to commute to his Atlanta headquarters. Pierce, 31, was the subject of a recent article in the Wall Street Journal, *citing his company as one of the fastest growing in the international field of wireless communications.*

In the article, Pierce described the beginnings of his company years ago in the garage of his Walnut Creek, California home. The company has gone from a loss of forty-three thousand dollars in its first year to a cash flow this year estimated to exceed forty million. The company is at present privately held but the Wall Street Journal *reported that rumors in the market suggest Almerol may soon go public.*

Pierce moved the company's headquarters to Atlanta after absorbing Wilton Wireless. He told the Wall Street Journal *that he has plans to open offices in New York and London.*

When contacted by the Island Gazette *about his new island home, Pierce said, "My wife Lynn and I have enjoyed vacationing here and we believe this will be a wonderful place for our son to grow up." The Pierces have one son, David Jr., 2.*

"We love to sail," Lynn Pierce announced.

The Pierces' new home is one of the island's loveliest and has been the site of many parties and charitable fetes. Lynn Pierce hopes to continue that tradition. She has long been active in volunteer activities.

Many of the photographs proved that Lynn Pierce's hope was fulfilled. Max looked at one in particular, knowing he glimpsed a moment that had meant much to this couple. Dave and Lynn danced on a terrace strung with glimmering Japanese lanterns. Pierce's normally stern, almost ascetic face was warmed by a sweet smile as he looked proudly at his wife, lovely in gold silk, her head flung back in laughter.

Barb's note read: *This was one of the biggest bashes ever. Tickets sold at $250 a couple to raise money for the Humane Society.*

Max reached for the dossiers on Dave Pierce, Lynn Pierce and Janet Pierce.

Emma, of course, had a cell phone in her shell-spangled bag.

"Thank you, Mrs. Clyde." Mavis quickly punched the buttons. "Billy? Mavis here. I'm out in the lot behind the station. Mrs. Clyde and Annie are here to get the van, but it smells like it's burned inside. Arson, for sure. The chief's gone to the Girard apartment to check out a tip. I thought I should stand by until someone can get here."

"First rule of police procedure," Emma murmured to Annie. "Contain all bystanders. In *The Mystery of the Movable Mugwump*—"

Annie tuned out. She was much more interested in *The Mystery of the Vandalized Van.* That explained the missing car keys. Last night, after Henny ran into the darkness, the murderer grabbed the keys, and then what? A bike in the back of the van? That almost had to be the answer. Otherwise, the murderer could have taken Henny's car. Annie was sure of one fact. The murderer had to have a means of escape from Marsh Tacky Road. It was too far to walk to any of the houses on Kathryn's list.

Keeping a good distance from the van—Mavis was watching her carefully, ready to speak out if Annie encroached on the crime scene—Annie walked past the end and studied the crushed oyster shells. Nothing there to help. This murderer didn't shed broken buttons, hairs or cloth fibers.

Annie glanced toward the gate. It stood six feet tall and was open now. A chain and lock dangled from a hasp. Obviously, the lot was locked at night, but the old-fashioned chain-link fence wasn't topped by barbed wire. On the island, keeping intruders out of the police lot obviously wasn't a concern. Or hadn't been until now. Gaining access late at night had been easy. There was a live oak at a far corner of the lot with spreading branches, an easy climb and drop. Then, armed with the keys, the murderer hurried to the van, unlocked the back door, sprinkled the contents with gas, tossed in a match. The murderer probably had a worried moment or two when the fire first flamed, but if no one came, and obviously no one had, it was a simple matter to give the fire fifteen minutes to burn, then slam the back door and leave, confident that the discards could no longer afford any clue to the route of the van.

Annie gestured to Emma. "Come on, Emma. There's no point in hanging around here. You can bet all they'll find in the van is a charred mess." Annie glanced at her watch. "Let's get back to the club. I need to get my car."

Max opened the dossier on Dave Pierce:

DAVE PIERCE, 52, born in Tuscaloosa, Alabama, father Timothy, a municipal judge, mother Anna Mae Harrison Pierce, primary school teacher. Only child. Straight A's throughout school career. Scholarship to Stanford University. Business degree. MBA Wharton School of Business. Worked with various companies in Silicon Valley until starting his own business. Type-A personality. Reputed to work seven days a week. Considered a fair but distant boss. One longtime employee said, "Dave has all the personality of a hammerhead shark but if there's moving prey, he's your man." Another said, "The man's a machine, but he's got a heart. When my mother was dying of cancer, he let me go on extended leave and my job was there when I came back." A high school counselor of David, Jr., said, "You hear a lot about absentee parents and money won't take their place. I only met Dave Pierce once. That was when David received the

award for Outstanding Senior Boy. But I can tell you his
kid makes a room shine. That takes love." A longtime
golfing buddy said, "His game went to hell after Lynn
died. He didn't play for a couple of years." The administrative secretary at his office, "Involved with Janet when
Mrs. Pierce was alive? Absolutely not. He isn't that kind
of man. But he was lonely after she was gone and Janet's
always been his right hand. She started to work for him
right out of college and she thinks he's God."

There were several photos of the second Mrs. Pierce,
Janet as a somersaulting high school cheerleader, competing
in water ballet in college, as a graduating senior at the University of California at Northridge. Always attractive, her
beauty increased with time as she matured from a plump-
cheeked girl to an elegant and sophisticated woman. In several of the pictures, before the death of Lynn Pierce, she
stood in the background at business gatherings, attentive
and interested, blond hair upswept, small gold earrings,
black suit and pumps.

JANET MURRAY PIERCE, 46, born in Long Beach, California,
father James a high school physics teacher, mother Stella
Fowler Murray an oil company secretary. Middle of
three daughters. Always the prettiest girl in her class.
Serious. Excellent grades. College scholarship, majored
in business. Her first job out of college was with Almerol. She devoted herself totally to the company. Or,
as one friend observed, "She caught Dave's attention
early. She was quick, bright and worked her guts out.
She put in a lot of twelve- to fourteen-hour days." By
the time the company moved to Atlanta, Janet was vice
president of operations. She often came to the Pierce
home at Broward's Rock for gatherings combining business and social events. The administrative secretary tried
to be nice: "Really, they're quite a match. Man machine,
woman machine. She's still involved in running the com-

pany, though she stays on the island now and tries to do the Mrs. Dave Pierce bit. Everybody always knew she was nuts about him, but he never tumbled to it. You have to give her credit for that. Of course, I knew he was a goner after the first wife died. He never could have survived without Janet. I suppose they're happy enough. But he used to whistle a lot when his first wife was alive. I haven't heard him whistle in years."

Max closed the folder. He glanced at the clock. Almost noon. There was still time to study the dossiers on Ruth and Brian Yates before meeting Annie for lunch. As he picked up the Yates folder, the phone rang.

The Pink Rolls-Royce glided majestically to a stop near Annie's Volvo. As Annie opened the door—the click was right on a par with that of a bank vault—Emma observed crisply, "We shall not permit ourselves to be stymied by this setback."

Annie jumped out. "Certainly not."

"Think of Marigold in *The Adventure of the Dancing Tarantula*—"

Annie was not really ready to do that.

"—when she was faced with the locked cellar door, remember what she did?"

Annie bent down, peered into the luxurious interior. Honestly, she'd not noticed until this minute that the leather was also pale pink. Why did she suddenly think of the healthy membranes in a wolf's mouth? Was it because Emma was awaiting an answer, confident, of course, that Annie knew the ins and outs of every one of her marvelous plots?

"Marigold is simply amazing!" Annie had never sounded perkier.

Was there a glint of humor in those icy eyes? A twitch of that firm mouth? "Isn't she, though," Emma agreed. "I suggest we follow her example of amassing information, then conferring. Let's meet at my house at four. We can plan our attack for tomorrow. I have to be at the club during the day but I'm confident we shall learn a great deal. And tomorrow night is the Fall Revel."

The Women's Club always celebrated the successful completion of another White Elephant Sale with a magnificent party at the Island Hills Country Club.

"Everyone will be there." Emma tapped on the steering wheel. It was, of course, shell-pink.

Everyone, Annie knew, meant everyone whose house had been on Kathryn's list.

Emma's gaze was steely. "I shall devise a plan this afternoon."

Annie turned on the air-conditioning in her car. A cloud of monarchs swept past, proving it was September, though the weather had yet to break and the steamy air still felt like summer. Last night's storm had simply added another layer of humidity. She picked up her cell phone and called.

"Lucy Kinkaid Memorial Library," a sweet voice announced.

"May I speak to Edith Cummings, please?" Annie backed the car, turned, headed out of the lot.

"Edith is on sick leave. May I take a message?"

Annie braked at the stop sign. "Oh, I'm sorry to hear she's sick. This is Annie Darling and I wanted to talk with her." That was accurate. But it would have been more accurate to say she wanted to get the lowdown on some island nabobs. And where did that odd but wonderful word come from? She'd have to ask Edith, who always knew everything as librarians are wont to do.

"Oh hi, Annie. This is Mindy Smith." A member of the Friends of the Library who was a very good customer. "Poor old Edith. She tumbled down the main stairs and twisted both ankles. So she's home for about a week. I've been meaning to call you. Do you have a first edition of *Hearts and Bones* by Margaret Lawrence? I love that book!"

Annie did, too. This title was the first in a series of brilliant historical mysteries set in the period following the American Revolution. The books chronicled the life of midwife Hannah Trevor, a woman surviving turbulent and terrible times. "I sure do. I'll hold it for you. Thanks, Mindy."

Annie was nearing the Seaside Inn. She punched in Edith's home number.

The phone was answered in mid-ring. "Hello?" Edith's raspy voice quivered with hopefulness. She would likely have welcomed a call from a government survey.

"Hi, Edith. This is Annie. How are you feeling?"

"I'm waiting for deliverance," the sour voice groused. "Not like the damn river. That would make you stick to the city forever. Then you read James Ellroy and you know the city's even scarier. Where to go? What to do? A treehouse? A moon shot? A yellow submarine? Is this the lottery people? I'll get on a plane to Marrakesh if I have to crawl there." A heavy sigh. "Hello, Annie."

"Hey, Edith. I'm sorry about your fall." Annie picked up speed, turned left. Edith didn't live far from St. Mary's. Or, by extension, from Kathryn Girard's shop and apartment. "Are you up for company?"

"You? Or a traveling circus? Maybe there's a friendly python who'd like to drop over. Wiggle over? Slide over? Undulate—"

Annie slid up to the curb, turned off the motor and waved at Edith, who was propped in a hammock on the front porch of her one-story wooden home, modest but cheerful with fresh white paint and bright green shutters. Edith waved and clicked off the cordless phone. She put the phone near a pitcher of sun tea on the table next to the hammock. Glasses, an ice bucket, a plate of assorted fruit-center cookies and a divided bowl with M&M's and raisins were within easy reach.

"Undulate, definitely," Edith announced as Annie ran up the steps. "I wondered if you'd come by. I may be stationary, but I'd like to do my part for Henny. I've heard you and Max are looking for clues all over the island." Edith adjusted a pillow behind her curly dark hair, grimaced as she moved one leg. "How's she feeling?" Henny was the current president of the library board and a longtime volunteer with the Friends of the Library.

"Lots better." Annie talked fast as she told Edith everything except the foray into Kathryn Girard's apartment.

The librarian's mobile face and lively black eyes reflected interest and intelligence. "The Campbells, Vince Ellis, the Pierces, the Yates. Tall cotton, Annie. Have some tea, Annie. Unsweetened."

Annie reached for the pitcher, refilled Edith's glass and fixed a glass for herself. "Thanks, Edith. Hmm, fresh mint." She twisted the mint, loved the fragrance. "Who else could afford blackmail?"

Edith grinned. "Well put."

And that reminded Annie . . . "Edith, why do they call rich people nabobs?"

"Nabob: A provincial deputy or governor in the old Mogul Empire in India. The Empire began in 1526 under the ruler Babur and ended in 1858. It was, by the way, the Moguls who built the Taj Mahal. Anyway, 'nabob' was used to describe the really rich in the 1890s and early 1900s in the United States." Edith grinned. "Four hundred years later! Don't you love it?" Then her face was stricken. "Annie, I've been meaning to call you. Do you remember during the Fourth of July festival at the library—"

Annie certainly recalled the recent holiday that combined spectacular fireworks and a particularly cunning murder.

"—when I told you"—Edith's voice was anguished— "that The Wizard of Oz was written as a sophisticated economic allegory?"

Annie had taken the news as simply one more assault on her childhood faiths: First Santa Claus, then the Yellow Brick Road. What next? Would Rudolph's nose turn out to be battery-powered? "Yes, I remember."

Edith put down her glass, clutched Annie's hand with

damp fingers. "I was wrong. Wrong! And yet I'd read this brilliant editorial in the *New York Times* applauding Frank Baum for his brilliant propagandizing on the gold standard and free silver. Do you know what it turned out to be?" Her voice rose.

Annie shook her head, certain she had no clue. Was she going to regain her faith in the Yellow Brick Road?

"An economics professor once used the book to illustrate *his* vision of an economic allegory, but people picked up his speech and soon everyone accepted it as fact that Baum's purpose was political. Well, the historian who wrote Baum's biography completely debunks the idea. Do you know why Baum wrote the book?" She yanked on Annie's hand.

Annie disentangled her fingers. "No. Why?" She knew Edith in this mood. There was information she had to impart.

"To please children. That was all. No political motive. No grand machinations to influence economic policies." Edith struggled to sit up in the hammock.

"It's okay, Edith." Annie leaned over, adjusted the pillow.

Edith sank back, her eyes mournful. "I'm a research librarian."

Annie understood. Everyone had pride. How would Annie feel if she didn't know the true author of *The G-String Murders* by Gypsy Rose Lee? Even though Gypsy Rose Lee's name was on the cover, Craig Rice wrote the book.

But Edith's total commitment to truth and her skeptical nature made her invaluable now. "Edith, nobody knows more about the island than you do."

For an instant, Edith's gaze was faraway, apparently still fastened on the baselessly tarnished Yellow Brick Road. Then those bright, observant eyes focused on Annie. She gave a modest shrug. "Oh, I suppose I know a bit." The disclaimer was careless, but the underlying confidence evident: Ask me, baby, ask me! The Oz debacle couldn't put Edith down for long.

Annie pulled her wicker chair closer to the hammock.
"Okay, Edith. What do you know about the Campbells?"

Max tucked the phone under his chin, tilted his chair
back. "Max Darling." Max admired the photograph of Annie
in its heavy silver frame. It was the next best thing to having
Annie here, her sun-streaked blond hair, steady gray eyes,
and special smile. Dear Annie, funny, fun, serious and pur-
poseful. She always tried hard to do her best. If that included an unfortunate propensity to encourage him to also
do his best, a matter upon which they had scant agreement,
well, marriage was meant to be challenging, right?

"Mr. Darling, this is Pete Garrett—"

"Oh Pete, Max here. Was that anonymous call helpful?"
Max doodled a cake, striped it like a lawn chair. He wrinkled his nose. There was a marvelous aroma of baking. Barb
could create wonders in the little kitchen next to the store-
room. But crème de menthe and white crème de cacao?

"We investigated thoroughly. Clearly, the apartment had
been disturbed since we checked it out last night. There is
now some basis to be especially interested—"

Max drew a clam with tight stitch marks where the shells
met. He circled the clam with dollar signs. Garrett obviously
had a future in a politically sensitive job.

"—in the houses Kathryn Girard apparently intended to
visit last night. Especially since"—this silence was dour—
"we have had a serious breach of police security. The Wom-
en's Club van suffered serious damage from an interior fire.
Obviously, Mrs. Brawley had no hand in that damage, as
she was under police surveillance as well as incapacitated.
The fact that the van's contents have been destroyed indicates an effort to prevent authorities from gaining information from the van's contents. Those contents must have come
from the houses on the list you gave me. Officer Cameron
told me"—Garrett hesitated, then plunged ahead—"that you
have very likely amassed some information about those indi-
viduals in your efforts to aid Mrs. Brawley and—"

Max spoke up, brimming with good citizenship. "Oh sure. I'll send over what we have right now."

Garrett's young voice held surprise, relief and appreciation. "That's awfully good of you."

"We're glad to help." Max put a bow on top of the clam. "We want to do everything we can to help you find out who killed Kathryn and chased Henny. Call anytime."

He buzzed for Barb.

She hurried into his office, dusting flour from a magenta apron. "I'm just putting on the icing. You can take a piece to Parotti's for Annie."

Max sniffed. "Crème de menthe?"

"I've been thinking about this cake for a while and laying in stores." Barb dusted off the flour. She glanced at the stack of folders. "It seemed like a good time. I thought I'd take a piece to Henny in a little while."

"On your way"—he pointed at the dossiers—"take copies of everything we've got to Chief Garrett."

Barb's eyebrows rose.

"We," Max said firmly, "are in full cooperation with the officers of the law."

"That," Barb observed, "is certainly a first." She gathered up the folders.

Max leaned back in his chair. If Barb got the stuff back to him in time, he'd read the Yates file before he met Annie for lunch. But he was already thinking of some questions that needed answers.

"I can tell you that Loretta Campbell didn't like her daughter-in-law worth a damn." Edith's hand bypassed the raisins for a handful of M&M's. "Raisins," she said indistinctly, "really louse up your teeth."

Annie took M&M's, too. After all, lunch was at least an hour away.

Edith crunched two more of the candies. "Loretta was president of the library board about five years ago. Nice lady, but lah-di-dah. Awfully proud of the Campbells and, of course, The Doctor. It's a wonder she didn't queer Gary's marriage. The second one. Lots of whispers about the first. People said he went around looking like a whipped dog. That wife beat it quick. I heard she went to Florida, worked in a nightclub. So you'd think Loretta would have appreciated Marie. Except Marie worked her way up from nothing. She was Gary's secretary. They got married as soon as the divorce was final. Maybe that's what put Loretta's nose out of joint. Maybe she thought Marie was a home wrecker. Apparently Wife Number One was a floozy. So wasn't Marie a better deal? But I've never forgotten a program a couple of years ago at The Haven. It was an awards deal, plaques to older kids who donated their time to work with little kids. Katy Campbell coached volleyball. I was working in the aisle, you know, helping get the kids in line to go on stage. I looked toward the Campbells. You know Marie, she's like a roman candle, bright, fizzy. She was watching Katy walk up the steps and, well, she was one proud mom. Sam was giving two thumbs up and grinning. Gary was clapping like a maniac. Then I looked at the old lady. Talk about a stone face. She watched her granddaughter go up those stairs, then her head swiveled toward Marie, and I swear, Annie, just for an instant, her face curdled like she'd tasted brine. One happy family, I don't think."

Annie lifted her glass. The tea was tart and refreshing. "Who do you think Kathryn was blackmailing? Gary or Marie?"

Edith picked up another handful of candies, popped two in her mouth. Her dark eyes were bright and sharp. "Hard to say. He's an odd duck. And I know there was something funny about Gary and the Little Theater. Gary's a Friend and he fixed the balusters on the second floor stairway. He did a beautiful job and Ned—"

Ned Fisher, the library director, had a finger in every island pie and never met a stranger.

"—tried to recruit him for the stage crew. Gary acted like he'd been invited to be the chief stuffed head in a taxidermist's shop. He backed away, those big eyebrows tufted, mouth twisted, muttering, 'No thanks. No thanks. Got to go.' After he left, Ned turned his hands up, asked me, 'What did I do, Edith? Does he think the Little Theater's a cabal?' " Edith took a big swig of tea. "Cabal! That's a good word. Did you know it came from the initials of Charles II's ministers, those conspiratorial old devils?"

Annie hadn't known. But no information forthcoming from a librarian would surprise her. After all, she'd read the Jo Dereske mysteries with librarian sleuth Helma Zukas, a human—and fun—almanac.

"And the funny thing is"—Edith pursued Little Theater—"Ned says he was looking over some of the old programs, long before either one of us came to the island, and Marie was a star. Played the lead in *Pajama Game*. But that was a long time ago."

Annie could picture Marie Campbell on the stage. She had an enchanting quality that made you feel a connection whether you knew her well or not.

But lives change. Fascinations can pall. And the Campbells' involvement in the local stage was a long time ago, apparently. "I can't see how dropping out of Little Theater could have anything to do with blackmail." Annie found a scrap of paper in her purse, wrote down: *Little Theater?* But ancient backstage rivalries hardly seemed worth pursuing. "Money."

Edith was a longtime mystery reader, as are many librarians. Edith's favorite authors included Margaret Scherf, Amanda Cross and Paula Gosling. She had no trouble following Annie's thoughts. "The old lady? But she was dying for a long time. And who would she leave her stuff to but Gary? I don't think that flies, Annie."

A well-hidden murder was such a wonderful reason for blackmail. Annie wasn't quite willing to dismiss Loretta Campbell's death. And Emma said Kathryn Girard was a member of the Hospital Auxiliary. Maybe she picked up a hint of something wrong from a nurse or nurse's aide or someone else in the auxiliary. Annie wrote down: *Hospital Auxiliary.*

Edith cautiously moved her legs. "Annie, would you mind shoving that little red pillow behind my right knee?"

"Sure." Annie leaned forward, adjusted the pillow. "More tea?"

Edith nodded weakly.

Annie plucked ice from a plastic bucket, poured the tea. She held up the plate. "Cookie?"

"Oh thanks. I'll have one or two." Edith languished against the pillow, wan as a gothic heroine.

Annie understood. Edith was long divorced and her son was at school. Spending a day alone with throbbing ankles would not be fun.

"How about the Pierces?" Annie had a swift memory of the green Porsche spurting from the Pierces' drive and a hand lifted in greeting.

Edith's eyes popped open, glittering with interest. She propped herself on her elbow. "I don't know much more about them than what everyone on the island knows. He's richer than Warren Buffett and she looks so expensive you expect her to shed diamonds when she walks. Actually, she seems pretty nice. She's all over the place. In the Friends, of course. I was detached from the library—lovely how Ned assumes I can do anything and will to cement relations with the rich—to work on a big promotion for the Prescott Art Center. And I can tell you that Janet Pierce did everything but throw down a cloak for Adelaide to walk on every time I saw them. Don't know why Janet would care so much. Dave could buy the island, much less the Prescotts. But Adelaide is old money, old family. Nope, can't help you with the Pierces. Who else is on that list? Vince Ellis? The Yateses?" Edith's face screwed up like a thoughtful monkey. "I guess you're sure about that?" She answered her own question. "Yeah, yeah, Kathryn's handwriting. Annie, it doesn't figure to me. Now, take Vince Ellis: He's a good guy. Works hard, tries to be the best single parent on the planet, and Meg's not even his kid. You talk about a heart-breaker. Arlene did a lot of stories out at The Haven and I got to know her pretty well. Bright, funny, sweet and crazy about that man. And he was crazy about her. Seems like everything was perfect for them until that last year. You know, they'd just brought Meg to live with them, maybe six months before Arlene died. I saw Arlene a couple of times that last month and she looked real bad, drawn and white, and her eyes were huge. She'd lost a lot of weight. Some-body told me she and her sister were real close. Arlene was so sweet with that little girl. I saw them on the beach one day and they had a way of turning their heads and looking at you and it was like Meg was a little replica of Arlene."

"It doesn't make sense, does it?" Annie thought about Vince Ellis and his losses. "I don't suppose," she said doubt-fully, "Vince had a girlfriend on the side."

Mystery cognoscente Edith looked at her sharply. "Oh, no way, Annie. Not Vince. Besides, he's never remarried."

That would seem to answer that. Though problems be-tween husbands and wives could involve more than infidel-ity and Vince's house was without any question on Kathryn's list. Annie wrote down: *Why was Arlene so unhappy?*

Edith peered at her pad. "You're on to something there. She was one miserable lady before she died. But Annie"—Edith's eyes were sad—"I don't think it will turn out to be Vince's fault." Her mouth quirked. "Though I've always had a weakness for redheads. Jeez, if Mike Shayne had a case on the island, I'd lay in a case of Martell's."

Brett Halliday's handsome Miami private eye had a taste for brandy.

"But," Edith sighed, "a woman's body in the back of a club van isn't exactly his style. Okay"—she leaned back on her pillow—"you've got Gary or Marie Campbell, Janet or Dave Pierce, Vince Ellis, which I don't think so, and Ruth Yates." Edith shoved back a tangle of curly dark hair. "Okay, okay, I know you tripped Ruth up about the gun, but honestly, Annie, Ruth's the original sad sack. Poor old Ruth. Hasn't she had enough trouble?"

Max arranged the photos in chronological order, Ruth Conroy Yates in her high school yearbook, walking across the stage for her bachelor's degree, her wedding, working in the church nursery, serving at a church tea, playing croquet with her husband, pricing donations at a church sale. Then and now, the pictures reflected anxious gray eyes, hair of an indeterminate brown, an uncertain but sweet smile. Her bony shoulders hunched defensively. Sticklike arms dangled at her sides. Her head was drawn tight to her neck like a turtle sensing danger. She was dowdily dressed in the pictures, a pink blouse and shapeless green skirt, a too-large navy-blue dress, a sundress with a cascade of ruffles.

Seven photos of Ruth, a dozen or so of Brian. Brian Yates either smiled all the time or was always camera-ready. Thick blond hair curled above cheerful blue eyes. Max riffled through, chose a few, Brian as president of his senior high school class, Brian leading scorer of his college soccer team, Brian at seminary, Brian at the reception after his ordination, Brian and his daughter playing softball, Brian speaking at the Art Center. Without exception, he beamed: face ruddy, eyes bright, mouth curved in an infectious grin.

When he and Ruth were pictured together, she faded into the background, not noticeable unless purposefully sought.

Nice man, Max thought. He always enjoyed talking to Brian. Actually, though he and Annie had known Brian and Ruth Yates since they came to the island, Max had almost no clear memory of Ruth Yates.

Max picked up the first dossier:

BRIAN ALDEN YATES, 52, first son of The Rev. Alden Alcott Yates and Josephine Cotter Yates, Scarsdale, NY. Father an Episcopal priest, mother a homemaker. Grew up in various cities (Scarsdale, New York; Alexandria, Virginia; Morristown, New Jersey; Dallas, Texas) where his father accepted church posts. President of his junior and senior classes at St. Mark's High School, Dallas; bachelor's degree in history from University of the South, divinity degree from Yale University. Served in dioceses in California, Texas and Georgia before coming to Broward's Rock ten years ago. Left a post as rector of a church to come to Broward's Rock as associate priest—

Max scrawled an oversize question mark on his pad and wrote: *A step down? Why?*

"—so that he could devote more time to his father, who had suffered a series of strokes and was bedridden."

Max drew through the question mark and queries.

Brian has turned down several opportunities to be interviewed by other churches, replying that he feels he's found his mission in his involvement on the island with a nursing home for disabled patients. In addition to duties at the church, he has been active in coaching softball and soccer, both at the local schools when his daughter was a student, and later at The Haven. Brian is married to Ruth Conroy, whom he met while an assistant priest at his first church in Laguna, California. Their daughter, Judith Ann, is married to Martin Fraser and lives in Denver, Colorado. Judy has two children, Mark Brian, 4, and Conroy Elaine, eight months.

The dossier on Ruth was much shorter:

RUTH CONROY YATES, 52, third of four children of Hampton Willis Conroy, pharmacist, and Lou Ella Taylor Conroy, homemaker. Ruth always made good grades but avoided extracurricular activities. She attended Long Beach University, majoring in childhood education. She lived at home after college and taught third grade at a Laguna Primary School. She met Brian Yates while as-

sisting in the Sunday School program at church. After
their marriage, she continued to teach until their daughter was born. Her activities have been limited to the
church or local schools.

Max slapped shut the folders. What could Kathryn Girard have discovered about the Yateses? He glanced at his
clock. Ah, almost time for lunch. Maybe Annie would have
some ideas.

"Ruth always looks like the last stagecoach out of Dodge
just left and there won't be another one." Edith's tone was
tart but her eyes were kind. "Usually I don't have any patience with scaredy-cats, but Ruth's really a sweetheart. She
was Ken's Sunday School teacher for four years and the kids
love her. What a softy. And she's shyer than a ghost crab.
She always reminds me of a crab. She scuttles. Brian bustles
around heartier than a musketeer, agreeing to this that or
the other, but half the time it's Ruth who ends up in the
trench doing all the work. Now, I understand he's got more
to do than anybody can manage, that's true of every priest,
but he moved his dad here and expected Ruth to manage
everything already on her plate, then spend hours attending
his dad. That was the same time their daughter was having
back surgery. Ruth got so skinny I thought she was going to
disappear, just like a ghost crab. About the same time, Brian's dad finally died. Ruth was worn to the bone. She looked
dazed for months, a real case of depression. But I can believe
that Ruth intended to shoot herself. It sounds just like her.
Whatever Kathryn Girard threatened, it figures Ruth would
hunt up a gun to shoot herself."

"But she didn't," Annie observed quietly. She finished
her tea. Almost time to meet Max. She resisted another
handful of M&M's. "Edith, can I go in the house and get
anything for you?"

"That's okay. Ned's bringing lunch. But Annie . . ."
Edith's face wasn't quite craven.

Annie knew what was coming. Edith was an ever-eager collector. Annie might as well show good grace. "What new books would you like, Edith?"

"How about the latest by Barbara Burnett Smith and Laura Lippman?"

As always, Edith's taste was impeccable.

Chapter 9

Parotti's Bar and Grill was the best of all worlds as far as Annie was concerned, fabulous food in a down-home atmosphere. Actually, the bait coolers along the back wall near the beer-on-tap barrels provided more atmosphere than nonfishing tourists could stomach, which made it even more popular with year-round islanders. The grill welcomed the early morning charter groups. Parotti's breakfasts were legendary, spoon bread with melted butter and maple syrup, big crisp sausage patties, smoked country ham with redeye gravy, fried grits, pancakes with fresh strawberries and whipped cream, sugary cinnamon-sprinkled rice with dollops of butter and cinnamon cake doughnuts.

Annie took a deep breath. Next to the salt marsh, this was her favorite smell, the tangy combination of fish, beer, sawdust and old grease. What was not to like?

Ben Parotti, tavern proprietor and ferryboat captain (the ferry's irregular schedule was sometimes dictated by how many people came to lunch), handed Max and Annie menus. He eyed Annie warily. "Hyperventilatin'?"

Annie grinned. Ben's recent marriage had transformed him from a grizzled leprechaun in tattered long underwear tops and stained corduroy pants to a stylish leprechaun in golf shirts and baggy white trousers, but had done nothing to ameliorate his penchant for describing spades not only as spades but in earthy, explicit language. Ben might now be spiffy, but he was the same old tactless despot of his own domain.

"Sucking in the silver scent of the sea." Annie waved airily at the bait coolers.

Ben's bushy eyebrows squiggled. "The missus keeps wantin' me to take 'em out. But I've always been in the bait business."

He looked so forlorn, Annie said quickly, "Parotti's wouldn't be Parotti's without the bait. Everything's just perfect. You've kept the best of the old and added just the right amount of new." She nodded at the red-and-white-checkered cloths that now covered the old wooden tables and the slender vases with stalks of tall goldenrod. (No need, he must have told his wife, to spend money on flowers when God puts them right along the road.) "And the menu's divine. I don't even have to look." She carefully did not glance toward Max, who was a sergeant major in the cholesterol police. "I'll have oyster chowder and spoon bread." Ben's chowder was made with real country cream and the spoon bread was delectable.

"Low country boil, a salad, and cornbread sticks. And a Bud Light." As Max handed Ben the menus, he shot her a look of reproach.

Annie returned to the path of virtue. "A fruit smoothie, raspberries and peaches and yogurt." She was suffused with righteousness. "And a salad."

Max tried not to laugh, then he did.

So did she.

"Annie, Annie. I love you." His vivid blue eyes were soft, warm and held a special light she knew so well.

"And I love you." He was always, to her, the handsomest man in any room, with his unruly blond hair and brilliant blue eyes and sunshiny smile that made her want to touch him. But maybe it was as well that Max managed not to be quite perfect. Yes, he ate right, but his favorite exercise was lounging in a beach chair, and as for his work ethic—well, maybe she had enough for both of them. And maybe their willingness to let each other be was the rock on which they'd built a happy marriage.

Annie propped her chin on her hand. "Marriages. Maybe when we understand these marriages—Gary and Marie, Dave and Lynn, Vince and Arlene, Brian and Ruth—we'll understand this murder. From the outside, everything looked rosy. Was it?"

Ben slid a tumbler of ice water in front of Annie, slapped down a frosted glass and beer for Max.

"We," Max said firmly, "are going to find out. But"—he reached down, opened his briefcase and lifted out the folders—"first we have to figure out who was being blackmailed. Gary or Marie? Dave or Janet? Brian or Ruth? The only one we can be sure about is Vince."

Annie held up two fingers. "Nope. We can be sure Ruth Yates was the blackmail victim, not Brian." She brought Max up to date on the gun. "Of course, she claims Kathryn took it. She may be lying."

Max munched a pretzel from the bowl in the center of the table. "So the gun belongs to Ruth."

"She claimed she was going to shoot herself. But she didn't." Annie sounded skeptical.

Max lifted his glass. "She's got one point in her favor. Kathryn wasn't shot. And obviously, Ruth could have shot her."

"Maybe Kathryn grabbing the gun made Ruth so mad that she bashed Kathryn. Maybe she made up the whole thing because she shot at me last night and wanted to make us think someone else has the gun." But that was the kind of cleverness at which Emma Clyde excelled, not gentle Ruth.

Max put the folders on the table, pushed them toward Annie. He retrieved his cell phone from his briefcase, turned it on and set it at the edge of the table. And he picked up a sack with a happy face drawn on it. "From Barb. A slice of awning cake." He held up his hand. "Don't ask, just look. But you'd better take it out with you. Ben's feelings would be hurt. Barb said she might call. She's very proud of the cake." He pushed the folders and the happy face sack to Annie. "Why don't you look this stuff over—" A muffled ring. Max picked up the cell phone.

"Oh hi, Laurel." His easy grin was both fond and slightly apprehensive.

Annie peeked in the sack, then put it on the floor beside her purse. She knew that if Barb made it, it was good. Annie opened the top folder. She could read faster than anyone she knew, except Henny, of course. She pulled out a notebook and scanned and listened to Max's conversation.

"Fred who? . . . Pago Pago . . . oh, of course, Tutila Island." Then he grabbed a pad and pen from his briefcase. "Mark Stone? Lives on Red-Tailed Hawk. Right. . . . He actually saw Henny's car?"

Annie closed the Campbell folder, wrote down two questions.

". . . Okay, I got that. . . . About five minutes after six some old bat driving like an idiot—"

So Serena Harris didn't want to be late for the Andy Griffith rerun.

"—came around the curve on his side and he had to yank over to the right and slid into the ditch."

Ben arrived with their salads. Since they were old regulars, he didn't even have to ask: vinaigrette for Max, blue cheese for Annie. The salad itself was part of Parotti's transformation. Instead of a wedge of iceberg lettuce and two tomato slices, the plate blossomed with arugula, spinach

leaves and Boston bibb as well as rice noodles, water chestnuts and mandarin oranges. Ooh-la-la.

Annie finished the dossier on Vince Ellis. The question
was obvious. She wrote it down with sadness.

". . . a broken axle. So what did he do? . . ."

Annie's spine prickled as she read about Lynn Pierce.
Arlene Ellis disappeared first. Did her death give Dave
Pierce a blueprint for murder? She added questions four,
five and six.

". . . he's sure? That's weird. You think he can be relied
on? . . . Car slid into a welter of ferns? But . . . Oh, of course.
Ferns indicate sincerity. Yes, I see. . . ."

Reading the Yates file took no time at all, but Annie's
pencil, poised above the pad, didn't move.

". . . you and Fred are certainly to be commended. . . ."

Annie found a clean sheet, scrawled: *Howard out in the
cold?* And shoved it across the table.

Max glanced down. He cleared his throat.

Annie watched with great interest. Max always seemed
to get uncomfortable when skirting the edge of Laurel's
love life.

"Uh, Mother, uh—"

Annie hissed, "Fall Revel."

"Are you going to the Fall Revel tomorrow night?" He
came to a full stop. "But I thought you and Howard—"
Laurel's most attentive beau in recent years was Howard
Cahill, a ruggedly handsome widower.

"Oh. Of course I believe in freedom." He saw Annie's
swift glance. "I mean, freedom for some. . . . No, no, certainly for you. And I know a cruise is simply a cruise, of
course it is. . . . Honeysuckle vines? What did he say? . . . He
knows he will always think of you when he sees honeysuckle?" Max's blue eyes were bewildered. "Oh, sure. Honeysuckle represents generous and devoted affection. Right.
I should have known. Well, I'll look forward to meeting
Fred. More for you to do?" Max looked at Annie.

Annie shook her head. "Not right now. Ask her if she can come to Emma's at four. Council of war."

"That's all for now. Can you meet us at Emma's at four? . . . Okay. See you then." He clicked off the phone. "Laurel and Fred found a guy who had car trouble, actually slid off the road and broke an axle, about twenty yards from the entrance to Marsh Tacky Road. He came around the curve and that's when he went into a slide. By the time he got out of his car, he'd seen Henny's car turn into Marsh Tacky and he just glimpsed taillights ahead of her. He was still there, waiting for a wrecker, and he saw our cars turn into the lane. Between the time Henny's car went in and we arrived, no car came out of Marsh Tacky Road. And nobody. Not on foot or with water wings or any way."

Ben plunked down Annie's chowder, spoon bread and fruit smoothie and Max's Low Country boil. "Everything okay?" He craned his head to read the labels on the folders.

Annie nobly ignored the syrup for the spoon bread— after all, she wasn't a pig, no way—but she poked a hole in one square, poured in melted butter, then took a delectable bite. "Mmm. Wonderful, Ben."

Ben deposited his tray on the next table and swung back to peer at them. He leaned against a heavy wooden chair, folded his bony arms and appeared set for life. "Everybody says that new police chief almost fell on his ass, but the mayor set him straight." Ben sniffed. "Suspectin' Henny! Why, she knows all about mysteries. If she set out to kill somebody, you wouldn't find her layin' out in the woods to be caught."

Annie slurped a succulent piece of oyster. That Ben had heard the village drums was no surprise. But she was impressed with his reasoning. The mayor saw Henny as too respectable to be a criminal. Ben had it right. Henny was too clever to be caught should she choose to commit a crime. That, however, was an argument best not offered to Chief Garrett.

"First thing I heard that, I knew you folks would get

busy. Well, I can tell you that Girard woman was mighty peculiar. She paid her rent in cash. Called me once to fix the commode. Wasn't nothin' in that place to make it a home. I heard"—he ducked his head, looked around the room, which was empty except for a group of earnest women studying bird manuals, dropped his voice—"that Louella Kendall—you know, she's a third cousin to my wife Jolene— told Kathryn she didn't want her comin' to the hospital no more. Louella's a head nurse and she don't take no nonsense. I tried to get Louella to tell me what it was all about and she treated me like I was askin' her to testify to the grand jury." Ben's eyebrows bristled. He looked like a snazzy, aggrieved leprechaun. "Anyway, you might see if you can get Louella to ante up. 'Cause I know you"—he looked at Max like he was a combination of Harrison Ford and Michael Douglas—"got a real way with the ladies."

Ben flicked a glance at Annie, shifted slightly so he could avoid her interested gaze. "Anyway," he said quickly, "I been over to the place this morning with the chief. And you know what?" Ben bent over the table, his whisper sibilant as a snake's. "Her stuff was all tossed around, but damnedest thing, there was this leather album and it was full of thousand-dollar bills!"

"Coo!" Annie exclaimed. Just for that moment, she was right on a par with Albert at Blunt's Detective Agency, Agatha Christie's creation for Tommy and Tuppence Beresford.

Ben looked at her in concern and reached over to lift the pitcher and refill her water.

Max nudged her under the table. "Ben, that's really interesting. It makes you wonder," Max said darkly, "what kind of money Kathryn Girard had to keep hidden." A dramatic pause. "And what Kathryn was picking up on Thursday afternoon."

There was a cogitative silence. Then, eyes glistening, Ben nodded sagely. "It does, don't it? Well, you and the missus enjoy," and he turned and moved across the floor faster than a pelican diving for menhaden.

"Max"—Annie put a little raspberry jelly on her spoon bread—"Ben's a canny old devil. Pretty soon everyone on the island's going to hear that Kathryn was a blackmailer." The fruit smoothie made an interesting combination of tastes with the spoon bread.

Max speared a piece of sausage. "It should make the folks on Kathryn's list damn nervous."

Annie took a last spoonful of her chowder and cut another piece of spoon bread. "But we have to figure out what Kathryn had on these people. And who was paying her at each house. Well, of course we know Vince and Ruth were blackmail victims. It's maddening. We know a lot about these people, but we don't know who was hiding what." She picked up her notebook, handed it to Max. "Here's what I want to know."

ANNIE'S LIST

1. Why did Loretta Campbell dislike her son's wife?

2. Why did Gary and Marie quit the Little Theater?

3. Where was Vince Ellis when Arlene took her last sail?

4. Was Dave Pierce having an affair with an employee when his wife died?

5. Was Dave Pierce on the island the day his wife disappeared?

6. How well does Dave Pierce swim? What was the weather like that day?

Max looked at her with interest. "No questions about Ruth Yates?"

Annie turned up her hands. "Okay, we know Ruth paid blackmail for something. But what could it be? There's nothing we've found out about her that seems the least bit likely. Can you see Ruth having an affair? Or stealing anything? I mean, if she was somehow filching money from the church, why would she have to lie to Brian and pretend the car needed fixing to come up with cash? Besides, she has nothing to do with church expenditures, all she does is volunteer her time. I can't figure out what she could have done!"

"We'll find out." Max was as cocky as The Saint, Leslie Charteris's urbane and unruffled hero. "Here's what I wonder about." Max handed her his list.

MAX'S LIST

1. Who was the doctor who attended Loretta Campbell when she died?

2. What caused Gary Campbell's divorce? And was he involved with Marie when he was still married?

3. Why did Arlene Ellis take her boat out on a stormy day?

4. How did the murderer get away from Marsh Tacky Road?

5. Everybody says Dave and Lynn Pierce had a great marriage. Why would he kill his wife?

6. Edith Cummings ties Ruth Yates's depression to her daughter's surgery and the death of Brian's dad. What really sent her into a decline?

When Annie handed the list back, he added:

7. Why did Louella Kendall boot Kathryn Girard?

"Actually, honey, those are good questions except for number five," Annie said kindly.

"Oh?" Max was too well adjusted to be affronted. Maybe.

"Well," Annie said hurriedly, "it's the behind-closed-doors thing. Nobody can ever really know about anyone else's marriage." She finished her fruit smoothie.

"Not so," Max protested. "You can't fake real love. And why would anyone want to? Dave Pierce wasn't running for good-guy-of-the-year. He's a powerful man accustomed to having his own way. Now, maybe he wanted to look good to his son, that's a possibility. But I can't think of any other reason why he'd put up a false front."

Annie understood the logic. "But you can't make me believe Arlene Ellis and Lynn Pierce went out in sailboats within six months of each other and had accidents. Not when both the guys ended up paying blackmail."

"We don't know that it's Dave who's being black-mailed." Max looked like a croupier who had just raked in a pile of chips. "How about Janet?"

"Where's Janet supposed to get the money to pay Kath-ryn?" Annie dropped her notebook into her purse. "She's married to a rich man, but that doesn't make her rich."

Ben materialized. "Coffee today? Dessert? The missus said to tell you we got blackberry dumpling with vanilla sauce and sweet potato pie."

"No, thanks, Ben." Max pulled out his billfold. He put a bill on the tray, shook his head at Annie as he gathered up the folders, slid his notebook into his briefcase.

Ben picked up the tray and turned away.

Annie had an inkling how Agatha felt about restricted rations. Ben's vanilla sauce was made from condensed milk and was to die for. But she had Barb's awning cake to sustain her. Besides, there would be other days at Parotti's. She might even drop back by in the afternoon to check with Ben about . . . Well, surely there would be something she needed to know. After all, Ben was an authority on currents, weather and boats. Boats . . . But first she wanted to know more about the days when Arlene Ellis and Lynn Pierce disappeared.

When they stepped outside, they blinked against the vivid sunshine. Parotti's was always dusky and dim.

"Mmm, you look nice," Max said.

Annie looked down in surprise. After her bike ride to

Kathryn Girard's to return the album, she'd stopped by home and changed into a scalloped white blouse and a light blue cotton skirt, the better to go calling on women who knew everything.

"You," Max said firmly, "not your outfit." He slipped an arm around her shoulders and drew her chose. "Maybe we ought to go home for a little while. . . ."

Annie grinned. "When," she said firmly, "we've finished our work."

Annie put down her car windows and used her cell phone. The breeze kicked up whitecaps in the Sound. Three sleek black dolphins arched over the water in their own aquatic ballet. Waves slapped against the ferry, recently repainted a soft green with a new name on the bow, *The Miss Jolene*. Ah, romance. A raucous chuckling noise announced a covey of laughing gulls hovering over the water.

Annie called information, punched for the number to ring.

"Prescott residence." A soft, gracious voice.

"Is Mrs. Prescott in? This is Annie Darling." Annie glanced at her list. It was hard to know where to start, but if she had to pick a murderer, a quick, ruthless, smart killer, she would put her money on Dave Pierce.

A catamaran ran before the wind, its red and gold sails brilliant in the afternoon sun.

"Hello, Annie? Adelaide Prescott." She spoke with the golden accent of South Carolina, as cadenced as a minuet, as lovely as a haunting melody. "Dora called me this morning. I'd be happy to visit with you. Can you come now?"

A white iron arch announced, HAPPY TRAILS. Max drove through, passed the first parked trailer with the posted sign, MANAGER. He was looking for Number 5. The crushed oyster-shell road wound around a lagoon. Old live oaks spread shading limbs. Sunlight dappled the sides of the trailers.

Number 5 was small and looked permanent, with a green shaded awning and a morning-glory-draped trellis. A small woman with iron-gray hair drawn back in a severe bun sat upright on a white stool in the shade of the awning, a blue bowl in her lap. Her hands flashed as she snapped green beans, tossing the ends to the ground.

Max parked across the road. As he approached, wary brown eyes appraised the car and him. Thin lips pursed.

"Mrs. Kendall, I'm Max Darling, a friend of Ben Parotti's." Max used his most genial, casual voice. "Ben thought you could help me with some information I'm seeking."

Those skilled fingers never stopped working. "Ben's a bigger gossip that any old woman. I don't hold with gossip." Cold eyes challenged him.

"No, ma'am. I don't, either." Max was as fervent as Joan Hess's Brother Verber decrying the evils of alcohol.

Her icy gaze didn't warm.

Max dropped his efforts to charm. He would have as much success trying to con Emma Clyde. "Ma'am," he said quietly, "may I draw up a chair and tell you why I'm here? It's a matter of life and death."

Adelaide Prescott lifted the Georgian teapot and poured. "It's such a pleasure to see you, Annie. I wish, of course, that we could have come together for a more cheerful purpose."

They sat in matching Queen Anne wing chairs, upholstered in rose and cream, in the elegant drawing room of the plantation house built in the 1780s. The cypress walls were as rich and ruddy as the day they were made. The tea table was near a fireplace with an elegant Adam mantel.

Annie held the fine Spode china cup. "You know everyone on the island."

Adelaide Prescott's soft round face would have looked perfect under the muslin mob cap of a colonial dame, shining white hair, shrewd brown eyes, pink cheeks, rosebud mouth. Shapeless as a dumpling, she loved beautiful clothes. Today the blue and green shells in her silk blouse were echoed in a frieze on her swirling green skirt. She stirred a teaspoon of brown sugar in her tea. "I keep confidences."

Annie leaned forward to speak, but Adelaide held up a plump white hand.

"That is why Dora thought of me." Fine white brows crinkled in thought. "I have what my mother used to call a listening ear. Perhaps it is because I've always preferred to listen rather than speak. People know that I keep to myself what I learn, so sometimes they tell me more than they should. And I've heard so many things through the years. Dora promised me that you will only use what I tell you to see justice done."

"We will do our best." Annie met her sharp gaze.

In a moment, Adelaide nodded. She sat very straight in her chair. "What do you wish to know?"

"Why did Loretta Campbell dislike Marie?" Annie sipped the tea; Darjeeling, quite perfectly brewed.

Adelaide's sudden smile was impish. "One of my mother's inviolate canons was never to speak of anyone unless one could speak well. I would so much rather have embraced Alice Longworth's attitude and now I have that opportunity. Dear me. Loretta. Loretta was small minded, selfish and stiff-necked. As a mother, she embodied the unfortunate maternal instinct to defend its young at all costs, whether justified or not. I always felt sorry for Gary. His father—"

The Doctor, that was how Loretta Campbell always referred to her husband.

"—was one of those booming men. A big head and a deep voice. Quite charming. Everyone liked him. I'm afraid Gary is more like his mother, inward and repressed. And"— Adelaide's eyes narrowed—"with such a terrible temper. Gary has a jealous nature. When he was in high school, he took a girl to a dance and she flirted with some other boys. At least that's how the story went, and Gary was so angry he pushed over the table with the punch bowl and stormed out. Then Gary made such an unfortunate first marriage.

My husband once told me that Helen Campbell had only to walk into a room and every man there would find his way to her. I thought Gary was so much better off when he married Marie. Yet, Loretta disliked Marie. I don't know why she was so hostile to Marie. I do recall"—she fingered the single strand of pearls at her throat—"that there was some talk about Marie and one of the dashing actors at the playhouse one summer. I don't remember his name now. It's a shame Henny is in the hospital, as she certainly knows everything about the Little Theater. However"—Adelaide's eyes brightened—"I understand Henny's doing quite well but that she has no memory of her search for the club van. When Henny—"

Annie's eyes widened. Henny's condition was to have been kept secret. Adelaide Prescott certainly seemed to be in the know. Was this word out all over the island, too?

"—is well enough for visitors, I would suggest you ask her." Adelaide beamed.

"You haven't spoken to Henny?" Annie asked.

"No. They say no visitors are permitted, so I assumed I shouldn't call, but I was talking to Janet Pierce a little while ago over some matters for the Art Center and Janet said she'd talked to Henny. You know young people, they just pick up a phone and call. Janet said Henny sounded wonderful, only a little bit of a headache, but that Henny said she wouldn't get her memory back about that evening. Henny told Janet the doctor said people with head wounds don't remember the events leading up to the trauma. Janet said Henny wasn't upset, but she was eager to get home. She told Janet if they'd let her out of the hospital, she'd get busy and solve the murder in a jiffy."

So much for the cordon of protection around Henny. The problem was that no one had told Henny she was supposed to be too sick to talk to anyone. And Henny didn't know about the list scrawled by Kathryn Girard. The list had been in Henny's pocket but that, too, would have been lost in the memory swept away by her injury. Who else had called

Henny? How about the Campbells and Vince Ellis? As for Ruth Yates, she'd been there.

"Why did Janet call Henny?" Maybe Max was smart to suggest the guilty Pierce might not be Dave.

"Oh, Henny and Janet are cochairwomen for the juried art show. A decision had to be made about the judges. Janet is always on top of things. A scone, my dear?" Adelaide pushed the plate nearer to Annie.

Annie smiled, took a scone and whipped cream and a dear little tart. After all, she'd had no dessert at lunch. But the awning cake awaited her in the car. Maybe she should drop by the store, give Agatha an extra snack.

"Have you known the Pierces long?" Mmm, the strawberry jam was homemade.

"Ever since Dave and Lynn came to the island. Such dear young people. And so much in love." Adelaide's voice was soft, her eyes sad. "That day she was lost, he took out a boat to look for her. Janet begged him to let the Coast Guard search and finally she insisted on going out with him. My grandson got up a group of boaters and they fanned out in all directions. They found Lynn's boat not far out, capsized."

"So Dave Pierce was on the island that day. And Janet." Annie sipped her tea.

Adelaide's eyebrows rose. She hadn't missed Annie's nuance. "Of course Janet was here. Dave and Lynn were entertaining a number of his business associates. Janet always came for those events."

And for a little dalliance with the boss? Because why else would Dave have killed his wife? "Someone told me Dave and Janet were having an affair."

Adelaide brushed some crumbs from her fingers. "That's nonsense. Oh, I know he married Janet. And it was within a year. But he was terribly lonely and she was always kind to him. I think, actually, it's a rather sad marriage. She is one of those women who devoted herself completely to her career and, of course, he was her career. And he is still a magnate but I think as a husband he must be less than wonderful. But few marriages are as perfect as his first. I shouldn't care to be Dave Pierce's second wife. I believe she is under great stress."

"Really?" Annie had a swift memory of Janet Pierce, tall, slender, lovely, self-possessed. Annie did not associate stress with Janet.

"That might explain—" Adelaide broke off. She frowned into her teacup.

Annie looked at her hostess sharply. Adelaide was an elderly woman and she'd spent her life either saying good things or nothing at all. What was it that she didn't want to say about Janet Pierce? It couldn't have anything to do with Lynn Pierce's death. Adelaide was quite open about that and obviously had no suspicion that Lynn's drowning could have been anything other than an accident.

"How," Annie asked carefully, "do you think stress has affected Janet?"

Adelaide put down her cup. She looked across the room through the bay window at the cordgrass rippling in the breeze and the murky green waters of the Sound. "I've not heard anyone suggest what I am going to say. And it may simply be a great coincidence, but the parallels seem striking to me." Her brown eyes troubled, she looked at Annie soberly. "I would never mention this except Dora impressed upon me the gravity of the situation. I shall trust that you will never tell anyone what I am going to say unless you prove it beyond any doubt."

"I promise." Annie knew it was a promise she had to keep.

"Janet"—Adelaide's tone was thoughtful—"embodies many admirable qualities. She is highly intelligent, organized and capable, as you might expect of a woman with her experience in the business world. Since marrying Dave, she has devoted an enormous number of hours to island charities and civic groups. But"—she stopped uncertainly—

"I have noticed an odd pattern. I assume you've heard of some of the thefts. . . ."

Annie felt as though a shade had flipped up in a window and she was looking into a brightly lit room. Thefts, of course! The ruby necklace from the Clark house, the double string of pearls from the Krichevsky house, the magnificent diamond and emerald ring from the Worrell house. The ring had disappeared only a month ago. All the thefts had occurred within the last two years. No one had been caught. The Clarks changed their domestic staff, which caused hard feelings. Henny had been outraged, insisting there was no reason to suspect the butler or maids.

Annie stared at Adelaide.

Slowly, the old woman nodded. "You see, each theft occurred while a party for a particular charity was in progress—"

"It could have been any guest, couldn't it?" Annie didn't see a trail leading to Janet Pierce.

"There are numbers of parties throughout the year. I find it curious," Adelaide said, "that the thefts all occurred during parties planned by Janet." She smoothed the rose and cream arm of her chair.

"Why would she do it?" Annie demanded. Stealing valuable jewelry from the hostess of a charitable bash would take incredible nerve. The possibility of being caught was surely great. If caught, the scandal could not only wreck her marriage, it would send her to jail.

"I have worked with Janet quite often the past few years." Adelaide's soft voice was thoughtful. "I have seen darkness in her eyes, the unhappy droop of her mouth. And once, it was after that sapphire bracelet was taken from the Riordan house—"

Annie had forgotten about that one.

"—I observed that the thief had to be someone very prominent socially, which made me wonder if there might be sickness involved, a compulsion of some kind. Janet said very sharply that she doubted that was the case at all, that probably the thief simply did it for the thrill, the kind of thrill some people take from sky-diving or mountain climbing. I think"—Adelaide's tone was suddenly firm—"that she was describing herself."

Annie felt like someone working on a puzzle, thinking the pattern was coming together, then finding another handful of pieces in the box with different shapes and colors. Was it possible that Lynn Pierce's death, so similar to Arlene's, was purely and simply an accident?

"In any event"—Adelaide's bright eyes sharpened—"there's a rather grand party tonight at the Pierce home, a fund-raiser for the Art Center. The Pierces have a number of out-of-town guests. I've known one of them for years, Wilma Shaw. Wilma grew up here and loves to return. Wilma lives in Coral Gables. She always travels with her jewelry. One of her necklaces was made in Spain from gold sent back by Cortés. It is her favorite and I know she'll have it with her."

Annie stared at her hostess. "Wouldn't it be incredibly reckless of Janet to commit a robbery in her own home?"

"That," Adelaide said gently, "would be the point, wouldn't it?"

Annie's picture of Janet Pierce, a little piece here, another piece there, was changing. Maybe Max was right and Dave and Lynn Pierce had had the world's greatest marriage. Maybe Adelaide was right and Janet was a wounded spirit. Maybe Janet was venting her jealousy—there's no way to compete with a ghost—by risking everything for a glow of excitement.

And, of course, for money. The jewelry was undoubtedly worth great sums, even sold to unscrupulous buyers. Was that how Janet became a blackmail victim? Did she offer stolen goods to a woman who made money from secrets?

The pieces seemed to fit.

Annie looked in admiration at her genial hostess. Was there a buccaneering glint in Adelaide's eyes? How else had she ever tumbled to Janet's secret?

Adelaide smiled. "I shall find the party tonight quite interesting."

Louella Kendall snapped the last green bean. "The doctor saw no call to do anything." Her wrinkled face folded into tight lines.

Max watched a grackle, iridescent feathers shining, retrieve bits of bean from the sandy ground.

"I don't know the rights and wrongs." She shook the bowl. "I always try to keep my patients alive, but sometimes it's real hard. Sad for them, sad for their families. I do my best for them." Her mouth thinned. "I knew that Kathryn Girard was up to no good. Always running to sit with the dying ones. That's not natural, is it? She couldn't wait, that sly look in her eyes. I finally told her to leave old Mrs. Campbell alone. Poor old thing would be so upset after Kathryn had been there. Once she was crying so hard and I asked her should I get her son and she said she just hated remembering, that she had to stop thinking about it. I told her best way not to think about things is to close the door on it, whatever it is. That's when I told Kathryn to leave her alone."

Another grackle darted near. "Did you tell the doctor how Kathryn upset Mrs. Campbell?"

The brown eyes flashed. "No, sir. I can run my own floor. Always have, always will. I told that woman not to go in Mrs. Campbell's room again. And she didn't."

"Did Kathryn ask a lot of questions when Mrs. Campbell died?" Max tried to keep his tone casual.

"That woman! It just showed how fake she was. She was out of town when Mrs. Campbell died. And when she got back, she didn't say a thing when I told her. Bored, she was." Louella smoothed back her sleek hair. "That was a long night. The family had been there and gone home. Thought she'd rallied. But she took a turn for the worse. Dr. Burford came at once. He's a good man. A good doctor and a good man. He'd known old Mrs. Campbell for a long time and he sat there beside her as she slipped away, held her hand. No, Kathryn Girard didn't care at all about Mrs. Campbell. That wasn't why I sent her packing. It was old Mr. Yates. Not"—she sniffed—"that she spent any time in *his* room. Oh no, why bother with an old man who was suffering so, frozen in his body like a mummy in a tomb, but still alive, his eyes begging you to help him and there wasn't anything we could do and his daughter-in-law spent so much time, talking to him, holding his hand and then she'd come out in the hall and cry. No, Kathryn didn't waste a minute with him, but as soon as he died, she—" Her lips clamped together.

Max knew he needed the right words, the perfect words. Louella Kendall knew her place. The doctor was in charge. But the floor belonged to her. Max said briskly, "That's when you told her not to come back. What did she do?"

Louella's eyes burned. "Some things you don't talk about. That nurse's aide, I gave her what for, running around saying the plug was pulled out on old Mr. Yates's respirator. That was nonsense. You don't keep the machine going after a patient dies."

Max understood almost as if he'd been there, and certainly Kathryn Girard had understood. "Kathryn must have been very interested in what the nurse's aide said. I imagine she asked the aide who had been in the room with him just before he died."

Louella stood, shook out her apron. "Isn't anybody can say Ruth Yates didn't do her best for her husband's daddy. It broke her heart to see him like that." Her old eyes were sad and troubled. Like she'd told Max, she didn't know the rights and wrongs and the doctor hadn't said anything.

Chapter 10

Annie looked at the happy-face sack in the passenger seat as she braked at the stop sign for Red-Tailed Hawk. She could go home and have a glass of skim milk. Max always urged her to drink skim milk. He said studies proved that people who drank skim were healthier than those who drank whole milk. Annie said she could do a study proving that people who ate chocolate were happier than people who didn't. She opened the sack, sniffed. Hmm, what an interesting smell. Or she could go by the hospital and check with Henny about the Campbells and Little Theater. Or—

The car turned right. Annie was familiar with automatic writing on Ouija boards as described by Mary Roberts Rinehart in *The Red Lamp,* but not automatic driving. Apparently she had listened more closely to Max's end of the conversation with Laurel than she'd realized. Now that she was so near, it wouldn't hurt to nip up Red-Tailed Hawk and see where Mark Stone's car skidded off the road.

A half mile ahead, she slowed and peered to the right

up Marsh Tacky Lane. In midafternoon sunlight, the dusty gray road curved into dimness beneath overhanging branches of live oaks and magnolias. Intermingled tire tracks were the only reminder of Thursday night's crush of cars and searchers.

About twenty yards past Marsh Tacky, Annie saw a crumpled mass of ferns in the east ditch. Annie turned and stopped. Putting on her hazards, she hopped out and walked to the ditch. Oh yes, there was a gouge from a right front tire. It appeared that Stone had gunned his motor trying to get back on the road.

Annie looked toward Marsh Tacky Road. Stone had a clear view from here. If he'd gone into the ditch just as Henny turned right and if he'd stayed there until Annie and Max arrived, there was no way anyone could have left Marsh Tacky without being seen by Stone.

Annie glanced at her watch. A quarter after three. She was due at Emma's by four. She had time to go by the hospital if she left right now. Back in the car, she clicked off the hazards and headed north. At the last minute, she veered left into Marsh Tacky. There might be something to this automatic driving. But the fact was, this mattered. When Chief Garrett heard what Mark Stone had to say, he might pitch on Henny again as murderess-in-chief, no matter Kathryn's ransacked apartment and the album full of money and the burned-out van. Garrett could argue quite reasonably that if Kathryn was a blackmailer, one of her victims could have broken into her place and set the inside of the van on fire. Of course, he was unaware of the gunshot outside Kathryn's store late Thursday night. Annie counted up the surreptitious entries into Kathryn's apartment: one, the murderer; two, she and Max; three, the ransacker; and four, the unknown who arrived just as she returned the album this morning. Of course, it was always possible that the murderer had made a second visit, but it seemed more likely that visitors three and four were blackmail victims who had heard about Kathryn's murder and were afraid there might be some damaging information in her apartment.

Annie drove slowly up the lane, noting trampled ferns and saw palmettos with broken fronds. The road angled north, curved south, turned west. Yes, there was the place where Henny stopped. The van had parked about twenty yards ahead. Nothing in the road recalled the van with the body and the abandoned old Dodge except tire tracks and footprints, some deep in gray dirt that had been wet and was now dry and dusty.

Annie idled the Volvo near the spot where Henny had stopped. She pulled out her notebook, flipped past the last page where she had written, *Jewels.* Tapping the clean sheet with her pen, squinting in thought, she finally printed neatly:

TIMETABLE

(Times are approximate.)

THURSDAY

6:00 P.M.—Serena Harris observes Henny's car turning into Marsh Tacky Road.

6:01 P.M.—Mark Stone is forced into the ditch by Serena's car.

7:15 P.M.—Annie and Max Darling arrive at Marsh Tacky Road.

7:20 P.M.—Annie discovers body of Kathryn Girard in back of van.

7:30 P.M.—Police arrive.

7:45 P.M.—Search begun for Henny Brawley.

8:05 P.M.—Emma Clyde arrives.

8:35 P.M.—Henny found by Boy Scouts.

8:45 P.M.—Henny taken to hospital, Annie accompanies her.

10:25 P.M.—Emma arrives at hospital, having arranged for auxiliary to guard Henny.

11:00 P.M.—Max picks Annie up. At home, they get their bikes and set out for Kathryn Girard's, knowing the police have already checked the apartment.

11:30 P.M.—Annie and Max arrive at Kathryn's store.

11:35 P.M.—Intruder shoots at Annie.

11:50 P.M.—Annie and Max leave apartment, Annie carrying the album, after searching Kathryn's suitcase, briefcase and carry-on.

FRIDAY

9:30 A.M.—Annie discovers Kathryn's apartment in a shambles, leaves photo album.

9:35 A.M.—Annie hides from unknown trespasser.

10:45 A.M.—Annie at hospital, finds Ruth Yates in Henny's room.

11:10 A.M.—Annie corners Ruth Yates outside Women's Club.

11:30 A.M.—Annie opens the door to the van at the police station.

Annie dropped the notebook on the passenger seat. Garrett was right about one thing, even if he was wrong in focusing on Henny. More than one person was involved in all that had occurred. For starters, the murderer was at Kathryn's when Annie and Max arrived on their bikes late Thursday night. It had to be the murderer, Annie reasoned, because of the gun and because the bullet was aimed at her. Whoever came out that door was willing to kill to escape unseen. That wasn't just a blackmail victim.

That meant the murderer left Marsh Tacky Road—Annie looked up the sun-dappled road—between, say six-ten P.M. and their arrival at seven-fifteen. But, Annie figured, sooner rather than later. The minute Henny disappeared into the park, the murderer ran, too, taking the van keys along.

The murderer reached Kathryn's apartment between the police check and their arrival at eleven-thirty P.M.

When did the murderer fire the van? Probably shortly after leaving Kathryn's store.

As for Kathryn's apartment, someone came after Annie and Max left and before Annie arrived the next morning. Someone else came Friday morning shortly after Annie. These would be the blackmail victims, who heard of the murder when the calls went out for volunteers to search for Henny. The person who arrived before Annie tossed everything about in a rage.

Annie was sure of her interpretation, but Garrett could argue the blackmail victims were equally likely to have fired the van. Would it do any good to point out that the car keys were taken from the van by the murderer? Probably not. Garrett could say there were other keys available and Annie knew that was true. An extra set hung on a hook just inside the Women's Club office. Those were the keys Emma had brought to the police station this morning.

Annie shifted into drive and followed the curve of the road to the sign marking the entrance to King Snake Park. The murderer must have come this way, most likely riding a bike. Was it to hide any trace of a bike that the van was burned? Or was it to make sure no one could identify any of the donations?

Annie parked by the entrance. She glanced at her watch. She still had time to take a look. She walked under the arch. An asphalt bicycle path curved to her right around the lagoon. The dirt trails to the left would have been muddy Thursday night. Besides, those trails led into a forest preserve in the opposite direction from the houses on Kathryn's list.

The bicycle path was shadowy. No-see-ums buzzed. A night heron sat immobile on the limb of a live oak. Shrubs rustled to her right. Annie froze, then breathed again when she saw the tawny coat of a deer and a fluffy white tail. She walked quickly, waving away clouds of insects, watching carefully for snakes. There had been no one here to see a murderer's flight Thursday evening except the inhabitants of the woods. Annie reached the far side of the lagoon. An alligator rested in the sun. Shiny eyes watched her.

The bicycle path veered to the right. Past a scrubby patch of ground, a sleek green fairway marked the edge of the golf course. Annie had played the course with Max, though her golf was of the sort that she could only play with very good friends. Or her husband. She had a penchant for losing balls, but, as she often explained to Max, only an idiot looks too far for a lost golf ball on an island teeming with snakes and alligators. The north-south fairway to the ninth hole was a dogleg to the west. The golf cart path, of course, skirted the course, beginning and ending at the clubhouse. The bicycle path wound through more woods and eventually crossed Laughing Gull Road.

A long rambling, two-story house backed up to the fairway with a good view of both the bicycle and golf cart paths. Max loved riding bikes and they often chose this path. It was, she realized with a shiver, made to order for a rider intent on escaping notice, miles and miles through a belt of forest, coming into open areas only to cross streets. This house was the only one near the eastern boundary of King Snake Park. A long room with ceiling-high windows overlooked a terrace and the paths.

Annie hesitated, then headed for the back door. It wouldn't hurt to ask.

Max maneuvered the golf cart around the lagoon on the fifth hole. A short stocky man in an avocado-green shirt and white Bermuda shorts dipped his head, bent his knees and waggled his putter. Then he straightened, stepped back, knelt to peer at the undulating green. Returning to the ball, he once again, slowly, carefully, resumed his stance, paused, putted. The ball headed straight for the cup. At the last instant, it veered to the left, rolled slowly past the cup, gradually gained momentum and tumbled into a deep sand trap.

His tall, lanky companion, russet shirt half tucked into pink shorts, marched up to his ball, perhaps ten feet from the hole, bent, stroked and the ball sped over the grass and plopped into the cup.

It took the older man three shots to get out of the trap and two more to hole the ball. His round face, always reddish, looked choleric.

Max waited in the shade of a live oak. It was not perhaps the most politic time to approach Horace Burford, M.D., whose late patients included the Rev. Alden Alcott Yates. Max waited until Burford had completed a superb iron shot that landed perfectly on the next green and his partner was in the rough trying to devise a shot around a two-hundred-year-old massive live oak. Burford was waiting in his cart when Max pulled up behind.

Burford mopped his face, glanced in Max's cart, which was empty of clubs. "You takin' up joyridin', Max?" Burford was an excellent doctor and was chief of staff at the hospital, capable, bullheaded, cantankerous and smart. Godzilla could likely have given him pointers on bedside manner.

"In pursuit of you, Horace." A thrashing in the rough heralded an attempt to shoot to the fairway. Max knew he had about forty seconds. "Horace, you've heard about the murder last night."

The doctor's white eyebrows bunched. "Damn fool cop can't seriously suspect Henny."

"He seriously does, Horace. But there are some other suspects now. Including Ruth Yates." Max stared into startled blue eyes. "That's why I want to ask you about the death of Alden Yates."

Just for an instant, the doctor's red, sweaty face was immobile. Then, flapping his orange bandana, he barked, "Alden Yates suffered a series of strokes and he died of heart failure." Cold eyes stared at Max. "Anybody who says differently will see themselves in court for slander. That includes you. Now, if you'll kindly leave me the hell alone, I'm playing golf, in case you hadn't figured that out."

Annie admired the red-tiled terrace bordered by camellias, Japanese quince and masses of blue and white impatiens. Everything about the house bespoke loving attention to detail, from the carefully edged flower beds to the baskets of ferns hanging from beams in a screened-in porch to bright green shutters and carefully trimmed ivy. On the first floor, a series of long, tall windows provided a magnificent view from a huge clubroom.

A low brick wall marked the end of the property. Terracotta vases filled with marigolds graced corner pedestals. The bicycle path ran on the south side of the low wall. The golf cart path skirted the west side of the wall. Annie walked swiftly. She was turning into a central walkway of the wide terrace when she paused, frowned and returned to the path. At the far west end of the wall, where the path curved into a swath of trees bordering the fairway, a vase leaned to one side.

So, all was not quite perfect. That made the house suddenly seem more approachable. Annie always felt intimidated by perfect housekeepers and perfect groundskeepers. They tended to be inflexible and ask searching questions, such as, "What do you do about mildew?" and "What is your schedule for mulching?" (Annie forced herself not to reply, in turn, "Pretend it isn't there," and "By the light of a quarter moon with a newt in one hand and a buckeye in the other.")

Annie's shoes clicked on the tiles. She walked slowly, trying to frame a reasonable question. "Were you looking out of your windows into the rain at a few minutes after six last night?" seemed a little abrupt, not to say peculiar. But surely the person who lived here must have heard sounds of the search, perhaps seen swaths of lights. Though that activity occurred some time after the murderer's escape.

But still . . . Some intelligent query, Annie assured herself with Hastingslike confidence, would occur to her.

She stepped onto the porch, lifted her hand to knock at the door leading into the club room, and looked through one of the eight-foot windows, admiring the bright chintz-covered chairs, a stark white fabric with a profusion of red poppies, the glowing heart pine floor and—

Annie's hand fell. She stood quite still and leaned toward the window.

The dead man lay on his back not far from the door, afternoon sun spilling around him. He had been a natty dresser, a cream polo of the very finest, softest weave of cotton, crisp khaki trousers, Italian loafers of burgundy leather. A table set for breakfast was a few feet beyond him, a glass of orange juice, a bowl with cereal. Thoughts whirled in Annie's mind: He must have been ready to have his breakfast when his murderer arrived. Edith would know the origin of "natty." Maybe the word popped in her mind because he was old with a bristly iron-gray crew cut and sharp features. He'd been dead for a while because the pool of blood had congealed and his blood-sodden shirt was stiff. He hadn't shot himself because the gun lay near his foot, but the police would do gunshot residue tests to be sure.

The gun. Annie swallowed. She couldn't be certain from here, but the grip looked white and shiny. What was it Ruth had said? Her father's gun, the grip pearl-handled with his initials.

Annie stepped stiffly down the steps, walked to a lawn chair in the shade of a yellow and white umbrella. She sat down, got out her cell phone and made three calls.

Max's Maserati squealed to a stop just as the police siren died. Garrett and Pirelli jumped out of the police car and Max shouted, "The terrace. Annie said to come to the back of the house," and he was running hard, knowing there should be no danger to Annie now, no matter what she'd found, but driven to be sure. He heard Garrett's yell, but he didn't care. Annie, Annie . . . Loblolly pines screened both sides of the rambling house. Somehow he kept his balance even though his loafers skated over needles slick as pond ice. He skidded around the end of the house, jumped a low wall onto the terrace.

Annie came up from the terrace chair and ran to meet him.

Max caught her in his arms. "I'm sorry, honey, I'm sorry."

She clung to him and let tears come because there is nothing so ugly as murder. She didn't know the man, but he had picked out a pretty shirt this morning and the shirt would never be worn again.

"You two sit over there and keep quiet." Garrett might look like a sunburned cupid, but his voice was tough and cold and the eyes that studied them were full of suspicion. He watched until they walked to the lawn furniture, sat down. Max gave Annie's arm a warning squeeze.

Annie pointed at the back door. "He's in there, Chief."

Garrett gestured to Pirelli, then walked swiftly to the door. He looked through the tall window as Annie had just a little while ago. He stood without moving for several minutes, then, pulling latex gloves from his pockets and slipping them on, he turned the doorknob. The door opened. Garrett stepped inside and Pirelli followed.

Annie knew they had much to do, Polaroid pictures, videocam, sketches, fingerprinting, the arrival of the medical examiner. But she was sure that she had seen the most important piece of evidence.

"Max, Ruth's gun is in there. I'm sure it's hers." She watched the men moving around the big room.

Max frowned. "Why would she be so stupid? She described the gun to you, didn't she?"

Annie had a swift memory of Ruth's forlorn eyes, shaking hands. Oh yes, Ruth had described the gun. What would Ruth do if she shot a man? Drop the gun and run? Oh yes, quite possibly she might. However, could Ruth be driven to murder? Gentle, unconfident, twittery, sweet Ruth? But this murder occurred because of another murder. And once a scarlet trail was begun, there could be no turning back. Never.

"She told me about the gun," Annie said wearily, "but she claimed Kathryn took it from her." Bluffs and double bluffs abound in mysteries. Was Ruth that clever? "Do you suppose Ruth left the gun deliberately?"

Max looked toward the house. "That would be a hell of a gamble."

"Maybe. Maybe not. If it ever comes down to a jury, there are grounds for reasonable doubt, aren't there? Ruth told me the gun was gone twelve hours before anyone shot this man." Annie massaged her temple. Could Ruth possibly have staged that sad interlude with Annie? Did Ruth have the wit to create such a complex web? After all, it was Ruth who first mentioned the gun. If she had shot at Annie outside Kathryn's store, then certainly it would be smart to tell Annie that the gun had been taken before Kathryn died. And when danger came, a call from a man who saw the murderer's escape, why not shoot him and leave the gun?

"Garrett won't buy it." Max shrugged. "But that's Ruth's problem, not ours. And Garrett's problem." He looked past Annie, lifted a hand in greeting and stood.

"There they are." Emma's crisp voice sounded bright and fresh. She plunged across the flagstones, her caftan billowing, her bright eyes scanning the house, the terrace, the woods and paths.

Laurel wafted alongside the big woman, murmuring huskily, "Poor dear man. I would never ever plant rhododendron. There could be no clearer signal of danger." Laurel looked even more slim and lovely than usual. Most women her age would look absurd wearing their hair in a ponytail. Laurel looked adorable and her striped cotton blouse and soft blue slacks emphasized a figure that men from seven to seventy regarded with extreme interest.

Annie glanced past them. Was Fred, the super sailor, in tow? Apparently not.

Laurel's midnight-blue eyes sparkled. "Celandine. Such an interesting plant. It reminds one of buttercups." Her seductive lips curved in delight. "And, of course, it whispers of joys to come."

Max almost spoke, thought better of it. Annie felt that was a wise decision. There might have been an interesting silence, but after a quick amused glance at Laurel, Emma said briskly, "Thanks for calling me, Annie. Bring us up to date."

When Annie finished, Emma frowned. "Crew cut? Spiffy dresser?"

Annie nodded.

Emma's square face was somber. "Poor old Jake. He was a damn fine golfer."

Max stared at the house. "Jake Chapman?"

Emma nodded.

Annie hadn't recognized the dead man, but now she remembered him from the club, always well dressed, a neat, spare, intense, precise man, the kind of man who would have a beautifully kept house and well-tended grounds.

"Why Jake?" Emma mused. "In *The Puzzle of the Pink Potted Plants,* the murderer's ex-lover got up to let the cat out at three in the morning and spotted his car turning into Mulberry Lane."

There was a moment of silence.

Emma's face tightened for an instant, then she continued graciously, "I'm sure you all remember what happened next."

Max tugged at one ear and was a picture of earnest concentration.

Annie frantically tried to remember: *The Puzzle of the Pink Potted Plants,* was that the one where Marigold looked at an open door transom and announced the murder's identity?

Laurel smiled ecstatically. "Pink larkspur? Fickleness is ever destructive. No doubt she called her old lover the next morning when she heard about the body in Mulberry Lane? Putting two and two together."

Emma favored Laurel with an approving smile. "Exactly. And that's what happened here, I'm certain."

Max folded his arms across his chest. "I know the women on the island always know everything as soon as it happens, but old Jake probably wouldn't have known about the murder until the afternoon paper. Okay, maybe he'd pick it up on the morning news. But why would he happen to be looking out his window at just the right time to see the murderer go by? Emma, I don't think it flies."

Annie announced excitedly, "He was going to eat breakfast in his clubroom."

Three pairs of eyes studied her.

Annie suddenly knew how Frances and Richard Lockridge's Pam North felt when confronted with slow mental processes.

"Don't you see?" Annie demanded impatiently.

No one spoke.

"If he ate breakfast there, it means he spent most of his time in the clubroom. And"—she squeezed her eyes shut for a moment, then opened them—"yes, the place at the table faced this way. Of course he'd see everything from the clubroom windows." She bounced to her feet. "The vase! That's what happened."

Now the silence was profound. Emma glanced meaningfully at Max. Laurel murmured throatily, "She seems quite calm. But is there an aura of red columbine, which might indicate a trembling and anxiousness? One can sense these things, I'm afraid." Even Max's dark blue eyes were concerned.

"The vase!" Annie gestured toward the wall at the end of the terrace. "Come on." She sped down the walk.

The silent trio followed and clustered around her at the west end of the wall. She pointed at the tilted vase.

"Don't you see? Maybe the murderer was in such a hurry the bike skidded and bumped the wall, knocking over the vase." She waved a hand at the immaculate grounds, the recently painted house. "Jake Chapman would have been furious. He must have hurried out on the terrace and followed long enough to recognize whoever it was and this morning, he called—"

"Why do you say this morning?" Max squinted into the late afternoon sun.

"The table's set for breakfast. Besides"—and Annie remembered the quick bark of the gun last night—"if Jake confronted the murderer right after the attack on Henny, he would have been dead before we went to the shop. And that's impossible or the gun couldn't be here. And I refuse to believe in two guns. No, whatever he saw, he waited until this morning to call and complain."

Emma clapped her hands. "Two guns. That could be true, Annie. In *The Mystery of the Albuquerque Anvil*—"

Annie cut in impatiently, "Emma, that was crazy. You had three guns, a bolo and an ax and then Marigold figured out the murderer soaked a bunch of cigarette butts and dumped a slug of nicotine in the bourbon. I mean, really!"

Emma glared. "It was perfectly logical. Marigold figured it out as soon as I got to page 279. The chief suspect, a chain-smoker, had made his ex-wife mad so she decided to frame him and she brought the bolo to kill his pet boa constrictor, the ax to smash open the chest where he kept the bearer bonds and the guns to sell to a collector."

"How thrilling," Laurel breathed, her eyes wide with admiration. "Dear Emma. You are simply amazing. I must devise a crest for all your books. Perhaps sweet alyssym, which always brings to mind excellence beyond beauty."

Emma's nod accepting the tribute was graciousness itself, but her pale eyes studied Annie like a taxidermist evaluating a carcass.

Annie stared right back. There were benefits from reading about Sara Paretsky's V. I. Warshawski. V. I. never wilted. "Lacking an ex-husband, a boa constrictor and a chest full of bearer bonds, I think we can dismiss two guns here. Broward's Rock is not Arsenal America. Most people don't have handguns. Rifles, maybe, for hunters. But not handguns. And who are we talking about? The Campbells. Vince Ellis. Dave and Janet Pierce. Ruth Yates. None of them hunt. No, there's one gun and it belonged to Ruth Yates."

"Ruth." Emma's tone was thoughtful.

Max waved away a cloud of no-see-ums. "All we know is that the gun in the clubroom sounds like the one that belonged to Ruth Yates. It will be up to Garrett to find out." He looked across the terrace. "Do you suppose Garrett's going to leave us out here until all our blood is sucked away?"

Since no-see-ums loved Max and ignored her, Annie said callously, "I'm in no hurry to talk to our new police chief."

Emma, her glance still cold, demanded, "What exactly brought you here, Annie?"

That, of course was precisely what Garrett was going to ask. "It's all perfectly logical," she said stiffly. "Nobody came out of Marsh Tacky Road into Red-Tailed Hawk, so the murderer had to come this way. So I came."

Max swatted away a mosquito. "You came, you saw, you knocked on the door. I believe it. Whether Garrett will is another matter."

"Sour red berries with big yellow flowers." Laurel smiled. "And spiny."

Max said gently, "Yes, Mother?"

"Barberry. A sure indication of sharpness of temper. Perhaps dear Annie should be tactful when she informs Chief Garrett about our investigations and Mark Stone's enforced vigil near Marsh Tacky Road last night."

Annie looked at Laurel's dreamy expression with respect. Laurel sure had a point. How much tact would it take to tell Garrett they'd outdone him from start to finish in the search for facts? More tact than Annie had ever commanded.

Emma waved a stubby hand. "Leave it to me. I'll explain everything."

Sometimes Annie resented Emma's generalship. But not right now. She welcomed any and all support.

A car door slammed. Horace Burford, wiping his sun-burned face with a bandanna, stomped across the terrace, black bag in hand.

Max was frowning. "Annie, you said Jake was going to have breakfast."

Annie nodded. "There was a glass of orange juice and a bowl of cereal. And the murderer came."

"Okay." Max waggled his arms and the no-see-ums whirled away. "I follow you this far. But are we talking mental telepathy, a crystal ball? Why did the murderer come?"

Emma jumped in. "Oh, that's simple. Jake called him. Or her. First thing this morning. Wanted his vase fixed, said how much it would cost. Annie's right. Jake had to have seen something last night. Nothing that would have alarmed him. But if someone rode past his house, careened into the wall—and you know the person who left Kathryn's body and tried to conk Henny must have been stressed—and went on, leaving the damaged vase, Jake would have been outside in a flash. He wouldn't have been likely to chase after the person at the moment, but he would certainly have called." Her broad mouth spread in a grim smile. "Oh yes, I like that. I'll use it in my next book. I'll call it *The Case of the Careless Caller*. I can see it all. The phone rings. The murderer answers. At this point, the murderer thinks everything is pretty well under control. Kathryn's dead. The murderer es-caped from her apartment with the blackmail folders. Henny Brawley's under suspicion for Kathryn's murder. So far, there's no indication Henny remembers anything of what happened in Marsh Tacky Lane. Everything's cool. Then, Jake calls. Jake's in a huff and he says, 'You knocked over my vase when you hit my wall last night. It's going to be expensive to fix it.' He didn't know it, but the minute he said that, he was a dead man."

Footsteps thudded. Two medics carried a gurney around the end of the house.

"Maybe." Max swatted at a bumblebee.

"I wouldn't do that." Annie watched the black-and-gold-striped insect.

"I'm simply giving him some direction." But Max took two steps back and didn't poke at the bumblebee as it curved near. "Okay, Emma. I'll agree that Jake Chapman saw something. Or someone. He calls this morning. The murderer comes over, shoots Jake and drops the gun. And, since Annie saw the gun, she's going to have to tell Garrett that it looks like the gun Ruth Yates described."

"But if I do," Annie said unhappily, "Ruth's going to be in terrible trouble."

Footsteps gritted on the terrace. Pete Garrett strode up to them.

Chapter 11

Pete Garrett's hard glare fastened on Annie. "You find a body last night. You find a body today. How come?" The phrasing wasn't elegant, but his point was clear.

Annie bristled. "That's not fair. I found Kathryn's body because I was hunting for Henny Brawley."

Garrett jerked his head toward the house. "And this one?"

Laurel moved closer to Garrett. "My dear"—Laurel beamed at him—"I don't believe we've met. I'm Laurel Roethke and I do so much appreciate the efforts of our wonderful enforcers of the law. It was my pleasure to observe you last night as you so efficiently performed your duties."

Garrett was not immune to Laurel's magic. For a moment, a light flickered in his eyes that had nothing to do with police work.

Annie observed her mother-in-law. How did Laurel do it? Was it her shining hair that glistened like burnished silver? Or those mesmerizing eyes, brilliant as a Greek sea? Or the curves subtly accented by her beautifully fitted clothes?

Garrett's growl to Annie was transmuted to an accolade to Laurel. "Ma'am."

Laurel's eyes held his for a long moment. "I know you understand that we all want to do our part for the community. Mrs. Clyde"—Laurel nodded toward Emma—"is so active and such a supporter of the mayor's. We felt it incumbent upon us to gather as much information as possible to aid you in your investigation. In my efforts, I discovered that no one was observed leaving Marsh Tacky Road after the arrival of Henny's car and before the arrival of my son and daughter-in-law. Obviously"—her laughter tinkled like a wind chime—"the murderer fled through King Snake Park. Annie was simply exploring the surroundings and she came to this house."

It took Garrett a couple of questions to sort it out, but he wasn't slow. "So"—and he looked Annie—"you came up here to ask this guy if he saw anything last night?"

"Let me show you," Annie urged.

A moment later, Garrett surveyed the tilted terra-cotta vase.

Annie pointed at the wall. "Jake Chapman saw somebody bump the wall last night. But he didn't know about the murder. This morning he called to complain about the damage and the murderer had to kill Chapman."

Garrett wheeled around and headed for the house. He was already crossing the club room when the interested quartet reached the door, Emma in the lead. Pirelli held up a hand, barring their entrance. Max looked over Emma's shoulder while Annie and Laurel peered in through the window.

Garrett looped a string around the telephone receiver. Using a pencil, he pushed redial. The receiver dangled from the string. They all listened. One ring. A second. It was answered in midpeal. A sweet voice said, "Ruth Yates."

Slowly, carefully, Garrett depressed the cradle.

Across the room, Horace Burford pushed back a chair. He stormed across the room, red face glowering. "What the

hell's going on?" He swiveled, glared at Max in the doorway. "I warned you, Max. Alden Yates died of natural
causes and that's all there is to it. I'll see you in court."

Max turned his hands palms up. "I haven't said a word
about Alden Yates. Ask Chief Garrett."

Burford stood quite still, his red face abruptly wary.

Garrett took two steps, stood inches from Burford.
"Alden Yates? Who was he?"

Burford turned away.

Garrett moved at the same time, kept himself face-to-
face with the doctor. "Who was Alden Yates? When did he
die? Where did he die?"

Burford reached for his bag, snapped it shut. "An old
man, a sick man. Brian Yates's father. Died of the results of
a series of strokes. That's all there was to it." He stalked
toward the door. Max and Emma stepped aside.

Garrett didn't follow this time. But he called sharply,
"Did you sign the death certificate, Dr. Burford?"

Burford's angry voice barked, "Damn sure did," as he
plunged out onto the terrace.

Garrett walked up to Max. "What do you know about
Alden Yates?"

"I don't *know* anything," Max said carefully. "There's
been some gossip. You might check and see who was on
duty at the hospital the night Alden Yates died."

Annie avoided looking at the area where Jake Chapman's body had lain. But she couldn't resist one quick
glance. The gun no longer lay on the floor. No doubt it had
already been boxed for transport to the forensics laboratory
in Columbia.

Garrett saw that quick glance. "What are you looking
at?"

"The gun's gone." She took a deep breath.

He was immediately alert. "What do you know about
the gun?"

She knew what she said might be the last nail in Ruth
Yate's coffin. But she had to speak. She had to tell Garrett

everything she knew about that gun. Or everything she thought she knew. She started with the gunshot outside Kathryn Girard's shop.

Garrett pounced like Agatha after fresh liver. "What were you people doing there?"

Annie and Max exchanged a swift glance.

Max said smoothly, "We were checking to see if anyone was at the apartment. There was no answer to our knock. But I'm sure you want to know what happened when we arrived." And the implication was clear: Don't push us and we'll give you some useful information.

Garrett's eyes glittered. He started to speak, stopped, took a deep breath. "What happened?"

Annie moved swiftly from the shot in the night to her discovery of the list in Henny's pocket, her arrival at the hospital to find Ruth Yates in Henny's room, Ruth's question about a gun, Annie's pursuit of Ruth and their tense exchange. "But," Annie concluded, "Ruth said Kathryn took the gun away from her. That means the murderer could have taken it from the back of the van."

"A pearl-handled grip?" Garrett demanded.

"Yes." Annie's voice was troubled.

Emma cocked her head like a pirate spotting a silver piece. "So Ruth said Kathryn took the gun. Damn clever lie. If it was a lie. In *The Mystery of the Moribund Macaw*, the murderer pulled a triple bluff. Marigold figured it out, of course."

Max rubbed a bright red mosquito welt. "Do you really think Ruth's capable of bluffing anybody? About anything?"

Laurel murmured, "Ruth is quite sensitive. And kindhearted. Really, she is so distressed at the proposal to kill the deer." The island was presently overrun with deer. Other suggested solutions included deportation or pills to prevent pregnancy. "She most emphatically opposes killing the deer."

Annie shot her mother-in-law a quick glance. Laurel always seemed so spacey, but sometimes she knew what mattered. Would a woman who didn't want Bambi killed have committed three murders? However, Marie Campbell fought for the deer, too. Did that make either or both of them less likely to have killed Kathryn?

Emma folded her arms. "Let's not forget that Kathryn's list included the Campbells, Vince Ellis and the Pierces as well as Ruth. Marigold never makes the mistake of dismissing suspects from her consideration merely because a piece of physical evidence is linked to only one of them. In *The Case of the Confident Captain—*"

"Ma'am." Emma might be the mayor's confidante, but she lacked Laurel's allure. Garrett said grimly, "You folks have been very helpful. But this is a crime scene and I'll have to ask you to leave. Now." He turned away, stepped into the clubroom.

Undaunted, Emma lifted her voice, reminding Annie of a load of gravel being dumped. "Chief, does this mean Henny Brawley is no longer under suspicion?"

Garrett's pugnacious face was expressionless. Finally, he said carefully, "At this point in the investigation, it would appear that Mrs. Brawley, who has been under police surveillance, could have had nothing to do with this murder. I would say that the focus of the investigation presently—"

Emma cut in. "Are you going to remove the police guard?"

Garrett gave an abrupt nod and closed the door. With finality.

Annie felt a surge of relief. At least Henny was no longer a suspect, although it was dreadful that it had taken a second murder to convince Garrett.

"Butterfly weed. I shall go home and prepare a card." Laurel clapped her hands in pleasure. "The flowers are quite bright and lovely. Orange."

"Let me go," Emma said absently.

Just for an instant, Laurel looked just a trifle miffed. "Yes, indeed," Laurel admitted.

Annie knew her mother-in-law would die before she'd

ask how Emma knew. After all, Laurel was the authority on the language of flowers. "Why, Emma"—Annie's eyes were wide with admiration—"how did you ever know?" She ignored Max's sharp glance—would she rain on Laurel's parade?—and said ingenuously, "That's simply wonderful."

"Oh, just one of those odd facts you pick up as a writer." Emma looked as satisfied as Agatha with a mustache of whipped cream. "Like the fact that Lusaka is the capital of Zambia or minestrone is 89.5 percent water or an impeller is the rotating part of a centrifugal pump."

Annie was so thankful that Henny was no longer at risk, she was willing to nod admiringly at Emma, though the writer's ego outpaced Hercule Poirot's.

Max grabbed her arm. "No guard. Come on. We have to get to the hospital."

Annie's sense of ease vanished. Abruptly she understood. Yes, it was wonderful that Henny was no longer a suspect, but that didn't mean all danger was past. Jake Chapman died because this murderer took no chances. Henny was perfectly safe if Ruth Yates was guilty. But what if Ruth didn't kill Kathryn Girard or Jake Chapman? Would this murderer gamble that Henny's memory would never return?

Not likely.

"Max, you're right. You go straight there. I'll get my car. Emma—"

Emma held up both hands. "Wait a minute. Here's what we'll do. . . ."

Water slapped against the hull of the yacht. Max rowed past the prow. In the moonlight, the name was clearly visible: *Marigold's Pleasure.*

"This way, sir." A dark figure moved along the deck. "If you'll throw the mooring rope, I'll fasten it. The ladder is amidships."

Annie got a kick out of climbing up the rope ladder. It was as close as she'd likely ever come to a Hammond Innes

adventure. When she and Max reached the deck, the crew-
man pointed to a lit stairwell. "Mrs. Clyde's guest is in
the saloon."

And she was.

Annie hurried across the gray and pink Persian rug.
"Henny, oh Henny."

Their old friend was ensconced on a silk sofa, soft pillows bunched behind her, a pale pink afghan over her knees.
Except for a small bandage and a very pale face, she looked
like the Henny of old, bright dark eyes sparkling with
interest.

"Thanks, Annie, Max." Just for an instant Henny blinked
away a tear.

Annie grabbed a thin hand, held it tight. "Emma's the
smart one. You'll be safe here. How did you get out of the
hospital?"

"Oh, it was vintage Emma." Henny gingerly touched her
head. "She bought a red wig so heavy I could barely walk
and a purple and yellow caftan. We waited until the hall
was clear, then I hurried to the stairs and went down to the
emergency room. Emma stayed in my room and I'm sure"—
Henny's smile was quick—"she talked at length about her
new book, *The Adventure of the Airborne Aardvark*, to the pillows we mounded in the bed. Then she stood in the hall
and wished me a good night, loudly. She was heading out
to a party, said she'd tell me all about it tomorrow. I walked
out to the emergency drive. Emma's housekeeper, Cleo Bin-
ton, was waiting for me. We drove to the ferry. Emma had
talked to Ben. Cleo and I waited until he returned from a
regular trip, then scooted on board and he pulled out with
only the one car. If anyone had followed, they'd think we
were going to the mainland. We started across the Sound,
then he veered around the end of the island and we rendez-
voused with *Marigold's Pleasure* and here I am." The vivacity
seeped from her face. "But I want to know everything.
Emma told me about the houses Kathryn listed. I don't remember putting the note card in my pocket." She gingerly

touched her temple. "I suppose I must have driven to the houses in turn and at some point spotted the van and followed it to Marsh Tacky Road. And someone at one of the houses had already killed Kathryn." Her eyes narrowed. "You know, I should be able to tell you who did it. I know all of these people. It seems laughable to suspect Ruth. She's disorganized and vague and indecisive, not exactly qualities for a successful murderer."

Annie almost pointed out that Ruth's arrest was imminent, so the degree of success could be in question.

But Henny churned ahead. "Now, Dave Pierce seems quite capable of murder in a crisp, cold, unemotional way. As for Janet, I've never dealt with anyone better able to plan and accomplish whatever goal she might have. And Gary Campbell"—Henny smoothed her afghan—"is one of those quiet ones. Nothing would surprise me about Gary. It always makes me uncomfortable the way he sticks so close to Marie, like she's going to vanish if he blinks his eyes."

Annie hitched a chair closer to the divan. Adelaide was sure Henny knew everything about local theater. "What ran Gary and Marie away from the Little Theater?"

Henny started to shake her head, stopped, touched the bandage. "Damn." She waited a minute. "I went on a train trip across Canada that summer. When I left, they were big in rehearsals, and when I came back, they had dropped out. No one made anything of it. They were always kind of aloof. He always seemed to draw a magic circle around Marie, never let anyone get close. At cast parties, he was right at her side. And I don't know why. I don't remember ever seeing her flirt with anyone. But maybe it was him. Maybe he never felt comfortable unless she was close at hand."

Max dropped into a cane chair. He picked up a book from the coffee table, held it so Annie could read the title, *The Case of the Coy Cook.*

Annie wrinkled her nose.

Henny waved her hand. "Not one of her best. But actually, it has some parallels here. A fellow like Gary Campbell, lots of money, upper-middle-class white male, lawyer, and the whole thing hinges on the guy's temper."

Temper. Annie looked at Henny sharply. That was the second time someone had mentioned temper in connection with Gary Campbell. "But why? What's he got to be mad about?"

"That I don't know. But I can tell you he's got a short fuse. Once at a Friends meeting, somebody interrupted him and he stopped and his face turned purple and I thought he was going to heave a chair across the room. You could see it in his eyes. Maybe that's why Marie's always right there. She took his hand and tugged. You know how little she is, but in a second she had him out in the hall and the whole thing blew over." Henny looked thoughtful. "That's funny. I hadn't thought about it until now, but she's the tough one."

Annie remembered Marie's lively, elfin face, not a face to associate with double murder. But there was strength in that face. Had she needed strength through the years to deal with her husband? And with a mother-in-law who loathed her?

"And that leaves Vince Ellis." Henny pointed across the saloon at a wall of framed photographs, all, of course, featuring Emma. "I've always liked that picture, the third from the bottom. It's one of the few times I've ever seen Emma laugh out loud."

It was an excellent shot of Emma and Vince and Arlene Ellis. Across time, there was no way to know what prompted the joke but Vince was staggering backward, one hand holding up his tie to simulate a noose. Arlene stood with her arms folded, shaking her head in remonstrance, trying not to laugh. As for Emma, her face was pink, her eyes watering and she could scarcely stand she was laughing so hard.

"Vince used to be so much fun," Henny said softly. "Before Arlene died, he was the happiest man in the world.

When you think about it"—she shook a finger at Annie—
"how many happy murderers have you ever read about?"

"Vince isn't happy now." Max's gaze was dark.

"I should know who did it." Henny moved impatiently
on the divan. "I've been thinking and thinking ever since
Emma told me. And then I try to imagine being afraid of one
of them and it seems crazy. Emma insists I'm in danger."

There was a silence and they all could hear the slap of
water against the hull.

"It depends," Max said judiciously.

"The case is solved," Annie said slowly, "if Ruth Yates
is the murderer."

"No." Henny was emphatic. "I've known Ruth ever
since she and Brian came to Broward's Rock. She is incapa-
ble of murder."

Max's face was grave. "I'm afraid we can't be certain of
that. I talked to the nurse who was on duty the night Alden
Yates died . . ."

When he finished, Henny shook her head, then winced.
"I don't believe Ruth killed anyone. Funny. It would be so
much better for me if she was guilty. Because I'm beginning
to remember, you know. In patches. And if it isn't Ruth . . ."
She suddenly looked much smaller, frailer, weary. She
looked around the elegantly appointed saloon. "I can't stay
here forever."

Death could come stealing quietly up the steps of her
isolated marsh home in the stillness of a rainy morning, in
the darkness of moonlit night.

"We'll figure it out, Henny. I promise." Annie wished
she had the ebullient confidence of Elizabeth Peters's Amelia
Peabody instead of an uneasy feeling that their opponent
was as cold and capable as Agatha Christie's villain in *N
or M*.

Annie glanced at the clock as they straggled into the
house. Almost two in the morning. Every night they came
in a little later. They had waited until Henny was locked in

her cabin and safely asleep before rowing back to the harbor. Now, as they flicked on the kitchen lights, Dorothy L. gamboled happily across the counter.

The answering machine light blinked steadily. Five messages. Annie crossed to the machine as Max shook out dry food for Dorothy L.—certainly it was fortunate Agatha couldn't see this—and filled tall tumblers with ice. Annie punched the button.

Message 1: Chief Garrett informed me that Pamela Potts arrived on the scene shortly after I left the hospital and she raised the alarm. Henny is now officially among the missing. I'm pleased with that. It should make our murderer highly nervous. By the way, I cleared Henny's departure with Dr. Cary and with our young police chief. Garrett may possibly learn something from this adventure. In fact, it's given me an idea for a book: *The Case of the Shamefaced Cop.* If Garrett had listened to us Thursday night in Marsh Tacky Lane, he might have fanned out and reached Jake Chapman's house and Jake might be playing his regular foursome in the morning. In any event, we dare not be sanguine about Garrett's focus on Ruth. In fact, I intend to get the word out that we intrepid investigators are convinced of Ruth's innocence and intend to pursue other suspects. To that end, I suggest Max delve deeper into the boating mishaps. Annie, I'll expect you at the White Elephant Sale in the morning. Everyone will be there. I'll stalk about making dark hints. You can furrow your brow, widen your eyes, and claim you never, ever believed—let your voice drop—and whisper a scandalous tidbit. You'll ferret out all kinds of discreditable histories. I've already spoken with Laurel. Do you know, directing this investigation is almost more fun than writing. Until tomorrow.

Max handed Annie a glass of water. She drank and glared at the answering machine. "Who does she think she is?"

Max grinned. "Marigold Rembrandt is America's Miss Marple. What does that make Emma?"

"A conceited, self-centered, patronizing show-off," Annie fumed. "Does she think she needs to tell me how to ask questions?"

"That's ridiculous," Max said staunchly. Was there a slight quiver of his lips? He ducked his head to pick up Dorothy L.

Annie looked at him suspiciously. "Emma may have written seventy-five books but that doesn't mean she knows everything. I fact, I could tell her a book to write. Or maybe I'll write it, *The Case*"—she savored every syllable—"*of the Missing Mystery Writer.*"

Max grinned. The cat curled against his chest and purred.

MESSAGE 2: Dear Annie, dear Max. I am impressed by your devotion to Henny's cause. I must rush to my easel and compose a tribute to you both, elder for zealousness, goldenrod for encouragement, and larch for audacity. I shall embrace magnolia as a reminder that I, too, shall persevere. Dear Fred is so encouraging. And insightful. When I see him, I can only think of monkshood, a tribute to his chivalry—

Max's dark brows knit in a frown. Dorothy L. looked at him with interest.

Annie resisted the impulse to hoot, "Chivalry? Is that what they call it?" Clearly in America the semantics of sex were undergoing a strange and wonderful transformation in the last years of the twentieth century.

—and of ranunculus, as I am surely dazzled by his charm. Mmmm. But tomorrow I shall broadcast the language of flowers in our pursuit of justice. Anon.

MESSAGE 3: The evening was quite uneventful. I can report—

Adelaide Prescott's soft Carolina accent invested the everyday words with grace and loveliness.

—a grand success for the Arts Center. I believe it may be the most successful fund-raiser to date. Certainly Janet Pierce deserves the gratitude of every lover of art on our island. In regard to our earlier speculations, I must inform you that nothing untoward occurred. Indeed, Janet Pierce was at her loveliest and most charming. I spoke to her at one point and Janet's smile was unforgettable. She said, "Mrs. Prescott, you will never know how much this evening means to me," and at that point Dave came across the room and he looked so proud, a pride which I well understand. The credit for the party's success all belongs to Janet. I trust you will dismiss our earlier conversation. My dear old friend was there with her remarkable necklace. I was in total error. Good night, my dear.

Max dropped Dorothy L. to the floor. She immediately wafted through the air to land beside the answering machine. She patted the cord.

"Dorothy L., don't even think about it. Max, she's still hungry."

Max opened the refrigerator, found a piece of steak. As he chopped it up, he looked at Annie quizzically. "Come on, Annie. Can you really picture Janet Pierce as a cat burglar? The woman eats and breathes social prominence. She would never jeopardize her social status, much less put herself in danger of going to prison."

Annie took another deep swallow of the cool water. It was nice to focus on something besides Emma Clyde's bossiness. "It would be a neat link between Janet and Kathryn, a thief who picked a fence with a penchant for blackmail."

"I don't buy it." Max put down the bowl with the steak and leaned against the kitchen counter.

MESSAGE 4: Clearly there has been an outbreak of idiocy on the island. It was absurd for Henny ever to have been suspected of murdering Kathryn Girard. But Ruth Yates!—

Miss Dora's raspy voice quivered with indignation. The snap, crackle and pop of the international connection punctuated a tirade that concluded:

—and I trust that you and Maxwell and Emma will bend yourselves to the task of clearing Ruth. I have worked with Ruth on many diocesan matters and I can state unequivocally that she has neither the intelligence, the aptitude nor the appetite for multiple murders. Do you think it would be helpful for me to so inform the new police chief? I shall await your response. Good night

In unison, Annie and Max shook their heads. Dorothy L.'s fur fluffed.

"Not you, sweetie." Annie pointed at Max. "You call Miss Dora tomorrow. Deflect her. Tell her it's all a ploy to fool the real killer."

Max yawned. "Maybe it would be a good idea for Garrett to get a picture of how people perceive Ruth."

Annie put their glasses in the sink. "I think it will be better if we leave him alone. He's going to get tired of everybody telling him he's got it all wrong."

MESSAGE 5: Annie, I can't believe you told that policeman the gun belonged to me. I told you Kathryn took it—

Ruth Yates's voice shook with anguish and fear. Annie lifted her hands as if to ward off blows as the frantic words pelted her.

—and I can't tell anyone about Kathryn, I can't, I can't, I can't—

Ruth was sobbing now and the words became difficult to hear.

—can't bear . . . never wanted to hurt . . . leave me alone . . . oh Brian, Brian . . .

When the connection ended, tears burned in Annie's eyes. "Max, this is awful. She's terrified." She reached for the telephone.

Max grabbed her hand. "Wait. Annie, it's too late. You can call first thing in the morning."

Finally Annie agreed, but her last vision before falling asleep was of Ruth Yates, her face streaked with tears, her finger pointing at Annie.

Annie paced back and forth in the kitchen, watching the clock. It wasn't good manners to call before nine in the morning but surely contacting a frightened murder suspect altered the rules of social intercourse. The minute the hour hand swung to seven, she picked up the phone.

The microwave pinged. Max opened it, lifted out her two slices of pizza and his carrot muffin. He hadn't said a word about cholesterol or fat grams when she'd chosen her breakfast.

As he put her plate on the table, Annie nodded her thanks and swept Dorothy L. onto a chair. Undaunted, Dorothy L. swarmed right back on the table, her blue eyes sparkling. Max picked her up, nuzzled her neck. "Are you still hungry?"

"Of course she's still hungry," Annie snapped. "Dorothy L. thinks mealtime is anytime she's—" Annie broke off.

"Brian Yates." He was a big bear of a man, but it was the first time Annie had ever heard his deep voice sound harsh and stricken.

Suddenly her own kitchen seemed about as comfortable as the Arctic tundra. "Brian, this is Annie Darling. I—"

"Haven't you done enough harm?" His tone bristled with anger. "I can't believe you'd call here."

Annie stiffened. "Wait a minute, Brian. I'm not the one who pointed a gun at Kathryn Girard. But Max and Emma and I are the ones who are trying to find out what really happened Thursday night. Now, if you want to help Ruth, you'll let me talk to her."

Max was watching, his eyes concerned. Dorothy L.'s head poked up next to Annie's plate. Annie grabbed the plate, put it on the counter by the phone, then turned on the speaker.

"I can't." Brian spoke so softly he could barely be heard. "She's in the hospital."

"The hospital?" Annie felt numb. What had happened? What had Ruth done?

Max pushed back his chair, came to stand beside her.

"After the police left, Ruth locked herself in her room. Chief Garrett said she had to come to the station tomorrow and she should have a lawyer. But she wouldn't talk to me." His voice was heavy with pain and disbelief. "Dr. Burford came when I was trying to get her to let me in. She hadn't eaten. She was crying. He told me to wait downstairs. I heard him knock on her door. He told her he had to see her and not to be a damned fool. In a minute, she opened the door and he went inside."

Max scrawled on a kitchen pad: *I told you what Burford said. It must be true, after all. Ruth must have killed Alden Yates!*

Annie leaned close to the speaker phone. "Was she sick? What did Dr. Burford say?"

"Nobody talked to me." His tone was querulous. "I went

upstairs and leaned close to the door, but I couldn't make out what they were saying."

Annie pictured Brian Yates easing quietly up the stairs to creep down his own hall, bewildered and desperate.

"When he came out, he said Ruth was suffering from exhaustion and had to be hospitalized and he was going to check her in himself. She came out of her room with a bag." There was a long, aching pause. "She didn't even look toward me."

Annie wanted to tell him not to worry. But how could she? If ever a man had reason to worry, it was Brian. Instead, she said, "I'll go see her, Brian."

"They won't let you in. Burford called a little while ago. He said Ruth wasn't to be disturbed. Not by anybody. Not me. Not her friends. Not the police." He took a deep breath. "They've got a guard at her door. A guard!" and the phone slammed down.

Annie clicked off the speaker phone, put up the receiver. "Max, it looks worse and worse for Ruth."

"I don't think there can be any doubt about Alden Yates. But don't you see?" He cut his muffin in half, added a smear of marmalade. "Even if she's innocent of the Girard and Chapman murders, she has to keep her mouth shut."

"And if she won't talk"—Annie slipped into her chair, picked up a piece of still-warm pizza—"Garrett's going to be convinced she's guilty."

"Maybe she is," Max said soberly.

Maybe she was. They ate in silence.

Annie finished her pizza, resisted the temptation to heat another slice.

Max looked up, saw her studying the refrigerator. "Agatha is inspired by your example."

Annie grinned and he grinned in return, looking, Annie decided, absolutely yummy, his blond hair still in tufts from a night's sleep, his dark blue eyes bright, his face attractively stubbled with blondish beard. If it were a usual Saturday morning (Death on Demand didn't open until ten and Agatha's breakfast dropped automatically from a measured container), they could pursue other pleasures.

Max's entire face brightened. He pushed back his chair, apparently losing interest in his muffin.

"We have duties, Max." But he was bending near and suddenly his lips touched hers and she lost interest in duties.

As Max's red Maserati curved around a bend on its way to the harbor, Annie turned into the winding dusty road to the Women's Club. Thanks to the White Elephant Sale, traffic was as thick as on the William Hilton Parkway on Hilton Head before the cross-island expressway opened. The main parking lot to the Women's Club was full and cars were tucked off the road between pines.

Annie waved hello to friends and acquaintances. As she walked along the road, she realized that for all their good efforts on Friday, there was still so much they didn't know. She'd answered several questions on her list: Yes, Dave Pierce was on the island the day his wife's boat disappeared and the weather was fine, and no, everyone said Dave and his secretary weren't having an affair. But she didn't know why Loretta Campbell was hostile to her son's second wife, who certainly seemed an improvement over his first, or why Gary and Marie Campbell quit the Little Theater, or where Vince Ellis was when Arlene took her last sail. As for Max, he'd learned that Dr. Burford was at Loretta Campbell's bed when she died, but what mattered was what the nurse's aide said after Alden Yates died. If the rumors were true, Max knew why Ruth Yates went into a tailspin after her father-in-law's death. Annie had figured out how the murderer left Marsh Tacky Road, but not in time to save the life of Jake Chapman. Max had yet to learn why Arlene Ellis sailed on a stormy day or what happened between Gary Campbell and his first wife, though how could that lead to murder so many years later?

Food booths rimmed the perimeter of the front lawn. A coffee booth was in full swing and the soft drink concession already had two lines five deep. Most of the booths would open at eleven, offering everything from steamed oysters and she-crab soup to seafood shish kebab and corn dogs. As she joined in a throng of eager shoppers hurrying toward the front door of the Women's Club, Annie hoped that before the day was over, she and Max and Emma would learn enough to unmask a murderer.

A banner fluttered over the main door:

WHITE ELEPHANT SALE
Trinkets, Collectibles, Cast Offs,
Treasures, Surprises, Trifles
Join in the Fun—$5
Drawing—3 tickets for $10, 7 for $15, 12 for $20

Annie had a fuzzy idea this might be a form of gambling and wondered vaguely if the drawing was illegal. Was it legal to charge different prices for the tickets? But Chief Garrett had more serious matters on his mind. The noise level inside the club rivaled a combined rock concert, cement mixer and Boy Scout jamboree. Annie stood in line, forked over five dollars and received a green palmetto stamp on the back of her right hand.

Balanced atop a footstool next to a huge wooden Indian, Pamela Potts, her blond pageboy gleaming, her blue apron crisp, yelped, "Annie, Annie," and waved her hands above her head like Gilligan sighting a cruise ship.

Annie wormed her way up the central aisle. She was temporarily delayed when two little boys upended a tackle box filled with marbles. On her hands and knees, she helped their mother and the boys grab marbles and sling them into the box. "George, Howard, if anyone falls and we get sued, your father's going to kill you. George, take that marble out of your mouth. Howard, put that peashooter away."

Once past the marbles, Annie had to wait while a distinguished old gentleman with white hair and handlebar mustaches struggled up the aisle clutching a mammoth stuffed moose head. His face was dangerously red.

A prong of antlers swung perilously near. Annie ducked. "Handsome—uh—handsome head," she said.

He glared at her. "Thinks she'll get rid of it. Well, we'll see about that!"

Ah, the happiness to be found at an old-fashioned White Elephant Sale.

Annie slid next to the wall and looked up at Pamela. "You called?"

Pamela's stare was dubious. "I didn't call. I waved."

Annie forced a bright smile. She must remember with whom she spoke.

"Annie"—Pamela's voice trembled—"what are you doing here?"

Annie stared in return. It was hard to know where to start. Should she explain that she was responding to Emma's command? That she was pursuing anyone and everyone with information about the people on Kathryn Girard's route the night she died? That she wanted—

"Henny's missing. I thought you of all people would be out searching for her." Pamela's blue gaze was bewildered. "I called the police this morning and they told me not to worry, that Henny was free to leave the hospital when she wished. Dr. Cary won't return my call. I went by Henny's house. I knocked and there was no answer. I got her key from the front porch and went inside. No one was there. But someone had fed her cat. I tried to talk to Emma and she said everything was fine. But Annie, it isn't fine! Where's Henny?"

Annie reached out and pulled Pamela next to the wooden Indian. "Pamela, it's important for everyone to think Henny is missing." Annie bent near, whispered. "The police have Henny in a safe place until everything comes out about Kathryn Girard's murder, but that's a secret. Get the word out that Henny's missing. It could be a big help."

Pamela might be earnest, Pamela might be dense, but

Pamela could be counted on. "Oh Annie, I'll tell everyone. I'll act as worried as can be." Her face immediately assumed the woebegone expression of a beagle at a cat clinic.

"Good work," Annie said stoutly. Annie moved on up the aisle, peering around a massive woman clutching a box of Fiesta pottery. She had to admit that Emma's original hope of putting pressure on the murderer might be their last, best hope. Surely the murderer had to be a little worried even though word of Ruth Yates's plight was no doubt seeping across the island. But Henny's disappearance should cause uneasiness. As for Emma, she was formidable. If Annie had committed two murders, carefully setting up Ruth Yates to be the prime suspect, she'd be damned worried if Emma marched about emphasizing that Kathryn's first stop had been at Ruth's but who was to say it had been her final stop? And, if Annie had any success today, maybe she'd pull some other strings that would make a double murderer very uneasy indeed.

Chapter 12

A rush of wind from the rotating blades of the Coast Guard helicopter rippled the waist-high grasses near the landing pad. The craft shut down and in a few minutes the crew walked briskly toward the fence. The pilot, tall, thin, with a brush of dark hair and an easy slouch, came through the gate.

Max stepped forward. "Lieutenant Farriday?" He held out his hand. "I'm Max Darling. I called you about the searches for two boaters lost off Broward's Rock, Arlene Ellis and Lynn Pierce."

Farriday's handshake was swift and firm. Green eyes studied Max with interest. "I told you what we knew." His tone was pleasant but dismissive.

"I know, Lieutenant. But I'd appreciate if it you'd give me a minute. I have a couple of questions." Max's tone was easy and confident.

Farriday pulled off his flight helmet. "All right." He strode toward the single-story building. He opened a frosted door, held it for Max. Leading the way into a small office that overlooked the airstrip, he gestured toward a straight chair. He tossed his helmet on his desk and settled into a swivel chair.

Max knew he had to get Farriday's attention and hold it. "In the last couple of days, there have been two murders on Broward's Rock. I'm looking for a link to the deaths of either Arlene Ellis or Lynn Pierce."

"Accidental deaths." Farriday frowned.

"I know that's what they appeared to be," Max agreed. "But I'm asking you now, could either have been murder?"

Farriday rubbed his bony nose. "When someone drowns, Mr. Darling, and no one is there to see it happen, then, sure, the death could be murder. Or suicide. Nothing in either of the searches gave any indication that the deaths were other than accidental. I don't see how you could have obtained any physical evidence to prove anything else." His gaze challenged Max.

Max leaned forward. "Vince Ellis and someone in the Pierce family were being blackmailed. That blackmailer was killed Thursday night. I know there's no proof that either Arlene Ellis or Lynn Pierce was murdered. If there had been, you would have contacted the police. But can you now look back and tell me if there's anything, anything at all, about either of those drownings that worried you?"

Farriday leaned back in his chair. "Mrs. Ellis." His voice was thoughtful. "According to her husband, she was a first-rate sailor." Farriday looked across the room at maps of the Sound and the ocean. "Warning flags were up the day she went out. Force 7."

Max understood. Force 7 indicated winds of twenty-eight to thirty-three knots. Any experienced boater would stay in the harbor or, if at sea, heave to. The Sound must have been broken with whitecaps, the water foaming and the sky a dirty gray with dark anvil clouds towering high.

"Why did she go out?" Farriday mused. "The storms delayed our search. I didn't expect to find her. Her husband was going nuts when we were grounded. Paced like a madman, kept begging us to take off. I felt sorry for him. But when I asked him why she'd gone out on a stormy day, he just looked at me and shook his head and walked away."

An experienced sailor taking a boat out on a day heavy with storm clouds—what did it mean? Was Arlene Ellis arrogant or foolish, or did Arlene deliberately set sail to die? Or did Vince Ellis kill his wife and stage a fake disappearance?

Farriday pushed back his chair, stood. "I don't guess, Mr. Darling. I deal in facts. Experienced sailors. Mrs. Ellis went out on a stormy day. Mrs. Pierce sailed on a fine day, fleecy clouds and winds seven to ten knots. Neither one came back. You figure it out. But"—and he walked to the door, held it—"I can tell you that I remember those two searches well and part of the reason I remember them is the husbands. It hurt to look at them. I don't know why their wives were lost, but I can tell you I never saw men who cared more."

Annie reached the steps to the low stage. Yesterday Emma had reigned in solitary splendor at a card table. Today, the stage was piled high with boxes, some with red stickers, others with green, yellow, pink and purple. Emma stood at one end, gesturing decisively to a covey of blue-aproned volunteers. Emma's hair was in tight orange coils and her caftan was a remarkable mélange of red, yellow and green spots. ". . . imperative that the tables be kept well stocked. Replenish the tables from these boxes. The boxes are color-coded according to price. Each item in a red box sells at a table stocked with twenty-dollar items, green fifteen, yellow ten . . ."

A marketplace in Marrakesh couldn't have resounded with greater hubbub. As Annie waited for Emma to finish, she looked out over the teeming club room. A piercing whistle came from an electric train set near the front door. A usually sedate vice president of the Broward's Rock Music Club had found a tambourine and was holding it above her head and clapping it as she did a fair rendition of Carmen in the aisle between a pile of vintage hubcaps and stacks of *National Geographic.* Two women clutched opposite ends of a quilt, their faces obdurate, their knuckles white. An enthusiastic volunteer stood on an overturned bucket and held home-preserved jellies above her head, chanting, "Two for five . . ."

Familiar faces were everywhere. This didn't surprise Annie. But she was surprised—and she had to hand it to Emma, who had a disgusting habit of always being right— to spot most of the people who had been on Kathryn Girard's pick-up list. But maybe it made all kinds of sense. Whatever happened, the murderer had to keep up a convincing pretense that everything was fine and today was the White Elephant Sale, the most important event of the year for members of the Women's Club. No one who belonged would dream of missing it and their spouses were always in tow to provide muscle. Marie Campbell, Janet Pierce and Ruth Yates all were members. Of course, Ruth and Brian were not present.

A bright smile lit Marie Campbell's elfin face as she held out a chunky pottery pig to a customer. She took the five-dollar bill and handed it to her husband to put in the change box. Gary Campbell was too long to fit comfortably on the folding chair behind the card table and he looked morose and uncomfortable. And wary.

Janet and Dave Pierce were on their hands and knees by the chugging train. Dave reached into a box and pulled out an engineer's cap. He popped it on his head and his grin made his usually stern face boyish and appealing. Janet, who wore the blue apron over a pale pink silk blouse and white silk slacks, clapped her hands in delight. Janet would never look girlish, her eyebrows carefully arched, her makeup too perfect. She had the elegance and grace of a model, but she was aging and blondes age hard. The sharp light slanting through a window emphasized the jut of her cheekbones and the lines at the corners of her mouth.

His red hair always a beacon, Vince Ellis held a blue stuffed rabbit with droopy ears in one hand and a Barbie Doll carry-all in the other. A tiny smile on her face, Meg Ellis sat stiffly on a wooden stool as a blue-aproned volunteer painted a pink butterfly on her cheek. Vince tucked the carry-all under one arm and used both hands to hold the bunny up and clap his paws. Meg giggled.

Annie had a sudden memory of Arlene Ellis on a picnic, tickled by Vince's imitation of an anteater. It was uncanny how much Meg looked like Arlene. But Meg was, so everyone had been told, the daughter of Arlene's sister, Amelia. Vince and Arlene adopted Meg after the deaths of Amelia and her husband. Meg came to the island about six months before Arlene drowned. Was there a connection between the deaths of the two sisters? Could Meg actually be Arlene's real daughter? Maybe it would be smart to check out the circumstances of Meg's adoption.

The stage steps creaked behind her. Blue-aproned volunteers flowed past. Emma said crisply, "The first assault is under way." Her orange curls quivering, Emma nodded toward the sales floor. "There goes Laurel."

Laurel was wending her way down the crowded center aisle. Today her white-gold hair curved around her face. She wore glasses with aquamarine frames that emphasized the blue of her eyes and the soft blue linen jacket. Her white linen skirt was so short it should have been against the law, at least in Annie's opinion. After all, she was somebody's mother. Actually, a particular, specific mother. Laurel's progress was slowed by the bulky man carrying the moose head. He stopped and bowed, his white mustache quivering. Oh-ho, maybe Fred the Sailor was about to be vamoosed. But Laurel, always adept, slipped past. The moose head immediately began bobbing down the aisle after her.

Would it, Annie wondered, ever get to be a bore to have men of all ages look moonstruck the minute you came into view?

Laurel looked back, lifted pink-tipped fingers to blow a kiss.

The moose head damn near went into a gallop.

Emma folded her arms. "If it isn't one problem with her, it's another."

Annie grinned. "Emma, you are a profoundly insightful woman."

"I am a profoundly determined woman." Emma's chin jutted. "It hasn't been easy. At least Laurel's going in the right direction. I told her to start with Vince Ellis. I swear, Annie, dealing with your mother-in-law is on a par with trying to make a cat dance."

Annie said dryly, "I'd rather teach Agatha to schottische."

"Understandably." Emma's blue eyes were icy. "However, I prevailed."

Annie looked into those penetrating blue eyes, decided not to voice her complete confidence that Emma had a trifle to learn about Laurel. Instead, she said brightly, "Really."

"I told her to approach Vince and the Pierces and the Campbells and simply inquire what goods they'd put out to be collected on Thursday, that the club wished to give them a donation slip even though the donations were destroyed in a fire while the van was in police custody. Don't you think that's brilliant?" Emma's broad mouth spread in a satisfied smile. "Marigold employed a similar approach in *The Case of the Disappearing Diva*. Damn fool woman ran away with a Houdini imitator who sold shoelaces door to door."

Annie blinked.

"The diva, not Marigold, for God's sake. But this will alert the murderer, assuming Ruth is innocent, that everyone knows where Kathryn was scheduled to stop Thursday night. That should cause some uneasy moments. And it's

such a clear challenge. Do you know what Laurel wanted
to do?"

Annie had an idea. "Flowers?"

"Flowers," Emma's tone was grim. "The woman is obsessed—"

What a clear perception Emma had. Annie might casually mention Emma's judgment to Max.

"—by the idea of communicating with flowers. She told
me she'd worked late into the night preparing cards. I'll
admit the drawings were"—the caftan rustled as she
shrugged—"somewhat fetching, yellow daffodils, Canterbury bells in white, pink and blue, and something called
coltsfoot. It has yellow flowers and damned if the leaves
don't look like a colt's foot. Laurel said she would present
each person with a card and inform them that she commiser-
ated with them utterly over the shocking murder of the
woman coming to their homes simply to collect donations
and that she knew they would feel a part of the community's
effort to solve this heinous crime"—Emma's sardonic tone
indicated she was quoting verbatim—"and she was confident they shared in the uncertainty engendered by the crime
and accepted the obligation to see justice done. To wit, daffodils, Canterbury bells and coltsfoot." Emma sighed. "I
swear—" She broke off, her eyes narrowed.

Laurel, with the moose head peeking over her shoulder,
held out a card to Vince Ellis.

Vince listened as she spoke, his face blank. He still held
the blue rabbit. Shaking his head, he turned away.

Laurel stood for a moment more, looking at his back,
then, with a bright smile, she walked toward the electric
train and the Pierces.

Annie reached out, grabbed Emma's arm. "As Marigold
often says, 'Inspector, however a solution is derived, justice
results.' " Marigold was often given to pompous pronounce-
ments after outwitting the police. Privately Annie thought
Inspector Donald Dilatory should have thrown Marigold's

ass in jail but such was not to be in a mystery by Emma Clyde.

Emma might be overbearing but she was also smart and Annie didn't have to tell her that Laurel's card would have the same effect as a request for a list of donations, a clear announcement to the murderer that Kathryn's stops were known.

Annie decided a change in focus might be wise. "Okay, Assault One is under way. Assault Two?"

"We'll let them stew today. I've told Pamela to get the word out that the police know Kathryn Girard is a black-mailer. Tonight at the Fall Revel, I'll make it clear that I am convinced of Ruth's innocence and that I expect every member of the club to join us in an effort to discover information about Kathryn. And now"—Emma spoke above the raised voices from the middle of the room where the quilt confrontation was escalating—"I'd better see to that."

Annie watched soberly as Laurel made her rounds. The results were very much the same in each instance. Janet Pierce's face crinkled in puzzlement. She looked at her husband and asked a question. Dave Pierce pushed up the engineer's cap, then shook his head. At the card table manned by the Campbells, Marie was arranging a display of pottery angels. Her smile was apologetic as she waved away the offer of the card. Even from here, Annie could lip-read her answer, "Oh. No, not at our house. I'm sorry." Gary Campbell didn't smile. His thick eyebrows bunched and his lips made a hard line. As Laurel turned away, Marie dropped her hand on his arm, spoke urgently to him. But his rigid face didn't relax.

Annie realized abruptly what a genius stroke it had been to burn out the back of the van. Now no one could prove that the van had made a particular stop or that anything in the back belonged to any particular person. Smart thinking by a thoughtful murderer. But the murderer couldn't burn away the reasons for blackmail. And if Kathryn had discovered secrets, so could Annie.

Annie spotted a longtime customer, Jessica Greer, pawing through a dusty stack of books. Jessica collected children's mysteries from the thirties and forties. Jessica was also a member of the Broward's Rock Little Theater and had played roles from Marie Antoinette to Auntie Mame.

The ferry rocked gently in its berth. On Saturdays Parotti kept pretty well to schedule, leaving on the hour, returning on the half hour. It was almost ten, so Max walked fast. Parotti's Boat Rental was next to the ferry office. Max pushed open the door.

Ben Parotti looked up with a bright smile, which ebbed as he recognized his visitor. "Everybody's at that damn sale. Only rented two boats all morning." Parotti was especially nautical today, white cap with gold braid, white jacket with gold buttons and navy slacks. The effect was marred a little by high-topped red sneakers. He saw Max's glance. "Don't go tellin' the missus. She give me some things called boaters and I felt like I was walking in a couple of barges. I'll take sneakers every time." He brightened. "She's gone to that sale. Thought your missus'd have you over there to help."

"I'll go over in a while." Max sat on an old bench that gave an alarming tilt.

Parotti popped up. With apparent ease, he grabbed an anchor from one corner, smacked it next to Max. The bench settled down. "Keep meaning to fix that. But the missus has kept me real busy in the grill. And when that woman gets an idea!" Parotti sighed. "But if she hadn't kept me up late working on that dadblamned shelving by the front windows, I wouldn't have salvaged myself a nice little treat. Even the missus was pleased."

Parotti loved to talk, but Max knew he couldn't afford to spend the morning. He needed to ask his questions and go, but Parotti was so pleased with himself, Max didn't have the heart to squelch him. The only thing Parotti loved better than a good story was a successful discovery of anything he could claim as salvage.

Max relaxed against the wall. Annie didn't expect him at the sale until lunch. "What'd you find, Ben?"

Ben pulled up a chair, hunched close to Max. "I'll tell you, I was never so surprised. I'm working on that damn shelf and I saw a shadow down by the pier. Well, you know I don't take kindly to anybody poking their noses into my stuff and I thought to myself, well, somebody's up to no good. Why else would a body be sneaking around on the pier at one o'clock in the morning? Nothing else is stirring anywhere. The party people are on the boats over in the marina by you folks. It's workin' boats here and nobody's got a call to be wandering around after midnight. So I decide to take a quiet look"—his leprechaun's face mirrored sheer amazement—"and you'll never guess who I saw heave somethin' into the harbor! In the middle of the night!"

Max played along. "The mayor?"

"Better than that." Parotti leaned forward, planted his hands on his knees. "Brian Yates, one of them preachers at St. Mary's. You know, he wears a collar but he's married." Parotti sounded faintly scandalized.

Max didn't try to explain the difference between preachers, ministers and priests, Anglican or Roman. "What did you do, Ben?"

"Well, I hunkered down behind a trash can and watched him hurry away, looking this way and that"—Parotti's head swiveled and his eyes darted—"like a man who damn sure didn't want to meet up with anybody he knew. I almost popped out to ask him what he thought he was doin', dumpin' trash in the harbor. We got laws about that!" Parotti glowered.

"But you didn't." Max grinned. A man intent on salvage wouldn't waste his time in confrontations, no matter how interesting it might have been.

Parotti grinned in return. "I figured it would be better to find out what was goin' on. I got a lantern and some tackle and a boat. Well, it took me a while, but I pulled it out, almost a full set of them wooden sticks with heads that the rich folks use to hit a wooden ball around. And they like to dress all in white."

It was Parotti for croquet.

"The missus is thrilled." Parotti basked in the glow of remembered approval. "She thinks maybe I should clear some ground to the side of the grill and people can whack the balls. She's plannin' to make herself a white outfit."

"Play croquet," Max murmured.

Parotti nodded vigorously. "Yeah. That's what she said, croquet. Sounds kind of like some kind of fish to me."

Max asked quietly, "Is there a mallet missing?"

Parotti looked at him blankly.

"One of the sticks." But why else would Brian Yates slip through darkness to the harbor? Did he know a croquet mallet had been found not far from the van? After Dr. Burford took Ruth to the hospital, had Brian searched the garage, afraid of what he might find, terrified of what he did find? Or was it colder and harsher than that? Had Ruth told him about the mallet and he'd set out to hide any link to her?

Parotti's nod was quick and bright. "I looked 'em over. I can make one to match."

"Ben"—Max's tone was grave—"I'm afraid you have to call Chief Garrett. Had you heard that Kathryn Girard was killed by a croquet mallet?"

Ben's mouth dropped open. "I'll be damned. But a parson?" His tone was scandalized. "Well, I never."

Max knew this might be the final push to convince Garrett to arrest Ruth Yates. Maybe she should be arrested. Whether Ruth was arrested or not, Max still had some serious questions about the deaths of Arlene Ellis and Lynn Pierce. As Lieutenant Farriday said, either could have been murder. Max didn't know which was more suspicious, Arlene's death on a stormy day or Lynn's death on a perfect day for sailing.

Parotti squinted at Max. "You mean I got evidence here?"

"Maybe, Ben." Max didn't often consider the force of serendipity. If he hadn't come to see Parotti, perhaps no one ever would have known about the cast-off croquet mallets. On the other hand, there was another maxim which often came true: Nefarious deeds attract interested eyes, or, the perils of surreptitiousness in a small town. "But maybe not. Call Garrett. If he takes the set away, I'll see that you get another one." After all, Jolene Parotti was making an all-white outfit.

"Done." Parotti gave a quick salute.

Max made a mental note to see about a set of croquet mallets. And now it was time to ask Parotti for knowledge only he might have.

"Ample" would be an excellent summation of Jessica Greer, shining golden hair in smooth poufs, plump pink cheeks, a bosom with Wagnerian soprano proportions and a smile broad as the horizon. "Annie!" Her rich, deep voice ooozed contentment. "Look what I've found." She held out *Beverly Gray's Career* and *Beverly Gray on a Treasure Hunt*.

"Wonderful!" Annie exclaimed. And it was wonderful what some customers were willing to pay for first editions of various Beverly Gray or Nancy Drew or Hardy Boys titles. "Are you trying out for anything this fall?"

The segue might not rank as her most graceful, but Annie knew her customer.

Brown eyes sparkling, Jessica beamed. "My dear, the Little Theater is putting on *Arsenic and Old Lace* and I'm Martha Brewster." She clapped a hand to her chest and dust puffed from the book. "I do hope Henny is on the mend. No one else could possibly play Abby as well and rehearsals start next week." Jessica peered at her anxiously.

Annie patted Jessica's arm reassuringly. "Henny's doing fine. She'll be there."

Jessica screwed her face up like a child missing a favorite doll. "I wish you and Max had tried out for Elaine and Jonathan."

Annie wouldn't have tried out for a month's supply of Godiva. She didn't have cheerful memories of playing those roles several years ago in a most murderous presentation of the play. "Oh," she said vaguely, "we keep intending to get active again, but you know how it is, you get really busy. You know, I was talking to Henny the other day"—Annie felt as creative as Emma—"and we were talking about some of the people who are really good that you don't see anymore. She said she remembers Marie Campbell especially. And Gary. I guess Henny has that right." Annie looked at Jessica. "I didn't even know they'd been in local theater."

"Oh well"—Jessica's sigh expressed sheer happiness—"I can tell you everything about the Players. My dear, I am a charter member—1947. My first year on the island." She looked about for a place to sit and tugged loose a cowhide footstool from beneath a mound of musty sheepskins which slid over a collection of Tupperware. Jessica pointed at a sawhorse painted in red and black stripes. "Doesn't that show spirit! Drag it up, my dear."

Annie perched on the sawhorse.

Jessica daintily spread her crinkly multitiered skirt. "Oh, the Little Theater. My, we've had some great ones. You wouldn't have known Roderick Ransome. So good-looking. Hair as golden as a splash of sun. And brown eyes. Now, that's a combination! Big dark eyes with eyelashes an actress would kill for. My husband didn't care at all for some of our love scenes." A throaty chuckle. "I was happily wed but Roderick was quite a kisser. Well, my husband put an end to that but I . . ."

Ten minutes later, Annie plunged into the river of reminiscences. "The Campbells. Marie Campbell. Gary Campbell." Annie enunciated each syllable.

Jessica's mouth formed a perfect O. Her eyes widened. "The Campbells! Why, that's what made me think of Roderick. Though he was a good kisser. And I always remember them. Roderick might have been the best. I'm sure that's what Marie thought." Just for an instant her tone was sharp.

Annie had a quick sense that she was as near to grasping quicksilver as she would ever come. The words shimmered in her mind. Roderick. Kisser. Marie. And old Mrs. Campbell's unrelenting dislike of her second daughter-in-law and coldness to her granddaughter.

Annie's tone was casual, with no hint that she might be linking a long-dead love affair to a recent murder. "I suppose that's why Marie and Gary quit the theater."

Jessica's eyelids fluttered. "There one night, gone the next. Left us with an understudy for Marie in *No, No, Nanette*. There was a lot of gossip at the time. And as it turned out"—she lifted plump hands in a dramatic gesture—"why, they could have stayed. Roderick had a chance to go out to the Pasadena Playhouse and he jumped at it."

"I don't suppose you have a picture of him anywhere?" Annie asked.

"I can tell you," she said archly, "what would have happened at my house if I kept pictures of Roderick around. But if you want to know what he looked like"—and now there was a flash of spite in her dark eyes—"why, go check out the pottery table." Her pudgy hand rose and she pointed.

Annie looked up the aisle at Marie Campbell and the teenage girl tugging on her arm, a teenage girl with hair as blond as a splash of sun and eyes dark as chocolate.

Ben Parotti lifted down a huge old leather ledger. "I don't hold with all this computer stuff. Good old-fashioned records, that's what I believe in. Used to be you could walk in the bank or the hardware store and find what you wanted on the shelf with a price on it and take it to the counter and pay quick as you please. Now half the time they say the computer's down and give you a look like a lost dog. Now"—he was flipping pages—"that was three years ago, wasn't it, when Miz Ellis went out? Let me see, yes, the middle of October as I recall and one of the biggest storms of the season. Hmm."

Max leaned against the counter, tried to read upside down.

"A weekend," Parotti muttered. "Would have had a lot of boats out, but I didn't rent any because of the storm. Some damn fool tourists try to bribe you. Always ask 'em if they want to pay for the hearse at the same time. Damn fools." He peered at Max from under beetling brows. "Didn't rent a one that day or the next."

"And none missing?" Max had already checked the marina overlooked by Death on Demand and the other shops that curved along the boardwalk. No boats had been stolen the dates the two women disappeared. The Pierces also owned a motorboat and a yacht. The Ellises had only the one sailboat. The Coast Guard records indicated that both Arlene Ellis and Lynn Pierce had been seen alone in their sailboats leaving the marina.

"Nope." Parotti rubbed his face with a gnarled hand. "Most people who steal boats know when to stay off the water."

"How about when Lynn Pierce disappeared? That was in April. April eighth." Max knew the dates by heart now.

Parotti flipped pages, stopped. "Man, half the world was out that day. Rented every boat I had. Says here wind at six knots, broken clouds, sun." He ran a blunt finger down the lines. His corrugated face squeezed in thought. "You know what, I was missing a boat that day, the *Susanna G.*, a Sailfish. It was gone Thursday morning." He looked at the top of the page. "That was April eighth." His narrow shoulders lifted and fell. "But it was gone that morning and as I recall Miz Pierce sailed around noon, didn't she? I remember the search didn't start till almost six. So I guess it don't have no connection. And somebody brought it back late that night. I found it the next morning, the morning of the ninth."

Max felt like a man who'd stubbornly clawed his way up a treacherous incline. Now, finally, there was a knob to hold on to. Lynn Pierce had sailed alone out into the Sound. But someone could have waited in an inlet, watched the marina and set sail after her.

A sudden poke in her back startled Annie. She swung around.

A huge man with silver-streaked black hair and a flaming red beard looked at her anxiously. He waggled a long bamboo fishing pole. "I'm sorry, Annie. I didn't mean to bump you." Toby Maguire was a reclusive island artist and about the last person Annie would have expected to see at the sale. His often truculent face blazed with delight. "This is a pole just like the one I had when my brothers and I used to sneak out of school to go fishing. I wonder if there might be an old galvanized pail anywhere."

Annie pointed toward a corner where she'd noted a metal scrub board and assorted pails.

"Gee, thanks, Annie."

As he brushed past, holding the pole high above his head like a knight's lance, Annie saw Vince Ellis take Meg's hand. The little girl looked up at him, her face alight with happiness. They turned toward the doors. Now Meg carried the blue rabbit.

Annie started after them. Vince had brushed Max off at the *Island Gazette* office. But Annie wouldn't ask Vince about Kathryn Girard.

Stepping outside, she shaded her eyes. The well-tended front lawn was ringed by food booths. A calliope played on a small merry-go-round. Children ran and shouted. Meg tugged at Vince's hand and pointed at a tent half filled with plastic balls. He nodded.

When Meg pushed through the plastic flap and jumped and slid on the balls, Annie hurried across the grass. She didn't want to ask Vince her questions in front of Meg.

Vince saw her coming. They'd known each other for a long time, laughed at play rehearsals, worked together on community promotions. He managed a smile but his eyes were remote. "Hi, Annie." He clutched the limp blue rabbit, the Barbie carry-all and a carved coconut wearing a Robin Hood cap and sunglasses.

"Hi, Vince." She looked through the clear plastic sheeting. Meg was rolling and squealing. "She's having a lot of fun."

His face softened. "She loves those silly balls. Every time we go to the mainland, we stop at that big McDonald's with the playland and she spends all her time jumping in the balls."

Annie curled her hands into tight fists and wished she could whirl away, plunge back inside, range up and down the aisles, hunt for a calico cat or a map of Spanish Texas or a jigsaw puzzle or any damn thing that had nothing to do with heartbreak and hurt. But Henny waited on a boat to be able to go safely home and Ruth huddled in a hospital bed knowing that arrest was coming ever nearer.

Annie's throat felt thick, but she managed to speak. "Meg looks just like Arlene."

Was it the sunlight that made Vince's eyes suddenly shiny? Or grief that would never ebb? He didn't answer, simply stared through the transparent plastic, his face gaunt and tired. But there was no hint of uneasiness or fear. There was only pain.

Annie wished for a tall glass of water or a fan. But she didn't think it was the sunlight, soft now in September, that was making her feel so hot. "I guess Arlene and her sister looked a lot alike."

"Arlene and Amelia." He took a deep breath. "Arlene adored her." There was a bitter edge to his voice.

Was he jealous of Arlene's dead sister? But Amelia was dead, had died the year before Arlene was lost. How could that have anything to do with Vince now? Annie asked abruptly, "What happened to Amelia?"

Vince didn't change expression, didn't move. When he spoke, his tone was indifferent. "Amelia? She was killed in a car wreck." He stepped away, poked his head inside the tent. In a moment, he and Meg were walking away.

Annie stared after them. Vince didn't mind talking about Meg. It hurt him to remember Arlene. But he sure as hell didn't want to talk about Amelia. Why?

Chapter 13

Picnickers sat on blankets, folding chairs, ice chests and even atop an overturned rowboat. Voices rose and fell as rhythmically as the rustle of the wind in the pines.

Annie took a last bite of corn on the cob as Max concluded, ". . . so it looks like Garrett's on the right track. How would anyone besides Ruth Yates have access to their croquet set? And I'll start believing in UFOs if the mallet that killed Kathryn doesn't match their set."

"Sure it'll match. But that set wasn't stashed in a safe. Anybody who goes to St. Mary's would know about the Yateses and croquet." Annie licked her fingers. "Ruth and Brian have had croquet parties every fall for years. They set up croquet at church picnics. And other picnics, too. Rotary. And at fund-raisers for The Haven. And I know for a fact they never lock their garage. I've picked stuff up or dropped off books. They don't even have an electric garage opener. You just grab the handle and pull up the door."

Max dipped boiled shrimp in cocktail sauce. "Okay, so

it's not a brain-drainer to get the mallet. The point is, Annie, the only reason the mallet would be a good murder weapon would be to tag Ruth or Brian as suspects. And how would one of Kathryn's other victims know that Ruth was paying blackmail, too?"

Annie studied her paper plate. Honestly, she loved food booths. How else could you ever come up with a lunch that included Spam and pineapple shish kebab, corn on the cob, Indian taco, spinach feta salad and banana fritters? Of course, everyone to their own taste. Max's plate was piled high with boiled shrimp, steamed oysters, green beans, corn bread and two slices of watermelon. One for her? She took a bite of Indian taco, wiped grease from her chin. "I could see a way," she said slowly, "if Ruth had donated the croquet set. I can see Kathryn's murderer spotting the croquet set and thinking it would be clever to use a weapon that could be traced back to someone else."

"Then what?" Max broke open an oyster shell. "How did Brian get the croquet set back? Remember, the contents of the van were burned. No, that won't work. Besides I can't imagine anyone planned to kill Kathryn without having a weapon in hand when she arrived."

"And if she arrived at Ruth's—"

Max picked up the story. "—and Ruth pointed a gun at Kathryn—"

Annie nodded. "—and Kathryn took the gun away and they were right by the garage and Ruth grabbed up a croquet mallet—"

"—and whacked her." Max added another shrimp tail to his tidy pile. "Maybe we're chasing after phantoms. Maybe Ruth's the one."

"Kathryn planned to stop at four houses." Annie ticked them off on her fingers. "The Yateses, the Pierces, the Campbells, Vince Ellis."

"But only one of them killed her." Max tossed a piece of cornbread to a green lizard perched on the old log they were using as a table. "And it's looking more and more likely that Ruth must be guilty."

The banana fritter was a taste of heaven, light, crisp, and sweet. The only possibly better dessert was bananas foster, which she always garnished with a few splashes of chocolate syrup. Sometimes she thought chocolate syrup would be good on anything, turkey, steak, asparagus. Well, maybe not asparagus. "You have a good point," she said reluctantly.

In fact, not even Marigold Rembrandt could likely invent a reason why one of the other blackmail victims would know that Ruth was a fellow victim. They sure didn't have annual victim parties or exchange billets-doux about Kathryn.

So why steal Ruth's croquet mallet? The answer came fast and clear: Nobody took it. But that would mean—

"Annie, Max!" Pamela Potts flung herself to the ground beside them. Pamela's large eyes gazed at them piteously. Her lips trembled.

Annie reached out, grabbed a shaking hand. "Pamela, what's wrong?"

"Do you know what I've heard?" Her voice was tight and thin.

Annie could not imagine what dire information had reduced calm and placid Pamela to this state. Had the President admitted to a ménage à trois with an extraterrestrial and an Arab terrorist?

"It's all over the sale room." Her tone was hushed. "Kathryn was a blackmailer. And she had four houses on her list Thursday night." A sniff. "The Yateses and the Pierces and Vince Ellis and the Campbells."

Annie almost gave a whoop of delight. Emma's strategy was working, at least to a point.

Pamela gulped; tears spilled down her pale cheeks. "Oh, it's all my fault."

Max clapped her on the shoulder. "Nonsense, Pamela. You are simply under a strain." He had that hearty male voice engendered by irrational female conduct.

Annie shot him a warning glance and squeezed Pamela's hand tighter. "Tell us what's wrong, Pamela."

Pamela gulped. "Emma asked me to find out all about Kathryn's friends and activities on the island." A sobbing breath. "Well, I did. And I knew a lot about it because she was active in so many things that I do." Pamela rattled off a list of at least a dozen charities and volunteer groups. "But the more I looked, the more I realized that Kathryn didn't really have any friends. So it's all my fault." She dissolved in a fresh paroxysm of sobs.

Max pulled out his handkerchief, thrust it toward Pamela. "Now, now. You can't take things so personally."

"Shh," Annie said softly. "Pamela, did you see a lot of Kathryn?"

Tear-flooded eyes gazed solemnly at Annie. "Yes." It was a choked whisper.

Annie said gently, "Did she ask you about people? Like the Yateses? And the Pierces? And Vince Ellis? And the Campbells?"

Pamela blew noisily into the handkerchief. "Not so much about the Yateses and the Campbells. And I never thought Kathryn meant anything bad. She was just so interested! She said it was so sad, you know, about Arlene Ellis and Lynn Pierce, and she asked me all about the Pierces and Vince Ellis. And it was sad and so odd, really, one sailing out one year and one the next. I thought she was just interested, the way anyone would be. But I guess I should have known there was something wrong with Kathryn. Ruth Yates acted so strange around her. Whenever Kathryn came in a room, Ruth left. And Ruth is the sweetest person in the world. And now they're saying the police suspect her of killing Kathryn. Oh, I feel terrible. I never meant—"

Annie leaned forward, gripped Pamela's shoulders, such thin, stiff shoulders. "Hush now, Pamela. You didn't do anything wrong. Everyone knows how kind you are and how hard you work for the community. You never gossip. I know that. Yes, you were willing to tell a newcomer about people on the island, but, Pamela, you have to understand that Kathryn was searching for information for her own use. You had no way of knowing what you were dealing with. Nothing that happened is your fault, none of it."

"Annie, do you really mean that?" Pamela's eyes were huge with hope.

Annie leaned forward. Gave her a hug. "Yes. I truly mean it. Now you go fix your face and get some lunch. The best thing you can do is circulate on the sale floor, tell everyone that Ruth may have an alibi."

Pamela scrambled to her feet. Once again earnest and competent, she said briskly, "I'd better get the word to the Pierces and Vince Ellis and the Campbells. Right?"

"As fast as you can." Annie spoke with utter conviction.

Max looked at her curiously. "Have you been hanging out with Emma too long? That's sheer fantasy, isn't it?"

Annie nodded happily. "Sure. But why not? Between Laurel and Emma and Pamela, the murderer should be having a bad day." Annie gathered up their trash.

Max stood and reached down to swing her to her feet. "Assuming—"

"I know," Annie interrupted. "Assuming Ruth isn't guilty. If she is, there's no problem. If she isn't, we need to wrap this up as fast as we can. And here's what I think we should do. . . ."

Max flipped on the lights in his office. He was almost past the artificial putting green when he stopped, looked at the ball waiting invitingly on a small rise twelve feet from the cup. He picked up his putter and addressed the ball. With one swift, short swing, the ball rolled directly to the cup and dropped in. One for luck. And they needed luck.

Settled behind his computer, he got on the Web, called up the archives of the *Island Gazette*. Thirty-eight entries about Vince Ellis; Max scrolled, found the obituary for Arlene Ellis. He read the column, noting on his legal pad: parents John and Toni Simms, Jasper, Florida.

A moment more and he had the obituary in the Jasper newspaper for Amelia Simms Lassiter and Richard James Lassiter of Long Beach, California, who died on July 7. No cause of death given, survived by their daughter Margaret, his parents, her parents and her sister. No surprises there. Nothing to indicate Margaret wasn't their daughter. And no reason why they shouldn't have been buried in Jasper, although the obituary listed their home as Long Beach, California. Max shrugged and accessed the Long Beach daily newspaper for the five days preceding the funeral.

Max didn't find an obituary for the Lassiters or any record of a car wreck involving them. But he printed out the story he did find.

Annie hurried up the steps. She held up her stamped hand to prove she'd already paid the entrance fee and stepped into the main room. The sale was in its early afternoon lull. At four, prices would be halved and the room would again be jammed. For now, the noise had subsided to a dull roar and it was possible to move with moderate speed among the lanes between tables. Annie was searching for either Marian Kenyon, who surely was on hand because she was nuts about any kind of flea market and always covered them for the *Island Gazette,* or for Adelaide Prescott, who supported every island cause. Annie spotted Marian in the farthest aisle, chin in hand, studying a collection of macramé. Adelaide was manning a booth in the twenty-dollar section. Women of all ages clustered in the aisle. Adelaide held up a triple-strand necklace of coral for Janet Pierce's inspection. Was the attraction jewelry? Or the presence of the island's social arbiter? Or the presence of the very beautiful wife of one of the island's wealthiest and most powerful residents?

When Annie arrived on the fringe of the group, Janet was paying for the necklace. "Definitely a bargain." She draped the strands over her head. "This reminds me of our honeymoon on St. Thomas." Her eyes were soft, her lips curved in a gentle smile. Annie realized that, trick of physiology or reflection of manner, Janet's slender face had a tendency to appear haughty in repose and this unguarded moment revealed a more appealing woman. "I'll have to show Dave." She scanned the crowd. "There he is. Thank you, Adelaide. I'll come and take over in a moment." She hurried up the aisle toward the stage where Dave was holding a box and talking with Emma.

In a moment, the onlookers had melted away. Adelaide looked after them. "Tails to a comet. I've had more than my share of attention through the years, but I've always been grateful for old friends because you know if they've been coming to your house since they were four, they come because they like you." A merry smile. "Or if they don't like you, they come because you're part of their lives. I doubt if Janet knows who her real friends are."

If she has any. But the thought didn't have to be voiced. Annie and Adelaide exchanged glances.

Annie went straight to the point. "Adelaide, you're on the Little Theater board, aren't you?"

Adelaide arranged a half dozen brooches in an arc. Her plump fingers patted the last one, a double row of blue rhinestones. "I heard the Campbells' house was on Kathryn's route."

Annie looked at her with respect. "Yes. So there's something to that old story about Marie and Roderick."

"I never believed those rumors." Adelaide's tone was thoughtful. "Although Gary Campbell isn't my idea of a dream husband, Marie always seemed to adore him. And still does. Actually, I thought Roderick Ransome made a fool of himself chasing after Marie. You know, it must have come as a shock to Roddy when she didn't respond. He was used to women clamoring for him."

Annie picked up a heavy bronze necklace. Perfect if you wanted to have a green neck. She weighed it in her hand. "Jessica Greer had it the other way around."

Adelaide's smile was amused. "She would. She adored Roddy and he paid no attention to her."

"So Gary and Marie abruptly leaving the Little Theater had nothing to do with Roderick Ransome?" Although in today's world, would anyone care about Kate Campbell's paternity? Well, yes, Gary Campbell might care intensely. And it would fully explain Loretta Campbell's hostility toward Marie and Kate. But no matter how blond Kate Campbell might be, Adelaide Prescott was nobody's fool and she didn't believe there had been an affair between Marie and Roderick.

"Neither Gary nor Marie ever came back to the theater after she quit *No, No, Nanette*." Adelaide upended a small box of costume jewelry, began to pick through the pieces. She looked up at Annie, her round face creased with concern. "Annie, I like Marie. I think she and Gary"—Adelaide paused, searched for the right words—"have gone through difficult times." Her eyes were dark with sadness. "Are you sure Kathryn was coming to their house?"

"Yes. I'm sure." Annie described the list in Kathryn Girard's handwriting that Henny had carried in the pocket of her slacks.

"That seems to be beyond question." She added softly, "I am so sorry. And surprised."

Max looked at the printout:

COUPLE FOUND DEAD AT HOME; DAUGHTER SAFE WITH SITTER

A teenage babysitter heard shots Thursday evening and found the bodies of her employers, Richard and Amelia Lassiter, in their car on the driveway in front of the home at 43 Montgomery Circle, according to police Lt. John Harrison.

Lt. Harrison, who did not identify the babysitter, said that it appeared that Amelia Lassiter had shot her hus-

band, then herself. The Lassiters' daughter Margaret, 2,
was asleep, according to police. The child has been taken
into protective custody pending notification of relatives.

Richard Lassiter, 34, was an independent financial
consultant and president of Lassiter Financial Services.
There was no answer at the office number today. Amelia
Lassiter was not employed. The Lassiters had lived in Long
Beach since 1993.

A near neighbor who declined to be identified said
there were often indications of marital discord at the Las-
siter home and that Mrs. Lassiter had been observed with
a bruised face and once told a neighbor she was limping
because she had fallen. She was twice treated at a local
hospital for injuries.

Lassiter was a graduate . . .

Max sighed and put down the sheet. He flipped open
his Rolodex to Vince Ellis, picked up the phone and dialed
Vince's beeper.

Annie stared at the assortment of glass animals. She
picked up a pale yellow unicorn. Not really an animal, of
course, though Laurel was one of those who believed pas-
sionately in unicorns.

"Unicorns are very popular," a gray-haired, double-
chinned volunteer chirped.

"Do you have a pink one?" Annie's eyes slid sideways
as she tried to keep an eye on the booth where Marie and
Gary Campbell sat.

The volunteer said regretfully, "I don't think there are
any pink unicorns."

Annie nodded solemnly. "No, I don't believe there are,"
and gently placed the unicorn on the table as Gary Campbell
strode down the aisle.

Annie hurried to the table. "Hi, Marie. Do you have any
cobalt-blue Fiesta?"

Marie's laughter pealed like a silver bell. "Annie, the only Fiesta was gone by five after eight this morning."

Annie picked up salt and pepper shakers, a rooster and a hen. How do you ask a woman if her daughter was fathered by a man other than her husband?

Marie drew her breath in sharply. Huge dark eyes stared at Annie. Was she fey? Or was there something in Annie's silence that alerted her?

The two women looked at each other, Annie's eyes full of inquiry, Marie's wide and searching.

"Do you remember Roderick Ransome?" Annie's voice was kind.

Just for an instant, a fierce anger burned in Marie's eyes, anger and something more, pain and resolve. Then her elfin face quickly reshaped, her eyes bright, her lips lifting in a swift smile. "I'd be glad to help." She looked past Annie. "Oh Gary, they need me outside. Something about the bedding plants I brought. If you'll hold the fort for a few minutes . . ." She bustled from behind the table. "Keep my Coke for me. I'll be right back," and she and Annie were moving toward the front door.

Annie glanced back. Gary Campbell stood in the aisle, holding two paper cups. He should have been a picture of Saturday casual, red-and-white-striped polo shirt, khaki slacks, white socks, Reeboks. But his rigid posture and strained face were out of place in the cheerful bustle of the sale. As she hurried after Marie, Annie knew that he was staring after them.

It was a relief to step out into the sunlight until she looked into Marie's angry eyes.

"Marie—"

"Not here," Marie snapped. "Damn you." She plunged ahead of Annie, walking swiftly across the lawn toward the cemetery. She led the way to a marble bench in the shade of a weeping willow. The distant sounds of laughter and children playing and the calliope were in eerie contrast to the centuries-old silence of the graveyard.

Marie stood beside a stone lion, one hand tight on a concrete mane. She looked small and beleaguered and dangerous. "I paid Kathryn Girard to keep quiet. Do you want money, too?"

For an instant, Annie found it hard to breathe, then her face flushed a fiery red. "Marie, someone killed Kathryn. And I don't think it was Ruth Yates. Kathryn planned to make four stops Thursday night. Your house was on her list." Annie knew she'd gone too far, said more than she'd ever intended. But maybe it was time to say it all. "I want to know what hold she had over you and whether you killed her to keep her quiet."

"I paid her." Marie's voice was low and strained. "I tell you, I paid her. I didn't kill her. I put the money in the top of a duffel bag filled with clothes. That's what she said to do. She said it would be the last time, that she was leaving and that she would keep her bargain. No one would ever know—" The muscles in her jaw ridged. "Damn you, I paid her. If you don't want money, what do you want?"

"The truth of what happened to Kathryn. If you didn't kill her, you have nothing to worry about." But as she said it, Annie knew that wasn't true.

"Just the police poking and prying, and if they do, the whispers will start. They've already started. Everyone's talking about us and the Pierces and Vince and Ruth. We thought when Loretta died that the past was finally done." She stared at Annie with haunted eyes. "Gary never should have told her, but he thought if she understood, she would be kind to Kate. But Loretta was selfish and cruel. And yes, Gary and I were fools, both of us. We love each other but we'd not been married long enough to be sure. I guess I've always needed reassurance, about everything. I've always been scared and felt alone. We'd only been married a year and I picked up the phone and heard him talking to Helen. She was his first wife and she was a witch. Bewitching." There was pain and puzzlement in her voice. "Beautiful. And bad. And he went to meet her. After all she'd done to

him. Cheated on him, laughed at him, started stories that
he hurt her. Roddy had been chasing after me, so I went
away with him that weekend." She looked at Annie defi-
antly. "And then when we were home again, we knew we
didn't care for anyone except each other."

Annie held tight to a strand of willow. "And Kate?"

"We wanted a baby. We'd been trying. Kate came—and
Gary loves her. He's her father." Her voice trembled. She
brushed back a tangle of dark hair. "Please don't hurt Kate.
She seems so strong. She's such a wonderful athlete. But she
struggles with depression. She missed some school last year.
She mustn't ever know. She must not know."

"Is that what Kathryn threatened? To tell Kate?" Annie
heard the curl of horror in her voice.

Marie's thin face looked pummeled, desperate. "Please,
Annie, I swear—" She stopped. Her eyes widened. She lifted
her hands in the immemorial gesture urging restraint.

Annie swung around. For an instant, she felt a hot stab
of fear.

Gary Campbell moved like a boxer, clenched fists hanging by his side, head lowered, a raging gaze pinned on
Annie.

Marie darted past Annie, caught his arm. "Gary, no."

He kept on coming, one heavy footfall after another, his
bald head gleaming in a swath of sun, his heavy brows
bunched, his deep-set eyes dark with fury, his bony face
twisted in a scowl.

Annie backed away, one step after another until she was
pressed against the stone lion, the ancient mane painful
against her back.

"Gary, I told her I'd paid." Marie's voice rose. "Don't
you see, we're all right."

"You told her nothing." His voice was deep and menac-
ing. He bent down until his head was only inches from
Annie's. "We had nothing to do with that woman's death.
We never saw her, never touched her. I'm warning you.

Leave us alone." Abruptly, he reared back, turned. Grabbing
his wife's arm, he pulled her with him.

As the Campbells plunged through the cemetery gate,
Annie understood about Gary Campbell's temper. And she
had a swift memory of the disarray in Kathryn Girard's
apartment.

Max leaned against a piling, looked out past the marina
at the whitecapped Sound. Lots of sailboats with wonderful
names, the *J. P. Vanilla, Out of Sight, Kiss Me, Kate, The Happy
Wanderer, Rock 'n' Roll*. Both Arlene Ellis and Janet Pierce set
sail from the marina.

Firm footsteps sounded on the wooden walkway. Vince
Ellis stopped beside Max. He didn't say hello. He didn't
offer his hand.

Max watched him carefully. "I found the story about
Arlene's sister."

Vince shrugged, his face stony. "That's old news, Max."

The answer made perfect sense and Max knew it. So the
truth about Arlene's sister surely had nothing to do with
Arlene's death. But there was something here that Max
didn't understood. "Then why did you answer my page,
meet me here?"

Vince's answer was quick and smooth. "Curious, I guess.
The weakness of most newspapermen."

"No, I don't think so." Max shook his head. "You aren't
curious, Vince. You're afraid. Vince, where were you when
Arlene sailed out that last day?"

For a moment, Vince's face was utterly blank. "Oh
Jesus." He stared at Max. "Do you think I would hurt Arlene? Oh Jesus," and he swung around and walked away.

"It's kind of an obsession." Marian Kenyon held up a
three-foot-long, two-foot-wide swath of macramé. "My sister
and I exchange macramé every Christmas and we're in a
heads-up competition to find the ugliest macramé in the
world. I think I just won." She pointed at an orange sunset

against purple water with a tilted pink silo apparently kept upright by a chartreuse cow peering through black Harry Caray frames at a pot of gold that had a faintly green tinge. Marian's lips curved in a beatific grin. "Doesn't it give you the willies?"

Annie cocked her head. "Do you suppose that's fungus growing on the gold, an economic judgment of some kind?"

Marian handed a five-dollar bill to the volunteer and tucked the macramé under her arm. She jerked her head toward a massive driftwood log near the stage. "I've heard you and Max and Emma and Laurel won't let go on the Girard kill."

Annie should have known Marian was tapping into island rumors. After all, that was her business, even if her boss wasn't interested in this story.

Annie settled beside Marian on the log. "You know that the police suspect Ruth?"

Marian scrunched her face in total disgust. "Yes. Sweetie, that's baloney. Next thing you know they'll try to pin it on Ben Parotti on the theory that somebody sighted a munchkin near the crime scene so it had to be Ben."

"Ben's house wasn't on Kathryn's list." Annie's tone was quiet, but it removed their talk from good-natured fun. Because, as Annie well knew, Marian had to have heard that the list of houses and the owners included Vince Ellis.

Marian's head jerked up. She gave Annie a level stare. "I don't care if they find Vince's address tattooed on her underwear, he didn't kill her." But uneasiness flashed deep in her dark eyes.

"Marian, who was Arlene's best friend?"

Marian blinked, obviously surprised. "Arlene? Besides Vince?" Her raspy voice had an unaccustomed softness. "Arlene had lots of friends. I guess I was one of her best friends. We worked together a lot and she liked to go to secondhand stores. Vince hates old stuff, so every few weeks Arlene and I rooted around in the backcountry. Once I found a tintype of Annie Oakley, I swear to God. I had it authenticated by Sotheby's. Arlene was nuts for old copies of the *Saturday Evening Post*, especially with Norman Rockwell covers. Vince said we had all the finer instincts of a bag lady."

"It sounds like lots of fun." Arlene and Marian obviously were friends. They laughed together. But Marian worked for Vince. Would Arlene share problems about her marriage with Marian? Not likely. "Could you tell me someone else Arlene spent a lot of time with?"

Marian squinted at Annie. "I don't get this. Why the big interest in Arlene?"

Annie took the politician's out. She answered a different question. "I'm looking for someone who talked with her the last week of her life."

"I talked to her." Marian sighed. "She was only coming into the office half days at that point." She looked at Annie, waved her hand. "You know, since Meg had come. She was staying home in the afternoons to be with her. I don't know"—her face drooped—"maybe that was a mistake. Maybe if she'd kept on working full-time, she would have pepped up. Vince and I both thought being with Meg would help. But Arlene just got thinner and thinner. She'd pretend to be typing and I'd look over there and tears were streaming down her face. I know about grief. You can't wrap it up in a box like a dried flower when the funeral's over. She and Amelia were so close. Arlene worried about her, and then to have her die in a car wreck. One day she's on the phone to Arlene, the next day she's dead. Arlene was just wiped out."

"But Arlene and Vince hadn't quarreled?"

Marian looked at Annie as though she'd suddenly sprouted polka-dot wings and started speaking in Gaelic. "Are you nuts? Vince did everything a man could do. Had me talk to her. Had her mother come. The parish priest. Every damn thing. And I've told him that, over and over. But he keeps on feeling like he should have been able—" Her lips snapped shut.

"She sailed out on a stormy day," Annie said slowly. "A very stormy day." Deliberately sailed to her death.

Marian's eyes were anguished. "She was depressed. In the bottom of a dark pit and everything was gray. She wouldn't have done it if she hadn't been depressed." She wiped away a rush of tears. "Poor Arlene. And poor Vince. Dear God, poor Vince."

Max stared at the computer screen. It had the information he wanted. But he wasn't sure he could bring himself to take advantage of it. The class roster in the *Kindergarten Year Book* was short indeed. In the group picture, a solemn Meg Ellis clung tightly to the teacher's hand. The teacher's name was Barbara McKay. Max knew Barbara, tall and chunky with a mop of curly brown hair, merry eyes and nonstop chatter. She and Annie played in the same tennis league. And Barbara loved mysteries.

Children rarely engage in subterfuge. Teachers know more than parents would ever imagine. Max clicked off the computer. He was still thinking hard when he pushed in the front door of Death on Demand.

Ingrid gave him an abstracted wave as she dealt with two customers quarreling over who first sighted the first edition of Nevada Barr's *Ill Wind*. The statuesque woman with blue hair said icily, "If you don't mind, I was reaching for the book." Her opponent, his fox-sharp face livid, exclaimed, "It has long been my contention that women without exception exhibit the intellectual attainments of earthworms and the unprincipled lusts of rabbits."

A piercing mew tingled his ears. Max looked into gleaming green eyes. "You're not supposed to be up there."

Agatha peered haughtily down from the wooden perch which had until recently held the stuffed raven.

Max pointed at the open display case. The glass had been carefully removed. "I heard about that, Agatha."

He would have sworn she was smiling. Smugly.

Max strolled down the broad center aisle and knew he

had a furred companion. He paused at the coffee bar, bent down and whispered, "Your secret and mine, sweetheart," as he shook out a small portion of regular dry food.

As he headed for Annie's office, he glanced up at the paintings, paused . . . yes, he knew the first one. And the third one. In Annie's office, he rummaged in a file cabinet and found the folder marked *Customer Preferences,* found McKay, Barbara. *Women's mysteries, enjoys humor.* Max reached for the phone, punched in the number.

"Hello." Barbara's cheerful voice was a song of greeting.

"Hi, Barbara, Max Darling calling from Death on Demand. Annie put her best customers' names in a bowl and pulled out yours. We have a special prize for you. May I bring it over?"

"Why, Max!" Sheer delight lifted her voice. "Oh please do. I love surprises!"

The sale room was beginning to fill as bargain hunters fanned out. One enterprising volunteer had begun a hoarse chant: "Half price, cookie cutters of goblins, shooting stars and anteaters; old photos of gunslingers, madams and riverboats; 1910 telephone book of Savannah; cookbooks of Gullah cuisine, Indonesian spices and Gold Rush Grub; a treasure map that marks the location of the magic sword needed to save the princess; a genuine Penny Dreadful, only missing three . . ."

Annie hurried toward the aisle near the far windows. Discarded boxes were piled at the far end just behind the costume jewelry booth. Janet Pierce smiled up at a customer. Her sleek golden hair glistened in the late afternoon sun spilling through the shining glass panes.

As Annie came nearer, she marveled at Janet's crisp appearance. Annie felt frazzled and knew her hair needed combing, her blouse was coming untucked and her skirt was wrinkled.

Janet lifted a welcoming hand. "Every year I swear I

won't do this again. I've forgotten how hard it is to work all day."

Annie felt a sudden kinship. Okay, Janet looked fresh but she was just as tired as everyone else. "Sold a lot?"

Janet waggled her hand. "Quite a bit. But Emma's never satisfied." She checked her watch. "Twenty more minutes, then I'm going home for a swim."

Annie planted her hands on the table, looked around conspiratorially, then asked, "Janet, what's this I hear about Kathryn Girard's van stopping at your house?"

Janet gestured toward the stage. "No reason to be so quiet about it, Annie. Trot up on the stage and ask over the PA system." Her voice was amused, but there was an undercurrent of irritation. "I swear, you're the fifteenth person who's sidled up to ask me that, very confidentially, of course. All I can tell you—"

"—is that someone's made a mistake." Dave Pierce's clear tenor voice was unemphatic, but possibly its very smoothness and control made his tone more impressive.

Janet's head jerked up. "Dave, isn't this silly!" She spoke lightly, but her eyes watched him anxiously.

Pierce was not looking at his wife. Instead, he faced Annie, a slender man with a stern face, cold eyes, short black hair touched with silver.

Annie was uncertain what gave Pierce his air of power. Was it the grim set of his thin lips, the firm jut of his jaw, the obvious quality of his sports coat and worsted slacks, the shine of his Italian loafers? Was it all of these or none of these? But no one would dismiss this man or ignore him, not now in the crowded aisle of a rummage sale nor in a corporate boardroom nor on the deck of a boat. "In fact, Mrs. Darling, I understand it is your mistake. You provided this so-called list to the police." His eyes bored into hers.

Janet's hands closed on a mess of jewelry.

Annie felt an instant of shock. But why should she be surprised? Chief Garrett had truthfully answered Dave Pierce's inquiry and it certainly should come as no surprise that Dave Pierce, once the rumors reached him, would investigate. This was not a passive man.

Annie was never quite certain what gave her courage. It might have been his derisive reference to the list as "so-called." It might have been the remembered horror of that terribly still form beneath the blanket in the back of the van. It might have been the memory of Henny sprawled face down in the forest. "The list exists." Her voice was uneven, but she met his gaze without wavering. "Four addresses, Mr. Pierce. One address is yours. The list was made by Kathryn Girard. There can be no doubt of that." Annie didn't need a handwriting expert to be confident. She had seen the list and she had seen Kathryn's distinctive scrawl on the notepad in her shop.

Janet's face was puzzled. "I don't understand it. I'd already made our donation to the sale, a pottery swan"—she pointed across the room at garden statuary—"and some old linen and a tea set with a chipped teapot. And I'm the one who takes care of that sort of thing. . . ." Her voice trailed off. She was not looking at Annie. Again her eyes turned to her husband, and Annie read uncertainty. And fear?

Dave Pierce's lips curved in a cold smile. "Nonetheless, it's clear that there has been a mistake. If the list, as you claim, is genuine, then the Girard woman wrote down the wrong address, certainly for our house." A shrug. "Perhaps for all the houses. Moreover, no one has reported seeing the van at any of these houses. The list may have nothing to do with her death. In any event, our house had nothing to do with her death." He stepped past Annie, dismissing her, and focused his gaze on his wife. "Are you finished here, Janet?"

"Almost. I'm sacking up the jewelry that didn't sell." Her slender hands quickly scooped up some brooches. "Dave, let's take a swim."

Annie apparently no longer existed to the Pierces. That made her mad. She stared at Dave's back, then took two steps and ostentatiously squeezed past him and parked herself right in front of the booth.

Ignoring Annie, Dave smiled at his wife. "Beach or pool?" Janet lifted a tray with an array of gaudy bracelets.

"How much are those bracelets?" Annie pointed at that tray. She didn't wait for an answer. "Of course, that's just costume jewelry. Not like the pieces that have been stolen the past few years."

Janet held the tray motionless. She was strikingly beautiful in the sharp sunlight, golden hair, smoothly planed face, bright coral lips. The sun sparkled too on the red and yellow and green and white stones, and the cheap jewelry blazed with color. She glanced at Annie, her face unreadable, then in a swift movement slid the bracelets into a box. "No treasures here. But do you know, I've been thinking about those robberies—"

Annie's eyes widened. Was there the slightest hint of a smile on Janet's face?

"—and it occurred to me that all the jewelry was stolen after Kathryn Girard came to the island. Do you suppose she could have been the thief?"

Barbara McKay's round face glowed with anticipation. "Max, no wonder Annie's bookstore is such a success. Why, this is the nicest surprise I could ever have." She held tight to the book, wrapped in a paper bright with red and yellow balloons that Max had found stuck behind a duster in Annie's office closet.

Max smiled, felt ratlike and sipped the excellent fresh iced tea with a sprig of mint. "She had fun drawing names this morning. She always wants her best customers to know they are appreciated."

They sat in Barbara's small den and Max knew Barbara deserved a gift, even if this one was a product of his creative fancy. Bookshelves filled all four walls and all the books were mysteries. He spotted titles Annie would love to have: *To Spite Her Face* by Hildegarde Dolson, *Death Tears a Comic Strip* by Theodora Dubois, *Cat's Claw* by D. B. Olsen.

Barbara removed the paper, folded it with precision and

stared at the book with incredulous delight. "Max, Max! A first edition of *Murder's Little Sister* by Pamela Branch. Max, I can't believe it!"

Annie probably wouldn't either when she returned to the shop to find the $260 book gone. Max grinned. "Actually, it was easy to pick a prize for you. We can't decide what to give Vince Ellis. He's the other winner. He shops at the store for mysteries for Meg. You know, we have a terrific collection of children's mysteries. But Annie wasn't sure which we should pick. She said Vince is very particular about what Meg reads."

"Oh, that dear child." Barbara's eyes were soft. "What a difficult time she's had." She saw Max's inquiring look. "Oh, you wouldn't know, but I had Meg in kindergarten."

Max brightened. "Then perhaps you might suggest some books she would enjoy."

"Nothing too scary, Max. The Boxcar mysteries and anything for that age group by George Edward Stanley. His books are lovely, happy and silly and funny. But you have to be careful." Her gaze was earnest. "Nothing that mentions a car wreck or loss at sea. That dear baby has had so much trauma, but she's a lucky little girl." Barbara threw her hands up. "Oh, that sounds silly after all she's been through. But Vince is the kindest, dearest father to her. And he knows that Meg's very fragile. On top of everything else, you know how depressed Arlene was. Meg's just now gaining a sense of security. And she's making friends and that's so hard for a little girl as withdrawn as she is. You know how children are! They are quick to shut out anyone who's different. And maybe, too, it frightens them when they hear adults talking about a mother and daddy dying." Barbara sighed. "At school, we've all made a special effort for Meg to help her make friends. It's finally working."

Chapter 14

Annie luxuriated in the warmth of the sun on her skin and the smell of coconut oil and the gentle lap of salt water as her rubber raft rocked. Sometimes it was wonderful to remember where they lived, in the land of soft light, sea breezes and— She jerked upright, flailed and the raft overturned, dumping her into the water.

Max, his blond hair sleek against his head, whooped with delight, then dove toward her. She clung to him. "Dammit, Max, I thought that was a jellyfish on my leg."

"I'll rescue you from that old mean jellyfish." His gaze was virtuous, but his hand was sliding down her back to her thigh.

"Max, we're in public." She twisted away.

"We're in the water," he corrected, moving purposefully toward her.

"Public water," she insisted.

He grinned. "Ready to go home?"

She grinned in return. "Soon."

He did an abrupt back flip and water cascaded over her head and sprayed out in sparkling drops.

Annie paddled to her raft and draped herself across the middle, her legs trailing behind her in the water.

Max took a deep breath and did another back flip.

Annie watched as the plume of water rose and fell. "That's all we've done today. Make a splash that comes to nothing. We still don't know who killed Kathryn Girard or Jake Chapman. It could be Ruth. Or one of the Campbells. Or Vince Ellis. Or Dave Pierce. Or Janet."

Max floated on his back toward her, rolled over and joined her on the raft. He blew in her ear, then said quickly, "Not so, Annie. We accomplished a lot today."

She pushed away a blob of seaweed. "Like what?"

Max grabbed a strand of seaweed. "We know what happened to Arlene."

"How could she do it?" Annie turned to look into his deep blue eyes. "How could she sail away and leave Vince and that little girl?"

"Winston Churchill called it the Black Dog. Depression. Arlene wasn't able to think about Vince and Meg, Annie. All she saw was blackness." He looked out toward the horizon, the soft green sea stretching to meet the sky. "It was a black day that she sailed."

They clung to the raft, their bodies touching with the warmth that transcends light and heat.

Annie's voice was small when she said doubtfully, "But Max, Vince's address was on the list."

Max nodded. "I told you about my talk with Barbara—"

There had been a moment of stiffness over *Murder's Little Sister.*

"—and when I got home, I checked with Pamela Potts. Kathryn did some volunteer work at the school. People talk. Teachers talk. Meg's problems were probably mentioned. Kathryn had probably already picked up on Arlene's death and so she nosed around."

Annie rested her chin on a ridge of the raft. "But if Arlene committed suicide, what hold did Kathryn have over Vince?"

"Not a hold, Annie. A threat." His voice was grim. "What would it do to Meg if the gossip got around the school, reached the parents of the little girls she wanted to play with, that Meg's mother killed her father? Think about it, Annie."

A V of pelicans flew overhead, then peeled into dives, down, down, down to the water. Annie pointed at the birds. "That's what Kathryn did. She saw something odd in someone's life and she pounced. It was the same kind of thing with the Campbells. A secret that they didn't want anyone to know, especially not Kate." Annie's shoulders tightened. "Gary Campbell could lose control, Max. He almost did this afternoon."

Max's face hardened. "I wish to hell I'd been there. And that goes for Dave Pierce, too." He was still bristling at Dave's overbearing treatment of Annie.

She looked at him fondly. With his wet hair plastered against his head and a golden string of seaweed looped over his right shoulder he didn't look like a knight ready to joust for his lady, but he was definitely Galahad to Annie. "They don't have that," she said abruptly.

He looked at her with interest, dark blue eyes thoughtful. And patient.

It was, Annie realized abruptly, the same expression Max bore when his mother had made a remark that didn't fit any known context.

Dammit, she wasn't loopy. "The Pierces. They don't have the kind of closeness we have. Janet was watching him like Agatha at a mouse hole. I think"—Annie frowned, trying to interpret that quick flash in Janet's eyes—"she was scared."

"That may be the most important thing we learned today," Max said slowly. "If Janet was telling the truth and she'd already made her contributions to the sale, then maybe Dave was the one Kathryn talked to."

Annie shivered. "He's tough, Max. When I looked at him, I knew what it would have been like to be a captive on a pirate ship, knowing the captain would cut out my tongue in an instant. Without a qualm. Without a thought."

"I agree, Annie." Max maneuvered the raft away from the lowering sun. "Okay, we've tried to find out who might have killed Kathryn and why. And we think we know." He ticked them off on his fingers: Ruth Yates, the murder of Alden Yates; Marie Campbell, the truth about Kate's paternity; Gary Campbell, ditto; Janet Pierce—"

Annie wriggled in excitement. "Max, she was laughing at me about the jewelry. And that's a hell of a motive if Kathryn figured out she was stealing all that stuff. But I'll bet you anything she's going to get the story around that Kathryn must have stolen the jewelry, and when nothing is ever stolen again, everyone will accept Kathryn as the thief." Annie's face fell. "But would Janet twit me like that if she killed Kathryn? That would be awfully reckless."

"Maybe, as Adelaide said, that's the point." Max sprinkled water on her shoulders.

"Which would make them both scary." Annie glanced at him and amplified, "Janet and Dave."

Max resumed his summation. "—Janet Pierce, the jewel thefts; Dave Pierce, his first wife's murder; Vince Ellis, the murder and suicide of Meg's parents. But maybe none of that counts."

Annie stood up in the water so abruptly that the raft upended and Max sank in the water. When he came up, spouting water like a geyser, Annie continued hotly, "None of it counts? What do you mean, none of it counts?"

"The reasons for blackmail. Maybe what matters more is the people who were being blackmailed. What's a big deal to one person, isn't to another. Would Gary Campbell kill somebody to prevent people from learning about Marie's weekend with Roderick Ransome?"

"But Max, it wasn't just a weekend. It was a weekend with long, long consequences." The sins of the fathers, or in this case, the mothers. . . . Old truths were like prehistoric remains. The flesh was gone, but the bones could not be ignored.

"I know. But the point is the people, not the facts." His voice was stubborn. "If you just look at facts, we can all go to the Fall Revel tonight and laugh and drink champagne; the investigation's complete."

Annie said slowly, "Ruth. The gun. The croquet mallet. A secret that could put her in jail. Two plus two equals four." Her eyes narrowed, then she said in a rush, "And you know what? I don't believe it for a minute. Ruth's gentle and indecisive and long-suffering. That's what you mean, isn't it, Max?"

"Right. We can have all the facts in the world, but what it comes down to is character. Tell me about this murderer, Annie." He looked at her intently.

Annie understood. There was a design to the death of Kathryn Girard and there could be no doubt that the impression of the murderer's mind was there to find. "All right, there are two possibilities. If Ruth Yates killed Kathryn, she grabbed up the croquet mallet in a rush of anger after Kathryn took the gun away. But if Ruth didn't kill Kathryn, it's a very different matter."

"Very different." Max rested his chin on his folded arms. The raft tilted up and over a swell. "In that event, the murderer figured that Ruth Yates was a blackmail victim because of her attitude toward Kathryn. The murderer decided ahead of time that Kathryn would die when she came to make her last call." He frowned. "But why kill her at all if she was going away?"

"This murderer," Annie said crisply, "must have had a reason. Maybe it wasn't possible to come up with the money, maybe Kathryn demanded it on too short notice or maybe the murderer didn't believe Kathryn's demands would stop. This is important, Max. We know the mallet killed Kathryn. The murderer must have taken it earlier in the week from the Yateses' house."

A shrimp boat, nets drawn up, passed a hundred yards away. "Here's what we know." Max was precise. "The mallet is stolen in preparation. The murderer kills Kathryn when she arrives and puts her in the back of the van. If Ruth is innocent, that's when the murderer saw the gun and took it. The murderer drives the van to Marsh Tacky Road. Henny arrives. The murderer attacks Henny, but misses. Henny runs away. The murderer—"

Annie interrupted. She was the one who'd found the tilted vase at Jake Chapman's house. "—takes the bike trail and bumps the vase at the Chapman house, maybe it was raining so hard the bike skidded, whatever. Late that night, the murderer goes to Kathryn's to see if there's any incriminating stuff and finds some files. We arrive and the murderer shoots at me. The next day, Chapman calls about the vase—"

Max broke in. "Wait a minute. When Garrett punched redial, the phone rang Ruth's house."

Annie nodded solemnly. "Yes, it did. That means one of two things: Either Ruth is the murderer and Chapman did call her and she was too upset to think about erasing any trace of the call to her, or"—Annie shivered—"the murderer knew Ruth was a blackmail victim, so after killing Chapman, the murderer dialed Ruth's number, setting her up to be the suspect."

"A cold devil," Max observed. "Damn cold. We'd better remember that." He ticked off the points on his fingers. "If Ruth is innocent, the person we're looking for is capable of careful planning, has no scruples about putting an innocent person in jeopardy and acts swiftly if threatened."

"Not Ruth." Annie spoke with conviction.

Max called the roll. "Vince Ellis? Marie Campbell? Gary Campbell? Janet Pierce? Dave Pierce?"

Annie knew who had her vote. "Dave Pierce." But was it prejudice or instinct? She continued almost without pause. "Vince is tough, too. And all he has left in the world is Meg. Gary Campbell has a hell of a temper. If he was the one who came out of Kathryn's place, he wouldn't wait a minute to shoot. Marie's a mother. Backed into a corner to protect Kate, she might do anything. Janet Pierce was a top-rank executive. She could plan an invasion of Mars. And I know she stole that jewelry. Oh Max"—it was a wail—"all we really know is that Ruth didn't do it and I don't know how we'll ever find out who did!"

They stood in the foyer, admiring each other.

Annie twirled, the tiered skirt of her black georgette dress flaring, then reached out to smooth Max's lapel. "Honestly, a white dinner jacket is as sexy as a baseball uniform. I like it so much better than an old black jacket."

Max's dark blue eyes studied her. "I thought we watched baseball because it's such a complex game, so much going on, both on the field and off, the runner at second trying to pick up the signals, the manager deciding between relievers on the basis of the lineup, right-handed bats or left, the infield charging if there's a suicide squeeze on. Am I under a misapprehension?"

Annie's smile was demure. "And those things, too."

His lips quirked. "Do I detect a shameless hussy?"

"You might." Her eyes sparkled.

"Good. How about—"

The phone rang.

"I'll check caller ID." Annie rushed to the kitchen. "It's Emma," she called out. "Hello, Emma."

Max lounged in the doorway.

Annie punched on the speaker.

". . . glad I caught you. Not that I think there's anything we can do. Garrett's arrested Ruth as a material witness. He'll probably have her arraigned for murder on Monday." Emma sighed. "Can't say I blame him. Ruth's fingerprints are on the gun that killed Chapman. Her fingerprints are on the mallet that killed Kathryn. And that damn fool husband of hers dumped the rest of the croquet set in the harbor and Ben Parotti fished it out and called Garrett. Turns out everyone on that list denied that Kathryn came by in the van. Except poor old Ruth, of course. I'm going to make an appeal to the community at large at the festival tonight. And Laurel and Pamela will work the crowd. But I'll have to admit I'm stymied. Problem is, there aren't any damn clues. I always provide Marigold with plenty of clues." She slammed down the phone.

Strings of white lights decorated a welcoming arch at the Island Hills Country Club. The lights spelled out FALL REVEL.

Women in shimmery dresses and men in white dinner jackets and black trousers were streaming onto the broad veranda. Japanese lanterns bobbed in the gentle breeze.

Annie and Max waved at friends, called out hellos, were in a group heading for the main ballroom as the band swung into a sensuous tango, the dance which had swept the island this past year. Many of the tables were already filled as guests moved slowly past a sumptuous buffet. The ballroom doorway filled and the forward pace slowed to a crawl.

"You hand in your tickets when you get in the buffet line." Annie was puzzled. "And there's plenty of room in the ballroom. I can't imagine what's holding everyone up."

Max craned to see. "There's a bottleneck just past the main door. I don't— Oh."

The couple in front of them turned. "Some kind of appeal," the woman said.

Annie stood on tiptoe. Laurel was holding out a card and accepting a five-dollar bill, which she dropped into a bowl. A banner was pinned to the wall behind her: RUTH YATES DEFENSE FUND. BUY A BOUQUET FOR RUTH.

By the time they reached the table, the bowl was half full. A ruggedly handsome man in his sixties with the stalwart air of Ezio Pinza in *South Pacific* stood with one hand on the back of Laurel's chair.

"Dear Max, Annie." His mother beamed. "I am so eager for you to meet Fred Jeffries. Fred, this is my son and my dear daughter-in-law."

Jeffries stepped around the table, pumped Max's hand, smiled at Annie. "Marvelous woman, your mother. She's opened up a new world to me." Then he added hastily, "Flowers, you know."

Annie smiled in return. "Camellias," she said pleasantly.

"Camellias?" Fred and Max spoke in unison. Laurel watched Annie carefully.

"So many meanings," Annie said carelessly. "But I know that camellias always signal good luck." As well, Annie knew, as a gift to a man.

"Luck," Laurel trilled. "How thoughtful of you, Annie. And certainly, we shall think camellias for dear Ruth." She clapped her hands together. "Of course, the moment I knew that the gun belonged to Ruth, I foresaw great tribulation for her. As soon as I got home, I set right to work." She pointed at the stack of painted cards. "Blackthorn represents so clearly dear Ruth's difficulty. The sweet-chestnut blossom demands that she be done justice. The gladiolus represents her friends ready-armed to defend her, and hazel reveals that our hearts are agitated. Lantana trumpets our unyielding commitment." She thrust a card at Max.

He dropped in a twenty and they moved on with a final smile to Fred, who once again stood behind Laurel's chair. Close behind. As they reached the end of the buffet line, Annie observed mildly, "I'm never quite sure about your mother."

"She's definitely *ma mère*," he replied.

"Oh, I don't doubt that." Her eyes swept his blond hair and lake-blue eyes and masculine version of Laurel's elegant regular features. Was her tone faintly regretful? Or resigned? "It's her incredible capacity to appear . . ." She paused, decided "looney tunes" lacked tact, and said, ". . . utterly guileless when she's engaged in a deliberate ploy."

"Ploy?" Max's eyebrows rose.

Annie pointed across the room. Pamela Potts, festive in a blue dress that she probably first wore as high school valedictorian, stood in the center of a clot of rapt listeners.

"I'll bet you the rest of my Pamela Branch firsts that Pamela Potts is busy spreading the fascinating news about the four houses on Kathryn Girard's list while Laurel tugs on everybody's heartstrings about Ruth. It's all part of Emma's grand plan to put pressure on the murderer. Emma thinks she can spin a plot the way she does for Marigold Rembrandt. I don't think so. But"—she shrugged—"we've done our best, so we'll give Emma her chance and we shall dance the night away."

Max grabbed her hand and in a moment they were on the dance floor. Annie loved to tango with Max. It always made her feel like a dark-eyed seductress with a rose in her teeth. When the music ended, they glided out onto the terrace with its magnificent view of the eighteenth green. They walked to a glass-topped table near the low wall. Moonlight silvered the green.

In the lagoon that served as a hazard, frogs croaked—not the frenzied chorus of midsummer, but a respectable enough din, from a frog perspective. Max was fond of pointing out that all those deep bleats meant, "Come on, sweetie, let's get it on." He would then sigh and exclaim, "Isn't nature wonderful!" Tonight he flicked a salute toward the lagoon, murmured, "Go for it, boys!" then looked at Annie. "What would you like to drink? Champagne?"

"No, thanks. I don't feel that festive tonight." Yes, it was wonderful to tango with Max, but Ruth Yates was in a cell and Henny must feel equally trapped, though *Marigold's Pleasure* was surely an elegant cage. "Club soda with lime."

Max touched her hair. "Maybe we'd better tango again. Asceticism doesn't become you."

She flashed him a bright smile. "Don't worry. I'm simply keeping the gray cells alert."

Max disappeared through the French doors into the ballroom now ablaze with color and sound and movement.

Annie hummed along as she slipped into the webbed chair. The lyrics for "That Old Black Magic" bubbled in her mind. That's what they needed, some old black magic—or white or pink would do. They needed magic because dogged application had so far yielded enough information for five Marigold Rembrandt mysteries and not a single hard fact pointing to a murderer. The hard facts, like the croquet mallet and the gun, pointed at Ruth and Ruth alone.

And here came Emma. Could anyone else look quite so majestic in a golf cart? Her hair, piled atop her head, sparkled in the moonlight. There had to be twenty rhinestone pins poked into the beehive that tonight shone with a purplish hue.

Emma parked the golf cart at the end of the path. She climbed out and her white silk caftan with a crimson band at the hem swirled around her ankles. She marched briskly up the steps, her head bobbing in response to greetings. The rhinestone pins flashed and the hem flared. She moved across the terrace like a queen greeting subjects, and paused only long enough by Annie's table to murmur, "I'll speak at eight o'clock. Watch our suspects."

Our suspects. That definitely had a proprietorial tone. Did Emma become possessive about the suspects in a Marigold Rembrandt adventure?

Annie described the moment when Max returned with their drinks.

He laughed. "And then are we to charge forward at a guilty cower and clap handcuffs on the perp?"

"Who knows? Marigold Rembrandt always triumphs." She glanced at her watch. "But that gives us plenty of time for dinner."

Annie loved the buffet: crab meat au gratin, scalloped oysters, glazed Cornish hens with orange and avocado slices, baked baby sweet potatoes, broccoli with peanut butter sauce, cheese grits, black-eyed peas and squash soufflé. There was a separate table for desserts: apple pie with rum sauce, chess pie, pineapple-studded white cake, chocolate chip pie, key lime pie and sherbets They settled at a table inside, near the stage. The band concluded a mélange of

Gershwin tunes. The musicians put down their instruments and filed off stage.

Annie spooned a smooth lump of chocolate chip pie. Max was eating rainbow sherbet.

Annie eyed his bowl. "Went all out there, didn't you?"

"A life on the wild side," he murmured. "It's—" He broke off, put down his spoon. "Here comes Emma."

Emma mounted the low steps to the stage and moved to the center. She lifted her hand and white spotlights closed on her. Head high, she gazed out over the dance floor to the tables, her square face confident. "Ladies and gentlemen, welcome to the annual Fall Revel, which marks the successful culmination of yet another superb Women's Club White Elephant Sale. Usually it is my pleasure to thank our committee heads and to report on the activities our fund-raiser will make possible in the coming year. Instead that report will be mailed to you. Tonight, I wish to focus on a crime which has directly affected our organization, the murder on Thursday evening of Kathryn Girard—"

If ever Emma held an audience it was this one. There must have been two hundred people in the room and the silence was absolute.

"—and the loss of one of the Island Hills Country Club's most accomplished golfers and outstanding members, Jake Chapman. I am making this extraordinary statement because one of the most respected members of our Women's Club, Ruth Yates, has become the focus, most of us believe quite incorrectly, of the police investigation into these murders. Let me recap for you the events of the last three days. On Thursday afternoon . . ."

Annie leaned close to Max, quickly whispered, "Emma better be careful. Dave Pierce probably has at least two lawyers in the audience and he'll go after her if she mentions him," then scooted her chair so that she had a clear view of the entire ballroom. As Emma's brisk voice continued, Annie quickly scanned the sea of watching faces. Vince Ellis stood motionless next to a potted palm. The shadow from a palm frond fell across his face, but didn't hide the hard ridge of his jaw. A blue spot bathed Gary and Marie Campbell, who sat alone at a table for four. Gary's dinner jacket fitted him awkwardly and his tie was askew. He hunched in his chair, his bony face alert, his arm tight around Marie's slight shoulders. She leaned forward, her elfin features bleak. Janet and Dave Pierce were the obvious host and hostess of a table for ten. Oh yes, the Pierces had a houseful of guests. And the vibrant redhead with the merry laugh and the incredibly large gold necklace must be Adelaide's old friend from Coral Gables. She was still wearing her ancient gold necklace, obviously. She nodded toward the stage and Janet leaned close to whisper to her. Yes, it would be quite an exciting story for a houseguest, a great mystery near enough to provide a thrill, but certainly not close enough to threaten. Janet's hands flashed as she talked, and she seemed to be enjoying relating her commentary. In marked contrast, Dave Pierce was totally, soberly, intently focused on Emma.

"—apparently the van was scheduled to visit Sea Oats Circle, Porpoise Place, Ship's Galley Road and Mockingbird Lane—"

So Emma was smart enough to skirt the possibility of slander by mentioning the streets but not the addresses.

"—and was found, as I'm sure most of you know, on Marsh Tacky Road. My request is for anyone who saw the van after four o'clock on Thursday afternoon to report where and when. You may call my number and leave your information. Please also leave your name and telephone number. My hope is that one of you"—that broad stubby hand swept the room—"may have observed some fact that will lead us to the identity of the murderer and . . ."

Annie's gaze swept the room. Vince Ellis folded his arms over his chest and slowly shook his head. Gary Campbell looked warily up at a man who had clapped him on the shoulder and was asking an excited question. Marie Campbell stared at their inquisitor with a fixed smile. Janet Pierce stirred her coffee. For an instant her bright social manner slipped away and her eyes were intent as she stared at her husband. Dave adjusted his glasses, his face creased in thought.

Annie whispered, "I'll give Emma some credit. She sure as hell has everybody's attention, but it won't prove anything even if somebody saw the van parked in one of their drives. Darn it, we already know where Kathryn was going. No, we need someone who was behind Jake Chapman's house. I wonder if she'll ask about that? We know the murderer passed his house sometime after six."

Annie almost pushed back her chair to go to the stage and join Emma when a heavy figure, head down, shoulders tensed, stumped across the dance floor and climbed the steps.

A sibilant hiss rippled across the room. Annie reached out, clutched Max's arm. Even Emma, who was well-known in mystery circles for her poker face and ability to win big pots at mystery conventions, appeared startled. But she quickly managed a welcoming smile. "Brian, I want you to know we all believe in Ruth."

Brian Yates wasn't wearing his clerical collar. Despite his wrinkled sports shirt and slacks, he had a somber dignity as he stared out at the once again silent ballroom. "They arrested Ruth. They say she killed this Girard woman to keep her quiet about my father's death. They say Ruth killed my dad. I want to tell you something." His eyes were dark with misery; his deep voice wavered. "Ruth loved Dad. Nobody ever had better care. Nobody. She was at the hospital a lot more hours than I was. She hated the way Dad was suffering. She hated it. After he died, she blamed herself but there was nothing that could have been done. Nothing that she didn't do for him. I deal with families in pain and I've seen it happen over and over again, taking blame where there's no blame. That's what Ruth did. I suppose that woman heard something Ruth said to someone, found out how upset Ruth was and took advantage of her. But I know Ruth never killed anyone. Ruth is about love. All she's ever done in her life is to give love. But someone who wanted to kill that woman came to our house and took away a croquet mallet. The police say Ruth's fingerprints are on it. Of course they are. I'm asking all of you to think back, remember this past week. If you came by Sea Oats Circle, who did you see there? I want every name of everyone who was seen at our house. Because one of them is the true murderer. Not Ruth. Never Ruth. And it's going to be up . . ."

Annie pulled on Max's arm. She rose and ducked behind a line of potted palms and hurried out to the terrace. Max followed and watched her as she paced up and down at the end of the terrace. "I couldn't stand another minute. It's terrible, Max. That poor man, his heart is breaking. And dammit, it's not going to work. None of that's going to save Ruth."

Max looked back toward the bright windows. "There's a chance someone saw the person who got the mallet."

Annie planted her hands on her hips. "All Brian is going to get is a bunch of names and nothing to connect that person to the actual crime. What we need is concrete, specific, physical evidence. . . ." She stared out at the golf course and facts whirled in her mind:

The weather was perfect the day Lynn Pierce took her final sail.

Someone stole a boat from Parotti's in the morning before Lynn sailed.

What kind of impact would it take to dislodge the terracotta vase on the wall behind Jake Chapman's house?

The murderer planned ahead, so Marsh Tacky Road was decided upon in advance.

King Snake Park abutted the golf course and so did Jake Chapman's house.

"Specific physical evidence." Annie's heart thudded. "Oh God, Max, I should have known when Emma came tonight in her golf cart! And it's just as you said, it all comes down to the people. Dave Pierce is cold and dangerous.

Gary Campbell blows up, but then it's over. It's Dave Pierce who is implacable."

Max's face crinkled. "Annie, what does Emma's golf cart have to do with—"

"Not Emma's golf cart." Annie spoke calmly because now she could see it all in her mind, the four houses where Kathryn Girard planned to stop, the golf cart path running behind the Pierce house, skirting the various holes, passing behind Jake Chapman's house and the bike path there, too, the bike path that led to King Snake Park and would equally well serve a golf cart.

Annie grabbed his arm, headed for the terrace steps. "Max, you know this course. Which house belongs to the Pierces?"

"The sixteenth fairway runs behind their house. Annie, are you sure?" He hurried to keep pace with her.

"We'll know in just a minute. A golf cart, Max. That's why the van was left on Marsh Tacky Road. That's why it didn't matter that Henny's car blocked the way. That's why Mark Stone didn't see anyone come out of Marsh Tacky Road. The golf cart was hidden on Marsh Tacky Road earlier on Thursday. But it was still raining and the path behind the Chapman house must have been slick or maybe the cart was going too fast. That's what happened, the cart slid into Chapman's terrace wall and knocked over the vase. It had to be a golf cart. A bike wouldn't have knocked the vase loose. And the only people who live on the golf course and who play golf and who very likely, just like Emma, have their own cart are Dave and Janet Pierce. If that's what happened, there has to be some trace on the cart. And Max, that's all we need. One piece of solid physical evidence and Ruth will be free. Because if it is the Pierces' cart that knocked over the vase, there can't be any other explanation. And I'll bet if Garrett looked hard enough, even with all the people who came to Marsh Tacky road that night to hunt for Henny, I'll bet there will be a track of the cart's wheels.

It had to have been put in deep shrubs so no one would spot it on Thursday."

They were passing the sand traps on the sixteenth green. The path curved deep into the shadows of tall pines. Max pointed through the pines at a two-story gabled building. "There's the back of the Pierce property. I think that's the garage. If they have a cart, that's probably where they keep it."

Their footsteps crunched on the oyster-shell walk as they left the cart path. The walk followed alongside the building, ended at the broad driveway. It was an old building, had probably originally served as a stables when the Tudor mansion was a country estate. Lights flooded the drive, spilled from the back of the huge house, hung in trees in the garden.

As they stepped into the blaze of lights on the drive, Annie checked the back of the house. Windows both upstairs and down glowed behind curtains. "I sure hope everybody's still at the club."

"It shouldn't take long," Max murmured. There were six overhead doors. He tugged at the first to no avail. "Damn. They're electric."

They hurried past the other overhead panels to a white wooden door at the end of the building. It was unlocked. Max turned a thumbs-up and opened it. He hesitated for only a moment, then found a light switch and turned it on. The long narrow space had probably once served as a tack room. Garden tools hung from pegs. A riding mower was at one end.

Annie moved swiftly to a door that led into the garage. She twisted the knob. The door opened and they stepped into the huge garage. Max found the lights. Two slots held a beige Mercedes and a black Jeep.

"Janet has a Porsche and it's not here. But how do you suppose they got all their guests to the club?"

Max shrugged. "They probably hired a limo. Maybe Dave took most of them and some went with Janet."

Annie gripped Max's arm. "Look. At the far end." Two

golf carts with jaunty red awnings were parked in the last slot.

Their shoes clipped on the cement as they hurried the length of the garage. Annie darted to the first cart, bent forward to study the front. But the front of this cart bore no scrapes or blemishes.

Max moved past her to the second cart. "Hey Annie, come here and—"

The fourth garage door rumbled as it slowly lifted and receded on its frame.

Annie's eyes jerked toward the opening, then she moved swiftly to stand in front of the second cart. She looked at the right front end and felt a surge of triumph. A deep red gouge made an ugly streak on the right front of the cart. The vases at the corners of Jake Chapman's wall were terracotta. Here was physical proof that no one could dispute. This cart was the force that knocked loose the vase and it was the damage to the vase that led Jake Chapman to make the call that ended his life.

Headlights beamed through the opening. Car doors slammed. Dave Pierce walked slowly into the garage, his measured pace perhaps even more threatening than the tight smoothness of his face and the glitter of his dark eyes. Janet Pierce followed, her face as white in the sharp lights as the silk sash around her slender waist.

A heavyset woman bustled importantly after them. "I know they're dressed right, Mr. Pierce. But I've never seen them before and I didn't think they should be messing around in the garage."

"You were quite right to call for me, Martha." Pierce didn't glance toward her. His eyes never left Annie and Max. "I'll take care of this. You may return to the house."

"Maybe it would be better if she stayed." Annie's voice was thin but steady. There had already been three murders: Lynn Pierce, Kathryn Girard and Jake Chapman. Martha was an insurance policy Annie intended to cling to.

"First, you have the effrontery to break into my garage.

Now you want to direct my staff." His cold voice was harsh. "At this point, Mrs. Darling, you and your husband owe me an apology. And it better be a good one or I'll bring charges against both of you."

"An apology?" Annie stepped forward, eyes blazing. "To a murderer? You might as well stop posturing. We have proof now." She pointed at the second golf cart. "Ruth Yates is going to be set free and you are going to be arrested."

Janet Pierce gasped. She stared at her husband, her eyes wide, her hand clutching the ruby necklace at her throat.

Dave Pierce's dark brows drew into a tight line.

Max reached out, drew Annie back where he could step in front of her. "Annie's right, Dave. You're finished. That scrape on the golf cart will have particles of terra-cotta from Jake Chapman's vase."

Janet Pierce gave a low moan.

Dave Pierce didn't even glance at her. "What the hell are you talking about?" Pierce's eyes blazed.

"You planned it beautifully." Annie felt her heart thud. Pierce was a dangerous man, a man who had almost gotten away with three murders. "Right from the start. But you planned Lynn's murder well, too, stealing a boat, sailing out and meeting her. Did you push her off her sailboat? Or did you knock her out and dump her overboard to drown?"

Dave Pierce stepped back as if he'd been struck, his face utterly still and empty.

The garage was abruptly quiet, a quiet laden with fear and anger and pulsing fury.

Annie reached out, grabbed Max's hand, but she talked even faster. "How did Kathryn Girard find out? Was it a good guess on her part because she had lots of experience in nosing out evil? Did she accuse you of Lynn's murder and you gave yourself away? But you have plenty of money." Annie's tone was scathing. "I guess you got tired of paying blackmail. So you worked it out. You stole the croquet mallet from the Yateses and hid the golf cart at Marsh Tacky Road—"

Janet Pierce moved like an old woman, her body stiff and jerky, one step at a time, moving away from her husband.

"—and when Kathryn came by the house, you killed her and put her in the back of the van. Everything went just as planned until Henny spotted the van and started following you. Did she honk to get your attention? Or did she spot the van turning into Marsh Tacky Road? That's when everything fell apart. There you were, trapped on Marsh Tacky Road, Henny walking up the road, Kathryn's body in the van. You tried to knock Henny out and missed. When she ran, you took the van keys and got the cart and started for home. And when you went around Chapman's wall, the cart skidded and knocked over the vase. And then you—"

Pierce's shoulders slumped. "My wife." The words were a deep, terrible whisper. "My wife." Pain scalded his face, grievous, unrelenting, unquenchable pain.

Annie stared at Dave Pierce. Abruptly, she understood.

Janet Pierce lifted her hands. In appeal? In defense? Slowly they fell.

Dave's eyes glittered with horror as he turned toward Janet.

Janet took a step back.

"Dave . . ." Her voice was unrecognizable, her face a harsh mask of despair. "Dave, I did it all for you. Dave, I love you. I've always loved you. I've done everything for you. It was an accident with Lynn. I swear that it was an accident." Janet sobbed. "An accident. But that woman, she accused me and then she said she'd tell you. I had to steal to keep her quiet." She shuddered. "She wanted so much money, more than I could ever get. And I couldn't ask you, not for that much money. So I had to steal the jewels. Each time she promised it would be the last, and then she'd smile that horrible cat smile and say she'd taken a fancy to another piece and she knew it would be easy for me. She called on Tuesday and said I had to get the Aztec gold necklace. She made me give her a signed note that I was going to steal the necklace. She promised she'd give the note back to me if I brought the necklace Saturday morning. I was so afraid. Dave, I did it for you. Dave, oh God, Dave."

Dave Pierce trembled, all of him, his entire body. "You sailed after Lynn. Did you fall overboard, cry for help? Lynn would have hurried to help you. And then you—" Anger burned in his stricken eyes, fierce and unrelenting.

"It happened so quickly." Janet pressed her hands hard against her ashen cheeks. "And then it was too late."

"My wife." Dave Pierce buried his face in his hands.

He was not calling to Janet.

Epilogue

Emma's eyes were not quite as frosty as usual. She sipped the mint julep. "Thoughtful of you, Annie."

"It's the very least I could do." Emma had a special fondness for mint juleps. Annie would have provided her with barbecued porcupine if that had been Emma's preference. Emma hadn't done a book signing in at least five years and here she was at Death on Demand and the bookstore was jammed from the front veranda to the farthest reaches of the coffee bar, the noise level reminiscent of the peak rush at the White Elephant Sale. Annie could scarcely keep the jubilation from her voice, but she didn't want Emma to get a big head. Annie eyed rigid six-inch spikes of orange hair. Well, at least no bigger a head than she already had.

"I should have figured it out." The pronoun was sharply emphasized. Emma was still piqued that Annie and Max solved Kathryn Girard's murder first. "But the very next day, two people called to say they'd seen Janet Pierce near the Yateses' garage. There's no doubt that the broad sweep of my net would have yielded proof. And if I"—again the emphasis on the pronoun was pronounced—"had solved the crime, I'd have been sure to have the police on hand. I would have much preferred to have Janet Pierce arrested."

Annie tried not to bristle. Of course, it would have been preferable.

Emma's glare was icy. "It's quite unfortunate that she slipped away in a boat. Since there's been no trace of her, she's presumed dead and I suppose some might see it as poetic justice that she met the same fate as her first victim. But it is highly irregular." A sniff. "If she'd been arrested, we might have learned more about the stolen jewelry. That is perhaps the most fascinating element. Think of it, this socially prominent woman driven to burglary! Can you imagine the enormous stress? Kathryn Girard went to the well one time too often. And it should have been a clue that Kathryn planned her pick-ups for Thursday but wasn't flying out until Saturday. There had to be a reason for that delay!" The author's spiked hair rippled as she nodded violently. "Well, of course there was a reason. Janet couldn't steal the necklace until Friday night. But Janet obviously decided immediately upon murder. And I will have to admit"—the tone was a bit reluctant—"that her plotting was superb."

Annie looked at Emma curiously. Would anyone other than a mystery writer see a plan for murder in terms of plot?

"Superb!" Emma's plump hand waggled. "Hiding the golf cart on Marsh Tacky Road, stealing the croquet mallet from the Yateses' house, taking the gun from the back of the van, using it to kill Jake Chapman. Of course, placing the phone call to Ruth's house after Jake's murder was nothing short of diabolical. Wish I'd thought of it," she said regretfully. "It would have worked so well in the *Riddle of the Rampaging Rhinoceros*. Oh well." She sighed, took a deep drink of her julep and waved her hand. "Where am I signing?"

"At a table by the coffee bar." Annie led the way up the clogged center aisle.

Behind the coffee bar, blue eyes intent, sleeves rolled up, Max filled coffee mugs as fast as he could. Henny cut slices of cake and Laurel poured glasses of wine. Agatha watched intently from the end of the coffee bar.

Emma settled at the table directly in front of the fireplace. Stacks of her latest, *The Adventure of the Purloined Python,* filled one side of the table and were arranged on the hearth behind her. Fans immediately formed two lines that stretched to the front of the store.

Annie was pleased to spot some familiar faces now free of fear and suspicion. Vince Ellis held a stack of Nancy Drews. He grinned as he listened to an animated, as usual, Marian Kenyon. Ruth Yates clung to Brian's arm. She looked up adoringly at her ebullient husband, who was, as usual, the center of an admiring audience. Gary Campbell was right behind his wife, watching Marie's eager, happy face as she spoke to a friend. At least those lives were now secure, Annie thought with a rush of relief. She'd heard that the Pierce mansion was up for sale and that Dave Pierce was living in Atlanta. There could be no real happiness for Dave Pierce, but he had his work and that could offer him sanctuary from sorrow.

Annie slipped behind the coffee bar. Max handed her a mug inscribed *The Clue of the Second Murder* by John Stephen Strange.

Henny lifted her mug, inscribed *Death Takes the Wheel* by E. and M. A. Radford. "Here's to Annie who"—she darted a glance at Emma, busily autographing—"outsleuthed Marigold Rembrandt, and—"

Annie smiled modestly.

"—by the way, what's the prize for this month's paintings?"

Annie glanced at the wall above Emma. "Something special, I think." She'd originally planned to give a new hardcover and free coffee for a month. But no one was ever likely to get the full answer. "It's not going to be easy," she warned. "This month the winner must not only correctly identify each painting by title and by author but—"

They all bent forward to hear as a peal of laughter sounded near the front of the store.

"—must also declare what quality the books share in common."

Henny's brown eyes glowed. "The prize?" she demanded.

Annie accepted the challenge. After all, how could anyone—even Henny—come up with the one quality, as decreed by Annie, that these five books shared? "Winner's choice," Annie said grandly, her wave encompassing the store.

Henny pointed at each painting in turn. "Number One, *The Thin Woman* by Dorothy Cannell; Number Two, *Going Nowhere Fast* by Gar Anthony Haywood; Number Three, *Miss Zukas and the Library Murders* by Jo Dereske; Number Four, *Murder on a Girls' Night Out* by Anne George; and Number Five, *Caught in a Rundown* by Lisa Saxton."

"That's the easy part," Annie said smugly. "What quality do they have in common?"

Annie had her first misgiving when a beatific smile lifted Henny's lips.

"Why, Annie, anyone would know that." A dramatic pause, then the one sweet, perfect word. "Charm!"